PENGUIN BOOKS

A Wish For Us

Tillie Cole hails from a small town in the North-East of England. She grew up on a farm with her English mother, Scottish father and older sister and a multitude of rescue animals. As soon as she could, Tillie left her rural roots for the bright lights of the big city.

After graduating from Newcastle University with a BA Hons in Religious Studies, Tillie followed her Professional Rugby player husband around the world for a decade, becoming a teacher in between and thoroughly enjoyed teaching High School students Social Studies before putting pen to paper, and finishing her first novel.

After several years living in Italy, Canada and the USA, Tillie has now settled back in her hometown in England, with her husband and new son.

Tillie is both an independent and traditionally published author, and writes many genres including: Contemporary Romance, Dark Romance, Young Adult and New Adult novels.

When she is not writing, Tillie enjoys nothing more than spending time with her little family, curling up on her couch watching movies, drinking far too much coffee, and convincing herself that she really doesn't need that last square of chocolate.

T0333102

A Wish For Us

TILLIE COLE

PENGUIN BOOKS

PENGUIN BOOKS

UK | USA | Canada | Ireland | Australia
India | New Zealand | South Africa

Penguin Books is part of the Penguin Random House group of companies
whose addresses can be found at global.penguinrandomhouse.com

First published by Tillie Cole 2018
Published in Penguin Books 2023
004

Copyright © Tillie Cole, 2018

The moral right of the author has been asserted

Copyediting by Kia Thomas
Proofreading by Sarah Burton

Set in 12.5/14.75pt Garamond MT Std
Typeset by Jouve (UK), Milton Keynes
Printed and bound in Great Britain by Clays Ltd, Elcograf S.p.A.

The authorized representative in the EEA is Penguin Random House Ireland,
Morrison Chambers, 32 Nassau Street, Dublin D02 YH68

A CIP catalogue record for this book is available from the British Library

ISBN: 978-1-405-96140-0

www.greenpenguin.co.uk

Penguin Random House is committed to a
sustainable future for our business, our readers
and our planet. This book is made from Forest
Stewardship Council® certified paper.

Dedication

TO ROMAN, THE BEAT OF MY HEART.

Author's Note

For the sake of the storyline, some of the places and locations (college, town, etc.) in this book are fictitious.

Although this book features a British male lead, the novel is written in American English.

'Music gives a soul to the universe, Wings to the mind, flight to the imagination, And life to everything.'

Plato

I

Cromwell

The club pulsed as the beat I was pouring into the crowd took over their bodies. Arms in the air, hips swaying, eyes wide and glazed as my music slammed into their ears, the rhythmic beats controlling their every move. The air was thick and sticky, clothes slick to people's skins as they crammed into the full club to hear me.

I watched them light up with color. Watched them get lost to the sound. Watched them shed whoever they'd been that day – an office worker, a student, a copper, a call-center worker – what the hell ever. Right now, in this club, most probably high off their faces, they were slaves to my tunes. Right here, in this moment, my music was their life. It was all that mattered as their heads flew back and they chased the high, the near nirvana I gave them from my place on the podium.

I, however, felt nothing. Nothing but the numbness the booze beside me was gifting me.

Two arms slipped around my waist. Hot breath blew past my ear as full lips kissed my neck. Spinning my final beat, I grabbed the Jack Daniels beside me and took a shot straight from the bottle. I slammed the bottle down and moved back to my laptop to mix in the next tune.

Hands with sharp fingernails ran through my hair, pulling on the black strands. I tapped on the keys, bringing the music down low, slowing the beat.

My breaths lengthened as the crowd waited, lungs frozen as I brought them to a slow sway, readying for the crescendo. The epic surge of beats and drums, the insanity of the mix that I would deliver. I looked up from my laptop and scanned the crowd, smirking at seeing them on the precipice, waiting . . . waiting . . . just waiting . . .

Now.

I slammed my hand down, holding my headphones to my left ear. A surge, a thundercloud of electronic dance music plowed into the crowd. Bursts of neon colors filled the air. Greens and blues and reds filled my eyes as they clung to each person like neon shields.

The hands around my waist tightened, but I ignored them, instead listening to the bottle of Jack as it called my name. I took another shot, my muscles starting to loosen. My hands danced over the laptop's keys, over my mix boards.

I looked up, the crowd still in the palm of my hand.

They always were.

A girl in the center of the club drew my attention. Long brown hair pulled back off her face. Purple dress, high necked – she was dressed nothing like everyone else. The color surrounding her was different to the other clubbers – pale pink and lavender. Calmer. More serene. My eyebrows pulled down as I watched her. Her eyes were closed, but she wasn't moving. She was still, and she looked to be completely alone as people crashed and pushed around her. Her head was tipped up, a look of concentration on her face.

I built up the pace, pushing the rhythm and the crowd as

2

far as they could go. But the girl didn't move. That wasn't normal for me. I always had these clubbers wrapped around my finger. I controlled them, in every place I spun. In this arena, I was the puppet master. They were the dolls.

Another shot of Jack burned down my throat. And through another five songs, she stayed there, on the spot, just drinking in the beats like water. But her face never changed. No smile. No euphoric high. Just . . . eyes closed, that damn pinched look on her face.

And that pink and lavender still surrounding her like a shield.

'Cromwell,' the blonde who was all over me like a rash said into my ear. Her fingers lifted up my shirt and tucked into the waistband of my jeans. Her long nails dipped low. But I refused to tear my eyes away from the girl in the purple dress.

Her brown hair was starting to curl, sweat from being sandwiched by clubbers taking its effect. The blonde who was one step from wanking me off in full view of the club snapped my fly. I keyed in my next mix, then grabbed her hand and threw it away from me, snapping my fly closed. I groaned when her hands slid back into my hair. I looked at my mate who had spun before me. 'Nick!' I pointed to my decks. 'Watch this. And don't mess it up.'

Nick frowned in confusion, then saw the girl behind me and smiled. He took my headphones from me and moved to make sure the playlist I'd set up played on cue. Steve, the club's owner, always let a few girls backstage. I never asked for it, but I never turned them down either. Why would I refuse a hot bird who was up for anything?

I swiped my Jack off my podium as the blonde smashed

her lips to mine, pulling me back by my sleeveless Cream-fields shirt. I wrenched my mouth from hers, replacing it with the Jack bottle. The blonde dragged me into a dark spot backstage. She dropped to her knees and started again on my fly. I closed my eyes as she went to work.

I sucked on the Jack as my head hit the wall behind me. I forced myself to feel something. I glanced down, watching blonde hair bounce below me. But the numbness I lived with every damn day made me feel virtually nothing inside. Pressure built at the base of my spine. My thighs tightened, and then it was over.

The blonde got up. I could see the stars in her eyes as she looked at me. 'Your eyes.' She reached out a finger to trace around my eye. 'The strangest color. Such dark blue.'

They were. Coupled with my black hair, they always drew attention. That and the fact that I was one of the hottest new DJs in Europe, of course. Okay, maybe it was less to do with my eyes and more to do with my name, Cromwell Dean, gracing the headline spot on most of the biggest music festivals and clubs this summer.

I zipped up my fly and turned to see Nick spinning my next mix. I cringed when he failed to transition the beats like I would have. Navy blue was the backdrop to the smoke on the dancefloor.

I never hit navy blue.

I brushed past the girl with a 'Thanks, love,' ignoring her hiss of 'Prick' in response. I took my headphones off Nick's head and put them on my own. A few taps of the keyboard later, the crowd was back in the palm of my hand.

Without conscious thought, my eyes found their way to the spot where the girl in the purple dress had stood.

But she'd gone. So had the pale pink and lavender.

I threw back another shot of Jack. Mixed another tune. Then zoned the fuck out.

The sand was cold under my feet. It may well have been the start of summer here in the UK, but that didn't mean the night wind didn't freeze your balls off the minute you stepped outside. Clutching my bottle of booze and my cigarettes, I dropped down to the sand. I lit up and stared at the dark sky. My phone buzzed in my pocket . . . again. It'd been going off all night.

Pissed off that I actually had to move my arm, I pulled out my mobile. I had three missed calls from Professor Lewis. Two from my mum, and finally, a couple of texts.

MUM: Professor Lewis has been trying to get hold of you again. What are you going to do? Please just call me. I know you're upset, but this is your future. You have a gift, son. Maybe it's time for a fresh start this year. Don't waste it because you're angry at me.

Red-hot fury shot through me. I wanted to throw my phone in the damn sea and watch it sink to the bottom along with all this messed-up shit in my head, but I saw Professor Lewis had texted too.

LEWIS: The offer still stands but I need an answer by next week. I have all I need for the transfer except your answer. You have an exceptional talent, Cromwell. Don't waste it. I can help.

This time I did drop my phone beside me and sank back into the sand. I let the rush of nicotine fill my lungs and closed my eyes. As my eyelids shut, I heard quiet music playing somewhere nearby. Classical. Mozart.

My drunken mind immediately drifted off to when I was a little kid . . .

'What do you hear, Cromwell?' my father asked.

I closed my eyes and listened to the piece of music. Colors danced before my eyes. 'Piano. Violins. Cellos . . .' I took a deep breath. 'I can hear reds and greens and pinks.'

I opened my eyes and looked up at my father as he sat on my bed. He was staring down at me. There was a funny expression on his face. 'You hear colors?' he said. But he didn't sound surprised. My face set on fire. I ducked my head under my duvet. My father pulled it down from my eyes. He stroked my hair. 'That's good,' he said, his voice kind of deep. 'That's very good . . .'

My eyes snapped open. My hand started to ache. I looked at the bottle in my hand; my fingers were white as they gripped the neck. I sat up, my head spinning from the mass of whiskey in my body. My temples throbbed. I realized it wasn't from the Jack, but from the music coming from further down the beach. I pushed my hair back from my face then looked to my right.

Someone was only a few feet away. I squinted into the lightening night, summer's early rising sun making it possible to make out the features of whoever the hell it was. It was a girl. A girl wrapped in a blanket. Her phone sat beside her, a Mozart piano concerto drifting quietly from the speaker.

She must have felt me looking at her, because she turned her head. I frowned, wondering why I knew her face, but then—

'You're the DJ,' she said.

Recognition dawned. It was the girl in the purple dress. She clutched her blanket closer around her as I replayed her accent in my head. American. Bible Belt was my guess, by her thick twang.

She sounded like my mum.

A smile tugged at her lips as I stayed mute. I wasn't much of a talker. Especially when my gut was full of Jack and I had zero interest in making small talk with some girl I didn't know at four in the morning on a cold beach in Brighton.

'I'd heard of you,' she said. I stared back out over the sea. Ships sailed in the distance, their lights like tiny fireflies, bobbing up and down. I huffed a humorless laugh. Great. Another girl who wanted to screw the DJ.

'Good for you,' I muttered and took a drink of my Jack, feeling the addictive burn slide down my throat. I hoped she'd piss off, or at least stop trying to talk to me. My head couldn't take any more noise.

'Not really,' she shot back. I looked over at her, eyebrows pulled down in confusion. She was looking out over the sea, her chin resting on her folded arms that lay over her bent knees. The blanket had fallen off her shoulders, revealing the purple dress I'd noticed from the podium. She turned to face me, cheek now on her arms. Heat zipped through me. She was pretty. 'I've heard of you, Cromwell Dean.' She shrugged. 'Decided to get a ticket to see you before I left for home tomorrow.'

I lit up another cigarette. Her nose wrinkled. She clearly didn't like the smell.

Tough luck. She could move. Last time I checked, England was a free country. She went quiet.

I caught her looking at me. Her brown eyes were narrowed, like she was scrutinizing me. Reading something in me that I didn't want anyone to see.

No one ever looked at me closely. I never gave them the chance. I thrived on the podium at clubs because it kept everyone far away, down on the dancefloor where no one ever saw the real me. The way she was looking at me now made nervous shivers break out over my skin.

I didn't need this kind of crap.

'Already had my dick sucked tonight, love. Not looking for a second round.'

She blinked, and even in the rising sun, I could see her cheeks redden.

'Your music has no soul,' she blurted. My cigarette paused halfway to my mouth. Something managed to stab through my stomach at her words. I shoved it back down until I felt my usual sensation of numbness.

I sucked on my cigarette. 'Yeah? Well, them's the breaks.'

'I'd heard you were some messiah or something on that podium. But all your music comprised was synthetic beats and forced repetitive bursts of unoriginal tempo.'

I laughed and shook my head. The girl met my eyes head-on. 'It's called electronic dance music. Not a fifty-piece orchestra.' I held out my arms. 'You've heard of me. Said so yourself. You know what tunes I spin. What were you expecting? Mozart?' I glared at her phone, which was still playing that damn concerto.

I sat back, surprised at myself. I hadn't talked that much to anyone in . . . I didn't know how long. I took in a drag, breathing out the smoke that was trapped in my chest. 'And turn that thing off, will you? Who the hell goes to hear a dance DJ spin, then comes to a beach to listen to classical music?'

The girl frowned but turned off the music. I lay back on

the cold sand, closing my eyes. I heard the soft waves lapping the shore. My head filled with pale green. I heard the girl moving. I prayed she was leaving. But I felt her drop beside me. My world darkened as the whiskey and the usual lack of sleep started to pull me under.

'What do you feel when you mix your music?' she asked. How the hell she thought her little interview was a good idea right now was beyond me.

Yet, surprisingly, I found myself answering her question. 'I *don't* feel.' I cracked one eye open when she didn't say anything. She was looking down at me. She had the biggest brown eyes I'd ever seen. Dark hair pulled off her face in a ponytail. Full lips and smooth skin.

'Then that's the problem.' She smiled, but the smile looked nothing but sad. Pitying. 'The best music must be felt. By the creator. By the listener. Every part of it from creation to ear must be wrapped in nothing but feelings.' Some weird expression crossed over her face, but hell if I knew what it meant.

Her words were a blade to my chest. I hadn't expected her harsh comment. And I hadn't expected the blunt trauma that she seemed to deliver right to my heart. Like she'd taken a butcher's knife and sliced her way through my soul.

My body itched to get up and run. To pluck out her assessment of my music from my memory. But instead I forced a laugh, and spat, 'Go back home, little Dorothy. Back to where music means something. Where it's *felt*.'

'Dorothy was from Kansas,' she glanced away. 'I'm not.'

'Then go back to wherever the hell you're from,' I snapped. Crossing my arms over my chest, I hunkered down into the sand and shut my eyes, trying to block out the cold wind that was picking up and slapping my skin, and her words that were still stabbing at my heart.

I never let anything get to me like this. Not anymore. I just needed some sleep. I didn't want to go back to my mum's house here in Brighton, and my flat in London was too far away. So hopefully the cops wouldn't find me here and kick me off the beach.

With my eyes closed, I said, 'Thanks for the midnight critique, but as the fastest-rising DJ in Europe, with the best clubs in the world begging for me to spin at their decks – all at nineteen – I think I'll ignore your extensive notes and just keep on living my sweet as fuck life.'

The girl sighed, but she didn't say anything else.

The next thing I knew, the sun was burning its light into my eyes. I flinched when I opened them. The screech of swarming seagulls slammed into my head. I sat up, seeing an empty beach and the sun high in the sky. I ran my hands down my face and groaned at the hangover that was kicking in. My stomach growled, desperate for a full English breakfast with copious cups of black tea.

As I stood, something fell from my lap. A blanket lay on the sand at my feet. The blanket I'd seen beside the American girl in the purple dress.

The one she'd been wrapped in last night.

I picked it up, a light fragrance drifted into my nose. Sweet. Addictive. I glanced around me. The girl was gone.

She'd left her blanket. No. She'd covered me with it. *'Your music has no soul.'* A hard clenching feeling pulled in my stomach at the memory of her words. So I chased it away like I did anything that made me feel. Caging it deep inside.

Then I took my arse home.

2

Cromwell

Jefferson Young University, South Carolina
Three months later . . .

I knocked on the door.

Nothing.

I dropped my bag to the floor. When no one answered, I turned the knob and let myself in. One half of the room was covered in posters: bands, art, a Mickey Mouse painting, a bright green shamrock painting – the themes were all over the place. It was the most random thing I'd ever seen. The bed was already messed up, black duvet cover bunched at the foot of the bed. Crisp packets and chocolate wrappers littered the small desk. Used paints and brushes were strewn all over the windowsill.

I was a slob, but not this much of one.

To my left was what was obviously my bed. I threw my overstuffed bag on the floor beside it then collapsed on the bed. It was tiny, my feet almost hanging off the end. I took my headphones from around my neck and put them over my ears. Jet lag was kicking in and I had a crick in my neck from where I had slept in a funny position on the flight.

Just as I was about to turn my music on, someone flew through the door. My eyes slammed onto a tall guy with blond, shaggy hair. He was wearing long shorts and a sleeveless top. 'You're here!' he said, putting his hands on his knees, catching his breath.

I raised a single eyebrow in question. He held up his hand for me to wait, then came closer and held out his hand. I shook it, reluctantly. 'You're Cromwell Dean,' he said.

I sat up on the bed, kicking my legs off the side. The guy pulled a chair from under his desk and brought it next to my bed. He spun it and sat down, resting his arms on the back. 'I'm Easton Farraday. Your roommate.'

I nodded, then pointed to his side of the room. 'Your decoration is . . . eclectic.'

Easton winked and smiled wide. I wasn't used to smiling people. Never knew why people had reason to smile so much. 'That's as good a word as any for me, I suppose.' He got off the chair. 'Let's go.'

Running my hand through my hair, I stood. 'And where the hell are we going?'

Easton laughed. 'Hell, boy. Gonna take me a while to get used to that accent.' He nudged me in the arm. 'Girls 'round here gonna be flipping out over it.' His eyebrows danced. 'That and the fact that you're a famous DJ and all. You get pussy by the truckload, huh?'

'I do all right.'

Easton put his hands on my shoulders. 'You lucky bastard. Teach me your ways!' He walked to the door. 'Let's go. You're gonna get the Easton Farraday tour of Jefferson Young.'

I looked out of the window at the quad. The sun was boiling hot. I was from England; no one was used to getting that much heat exposure. Although technically, I was from South Carolina. My mum was from here, but I'd never known the place. We moved to the UK when I was only seven weeks old. I might have been American born, but I was British through and through.

'Why not?' I said, and Easton led me out of the door.

I followed him down the corridor. We passed a few people, and every one of them said hello to Easton. Hand slaps, hugs, and winks were handed out to both boys and girls from my new roommate. I saw the guys eyeing me weird. Some obviously trying to suss me out, others clearly recognizing me.

Easton tipped his chin at a guy and a girl approaching. The guy looked at me. 'Shit. Cromwell Dean. Easton said you were coming but I thought he was just full of it.' He shook his head. 'Why the hell are you here at JYU? It's all anyone can talk about.'

I opened my mouth, but Easton answered for me. 'For Lewis, right? Everyone who ever picked up a damn instrument is here for him.'

The guy nodded, like I'd answered his question, not Easton. 'I'm Matt. Easton's friend.' Matt laughed. 'You'll soon see that you're rooming with the most popular guy on campus. We're small-time at this college, but this guy's mouth is big. Took all of three weeks for everyone to know him freshman year. Only a few more before the faculty, seniors, and everyone in between knew his name.'

'Sara,' the redhead next to Matt said. 'You'll no doubt be drafted into our group.'

'You gotta spin on Friday,' Matt said.

Easton groaned and punched Matt in the arm. 'I had a plan, Matt. You gotta work up to asking that shit.'

My gaze darted between Matt and Easton. Sara rolled her eyes at them, then Easton turned to me. 'We got an old abandoned barn-slash-warehouse thing a few miles off campus. Old alumnus owns the land and the barn. He lets us use it for parties. Ain't many places around here to party – we had to get creative. It's all rigged up. One of the seniors from last year went all out with lights, a dancefloor, and a podium. Wanted to piss away Daddy's money for cheating on his mom. Place is a college dream.'

'Cops?' I asked.

Easton shrugged. 'It's a college in a small-ass town. Most of us are from the local areas. Jefferson never had a big pull for anything but being cheap for locals' tuition, until Lewis came this year. Most of the cops went to high school with someone here. Old friends. They don't bother us.'

'We kind of have a "don't ask, don't tell" situation with them. The Barn is far enough away from civilization that ain't no one complaining about the noise,' Matt said.

My head was throbbing. I needed a cigarette and about fourteen hours of sleep. 'Sure,' I said when I saw three sets of eyes all watching me, waiting for my answer.

'Holy shit!' Matt threw his arm around Sara's shoulders. 'I can't believe it. Cromwell Dean is spinning at the Barn!' He turned to Easton. 'It's gonna be epic.'

Easton saluted, then put his hand on my shoulder. 'Gonna give Crom a tour. Catch you later.' I followed Easton down the stairs that led to the quad. He took a deep breath when the humid air slammed into us like a freight train. Easton spread his arms. 'This, Cromwell, is the quad.' People lounged on the grass, music playing from phone speakers. Students were reading, chilling out in couples. Again, everyone said hi to Easton. They just outright stared at me. Guess that's what happens when you transfer in sophomore year to a rinky-dink university from another country.

'The quad. For chilling, skipping class, or whatever,' Easton said. I followed Easton to the cafeteria, then the library – which he told me wasn't for books, but for shagging behind the stacks. We got to a truck. 'Get in,' he said. Too tired to argue, I got in, and he pulled out onto the road, heading away from the college.

'So?' he asked as I lit up a cigarette and took a deep drag. I closed my eyes as I exhaled. Nine hours on a flight without nicotine was a bitch.

'Share the joy, Crom,' Easton said. I passed him a cigarette. I wound the window down and looked out at the sports fields and small stadium for the American football team.

'So?' Easton repeated. 'I get Lewis is a big draw for you, but even so, your life is made, isn't it?' I rolled my head against the headrest to look at him. He had a tattoo on his arm. Looked like a star-sign symbol or something. Never understood why people only ever got one. The minute I got my first, I booked in for the rest. A ton later and I still wasn't finished. I was addicted.

His speaker was playing a playlist from his phone. As if on cue, one of my mixes came through. He laughed. 'In case you were wondering, that was just God backing me up on my question.'

I tipped my head back and closed my eyes, just taking in the smoke. 'Did a year of uni in London. It was okay, but I didn't want to be in England anymore. Lewis invited me here to study under him. So I came.'

There was a brief silence. 'But I still don't understand. Why finish at all? You have a career that's taking off. Why bother with college?'

A knife in my stomach twisted, my throat clogging up. I wasn't going there. So I just kept my eyes closed and my mouth shut.

Easton sighed. 'Fine. Be a mystery. Just add that to the list of things the chicks will get wet over.' He shoved my arm. 'Open your eyes. How can I show you the sights of Jefferson Town if they're shut?'

'It can be an audio tour. The way you never shut your mouth, you could make some serious coin doing it.'

He burst out laughing. 'True.' He pointed at the small town we were entering. 'Welcome to Jefferson. Founded in 1812. Population two thousand.' He turned down what had to be the main road. 'You have all the usual places.' He said that in a horrendous English accent, which I assumed was for my pleasure. 'Dairy Queen, McDonalds, all that stuff. A few redneck bars. Some small diners. A coffee lounge – has some pretty good open mic nights if you're looking to chill. Some good local talent.' There was a cinema that had four screens, some touristy stuff, and finally, we passed the Barn. It was exactly that, but Easton promised me inside resembled something you'd find in Ibiza. Having played in Ibiza the most out of anywhere I'd spun, I doubted that. But it was a place to play, and in this town, it was something.

'What are you studying?' I asked.

'Art,' he replied. I thought of the posters and paintings

on the wall of our room. 'I like mixed media too. Anything with color and expression.' He cocked his head my way. 'I'll be running the lights on Friday. You on the decks, me on the lights. It's gonna be sick.' He waggled his eyebrows. 'Think of all the chicks we'll get.'

Right then, all I could think of was sleep.

3

Cromwell

Easton was practically bouncing on the driver's seat of his truck as we approached the Barn. It was only ten at night. I wasn't used to hitting the decks until twelve at the earliest.

Easton was right. The place was bouncing, people spilling all over the grass outside the wooden building. Dance music pounded through the cracks in the wooden panels. I winced on hearing one awful mix slide into another tune.

Easton must have seen my expression. He pulled the truck to a stop and put his hand on my arm. 'You're our savior, Crom. You see what we've had to put up with? Bryce is protective over his decks. You've been warned.'

I lit up a cigarette and got out of the truck. All eyes had been on it from the minute Easton pulled up. It got even worse when I got out. I ignored the stares and hushed whispers and moved to the bed of the truck.

I pulled out my laptop bag, throwing it over my shoulder. My sleeveless t-shirt was sticking to my chest. The weather made me feel like I was living in a permanent sauna. The denim of my jeans clung to my legs. I followed Easton toward the barn. All the girls were checking me out. With two full sleeves and tattoos creeping up my neck, there were only ever two reactions to me. Girls either flooding their knickers as soon as they clapped eyes on my ink, or complete revulsion. From the looks coming my way, it was mostly the former.

A brunette stepped in front of me, stopping me dead. Easton laughed beside me. She pushed on his arm, then said, 'I'm Kacey. You're Cromwell Dean.'

'Good observation,' I said.

She smiled. I ran my tongue over my lips and saw her eyes snap to my tongue ring. 'I'm . . . um . . .' She blushed. 'I'm looking forward to hearing your set.' She took a sip of her beer and nervously tucked her hair behind her ear. 'I've got some of your mixes on my jogging playlists, but I've heard it's like nothing else to hear you live.'

I looked at Easton. 'If you want me to save everyone from the ear-bleeding mixes that this Bryce is playing, we'd better go.'

'Catch you later, Kacey,' Easton said. I nodded at Kacey then moved around her toward the door. Easton nudged me. 'She's a good one.' He smiled wider. 'Hot too, huh?'

I ducked my head, hiding my face when I noticed *all* the people staring. I hated attention. I knew it sounded stupid, the DJ hating attention. But I just wanted people to want my music, not me. I didn't want their interest in me as a person. I just wanted to play.

Had to play for my sanity.

The rest was hard to deal with.

There wasn't much to me anyway. I really wasn't worth knowing.

Easton laughed at me shunning the attention and threw his arm around my neck. As loud as he was, he would never understand. The arsehole had no concept of personal space. But I couldn't help but like him. I didn't have friends. And I had a feeling he wouldn't go away even if I asked him to.

'Shit, Crom. You feeling like an animal in a zoo or what? We don't get many celebrities here in Jefferson.'

'I'm not a celebrity,' I replied as he led me toward the podium.

'In the electronic dance music world you are. And here at JYU you are.' He leaned over to another girl who was hanging by the stage. I swear, the guy was a chick magnet. He turned back to me. 'What's your poison?'

'Jack. Full bottle.'

'Nice,' Easton said, smiling in approval.

The girl went running off. I opened my bag and grabbed my headphones. Loosening my neck, I pulled out my laptop. Easton watched me like I was some living breathing science experiment. I raised my eyebrow. 'It's like watching a master at work or something,' he said.

Easton tapped the current DJ on the shoulder. Bryce. Bryce looked at me from the side of his eye then stormed off the podium. Easton laughed as the moody wanker pushed by me. I climbed the steps to the podium and set up my laptop. I plugged it in to the system, then let myself look up.

The place was jam-packed. Hundreds of eyes locked on me. I took a deep breath as the rising heat from the dancing bodies stuck to my skin, as the vibrant colors that surrounded them assaulted my eyes.

A bottle of Jack appeared beside me. I took a long swig then slammed the bottle back to my right. Easton, to my left, flicked his chin at me. He was downing a bottle of tequila like it was water. I peered over my laptop at the bodies lined up and waiting.

I lived for this moment. The pause. The held breath before the chaos.

I tapped the keys. Lined up the tune. Then, with a flick of my hand, sent the crowd into euphoria. Easton bathed the barn in green laser lights. Strobes followed, making the dancing crowd look as though they were moving in slow motion. Drinking. Smoking. Some high off their tits.

Easton threw his head back in laughter. 'This is insane! Cromwell Dean is in the Barn!'

The beat became the rhythm of my heart as it pounded against the barn's walls. Easton wasn't lying. Inside, this place was good. I took sip after sip of my Jack. Easton sucked on the tequila like it would run out if he didn't get it all down quick.

I shrugged. It was his life, and his killer hangover that'd smack him square in the eyes tomorrow. I glanced at my Jack. Who was I kidding? I was planning on joining him.

Easton nudged my arm. He flicked his chin at the front of the podium. Kacey, the brunette bird from outside, was looking up at me. She smiled, and I nodded my head at her. As I scanned the crowd, I saw people laughing in groups, couples kissing, dancing. I never had any of that in my life. I had my music. That was it. My stomach caved in sudden sadness, catching me off guard. I immediately threw the feeling away.

I wouldn't let it in.

Focusing back on my music, I threw in some beats to the mix, adding depth. Bass drums bouncing so hard they shook the building. Easton leaned over me to the mic. I never spoke. My music did the talking for me. Never even had anyone singing over my tunes. Just beats and the rhythm. 'Is that what you call losing it?' Easton shouted, and the crowd screamed.

He jumped onto the table holding my decks. I shook my head, smirking at the walking ego that was Easton Farraday. 'I said . . .' He paused, then screamed, 'Is that what you call fucking losing it?'

I slammed them with a bass beat so hard and fast it controlled them, brought them to their knees. Bodies bumped and smashed into each other as they moved. As they jumped and drank and some practically shagged on the floor. And I was lost to it. Like always, up on this podium, I was gone. Taken from the darkness inside my head and thrust into this. This numb nirvana.

I closed my eyes to pull myself from Easton's lights. My bones vibrated with the bass I was pushing. The sound sailed through my ears and injected itself straight into my veins. Bursts of reds and yellows danced behind my closed eyelids. I snapped my eyes open, only to see Easton stumbling around the podium. His arm was around a girl's neck as she practically ate his mouth. He backed her away until they were on the dancefloor and heading outside.

Hours passed in the blink of an eye. I played until I was done with my mixes. Bryce, the prick from before, was taking over before I'd even got off the podium. I took my Jack and snuck outside; the crowd were too off their faces to even notice the DJs had switched.

I'd completely ruined them.

I hit the outside air and found a quiet spot beside one of the barn's walls. I slumped to the ground and closed my eyes. The sound of laughing made me open them again.

This place was nothing like uni back in London. Jefferson Young was tiny, and everyone knew each other. My uni in London was massive. It was easy to get lost in the crowd. I'd lived alone. No dorms. Just a studio flat near the campus. No friends.

It was a different world out here. And I knew that having barely seen any of it.

For the past few days I'd barely left my room, sleeping off my jetlag and mixing my tracks for tonight. Easton tried to get me to hang with him and his mates, but I didn't. I wasn't exactly a social person. I was better on my own.

I closed my eyes again, just as I felt a warm body sit beside me. It was Kacey, a Corona in her hand. 'You wiped?'

'Knackered,' I said and heard her small laugh. Probably at my accent. Easton had been doing the same thing all week.

'You were amazing.' I looked over to her, and she dipped her head away. 'You must feel a million miles away from home, huh? Jefferson's not exactly London. Not that I've ever been, but . . . yeah.'

'Distance is good.'

She nodded like she understood. She didn't.

'Your major is music?' She shook her head. 'Obviously. It must be.' She cast her gaze over the people stumbling out of the barn. I'd leave too if I had to listen to that crap the other DJ was spewing out. 'I'm majoring in English.'

I didn't talk back to her; it just wasn't me. Instead, I drank my Jack in silence as she drank her Corona. A few minutes later, Matt and Sara came over. Matt crouched next to Kacey and spoke to her in low, urgent tones. She sighed. 'I need to call her?'

Matt nodded.

'Christ.' Kacey pulled out her phone and stood up.

'What's wrong?' I asked.

'Easton,' Matt answered. 'He's wasted. Refusing to move.' He pointed at Kacey. 'She's calling his sister. She's the only one who can handle him in this state. Asshole gets violent as all hell when you try to cut him off. Likes to party, but can't really handle the party, if you know what I mean.'

'Back off!' Easton's drunken voice rang out across the field. People gave him a wide berth as he stumbled our way, still clutching his tequila bottle. It was empty. 'Cromwell!' He stopped beside me and swung his arm around my neck. 'That set!' he slurred. 'Can't believe you're here, man. In Jefferson! Nothing ever happens here. It's a boring shithole.'

He slumped down next to the barn. Matt tried to get him to his feet. 'Fuck off!' Easton snapped. 'Where's Bonnie?'

'She's coming.' Easton dropped his head but nodded to show he'd heard.

'He's my ride,' I whispered to Matt.

'Shit. Our ride is full. Bonnie will take you home. She always takes East back to y'all's room anyway. She's nice. She won't mind.'

'I'm going to get my things.' I ducked back into the barn and got my laptop. I pushed my hair from my face as I exited the barn. I scanned the grounds. I was hoping coming here would make me feel better. Would take this dark pit, the one forever trying to cave in my stomach, away. I'd played my music to a packed crowd. Spoke to people, but I could feel the sadness I'd pushed down low fighting to be freed anyway. Ready to consume me. To bury me in the past.

Coming here had made no difference at all.

I noticed a silver 4x4 parked across from me. The headlights blinded me as I approached. I winced. My hangover was well and truly setting in. Matt was helping Easton off the floor, some new bird in tight jeans and a white cardigan on Easton's other side.

This must be the sister. I made my way over as Matt shut the car door. Easton lay sprawled, knocked the hell out, on the back seat.

'You're okay to get him home?' Matt asked the girl, before he hugged her and let her go. Sara did the same.

'Yeah,' she said.

'Cromwell!' Matt ushered me over with a wave of his hand. The sister didn't turn as I approached. Her back was rigid. 'Over here. Bonnie's taking Easton home.' He looked down at her. 'You won't mind taking Cromwell, will you? There's no room left in our ride. East brought him here.'

I didn't hear her reply. Instead, I moved to the boot of the car and put in my stuff. Matt waved at me as he walked away, taking Sara with him. Kacey put her hand on my arm. 'Nice to meet you, Cromwell.' She walked away with everyone else, looking back over her shoulder one more time as she did.

Just as I was about to open the passenger-side door, Easton's sister turned to face me. I couldn't believe my eyes.

25

A hazy memory hitched a ride on the warm breeze and bitch-slapped me across the face.

Your music has no soul . . .

She sighed, clearly seeing my pissed off reaction, then said, 'Hello again.'

'You.' I laughed dryly at the way the bastard universe liked to work against me.

'Me,' she said, seemingly amused, and shrugged. I watched her as she walked to the driver's side. Her dark brown hair was off her face, just like it had been in Brighton. She wore it in a ponytail, the tail hanging down her back until it stopped halfway down her spine.

She got in, then the passenger-side window rolled down. 'You getting in or are you walking home?'

I rolled my tongue ring in my mouth, trying to unclench my fists. No way would I show her how much that one bastard line she'd said on a cold-ass summer morning in Brighton had got to me. I refused to let it affect me like that again.

Bonnie, as she was apparently called, revved the engine. I huffed a disbelieving laugh. I opened the back door. Easton was snoring. His arms and legs took up every bit of space.

Bonnie leaned back, looking at me through the seats. I avoided her eyes. 'Looks like you're gonna be up front with me, superstar.'

I gritted my teeth and took a long deep breath. I searched for where I'd been sitting. The Jack was still there. I ran over to get it then slid into the passenger seat. I was going to need alcohol for this journey.

'Jack Daniels,' she said. 'Seems like you and he are close friends.'

'The best,' I said and slumped in the seat.

The silence in the car was deafening. I reached over and switched on the radio. Some folk song was playing. No thanks. I flicked on the next song on her playlist. When Beethoven's Fifth Symphony started, I decided to just turn the damn thing off.

'Your choice in music leaves a lot to be desired.' I took a long drink of my Jack. I didn't know why I'd even opened my mouth. I was never the first to speak. But as her words from that night circled my head, I'd felt the anger rise up inside me and they'd just spilled out.

'Ah, that's right. No classical. And now no folk. Good to know that good music offends you.' She took her attention off the road for a split second to look at me from the side of her eye. Her eyebrows pulled down. 'You're here for Lewis, right? Why else would you be in Jefferson?'

I took another drink, ignoring the question. I didn't want to talk to her about music. I didn't want to talk to her, full stop. I pulled a cigarette from my pocket and put it in my mouth. I went to light up, but she said, 'No smoking in my car.' I lit up anyway and took a long drag. The car stopped so fast I almost lost my Jack to gravity. 'I said, no smoking in my car,' she snapped. 'Put it out or get out. There's your two choices, Cromwell Dean.'

My body tensed. No one ever spoke to me like this. The fact that she'd pissed me off made it worse. I met her eyes and took a long, sweet suck on my cigarette then flicked it out of the window she'd opened for me. It was the first time I'd looked at her straight-on. She was all brown eyes and full lips. I held up my hands. 'All gone, Bonnie Farraday.'

She pulled back out onto the road and suddenly we were at Main Street. Students were staggering home in twos and threes, walking back to the dorms from the Barn. I didn't want to talk to her, but the silence in the car was even worse. My hands clenched on the thighs of my jeans. 'Not your scene?' I asked tightly.

'I was busy tonight. Studying before classes start on Monday.' She pointed behind her to her snoring brother. 'Or at least I was trying to, until my twin decided to get wasted, as always.'

My eyebrows lifted. She saw. 'Yeah. Easton's older by four minutes. Look nothing alike, do we? We *are* nothing alike. But he's my best friend. So here I am. Bonnie's taxi service.'

'Easton said you were both local.'

'Yeah, from Jefferson. As South Carolinian as they come.' I felt her eyes on me. 'Weird though, huh? That you're here after our meeting in England?'

I shrugged. But it was. What were the chances of that?

Bonnie pulled the car into a space in front of the dorm. She looked back at her brother. 'You're gonna have to help me carry him up the stairs.' I got out of the car and moved to the back seat. I pulled Easton out and threw him over my shoulder. 'My laptop,' I said, jerking my chin to the boot. Bonnie moved to the boot of the car and took out my stuff. I managed to carry Easton up the stairs and throw him down on his bed.

Bonnie was behind me. She was out of breath, huffing and puffing from the stairs.

'Maybe you should start some cardio. Stairs shouldn't be that hard.' I was being a dick. I knew it. But I couldn't seem to stop myself. That night in Brighton she'd well and truly pissed me off. Apparently, I couldn't let it go.

Ignoring me, Bonnie put my things on my desk. She took a glass off Easton's bedside table then left the room. She came back with it full of water and placed it beside him. She left two tablets beside the water and kissed his head. 'Call me tomorrow.'

I lay on my bed, my headphones around my neck, ready to zone out. Bonnie passed me and stopped. 'Thank you for carrying him up.' She took one last glance at him. Her eyes seemed to soften for some reason. It made her look . . . prettier than normal. 'Can you keep an eye on him, please?'

I pulled that thought out of my head. 'He's a big boy. I'm sure he can look after himself.'

Bonnie snapped her head to me. She appeared shocked, then her face frosted over. 'I see you're as charming as ever, Cromwell. Have a good night.'

Bonnie left. As she did, Easton stirred and cracked open an eye. 'Bonnie?'

'She left,' I said, throwing off my shirt. I stripped down to my boxers and got into bed.

Easton had turned back over. 'My sister. She tell you that?'

'She did.'

He was asleep in seconds.

I opened my music on my phone. And like every night, I let the comfort of dance music fill my head. The colors were different with EDM. They weren't the ones that made me remember everything.

And I thanked whoever the hell was up there, God or whatever, for that fact.

4

Bonnie

I shut the door of my SUV and made my way to my dorm room. With every step I thought of Cromwell Dean. I knew he was here, of course. The minute Easton found out he was rooming with him it was all he would talk about.

I, however, couldn't believe my ears.

Easton never knew I met him in Brighton. No one did. Quite honestly, I still couldn't believe that I'd spoken to him the way I did. But the way he'd spoken to me . . . dismissed me. He'd been so rude, I couldn't help it. I had seen him stagger down to that beach, Jack Daniels in hand. I had watched him in that packed club. Watched as people danced to his music like he was a god. And all I felt was . . .

Disappointment.

Cromwell Dean. Most of the world knew him as a DJ, but I knew him for something else. I knew him as the classical prodigy. And unbeknownst to Cromwell Dean, I had seen him. Seen him as a child conducting a symphony so beautifully that he inspired me to be a better musician. Seen raw footage of an English boy with the talent of Mozart. My music teacher had shown me the video of him in one of my private piano lessons. To show me what someone my age was capable of.

To show that there were others in the world that had

as much passion for music as I did. Cromwell Dean had become my greatest friend, even though he didn't know I existed. He was my hope. Hope that outside of this small town, people held music in their hearts the same way I did. Someone else bled for notes, melodies, and concertos.

Cromwell had won the BBC Proms Young Composer of the Year aged sixteen. His music had been played by the BBC Symphony Orchestra on the final night of the Proms. I'd watched in the middle of the night, on my laptop, tears streaming down my face, overawed by his creation. The camera had shown him watching the orchestra from the front row.

I'd thought him as beautiful as the symphony he'd composed.

Then, only months later, he disappeared. No more music was made. His music died along with his name.

But in all that time, *I* never forgot his name. So when he began making music again, my excitement was uncontainable.

Until I heard it.

I had nothing against electronic dance, per se. But to hear the boy I had idolized for so many years mixing synthetic beats instead of the real instruments he played like a master destroyed my heart.

I had gone to listen to him when I was in England. I couldn't help myself. I melded in with the crowd. I closed my eyes. But I felt nothing. I opened my eyes and watched him, feeling nothing but sympathy toward the boy I had once seen conducting the music he had crafted so stunningly. Hands dancing with the baton as he was carried away with the sweeping strings and soaring woodwind.

The music he had poured onto the page from his soul. The imprint of his heart that he left in the theater that had been gifted the performance. And the people who'd been blessed to hear it.

Up on that podium, his eyes were dead. His heart was absent from the beats, and his soul wasn't even in the room. He may be the fastest-rising DJ in Europe, but what he was playing wasn't his passion. It wasn't his purpose.

He couldn't fool me.

The Cromwell Dean I'd watched as a child had died with whatever made him lose that need to create such life-changing pieces of music.

'Bonnie?'

I blinked, my eyes clearing only to stare at the wooden door of my dorm hallway. I turned to see Kacey entering her room beside mine.

'Hey,' I said and put my hand on my head.

'You okay? You were standing with your hand on the doorknob for a few minutes.'

I laughed and shook my head. 'Got lost to my thoughts.'

Kacey smiled. 'How's Easton?'

I rolled my eyes. 'Drunk. But, thankfully, asleep and safe in bed.'

Kacey came closer. 'Did you give Cromwell a ride home?'

'Yeah.'

'What was he like? Did he speak?'

'A little.' I sighed, tiredness kicking in. I needed to sleep so badly.

'And?'

I eyed her and shook my head. 'Quite frankly, he's kind of a dick. He's rude and arrogant.'

'But hot.' Kacey blushed.

'I don't think he'd be a good one to go for, Kace.' I remembered the girl he had disappeared with in Brighton. In the middle of a set. His crass words to me on the beach: *I've already had my dick sucked . . .*

Kacey wasn't really a friend; she just lived next to me. She was sweet. And I was sure Cromwell Dean would chew her up and spit her out when he got what he wanted from her. He seemed exactly the type.

'Yeah,' Kacey said in response. I knew she was only being polite pretending to heed my words. 'I'd better get to bed.' She cocked her head to the side. 'You too, sweetie. You're looking kinda pale.'

'Night, Kace. See you tomorrow.'

I pushed through to my single room. I dropped my purse on the floor, put on my PJs, and climbed into bed. I tried to sleep. I was tired, my body aching with exhaustion. Yet my mind wouldn't turn off.

I couldn't get Cromwell out of my head. And worse, I knew I'd be seeing him on Monday. We were in most of the same classes. I was majoring in music. There had never been any other choice for me. I knew Cromwell was the same. Easton had told me.

I closed my eyes, but all I saw was him lounging on the passenger seat of my car, the Jack in his hand. Him smoking when I'd asked him not to. The tattoos and the piercings.

'Cromwell Dean, what happened to you?' I whispered into the night.

Reaching over to my cell, I brought up the video of the music that had been in my heart for so long and pressed play. As the string instruments danced and the wind section took the lead, I shut my eyes, and sleep found me.

I wondered if music like this would ever again find the heart of Cromwell Dean.

'Sis?' I turned around on my chair to see Easton entering my room.

'Well, hello,' I said. Easton dropped onto my bed. He ran his fingers over my guitar before putting it on the floor.

'Sorry about last night,' he said and met my eyes. 'It was Crom's first night on the decks and the place was insane. I got swept up in it all.' He shrugged. 'You know me.'

'Yeah. I know you.' I moved to the small fridge in my room and handed him a soda.

'Sugar. Thanks, Bonn. You know how to cheer me up.'

'You know I don't even drink that stuff. I have it here for your hangover emergencies.'

He winked at me. 'Cromwell said you drove us home.' I nodded. 'What do you think of him?'

I pushed his legs out of the way so I could sit beside him on the bed. 'What do I think of him?'

'Yeah,' he asked and downed the soda. He got up and grabbed another before sitting back down. 'I get he comes off rude. But I like the guy. Just don't think he has many friends.'

'He just got here.'

'I mean in England too. No one ever calls him. I've seen a few texts, but he said they were from his mama.'

'He shouldn't be so rude then, should he?'

'He was rude to you?'

'He was drunk,' I said, completely excluding the fact that he was a lot worse when I met him in Brighton.

Easton nodded. 'You should have been there, Bonn. The guy is insanely talented. It's like he just zones out and plays straight from his soul. And shit, he's gonna be in your class, yeah? You'll have to watch out for him.'

'I get the impression he doesn't need anyone to watch out for him, East.'

'Even so.' He jumped off the bed and held out his hand. 'Come on. Mama and Papa will be at the diner already.'

I took his hand and got off the bed. He looked at me, watching closely. 'You okay? You seem tired. You've stayed in more than usual this summer.'

I rolled my eyes. 'Easton, I *am* tired. I had to come get you after pulling an all-night study session.' I could feel my cheeks heat at the excuse. 'I wanna impress Lewis on Monday, you know? To get someone like that here . . .' I shook my head. 'It's not every day someone with that talent becomes your teacher.'

Easton threw his arm around me. 'You're such a nerd.'

I pulled away from him and threw some Altoids in his direction. 'Eat a few of those before we get to Mama and Papa. You smell like a liquor store.' Easton caught them and led us out of the door.

On Monday, classes would begin. I was pretty sure Cromwell Dean wouldn't even look my way. And Easton had it *way* wrong. That guy didn't need someone to watch out for him.

I was sure he'd only be a dick if I even tried.

5

Bonnie

The class was buzzing. Last year, there had never been energy like this. The class was small, but I could feel everyone's excitement as if I was standing in the center of a packed stadium.

My friend Bryce leaned over. 'Weird, huh? How a professor can cause this much hype.'

He wasn't just any professor though. Professor Lewis was a world-renowned composer. He'd traveled the world. Performed in concert halls and theaters that someone like me could only dream of. His personal struggles with drugs and alcohol were widely known. It's what had taken him from his life's work and back to Jefferson. His hometown. In an interview with the school paper, he'd said that he needed to be grounded in the place he knew best. Wanted to give back to his local community by taking tenure here.

The music world's loss was our gain.

I tapped my pen in a see-saw motion on my open notebook. The door opened, and a man I'd seen countless times on TV walked through. The room was silent as he walked to the table at the front of the classroom. He was young. Younger in person than I'd expected. He had dark hair and a kind smile.

He had just opened his mouth to speak when the door

opened again and a tall, heavily tattooed frame walked through.

Cromwell.

If Professor Lewis's entrance had inspired silence and awe, Cromwell Dean's entrance brought hushed whispers and fifteen sets of curious eyes fixed on him as he walked, head down, toward the back seats.

He walked slowly up the stairs and sat near the back. I didn't turn like everyone else. I looked at Professor Lewis, noting the lines of annoyance on his forehead.

Lewis cleared his throat. 'Mr Dean. Nice of you to join us.'

This time I did glance back at Cromwell. Just to see if he had any hint of remorse. He was slouching in his seat, staring blankly at Lewis. He looked the epitome of arrogance, rolling his tongue ring against his teeth. He was dressed in black jeans that had a chain hanging from the waist, and a simple white shirt with a low neck and tight short sleeves that gripped his muscled biceps. His tattoos climbed like vines up his arms and neck.

Some people would think them art. I thought they looked like they were strangling him.

His hair was messy and falling over his forehead. He wore silver rings in his ears and a single one through his left nostril.

Just as I was about to turn away, his eyes found mine. The color of his irises was strange. They were a turbulent kind of blue. Not like the blue of the sky, but a deep navy like the dangerous depths of a violently thrashing sea. He sighed heavily. I was sure it was at my presence. I hadn't told him I was majoring in music too.

'Mr Dean? Can we start?' Lewis asked.

He nodded his head. 'I wasn't stopping you.' My eyes widened at his response.

Cromwell's English accent was thick and obvious against Lewis's South Carolinian. As if Cromwell needed one more reason to stand out. His sullenness and tattoos were enough to do that in this small town. I took my sweater from around my chair and put it on. The room suddenly felt chilly.

'Let's not beat around the bush,' Lewis said as he addressed the class. 'I run a tiring program, and I expect y'all to comply and give it your best.' He came to stand in front of his table. He sat back on the tabletop and said, 'you should have all read the course syllabus by now. If you have, you'll know that the largest percentage of the grade comes from a year-long composition project. This will be undertaken in pairs.' He smiled, an uncontained excitement in his brown eyes. I thought I saw him briefly flick his gaze to Cromwell, but I couldn't be sure.

'I have already picked the pairs.' He reached into his briefcase and held up a piece of paper. 'You will see who you've been paired with at the end of class. And before you ask, no, the pairings are non-negotiable. And yes, both of you must complete the assignment or risk getting an incomplete. No one wants that on their record.'

He moved back around the desk and clicked on the projector. The TA turned off the lights. 'You will each get fifteen hours of one-on-one sessions with me per semester.' He looked over his shoulder, stern faced. 'Don't waste these hours.'

I looked at Bryce, feeling the blood rushing through

my veins. 'One-on-one sessions,' I said excitedly, and Bryce smiled wide.

'We'll have seminars every other week to discuss our compositions, both individual and the one done in pairs. Because the class is *all* about composition.' Lewis smiled and dropped his hard persona for a moment. 'I intend to create masters in this room. You will all know of my personal demons.' I held my breath. Everybody knew about his issues, but I didn't think he'd actually talk about them in class. 'I tried my best to bring my music to the world, but it wasn't my destiny.' He smiled again, an expression of peace washing over his face. 'I've found happiness in helping others realize their talents. My fate, it seems, is teaching. Helping others find their meaning in this world. Their passion.'

A soft silence enveloped the room. I blinked, realizing my heart was full and so were my eyes.

'There'll be a showcase at the end of the year. Your compositions will be performed then.' He stood and put his hands in his slacks pockets. 'What I failed to learn in my time as a composer is to lean on others. Share ideas and push one another to make your art the very best it can be.' He pointed at the class. 'Y'all are here because you are talented. But news flash: so are millions of other people. This project will help you learn from one another and improve your craft. It's the assignment I'm most intrigued by.'

Professor Lewis turned back to the projector screen and finished talking through the rest of the course requirements. When the talk was done, he said, 'Class dismissed. I suggest you find out who your composition partner is and go for a coffee or something. Use your time wisely. Get to know your partner well.' He smirked. 'You'll be spending a lot of time with them this year.'

Students piled to the front to check the paper the TA had pinned on the wall. Others introduced themselves to Lewis. Bryce checked his name then walked across to Tommy Wilder. I frowned. Bryce and I normally worked together. He came over and shook his head. 'Dream team's getting split up this time, Bonn.'

My heart sank a little. I saw in Bryce's expression that he was disappointed too. I was comfortable with Bryce. He wasn't the most talented. But he was sweet. I knew he liked me as more than a friend, and I would never go there with him. But he was comfortable for me to be around. He didn't ask too many personal questions.

I waited for the crowd to clear. A few people looked at me before they walked away. I wondered why. But when I read the list, I had my answer.

I exhaled a long slow breath. I stared disbelievingly at Cromwell Dean's name next to mine.

When I turned around, only Professor Lewis remained in the room. 'Bonnie Farraday, I presume?' He was holding his register with my student picture next to my name.

'Yes, sir.' I bit my lip. 'I know you said there would be no switching of partners for the project—'

'I did. And I meant it.'

My stomach dropped. 'Okay.' I turned to leave.

'You're the top of the class, Bonnie,' Lewis said. 'Cromwell is brand new to the college.' He sat down on the edge of the table beside me. This close, I could see a smattering of gray in his dark hair. I guessed he was in his forties. 'He was top of his classes in the UK. He is bright and extremely talented. But being a new student in a new college can be daunting for anyone. No matter how unaffected they appear.' He folded his arms over his chest. 'I was told by the faculty that you were a good choice to team him up with.'

'Yes, sir,' I replied again. For once I hated that the faculty regarded me as someone reliable and conscientious.

Just as I was about to leave, I said, 'Welcome back to Jefferson, Professor. You've been a real inspiration to many of us here.'

He smiled then turned back to his work.

I left, checking the hallway for any sign of Cromwell. I sighed when there was none. He had fled the room without even checking the board. I bet he didn't know I was his partner.

Drained of all energy, I leaned back against the wall. I had two free periods, and I was making it my mission to find him.

I was determined. I wouldn't let his bad attitude be my demise. If I had to work with him, I would. But nothing about this partnership made me think it would go well.

Absolutely nothing.

6

Cromwell

I moved to my desk and logged on to my laptop. Easton was at class, so I dropped my arse onto my chair and flicked on all my mixing boards. I threw my headphones on and fired up the mix I'd started a few days ago.

I closed my eyes and let the beats sink into my body. Bursts of pinks and greens flashed before my eyes. I moved my hand to the mixing table without even looking and turned up the pace. My heartbeat chased the bass as the rhythm sped up. Triangles and squares danced in jagged patterns. Then—

My headphones were taken from my head. I spun around, jumping from my seat. Bonnie Farraday stood behind me, my headphones in her hands. Ice-cold fury had immediately run through me, but it dropped when I saw it was her. That surprised me. My anger was pretty much what I was fueled by these days. I couldn't understand why it calmed.

I didn't like feeling confused.

I held out my hand. 'Give them back.'

Bonnie slowly pulled the headphones to her chest. I closed my eyes to keep calm. When I opened them again, Bonnie had her arms folded across her chest. She was wearing skinny jeans and a white t-shirt. She had a sweater over her shoulders like one of the posh kids I'd see strutting through the streets of Chelsea in summer. Her brown hair was back in a long plait. And when I looked at her face, she looked anxious.

'What are you doing here?' I asked. I reached behind me to turn off the mix that was now blasting through the speakers. It wasn't finished. No one heard anything I was working on until it was done. I had a new set to put on the streaming sites. Little Bonnie Farraday was messing up my schedule.

'Did you even look at the assignment list?'

I frowned. 'What assignment list?'

Her eyes looked up in exasperation. 'The one Lewis talked about for pretty much the entire class.' She walked forward and pressed my headphones into my chest. I looked down at her. She was only about five foot three, if that. She was tiny compared to my six foot two. Easton was just an inch or two shorter than me. He'd clearly got all the good stuff in the womb.

'You and me, superstar, are partners. In composition class. For the next year.'

I stared at her. Locked in on her brown eyes and felt the Fates laughing at me. I couldn't seem to escape this girl. 'Of course we are,' I sighed and turned back to my laptop. I'd only just tapped a key to bring the screen back to life when Bonnie shut the laptop again.

Her hand rested on the computer. I didn't even look up, just said through gritted teeth, 'Bonnie. I'm only going to tell you this once. Get off my laptop, and leave. I'm working.'

Her hand didn't move. She didn't move. I roved my eyes up to meet hers. 'Don't mess this up for me,' she said, face calm. But her words, spoken in that thick country twang, were anything but. I heard a shake in her voice that made my chest tighten.

I pushed the feeling aside and raised my eyebrows. 'And how can I mess this up for you, Farraday?' My tone was shitty. Condescending. I knew it. But she was starting to piss me off.

Her cheek twitched in annoyance, but she still didn't remove her hand from my laptop. 'I've worked too hard to get this far, and I won't let someone like you, someone who breezes by in life, screw it up for me.'

She seemed desperate, somehow. Still, fire lit me up inside. 'You don't know a thing about me.'

'No, I don't,' she said back. 'And I don't need to. I don't care whether you like me or not. But we're stuck together for the duration of this assignment.' She swallowed, then her voice softened. 'To have someone like Lewis teach me is a dream come true.' Her hand slipped off the laptop. I stared at the spot it had just been on. 'Don't take it from me.' There was a small catch in her voice.

I didn't know why, but it made that damn stabbing feeling I chased away so often slice through my stomach. Bonnie reached into her bag and pulled out a piece of paper. 'The TA was handing these out as we left. You were gone before he could get one to you.' I didn't even look at the piece of paper as it landed on my desk.

Bonnie sighed in frustration. 'It says we have to have a rough outline of our project done for Friday's seminar.' She tucked a piece of hair behind her ear. 'I won't be around for a few days, so we need to talk about this now.'

The thought of working with Bonnie made an uneasy

feeling sprout inside me. I didn't like to feel anything. I was happy numb. But for some reason Bonnie Farraday sparked life back into my dead soul. 'I'm busy.' I sat back down, throwing my headphones back over my ears. I had just taken the volume off mute when my laptop lid was pushed down again. This time harder. I had to count to ten . . . really bloody slowly.

The anger I lived with daily was waking up.

I slid my headphones off my head and put them around my neck. I turned. Bonnie was still beside me, fuming. She closed her eyes, and her shoulders sagged. 'Please, Cromwell. I know you're pissed at me for what I said to you in Brighton. I can hear it when you speak to me. But we have to get this outline done.'

Even at the reminder of that, fire boiled my blood. 'I'm not pissed off at you. I feel nothing toward you,' I said coldly. I didn't want her to think her words had had any impact. Especially how much.

'Right. Okay then . . .'

My jaw clenched as she started rubbing her arms. Like I'd hurt her. That annoying stabbing feeling was back in my stomach again. She moved toward the door then stopped dead. She spun and faced me, chin tilted upwards. 'Come with me for a coffee. We'll hash this out. I'll write it all up. You don't have to do anything but contribute to the idea. We just need to decide what we're gonna do.' I blew out a long breath. I simply wanted to be alone. I was better off alone. 'Just come, please. Then you can get back to your drum pad.' She was persistent. I'd give her that.

I really didn't want to go, but oddly, I found myself getting up. 'You have an hour.'

Bonnie's shoulders sagged in relief, then I followed her out of the door. I locked it. With a key. I turned, and she must have known what I was thinking. 'Easton gave me one. I'm normally the one who picks him up and brings him back home from parties. It made sense for me to have one.' She glanced down. 'I won't use it again without permission.'

Something stirred in me when her brown eyes dropped. I quickly pushed it away.

Bonnie led us out of the quad. She didn't walk beside me, just slightly in front, which was fine with me. A few girls smiled at me, and I made a decision that I'd get my end away sometime this week. Looked like it wouldn't be hard to pull around here. I'd gone too long without, and I was getting agitated too easy. Distracted.

Mainly by Bonnie.

Bonnie stopped at her car. 'If I only have an hour, I'll drive us there. It'll be faster.'

Students looked at us as Bonnie pulled away from the campus. 'We'll be officially dating by tonight, just so you know,' she said.

I snapped my head to her, eyes narrowed. 'What're you on about?'

She pointed at the students. 'Downside of a small local college. The rumor mill is worse than TMZ.'

I leaned back in the seat and watched as Main Street came into view. 'Great. That'll help me get laid.'

Bonnie laughed without humor. 'Not so much. You're the shiny new toy here. Girls thinking you have a girlfriend will only make you even more attractive than you are to them right now.'

'Good to know.'

Bonnie parked outside Jefferson Coffee. She got out of the car, her bag of notebooks and Christ knew what else slung over her shoulder. I had about ten dollars in my wallet and my hands stuffed into my pockets.

I traveled light.

I hadn't been here before, but the place was like any other hipster coffee shop I'd seen, all red walls, with a small stage in the back.

'Hey Bonnie!' about five different people said as she led us to a table at the back of the room. She smiled brightly at them, losing that smile when she sat down and looked up at me.

My fist clenched. I didn't like that fact. And I hated that I seemed to care.

I sat down, and a guy came over. 'The usual, Bonnie?'

'Yeah. Thanks, Sam.'

'No Bryce today? Never normally see you without him on a school day.'

'New partner.' She said it like she was announcing a death.

He looked at me. The prick nodded as though he could see why she was so pissed off. 'The biggest coffee you have,' I said. 'Black.'

Bonnie opened her notebook. 'Okay. I think we should start with what we can play. That'll help us know what our strengths will be.'

'I only do electronic music. So I'll have my laptop. Drum machine and all that shit.'

Bonnie looked at me blankly. 'We can't compose a showcase piece with your laptop and synthesized beats.'

47

I lounged back in my chair. 'That's what I've got. I work electronically. Lewis knows it. He offered me the scholarship. He scouted me out. Think I'd find this bumfuck place on my own?'

'You don't play anything else? No actual instruments?' There was a questioning lilt to her tone. Like she was privy to something about me I didn't want her to know. It unsettled me.

I shook my head, stretching my arms and putting them behind my head. I wanted to tell her that mixing electronic beats *was* playing an instrument, but I didn't even open my mouth.

'I play piano and guitar. A little violin too, but I'm not that great at it.' Her eyes narrowed on me. Like she was studying me. Testing me. 'You can read and write music though, yeah?'

I nodded, thanking God when the coffees turned up and she stopped bloody talking. I drank mine like it was a soda. Sam saw and indicated he'd be back with a refill.

'Lewis wants us to at least have an idea of a theme. What the piece will be about. What we're trying to say.' She tipped her head to the side. 'Any ideas?'

'Nope.'

'I thought something like the seasons? Maybe something to do with nature? The idea of time moving, us being useless to stop it.'

I rolled my eyes. 'Sounds like a riot. I can just hear the sounds of birds threading through my bass beat on my laptop.' I was being a dick again. At least more than usual. I couldn't help it around her.

She rubbed her eyes tiredly. 'Cromwell. We need to just

get through this, okay? Neither of us has to enjoy it. But we can work together. Plenty of musicians do it, have done it, and have created something good.' She took a drink of her coffee. 'I preferred the idea of the seasons changing. That way we can incorporate more instruments and tempos.'

'Fine,' I said as Sam came back to the table and refilled my cup.

Bonnie sat back in her seat, sipping on her coffee. She stared at me over her cup. 'Like what you see?' I asked, smirking.

She ignored me. 'Lewis told me you were top of all your classes in London.' I froze, my muscles locking.

'Someone should tell Lewis to shut his fucking mouth.'

'I'll leave that to you.' She rested her chin on her hand. 'So how did you come here anyway? Visa?'

'Dual citizenship. I was born here. In Charleston.'

'You're American?' she said, shocked. 'I didn't know that.'

'No. I'm British.'

She huffed in frustration. 'You know what I mean. You were born here?'

'Moved to England at seven weeks old. Never even visited here since. So I'm about as American as good old Liz.'

'Who?'

'The Queen.'

Bonnie ignored that. 'So your parents are South Carolinian?'

'Mum is.'

'And your dad?'

'Are we done here?' I snapped. We weren't going anywhere near my home life. I pointed at her scrawl on the

49

notebook. 'Seasons. Lots of instruments. Mixed tempos. Probably going to be a piece of utter shite, but it's what we've got. We're done.'

Bonnie sat back in her seat. Her mouth was open and her eyes were wide. I had a flash of regret on seeing her face turn pale, but I frosted over again, like always. I'd gotten good at it now.

'Yeah. Whatever, Cromwell,' she said warily, pulling herself together. 'I can take it from here.' I got up and threw my ten-dollar bill on the table. My chair scraped on the wooden floor, I got up that fast. The whole coffee shop looked over. Before Bonnie could offer to drive me home, I got the hell out of Dodge.

I walked down an alley, which brought me to the park that led to the campus. My muscles were jumping. I pulled out my cigarettes and sparked up, ignoring the shitty looks from the mums out with their kids. By the time I arrived at a large field, I'd inhaled three of the things and was suitably nicotined up. I sat down beside a tree and looked at the guy doing some kind of Tai Chi in the distance.

He looked like he belonged in a postcard.

I glanced up at the sun. The wind was still, and I laughed with bugger all humor when I heard birds singing above me in the branches.

Birds.

'Seasons,' I muttered under my breath. What a crock of shit.

But even as I sat there, trying to push the lame and done-too-many-times concept from my brain, I pictured a flute in short sharp bursts introducing the piece. I saw a single violinist bringing in the main melody.

Spring.

Yellow. All the shades of yellow on the spectrum.

I opened my eyes and curled my hands so tightly into fists that my fingers ached. Turning my torso, I sent my fist into the tree trunk I'd been leaning against. I pulled back my hand to see blood seep from the cuts the rough bark had caused.

I shot up from the grass and made my way back to the dorms, the blood dropping on the path back home. I needed my beats. I needed my mixes.

I needed to forget.

I threw the headphones that had been hanging around my neck over my ears and let the high volume drown out the colors and thoughts and images plaguing my head.

I pressed on a new playlist on my phone and lost myself in the heavy sound of garage and grime. It wasn't the music I made. I didn't even like it. I just needed to get my head away from Lewis, my parents, and Bonnie Farraday and her questions.

Easton was lying on his bed when I walked into our room. I took my headphones off. Easton stood and whistled low, shaking his head. 'What have you done to piss off my sister, man?'

'I was just my usual charming self.' I moved to my laptop and started back up what Bonnie had interrupted. But I saw Bonnie's shocked, hurt face in my head and it stopped me in my tracks.

Easton lay down on my bed. He was throwing an American football in the air and catching it again. 'Yeah, well if your intent was to have her seeing red, good job.' He stopped throwing the ball. 'So you're having to work together?'

'Looks that way.' I added the faint sound of a violin over the tempo dip I'd been struggling with. A violin. The sound worked perfectly. I'd never opened my file of actual instruments. Never added them into my mixes before.

I took a deep breath.

Until now.

I forgot all about Easton beside me, too focused on the fact that I'd added in a bloody violin to my mix, until he said, 'I get that she can be feisty, but take it easy on her, okay?' His words sank in, the warning clear in his tone. 'Not sure she can handle your kind of crazy.' He shrugged. 'Small-town girl and all that.'

He swung his legs off the bed. 'We're going to a bar tonight. And this time you're not getting out of it. Jet lag's gone. You've been miserable long enough. Now you're just being an unsociable bastard. And I can't have that. I have a reputation to protect.'

'If there are girls there, I'm in.' I couldn't believe that I'd actually agreed. But I kept seeing Bonnie in my head, and I knew I needed her gone. I needed to get laid. That's what all this was. Why she was getting to me so much.

'Finally!' Easton said and clapped me on the back. 'I knew I liked you for a reason.' He threw the ball across the room into a basket. 'Just bring your fake ID. You'll be the perfect wingman.' He rubbed his hands together. 'I'm gonna see the master at work. Been waiting for you to show me the way.'

'Not sure you need my help.'

Easton pretended to consider it. 'Sure as hell don't, but you and me, bro. We're gonna be on another level with the chicks here.'

I moved to my closet, took out a clean t-shirt, and raked my hands through my unruly hair.

Tonight, I'd dip my wick, get plastered, and forget about the world.

It was too bad that, for the rest of the night, wide brown eyes and the sound of a single violin kept nagging at my brain.

7

Bonnie

'Bonnie, Cromwell, I need to see you after class.' My head lifted from my notes as Lewis spoke. I glanced back at Cromwell.

He hadn't so much as looked at me since last week at the coffee shop. In fact, he seemed to be outright avoiding me. However, now, he even avoided my stare. He leaned back on his chair, not even acknowledging that the professor had spoken.

Class was dismissed and I gathered my things. 'You okay?' Bryce asked, casting an accusing glance back at Cromwell.

'Yeah.' I knew it must have been about the piece we had to compose. Even I knew when I submitted it that it was weak. I gave Bryce a tight smile and a hug. 'I'll see you later, okay?' He eyed Cromwell again. 'I'll be fine,' I insisted.

'Mr McCarthy, this is a private chat,' Lewis said.

Bryce nodded at Lewis and left the room. I walked down to the professor's table, where two seats waited. I sat down on one. I heard Cromwell's heavy footsteps slowly walking down the stairs. A minute later, he slumped into the seat beside me. His cologne sailed into my nose.

It was deep, infused with a strong hint of spice.

This was the first time I'd had a close chat with the

professor. Our private sessions wouldn't start for another week. Lewis took out the outline I'd submitted and laid it on the table before us. 'I just wanted to talk to you both about your potential composition.' I swallowed, nerves swarming in my stomach. 'The premise is good. The outline is well written.' He looked at me, clearly knowing it was me who wrote it. 'But the whole thing just lacked . . . for want of a better word, *feeling*.' I took in a long sharp breath as Lewis delivered that blow. I didn't look at Cromwell. It was the same line I had delivered about his music in Brighton.

Lewis dragged a hand down his face and turned to Cromwell. He was staring at the floor. Anger built inside me. This boy never seemed to care about anything. How he was picked to come here, with his current attitude to music, and study under Lewis was beyond me.

'Vivaldi's most famous work was *The Four Seasons*.' He read some of the proposal. 'I want my students to be original. I want you to explore self-expression in your creations. I don't want a recreation of another master's work.' He leaned forward, and I could see the passion for the subject reflected in his eyes. 'I want this to be your work. From your heart. Put into music what makes you tick. Trials and tribulations you've faced.' He sat back. 'Tell me who you are. Put everything you are into the piece.'

'We'll do better,' I said. 'Right, Cromwell?' When he didn't say anything in response, I felt like screaming in frustration.

Lewis got up from his seat. 'Take the room. There's no one in it until this afternoon. See if you can come up with anything else.'

Lewis left, and the room plunged into a deafening silence. I dropped my face into my hands and took a deep breath. It did nothing to calm me down. But when I looked up at Cromwell and his zero-shits attitude, my heart broke for the musician I'd thought he was. The one who apparently no longer lived within him. 'Do you really not care?' I whispered.

He met my eyes. His seemed lifeless. Cold. 'Not really, no.' His accent made his reply feel mocking and patronizing.

'Why are you even here?' I got up from my seat and had to rub my chest when my heart thudded and flipped around from the frustration that was building inside me. 'You don't play instruments. You don't care about composition. I've seen you in our other classes, and you seem to enjoy them as much as you do this one.' Now I was on a roll I couldn't stop. I paced, but I had to stop and put my hands on my hips when a sudden anger stole my breath. 'I've asked you to meet me three times this week. You said you couldn't do any of them. Yet I know you've been going out with my brother, getting trashed and screwing half the female student body.'

Cromwell's eyebrow rose. His lip kicked up into a ghost of a smile. It was a big mistake. It broke me. 'I've heard you spin, Cromwell. Don't forget that.' I laughed. What else was there to do? I could see my dreams for this year slipping away like sand in an hourglass. 'I took a train to Brighton to watch you, and all I got was disappointment.' I grabbed my bag. 'From what I can tell you have no desire. No passion for music, and you've been squeezed onto an already full program for God knows what reason. I have no idea what Lewis sees in you, but whatever it is, he will be sorely disappointed when it fails to materialize.' I made sure he was looking right into my eyes. 'I know I am.'

Calmer now I'd exorcised my anger, I stood in front of him and said, 'Meet me tonight at Jefferson Coffee. We can try and fix this and make sure we both get a passing grade. Meet me there at seven.'

I didn't even stop to get a response. Nobody had ever gotten under my skin the way he did. I burst out into the warm day; the summer's blistering weather was starting to gradually cool. I propped my hand against the wall and made myself breathe, only moving when I heard voices coming from behind me. Slowly, trying to calm my racing heart, I walked to my dorm and lay down on the bed. I closed my eyes, but all my brain wanted me to see was Cromwell.

I thought of the video I had seen of him all those years ago. Where had that boy gone? What had happened to him to make him lose his passion? The boy I had seen on the many clips I'd sought out over the years had all but died. He'd once played with such meaning, such purpose and soul. Now, everything about him was cold. He played music that meant nothing. Made me feel nothing. Told the world nothing.

And my dream of doing well in this course was now firmly in his hands.

'Another one, Bonn?' I looked up from staring out of the window to Sam, who was standing beside me with a nearly empty coffee carafe.

'No.' I gave him a tight smile. 'I think I've been stood up . . . again.'

'Cromwell?'

'How did you guess?'

'Just a hunch.' Sam smiled. 'At least you drink decaf. You'd be up all night if it was caffeinated.'

I smiled again, but I was sure he could see the sadness in my face. 'I'll just get my things and go. What time is it anyway?' A quick glance around the coffee shop showed me they were closing. Chairs were upside down on tables, and the floor was partially mopped. 'I'm sorry, Sam. You should have told me sooner to go.'

'Not a problem. You seemed deep into your work. I didn't wanna disturb you.'

'Thank you.'

'It's eleven thirty, by the way. Just in case you were still wondering.'

I gave him another tight smile, then threw my bag over my shoulder. I pulled my sweater on. I was cold. And tired. I'd walked here from the dorm, needing the fresh air and exercise.

I made my way down Main Street and stopped when I passed Wood Knocks. It was the bar most people went to. They had a small club underneath when it hit midnight. If the Barn wasn't on, then it was Wood Knocks that everyone went to. The dancing, cheap beer, and the casual attitude toward the mass of fake IDs were just a prelude to getting laid, really.

'Shots, motherfuckers!' I recognized my brother's voice in an instant. I peered through the window and saw Easton standing on the table, his loud voice ricocheting off the walls. I couldn't believe he was so drunk again. Just another thing that was worrying me. He was partying too much.

'Cromwell, get your "arse,"' he said in a terrible English accent, 'here right now, boy!' He searched the crowd. 'Where is he?'

A disbelieving laugh spilled from my lips. I walked away, leaving my brother searching the packed crowd, before I could see Cromwell's face. If I did, I didn't trust I wouldn't make a fool of myself by storming in there and ripping into him for leaving me in that coffee shop for nearly five hours doing our joint work on my own.

I picked up my pace as I made my way back to campus, pushing myself more than was wise. I arrived at my dorm, but as my hand hovered above the doorknob, I changed my mind and headed for the music department instead. Even before Lewis had arrived at the college, the rooms were open to students around the clock. The faculty understood that the time of day wasn't a factor when inspiration hit. Most artistic people were night people. At least the ones I knew.

I swiped my card and made my way down the hallway to a practice room. I had just dropped my purse to the floor when I heard the sound of a piano drifting down the hall.

I stood near the door and closed my eyes, a smile etched on my lips. It was always the same. Whenever I heard music, something happened inside me. Music always seeped into me like damp drizzle on a cold day. I could feel it down to my bones.

Nothing in my life made me as happy as hearing an instrument being played as perfectly as the piano was now. I loved all kinds of instruments. But there was just something about a piano that simply made me *feel* more. Maybe it was because

I would never play it as beautifully as the person playing it now. I didn't know. All I knew was that the sound gripped hold of my heart and made it so I never wanted to let it go.

The piano stopped. I opened my eyes. I moved to go to the piano in my own room, but then the sound of a violin began. I stopped dead in my tracks and exhaled a short puff of air. It was perfect. Every movement of the bow. I listened harder, trying to place the piece, or even the composer. But I couldn't . . .

And then somehow I knew – it was an original piece.

When the violin stopped, and the sound of a clarinet floated down the hallway, I realized that the sounds were coming from the largest room, where the loan instruments for the music education majors were stored. I closed my eyes and listened as whoever was in there played them all in turn.

I wasn't sure how long I listened. But when a silence rang out, my ears mourning the absence of the most breathtaking music I had ever heard, I let out a deep exhale. It felt as though I hadn't breathed through the tour of each instrument.

I stared at the closed door. The window panel was covered with a shutter. I stood, gathering my thoughts, and the piano played again. But unlike the other piece the musician had played, this one was different. It *felt* different. The slow notes were somber, the deeper tones the principal of the show. My throat clogged with the sadness the music evoked.

My eyes shone as the piece kept playing. Before I knew it, my feet were moving. My hand softly lay upon the doorknob, but it didn't turn.

It didn't turn because I could see the piano through a gap between the shutter and the door. My lungs forgot how to breathe as I looked at the pianist, the master of those beautiful sounds.

I had seen so many performances in my lifetime, yet none had compared to the rawness of what I had heard tonight. I followed the fingers dancing like birds on a lake. My eyes tracked up a pair of tattooed arms, over a white sleeveless shirt, over stubble-dark cheeks and silver piercings.

Then they locked on a single teardrop. A falling drop that rolled down the tanned cheek to splash on the ivory keys that were pouring with sounds of pain and hurt and regret.

My chest was stricken, reacting to the wordless story the music was telling. As I stared at Cromwell's face, it was like seeing it for the first time. Gone was the arrogance and the anger he wore like a shield. The shield was lowered, and a boy I didn't recognize was laid bare.

I'd never seen anyone so beautiful.

I stayed there, heart in my throat, as he played, face stoic but traitorous tears displaying his pain. His fingers never hit a wrong note. He was perfect as he told me a story I would never know, yet completely understood.

His fingers slowed, and as I looked closer, I saw they were shaking. His hands danced their way to the finale, a long, haunting note drawing the beautiful melody to a close.

Cromwell's head bowed, and his shoulders shook. My lip trembled as I felt the depths of his despair. He wiped at his eyes and tipped back his head.

I watched him breathe. I watched him in his silence. I watched in reverie as I let it sink in – Cromwell Dean *was* the hope I had always dreamed him to be.

Cromwell took a deep breath. My heart beat faster than I thought possible at the sight. The doorknob moved under my hand, and the door crept open, exposing where I stood.

Cromwell looked up at the noise, the creak of wood like a thunder-clap in the silent aftermath of his sorrow. His beautiful face drained of blood when he met my eyes.

I stepped forward. 'Cromwell, I—'

He stood from the piano stool; the abrupt movement sent it crashing to the floor. He swung around, hands clenched by his sides and dark blue eyes lost. Cromwell's mouth opened like he would speak, but nothing came out. He glanced about the room, at the instruments he had played, as if they were betraying his secret.

'I heard you.' I stepped further into the room. My bottom lip shook with fear. Not fear of him, but fear of what this all meant. Of who Cromwell Dean truly was. Of what he possessed inside of him.

Of who he could be.

'Your talent . . .' I shook my head. 'Cromwell . . . I never imagined . . .'

Cromwell turned away from me and edged around the room like he was trying to escape. I held out my hand, wanting to touch him, to offer him comfort as he breathed too quickly, as his lost eyes searched desperately for what to do next. Cromwell darted across the room toward where I stood, to the only exit. His eyes were wide and his face was pale. He stopped only a couple feet in front of me, shoulders sagging and body exhausted.

He appeared completely broken.

Cromwell's piercings glinted in the one dim light he had been playing under. A reluctant spotlight. Not daring to shine too brightly on an artist who didn't want his gift to be seen.

This close I could see his skin was mottled, the wet residue of his tears kissing his cheeks. He stepped closer again, edging his way to the exit. I'd never seen him this way. Gone was the arrogance. Gone was the attitude.

This was Cromwell Dean laid bare.

His breath blew across my face. Mint and tobacco and something sweet. 'Bonnie,' he whispered. My name from his lips cut me. His raspy voice sounded like it was crying out for help.

'I heard you.' I met his watery stare. My heart thudded in my chest. The silence in the room was so profound I could hear the two very different beats of our hearts slamming between us.

Cromwell stumbled away until his back hit the wall. His blue stare focused on the piano across the room. I wasn't sure from the look in his eyes if he saw it as an enemy or a savior.

Cromwell suddenly pushed off the wall and rushed to pick something off the top of the piano. He tried to get past me. As his arm brushed past mine, I acted on instinct and took hold of him. He stopped dead and bowed his head. His wide shoulders were slumped. I blinked away tears seeing him so undone. So tortured.

So exposed.

'Please . . . let me go,' he said.

My heart lurched at the desperation in his voice. I

should have done what he asked, but I kept tight hold. I couldn't let him leave so upset. In this moment, I found I didn't want to let him go.

'The way you can play . . .' I shook my head, speechless.

Cromwell sighed, his breath shaking, then brought something over his heart. I stepped back so I could see what it was. A set of dog tags was clenched in his trembling hands. He held them so tightly that his knuckles were white.

Cromwell screwed his eyes shut, and my body tensed with sympathy as a tear fell from his eye. I wanted to smooth it from his face, but I held back. I wasn't sure he would let me go that far. When he opened his eyes, the look on his face was nothing but tortured. 'Bonnie . . .' he whispered, his accent thick as he met my eyes. I'd always thought his accent was patronizing. Right now, broken and hoarse, it was only endearing.

Then he pulled from me and fled to the door, footsteps heavy on the wooden floor. 'Cromwell!' I called after him. He paused in the doorway, but he didn't turn. I wanted him to stay. I didn't know what I would say, but I didn't want him to leave. It felt like I waited a lifetime, heart in my throat, for him to decide what to do, whether to turn and come to me. But then the door opened and closed, and he left me alone.

I tried to catch my breath. I tried to make my feet work to go after him. But I was grounded, unable to process the memory of Cromwell so destroyed at the piano. It was ten long breaths before I could move.

I walked to the piano and picked up the stool from

where it had fallen. Sitting down, I ran my fingers along the keys. They still held a flicker of heat from where he played.

My fingertip dipped into something wet as I placed my hands. It was a fallen tear from Cromwell's eyes.

I didn't wipe it away.

Repositioning my hands, I began to play something I had written myself. I closed my eyes and opened my mouth, letting my biggest joy fly free. The answered prayer that was lyrics to a melody. A sung poem. Delivered from the heart yet sung from the soul.

I sang softly, a song I'd written just for me. One that was as timely as it was meaningful. One that had become my anthem. One that kept me strong.

It was meant to be sung with an acoustic guitar, yet something made me sit here, at this beautiful instrument. My hands moved along the ivories with practiced skill. But when the song came to a close and I shut the piano's lid, I knew my playing hadn't been worthy of this instrument after what Cromwell had brought to life from its keys.

I looked up at the door, the ghost of Cromwell's broken voice and haunted eyes still lingering in the air. I took in a deep inhale and tried to find the dislike for him that had settled upon me from our very first meeting.

Only now it wasn't there. Even with the rudeness and the arrogance that I saw from him most days. I now knew there was a pain behind his blue eyes, tattoos, and dark hair. In an instant, it made it impossible for me to think of him as I once did.

A tear dropped down my cheek. Cromwell Dean was in

so much pain that it took away his joy to play music that he'd once loved. Pain that caused him to shed tears.

I ached. Because I knew what that kind of pain felt like.

In the most unlikely of places, at the most unlikely of times, I'd found common ground with Cromwell Dean. But would we ever share those secrets . . . ?

I sighed.

Probably not.

8

Cromwell

The breeze slapped my skin as I rushed through the quad, past some old alumnus memorialized in a cast-iron statue in the center. My eyes darted around me, at the darkened edge of the grass and the illuminated benches under vintage streetlamps.

I breathed in my cigarette smoke, forcing it into my lungs, waiting for the rush of nicotine to calm me down. But it didn't work. I let my feet lead me wherever they wanted me to go. But it didn't stop the shaking of my hands. It didn't stop the erratic beat of my heart, and the tears that just wouldn't fucking stop.

My fingers ached as I clutched the metal in my hands so tightly I wondered if they would ever get the feeling back in them again. I walked and walked until I found myself at the lake. It was silent, no sign of life but the docked boats and the dim lights from the far-off lakeside bar that sat on the edge. My feet led me to the end of a dock before they gave out and I dropped to my knees.

The sound of the lake lapping against the dock's wooden posts hit my ears. Pale purples lit up my eyes, and the taste of cinnamon burst in my mouth. I groaned low, not wanting any of it. Not wanting the colors or the tastes or the feelings . . .

'Son,' he whispered, his eyes shining. 'How . . . how did you play like that?'

I shru'ed, dropping my hands from the piano. Dad's hand came on my head, and he crouched beside me. 'Has someone taught you that?'

I shook my head. 'I—' I quickly shut my mouth.

'You what?' He smiled. 'Come on, buddy, I promise I'm not angry.' I didn't want to make him angry. He'd been away with the army for months and months and he'd just got back. I wanted to make him proud, not angry.

I swallowed the lump in my throat and ran my fingertips over the keys. They didn't make a sound. 'I can just play,' I whispered. I glanced up at Dad. I lifted my hands. 'They just know what to do.' I pointed to my head. 'I just follow the colors. The tastes.' I pointed at my chest, my stomach. 'How they make me feel.'

My dad blinked then suddenly hu'ed me to his chest. I missed him when he was away. It wasn't the same when he was gone. When he pulled back, he said, 'Play again, Cromwell. Let me listen.'

So I did.

It was the first time in my life I'd ever seen my dad cry.

So I played some more . . .

I gasped, sucking in the humid air. I moved my feet, my back hitting the wooden post. A man was canoeing in the distance. I wondered why the hell he was here at night. But then I thought maybe he was like me. Maybe when he closed his eyes, he never got rest. Instead, he only saw the memory of what destroyed him. As I looked at the water rippling beneath the oars, I wished I was him right now. Just going. No destination in mind. Just bloody going.

Bonnie's face popped into my head as I felt the dog tag's metal cutting into my palm. I glanced down at my fingers and relived them playing the keys. Tattoos of skulls, and of the ID number that meant the most to me in the world, looked back at me. They mocked me.

It had to have been Bonnie Farraday who had walked in. At midnight, when everyone else was out at the bar or in bed, it had to be her who stood at the door. The one girl who had managed to get under my skin. To make me feel things I had never wanted to feel. I shook my head and ran my free hand over my face.

It had started with a message in my mailbox . . .

Drop by my office at five,
Professor Lewis.

I'd gone there and taken a seat in the chair opposite his. He had stared at me quietly. I'd met him a couple of times in my life. Mostly when I was young . . . then just before . . .

The first time I'd met him, I'd gone with my parents to see him conduct his work at the Royal Albert Hall. He'd heard of me and had invited us all along.

Then years passed and I heard nothing again. Not when I'd wanted him anyway.

Right now, I barely knew him at all. 'How are you doing, Cromwell?' he asked, his accent similar to my mum's. Although hers had been diluted through too many years in England.

'Fine,' I muttered and looked at the certificates on the walls. At a picture of him conducting an orchestra playing his music at the BBC Proms in the Royal Albert Hall.

I remembered how the place had smelled. Wood. Resin from the bows.

'How are you finding Jefferson?'

'Dull.'

Lewis sighed. He leaned forward, his face apprehensive. It became clear why a few seconds later. 'I noticed the date this morning.' He paused. 'I know it's the anniversary of your father . . .' He cleared his throat. 'I know I only met him a couple of times. But we spoke often. He . . . he believed in you so much . . .'

I paled. I didn't know my father spoke to him often. I closed my eyes for a second and inhaled.

It was as simple as a Google search to see how and when it happened. People I didn't know – or barely knew – could find out every detail if they got hold of my father's name. They could read his death like they knew him. Like they were there when it happened . . .

But I couldn't do it right now. I wouldn't face this with a professor I didn't know from Adam. He might have offered me a scholarship, but the guy didn't know me. He had no right to stick his nose in this.

I jumped to my feet and stormed out of the door. 'Cromwell!' Lewis's voice trailed off to nothing as I got the hell away.

Students gave me a wide berth as I stormed down the corridor. I shouldered some arsehole, who spun on me. 'Watch it, douchebag.'

I slammed my hands into his chest and threw him up against the wall. 'You watch it, wanker. Before I rearrange your face.' I needed to hit him. I needed to get this surge of anger out of me before I did something I'd regret.

'Cromwell!' Easton's voice cut through the gathering crowd. I yanked the prick in my hands off the wall and threw him to the ground. He looked up at me, wide eyed.

I turned and burst through the door, looking from left to right, just wondering where the hell to go.

Easton caught up with me. He jumped in front of me. 'East, I swear to God. Get out of my way.'

'Come with me,' he said.

'East—'

'Just come with me.'

I followed after him.

Some chick waved at me. 'Hi, Cromwell.'

'Not now,' I snapped, then jumped into Easton's truck. Easton pulled out of the campus, and for once in his life had the sense not to open his mouth.

My phone vibrated in my pocket. My mum was calling. She'd been trying all day. Gritting my teeth, I answered.

'Cromwell,' she said, relief in her voice.

'What?'

There was a pause. 'I was just checking you were okay today, honey.'

'I'm fine,' I said, shuffling in my seat. I needed to get the hell out of this truck.

My mum sniffed, and ice-cold fury swept through me. 'It's a hard day for us both, Cromwell.'

My lip curled in disgust. 'Yeah, well, you got your new husband to make it all better. Go pour your heart out to him.'

I hung up, just as Easton pulled up to a wooded area covered with thick green trees. I jumped out of the truck and stormed forward, not knowing where I was going. I burst through the trees and came to water. I stopped dead.

I closed my eyes and just stood there trying to calm the

71

hell down. I breathed in, tensing my stomach when I felt all the pain I knew would come today.

I dropped to the ground and stared out over the water. I didn't even know this place existed, never mind so close to campus.

Easton dropped down beside me. I shoved my mum's phone call from my head. Pushed the anger over the nosy bastard that was Lewis aside and just breathed.

'I come here when I get like you are now.' Easton leaned forward, putting his arms around his legs and his chin on his arms. 'Peaceful, you know? Like there's no one else out here but you.' He laughed once. 'Or us.'

I put my hands in my hair and hung my head. I squeezed my eyes shut, but all I could see was Dad's face. The last time we spoke. The raised words and his expression as I turned my back on him and walked away. I couldn't stand it.

I looked out over the lake. I was born in this state, yet I had absolutely no connection to it. The view right now looked nothing like home. It wasn't green enough, and the weather was too hot. For the first time since I'd been here, I felt homesick. But I didn't know what for. That place hadn't felt like my home for a long time. My relationship with my mum had deteriorated and I had no friends. Not real friends, anyway.

It was an age before I calmed down. Easton had disappeared a while back. When he dropped beside me again, he held out a beer. He put the six-pack between us. I pulled off the cap with my teeth. The minute the beer hit my lips, I exhaled.

'You good?' Easton asked.

I nodded. He clinked his beer to mine. 'Wood Knocks. Tonight. We'll get out of our heads. Help you forget.'

I nodded again, then drank another three beers.

I'd have done anything to take myself away from feeling like this.

Some bird's hands moved down my stomach, dipping under the waistband of my jeans. I let my head fall back against the wall. Her lips sucked on my neck as she took me in her hand. 'Cromwell,' she whispered against my skin. 'I'm gonna enjoy this.'

I stared out into the blackened room. Some cloakroom where students could store their coats in winter. Sawdust covered the floor. Peanut shells were down there too. The girl held me in her hand. Her lips kept pressing against my neck. It was annoying me. 'You're so hot,' she whispered.

I wasn't doing this.

I rolled my eyes, pushed her off me, and moved her hand away. I ducked out of the cloakroom and into the mass of students Easton seemed to have gathered in the hour between us getting back to the dorm and coming here.

I could hear him. I was sure Easton's voice could be heard from space. I burst out onto Main Street and looked around. There was hardly anyone around. Everyone was inside.

The shops and diners seemed to tilt slightly. I rubbed my hand down my face. I'd drunk too much.

'Where's Cromwell?' I heard the girl's voice ask from inside. I took off toward campus before anyone could see I'd smoke-bombed. My feet were heavy as I trudged my way back home. But when I approached my dorm, it was the last place I wanted to be.

I didn't think. I didn't even know where I was going until my feet stopped at the music rooms. I stared at the closed door and the card reader that let you in. I breathed hard, as if I'd just run a marathon. I tried to turn around, but my feet wouldn't listen.

My head fell against the door, and I closed my eyes . . .

I lifted my hands off the piano and blinked. My head always went somewhere else when I played. It transformed. Turned to color and shapes. Until I finished, and the world came back into view.

The audience burst into applause. I stood up and looked out over the crowd. I saw my mum, clapping, on her feet with tears in her eyes. I gave her a small smile then left the stage.

As I loosened my bow tie, the concert's director tapped me on the shoulder. 'Amazing, Cromwell. It was amazing. I can't believe you're only twelve.'

'Thank you,' I said and walked toward the backstage area where we could get changed.

I stared at the floor as I walked. I was glad Mum could see me tonight, but the person I wanted to see me wasn't here.

He was never here.

As I turned the corner, a flash of movement caught my eye. I lifted my head. The first thing I saw was khaki green. My eyes widened. 'Dad?'

'Cromwell,' he said, and I couldn't believe my eyes. My heart beat faster as I ran to him, throwing my arms around his waist.

'You were unbelievable,' he said and hugged me back.

'You saw?'

He nodded. 'I wouldn't have missed it.'

When I looked up, I was inside the music building. My

74

student ID was in my hand. I was in a music room, with a large rack of instruments at one end.

My hands itched to touch them. I wanted to blame it on the alcohol. I wanted to blame it on any damn thing else but the fact that I needed to be here. That I needed these instruments.

I wandered to the piano and ran my hands over the closed lid. My gut felt like it was tearing in two. I pulled my hand back, trying to turn away. But I couldn't. I sat down on the stool and lifted the lid. Ivory and black keys stared up at me. And like always, I could read them. I didn't see them as mute, I saw them filled with notes and music and color.

My hands trailed along the keys, and my lip hooked up at the corner. I ripped my hand away. 'No,' I snapped to no one but myself. My voice was lost in the room.

I closed my eyes, trying to stop the ache in my chest that had been there for three years. I could control it. I was good at that now. Pushing it away. But since this morning, I'd had to fight it harder than usual. It had killed me all day.

It was getting hard to fend off.

Play, son, a voice whispered in my head. My hands fisted as I heard the echo of my father's words in my mind. *Play* . . .

I gasped, releasing all the fight I had bottled up inside.

The room was silent. A blank canvas waiting for color. My hands rested on the keys. I held my breath then pressed down on a single key. The sound rang out like a siren. A burst of green so vivid it bordered on neon. Another came, bringing a faded red. Before I could stop, my hands were dancing over the keys as if I'd never stopped. As if I hadn't moved on three years ago.

Bach's Toccata and Fugue in D Minor spilled out from my hands, every bar burned into my brain. No sheet music was needed. I just followed the colors. Vibrant red. Pale blue. Ochre. Tan brown. Lemon yellow. One after the other. A tapestry in my mind.

When the piece came to a close, I turned on the stool. I didn't think this time. I didn't put myself through the torment. I just crossed the room and picked up whatever I came to first. At the first stroke of the string on the violin, I closed my eyes and just went with it.

This time it was my own music that poured from me.

One after the other, I moved through the instruments, the music like a drug being injected into my veins. I was a junkie who'd been clean for three years, finally getting his fix back. I was unable to stop. Overdosing on the color, the tastes, and the rush of adrenaline it sent sailing in my blood.

I didn't know how long had passed. But when every instrument had been played, I made for the door. But my addiction wasn't done with me yet. I wanted my feet to just cooperate tonight. I wanted to leave this behind and chalk it up to being too drunk.

But I no longer felt plastered. The alcohol wasn't what was leading me right now. It was me. And I knew it.

Like it was a magnet, I made my way to the piano again. I reached into my pocket and pulled out his dog tags. I couldn't bring myself to look at his name. Instead I put them on top of the piano and let them just be with me.

Let *him* be with me.

I breathed in and out five times before my hands landed

on the keys. My heart was a bass drum as I let them take control. And when they did, it was a damn dagger to the chest.

I'd only ever played this song once. Exactly three years ago to the day. I'd never written down the score. It didn't matter. It was committed to memory. Every note. Every color. Every heartbreaking feeling.

This piece was all dark colors. Low notes and tones. And as the sounds surrounded me, my face contorted, remembering Mum walking into my bedroom at three in the morning . . .

'Baby . . .' she whispered, hands shaking, face pale and wracked with tears. 'They've found him . . . he's gone.'

I'd stared at her, not moving a muscle. It wasn't true. It couldn't be true. He'd been missing, but he was going to be okay. He had to be. After how things had been left. He *had* to be.

But watching my mum fall apart, I knew it was real. He was gone.

As the sun had started to rise, I'd gone into the room that had my piano – my twelfth birthday present. And I'd played. I'd played, and as I did, the reality started to sink in.

He was gone.

I curled over as I played, the pain in my stomach too hard to bear. The music was dark, slow, and like nothing I'd played before. He couldn't be gone. Life wasn't that unfair.

He's gone . . . My mum's words circled my head. As I hit a crescendo, a bellow ripped from my throat. Tears came thick and fast after that. But my hands never stopped moving. It was like they couldn't.

I had to play.

It was like they knew this was it. That I'd never play piano keys again.

As the piece fell away, the last note coming to a close, I opened my eyes and looked down at my hands. It was all too much. My hands on this piano. Playing again after all this time. The colors, the taste of metal . . . the massive rip in my chest.

Teardrops fell onto the keys. Dad's face came into my mind. The last look he ever gave me – pain and sadness. A face I never saw again.

He'd taken the music with him.

My hands slipped from the keys. I couldn't breathe. The room was too silent and still, and—

The sound of the door opening made me look up. I felt the blood in my face drain as I saw who stood in the doorway. Bonnie Farraday was staring at me, her face pale and brown eyes sad. And it had ruined me. In that moment, I hadn't wanted to be alone. But I had no one to lean on. No one to turn to. I'd pushed everyone away.

And then she'd appeared. Her eyes filled with tears. Bonnie had been there with me when I was breaking apart. I hadn't known what to do. I needed to leave, needed to push her away too. I didn't need anyone in my life. I was better off alone. But in that moment, I wanted her near. Then she touched my arm and I'd nearly given in.

When I looked into her eyes as tears fell from mine, I knew I had to get out of the room. I broke into a run, hearing Bonnie's voice as she called my name. I ran until I reached the small clearing Easton had shown me earlier. I slumped down on the grass and let the warm breeze wrap around me. As I lit up a smoke, I caught sight of my hands.

They seemed different. Fingers freed, somehow, like I'd finally given in to what they wanted after all these years.

I'd played. I'd let the music back in.

As I took a drag of my cigarette, I tried to push the feeling of it from my head. But the echo of the notes still lingered in my ears. The shadows from the colors were still living in my mind, and the phantom feel of the keys beneath my fingers was still etched on my skin.

Muscle memory refusing to let go.

Frustrated, I lay back and looked up at the night sky. The stars were out in full effect. I closed my eyes, trying to push everything away and get back to the emptiness I'd embraced for so long. It didn't work. Nothing would leave me.

Especially not the southern accent of Bonnie Farraday, and the look in her eyes. *The way you can play . . .*

Her voice was violet blue.

I closed my eyes.

It was my favorite color to hear.

9

Cromwell

I stared at her in her seat next to the prick that was Bryce. She smiled and laughed with him as Lewis prepped for the lecture. *Look away, arsehole,* I told myself. I did. Only for her laughter to make my eyes snap back in her direction.

Her laughter was pale pink.

As I watched her now, my stomach clenched. My phone flashed on as I pressed the unlock button. And like I had all weekend, I stared at the simple message that had come through.

BONNIE: Are you okay?

The simple question made something happen in my chest. It felt like it was cracking more and more with every time I read it. *Are you okay?*

I hadn't seen Bonnie all weekend. She hadn't come to see Easton, who was mostly sleeping off his hangover from Friday night. I'd watched the door from behind my laptop, just waiting for her to turn up. I waited for Easton to move, just in case he was going to meet her. But she never came, and East only left to get food.

I told myself it was a good thing. That I didn't want to see her after making such a fool of myself. But then I'd lain awake all night staring at her simple text. *Are you okay?*

I didn't reply.

I busied myself with work. Got my mixes uploaded. The tunes were already the top stream in EDM. It should have made me happy. But every time I listened to them, all I saw was dullness in my mind. Now I'd played the instruments I'd once loved so much, everything seemed lifeless in comparison.

I had to forget it ever happened. But when my eyes wandered to Bonnie again, to her pretty face and thick dark hair, I felt like I was back in that room, with Bonnie's hand on my arm.

She'd tried to speak to me when I came in today, but I'd walked past her without a word. I wasn't sure I could look at her again without feeling like I wanted the ground to swallow me up.

But then I had to look at her . . . and I couldn't bring myself to look away.

I leaned back in my seat and forced myself to listen as Lewis droned on about the effectiveness of change of tempo in composing. It bored me. I didn't need to be taught this crap.

After nearly falling asleep, I checked the clock. There were only ten minutes left. I watched the clock as the minutes counted down. My phone buzzed on my desk. My stomach rolled when I read who the text was from.

BONNIE: Can we meet after class?

My heart kicked into a sprint. I looked at her a few rows down. But she didn't look back. I knew I shouldn't go. What the hell would I say? And if she even mentioned Friday night, I'd have to get the hell up and leave. There was nothing to be said. I was drunk. That was all it was. That's the story I was sticking to.

I didn't want to talk about it. I couldn't.

I lifted my phone to type that I couldn't make it. But instead, found myself saying: YEAH.

'One-on-one sessions start this week,' Lewis said, pulling my attention back to him. He pointed at the wall. 'Sign-up times are on the wall. Fill it out before you leave.' I tried to calm my pulse, but it wouldn't slow down at the thought of having to face Bonnie.

The students rushed forward to fill out the times. I stayed in my seat, gathering my things slowly. Bonnie was down at the front with Bryce. 'Come meet me for coffee one night, Bonn,' he said. For some reason a damn fire burst to life in my chest at him asking Bonnie out.

Bonnie tucked her hair behind her ear and moved to the sign-up sheet. She filled it out, then turned back to Bryce. 'I . . . I'm not sure,' she stuttered.

He caught her hand in his and I just about combusted. She looked down at his fingers on hers, and I froze, wondering what she would do. 'Come on, Bonn. I've been asking you since last year.'

She smiled up at him, and the sappy look on Bryce's face really pissed me off. 'Farraday,' I said, without thought. Bonnie looked up at me in surprise. 'I don't have all day. If you want to meet now, let's go.' I flashed a look to Bryce. 'I don't want to have to watch you turn him down.'

Bonnie flushed. Bryce looked like he wanted to murder me. I'd welcome him trying. Bonnie pulled her hand away from Bryce. 'I'll see you tomorrow, Bryce.' I heard a small shake in her voice. The way she glanced up at me nervously, I knew she didn't know what the hell to say about Friday night either.

Bryce nodded his head then made for the door. Not without giving me a dirty look first. Arsehole. Bonnie got in front of me. 'Cromwell, you don't have to speak to him that way.'

My nostrils flared. I didn't like how she was protecting him. Did she like him? Was that why? 'You wanted to meet.' I pointed at the folder she was holding, clearly labeled with 'Composition project.' I ran my hand through my hair. 'He was holding us up.'

Bonnie took in a deep breath, but then she really looked at me. Her brown eyes were wide and I saw sympathy flare in them. Embarrassment took me in its hold. I thrust my hand in my pocket and pulled out my packet of cigarettes. 'I'm going for a smoke. I'll be outside.'

I slipped my headphones over my ears and burst out the door. I was halfway through my cigarette when – Stacey? Sonya? – some bird I'd shagged last week came up to me. 'Hey, Cromwell. What are you up to?' Her voice was dripping with invitation.

I took another inhale and blew out the smoke. Bonnie chose that moment to come out of the door. 'Hey, Suzy,' she said, then looked at me. 'Are we going?' Bonnie's eyes dropped in unease, and the sight made my stomach fall.

I shrugged at Suzy. 'Got plans.'

I finished off my smoke then followed Bonnie to her car. I assumed we were going to the coffee shop. Bonnie seemed to live there. When the door shut, I tensed. I didn't want her to mention the other night. I prayed that she wouldn't.

Before she started the car. Bonnie stared out of the window. 'Cromwell . . .'

I was about to snap at her. To tell her to get lost like I did to anyone who challenged me on what I was feeling. But when her brown eyes fixed on me, and I saw the concern on her face, all the fight drained away. 'Don't . . .' I whispered, my voice sounding way too loud in the quiet car. 'Please . . . just leave it alone.'

Bonnie's eyes shimmered. She nodded. Her hands fell to the wheel, but before she pulled out of the parking spot, she said, 'Just tell me you're okay.' She didn't look at me. She kept her attention straight ahead. 'I just need to know you're okay.'

My leg bounced as her words cut through me. Because she sounded like she meant it. The crack in her voice . . . the shade of lavender that surrounded her told me she meant every word. 'Yeah,' I said, and her shoulders relaxed. The truth was, I was anything but okay. But that tether inside of me that kept everyone away pulled tight, straining on my throat to keep it the hell shut.

It was on the tightest leash whenever I was around Bonnie.

She smiled, and the leash momentarily slackened. But as she pulled out of the campus in silence, it gradually brought me back to heel.

When we arrived at Jefferson Coffee, we sat at what was looking more and more like Bonnie's usual table. Sam, the guy from before, came with the drinks. 'I assumed it was the same as before,' he said, pouring me a strong black coffee.

When he walked away, I looked at Bonnie across the

table. She had been staring at me. Ducking her eyes, she got out her folder. She opened it and put a sheet of music before me. She seemed embarrassed. 'I . . . I had some thoughts on the beginning of the composition. I've had this in my head for a while.' She nervously took a sip of her coffee. 'I know we don't have a theme or anything yet, but I thought I'd show you this.'

I glanced down at the music and read it. My eyes scanned the notes. I didn't say anything.

'You hate it.'

I lifted my eyes to Bonnie. I didn't hate it. It was just . . . nothing special. The colors didn't flow. Like if you saw a generic painting hanging on a wall somewhere. It was good, but nothing life-changing.

I decided not to speak at all. If I did, I'd only upset her. My jaw clenched in annoyance when I realized I didn't want to see her upset. The girl was messing with my head.

I stretched my arms over my head. I saw her watching. When I met her eyes, she moved them down to the music. 'Is it awful?'

'Not awful.'

'But not good either,' Bonnie said knowingly and sat back in her seat. She looked dejected. Her mouth opened, like she wanted to say something. I knew it would be about Friday night. The anger that usually controlled me began to rise in anticipation. She must have seen something in my face, as she said, 'Cromwell, I think we should go to Lewis and ask for new partners. This' – she pointed between us – 'isn't working.' She kept her eyes down. 'We're not on the same page when it comes to music.' Her finger traced a vein of wood on the table. 'Are . . .' She swallowed. 'Are you still only wanting to contribute using electronic, or have you changed your mind?' I closed my eyes and took a deep inhale. I had asked her not to go there.

I couldn't fucking go there.

And she was right. We weren't well suited. Our tastes were different. I wouldn't go down the classical route. Yet even knowing that, the thought of her partnering with someone else, someone like Bryce, had every cell inside me fighting back. 'There's no switching.'

The fight left Bonnie, and she leaned forward. 'Then help me.' She ran her hand over her forehead. She looked tired. A deep breath followed. 'Again, do you still only wanna do your side electronically?'

'Yes,' I said through gritted teeth.

I saw the disappointment settle in her eyes. 'Cromwell . . .' She shook her head. 'The way you can play . . .' She reached out over the table and ran her fingers over mine. Her fingers were so soft. Her voice was quiet. Soothing. Sad. 'I don't know why you won't play. But what I heard the other night . . .' Tears welled in her eyes. She put her free hand over her heart. 'It moved me. So much.' My heart beat out of control. I couldn't calm it down with her touching me. With her telling me how my music made her feel. I saw her. I saw the hope in her pretty face. Hope that I'd talk to her. That I'd say yes to composing with orchestral instruments.

Then my father's face flashed into my head, and I frosted over like a branch of a tree when a snowstorm hit. Anger infused my muscles and I ripped my hand back, rolling my tongue ring just to keep from exploding. 'Not happening.'

'Cromwell, why—?'

'I said it's not happening!'

Bonnie froze. I looked around the coffee shop and saw all eyes on me. I leaned in close. 'I asked you to forget what you saw and not bring it up again.' I screwed up a napkin in my hand. 'Why can't you just do as I ask?' I had intended for my voice to be hard, to scare her away. Instead it was broken and raw.

'Because I've never heard anyone so talented in my entire life, Cromwell.'

Each one of her softly spoken words hit me like a missile, trying to tear down my protective wall. 'Drop it,' I said. I felt my throat tighten, the leash pulling tightly.

The clearing of a throat broke the tension. I kept my eyes on Bonnie, seething, as Sam, the wanker with the coffeepot, asked her, 'Everything okay, Bonn?'

'Yeah,' she said and smiled. My stomach squeezed again. It was the second time today I'd seen her smile. And neither time was at me.

That bothered me more than it should.

I could feel Sam eyeing me. 'You going to the concert this weekend?' he said.

'Yeah,' she said. 'You?'

'Gotta work. Oh, before I forget, Harvey wanted to speak to you.' Bonnie got up and followed Sam. I had no clue who Harvey was. I finished the last of my coffee and looked down at the sheet of manuscript paper that was still lying on the table, staring at me. My hand tapped on the table as I stared back at it. I glanced around the shop and saw Bonnie near an office, talking. I fought against the need to grab the pen, but in the end the need to amend the composition won out. I crossed out the notes she'd roughly penned and replaced them with ones that flowed better.

When I finished, I stared down at the sheet and quickly got to my feet. My heart slammed too quickly in my chest. I shouldn't have touched it. But I had to write them down. The notes, the melodies. Everything.

I needed to leave. I meant to take the sheet with me and bin it on the way out.

'Shit,' I hissed as I burst through the door and realized I'd left the music behind. I looked left and right, deciding where to go. But then a text came through my phone.

SUZY: You around now? My roommate's out all day.

Through the window, I saw Bonnie walk back to the table and pick up the manuscript paper. My heart was in my mouth as her eyes scanned the pages. Her hand went to her chest, making mine tighten in response. Then she raised her eyes, scanning the coffee shop. I knew she was looking for me. My pulse raced and my feet itched to walk back in and work with her. To show her what her music had inspired in me. To show her where I'd take the piece. What instruments I'd use. How I'd conduct.

But the tether that held me back, the one that controlled me, that kept me from sharing anything, pulled tight, keeping me still. Keeping all my anger locked inside.

My phone buzzed again.

SUZY: ???

I looked up at Bonnie and saw her pretty face. Saw her eyes drinking in the notes I'd written. And I knew that it was her that was challenging the walls I'd kept around myself for the past three years.

And I had to let it go, or I wasn't sure I'd be able to cope with what would spill out.

ME: Give me fifteen.

I tucked my phone in my pocket, blocking everything out, and took off for campus before Bonnie found me again. I forced the numbness to take control and push Bonnie from my brain. But only a few meters down the road I saw a poster for the concert being held in the park this weekend. South Carolina Philharmonic. My jaw clenched as I fought the need to go and see it.

And, Bonnie would be there. That was reason enough not to go. I had to keep her at a distance. To only work with her on the project. She'd seen too much of me already. Knew too many of my secrets.

I just had to get back to my mixes. And my high walls that kept everyone out.

That was all I had to do.

'You didn't sign up.'

I sat in Lewis's office. A grand piano sat in the corner. A vintage violin with aged cracked wood and a fragile bridge was displayed on his wall. A guitar sat in a stand and cello lay on its side against the far wall.

I pulled my eyes away when a sense of home flowed through me. I looked at all the pictures of him conducting and realized how young he'd been when he started out. I wondered if he'd always loved music. If it was in every breath he took too.

'Cromwell,' he said, pulling my attention.

'I don't need one-on-one sessions.'

A muscle twitched in his cheek. He leaned his arms on the table. 'Cromwell, I know you've been focused on dance music for a while now. If that's what you want to focus on, then fine. We'll focus on that.'

'You know how to teach me things about EDM?'

Lewis narrowed his eyes on me. 'No. But I know music. I can tell you what is working and what isn't.' He paused, assessing me. 'Or we can work on some of your old strengths.' He pointed across at the instruments. 'Piano. Violin.' He huffed a laugh. 'Anything really.'

'No thanks,' I muttered. I checked the time on the clock. It was nearly the weekend. As soon as this meeting was done, a bottle of Jack waited for me. This week had pulled me apart, and I was ready to let it go. Ready to embrace the numbness that came with being trashed.

'Do you still compose?'

I rested my hands behind my head. 'Nope.'

Lewis's head tipped to the side. 'I don't believe you.'

Every part of me tensed. 'Believe what you want,' I snapped.

'What I mean is, I don't think you'd be able to stop yourself composing.' He tapped his head. 'As much as we want it to, this never switches off.' He clasped his hands on the tabletop. 'Even when I was at my most messed up, with the drink, the drugs, I still composed.' He smiled, but there was nothing happy or humorous about it. Instead it looked sad. It looked like I felt inside. 'I came out of rehab with an entire symphony.' He lost his fake smile. 'Even if something makes you hate music, whatever it is can often be the catalyst for your next great work.'

'Deep,' I muttered. Lewis slumped in dejection. I was being a dick again. But everything this week had just been too much. I was tired and wrung dry.

I just needed a damn break.

It was funny. I didn't know if it was being with Lewis, but in that moment I thought of my father, and how me being this way toward someone would have broken his heart. He didn't raise me this way.

Manners cost nothing, son. Always be gracious with those who want to help.

But he wasn't here anymore. And I'd coped with that fact in the only way I knew how. I checked the clock again. 'Can I go now?'

Lewis looked at the clock and sighed. As I got up, he said, 'I'm not trying to counsel you, Cromwell. I just want you to realize the gift you've been given.'

I mock-saluted him. I couldn't take one more person telling me about my talent. It was hard enough to push it aside without Lewis and Bonnie fanning the flames that I tried to keep extinguished.

'Your father saw it,' he said as my hand hit the doorknob.

I turned my head to face him, and, having no more fight, the floodgates fell. 'You mention him again, and I'll stop coming. I'm this close to dropping out of this shit-hole anyway.'

Lewis held up his hands. 'Fine. I'll stop mentioning him.' He got off his chair and came toward me. He was pretty tall. He stopped a few feet away. 'But as for the dropping out. You won't.'

I stood off the door, shoulders back. 'Yeah? And what do you know about—'

'Enough to know that even though you're carrying a chip the size of Alaska on your shoulder right now, you won't leave.' He pointed to the room. 'This is your arena. You're just too pissed and hurt to accept it right now.' He shrugged. 'You do see it, but you're fighting it.' The knowing look in his eyes almost brought me to my knees. 'You're a good DJ, Mr Dean. Lord knows it pays well these days, and I will no doubt see your name in lights in the future. But with the gift you have, you could be a legend on *this* stage.' He pointed at the shot of him in the Albert Hall. He sat down. 'I suppose the decision will be up to you.'

I stared at the picture for a second, at Lewis in a tux commanding the orchestra playing the music he had created. I felt the lead ball in my stomach, the one that tried to plow through my wall. Whatever lived inside me, that made me this way with music, was clawing to get out. It was getting harder and harder to subdue.

'I hope it will be the latter path you find yourself on, Cromwell. God knows I know what it's like to live a life with that kind of regret.' He flicked his hand and started up his laptop. 'Let yourself out. I have compositions to look at.' He looked at me over his screen. 'I'm waiting on your and Ms Farraday's outline. I won't wait forever.'

Cock, I thought as I slammed his office door shut. I was about to turn left to the main exit, but my head turned to the right, toward the sound of a string orchestra. I wandered down the corridor. It was an alternative way out of the building. I let myself believe that as I stopped at the door of the orchestra's practice room. I leaned against the doorframe, arms crossed.

As the cello took the lead, I let down my walls for a second and let the sound wash over me. A peace I hadn't felt in years settled through me. I stayed listening as they played Pachelbel's Canon in D. It wasn't the hardest piece, and they weren't the best. But that didn't matter. It was the fact that it was *being* played that did.

And I was listening. I saw magenta and salmon-pink hexagons as the cello played. Then starbursts of peach and cream, flickered shards of mauve and rose as the violins took the melody. I tasted floral on my tongue and felt my chest pull tight, my stomach building with light as the strings danced and sang.

As the piece finished, I opened my eyes, breathless, and pushed myself off the doorframe. I looked to my left. Lewis was at his door, watching me. A surge of anger lit me up that he was there, seeing me, and I rushed out of the building and walked to my dorm. The minute I entered my room, the smell of paint smacked me in the face.

'Shit.' I threw my bag on my bed.

Easton turned from the canvas he was painting on. 'Top of the morning to ya.'

I shook my head. 'Dick. I'm not Irish. I'm English.' I slumped on my bed, but the minute I did I was restless. Bastard Lewis messing with my head. Bonnie Farraday and her hand on her chest as she read my music was etched into my brain. But not as much as the imprint of her hand on my arm was from last Friday night.

They were pushing and pushing me to breaking point, and I couldn't friggin' stand it.

'There's a difference?'

I rolled my eyes and jumped back off the bed. I looked at the painting he'd done. There was color everywhere. It was blinding. Like Jackson Pollock on crack. 'Jesus, East. What the hell is that?'

He laughed and put down his paints. He was covered. He spread his arms wide. 'It's me! How I'm feeling on this fine sunny day.' He came closer. 'It's the weekend, Crom. The world is ours!'

'Tone it down.' I stared at my mixing table and realized that I had bugger all desire to create new mixes right now. 'Let's go get food. I need to get off this campus.'

'I like your style.'

We walked out of the dorm and headed to Main Street. Of course.

'Your mama's been emailing again,' Easton said as we headed to Wood Knocks. I looked at him, eyebrows pulled down. He held up his hands. 'You left your laptop open. Kept coming on every time she messaged you.'

'Great,' I muttered.

'Got a new stepdaddy, huh?' I gave Easton the side-eye. 'Saw it on the subject line.' He smirked. 'It's his birthday near Christmas. She wanted to know if you were going home to celebrate.' I stopped walking and stared at Easton. 'Fine!' he said. 'That's all I read. Promise.' He winked at me and smiled.

The answer to that would be a huge no. I wouldn't be going home for Christmas. Just thinking of her new husband in my dad's home tore me apart. I was staying far away.

We walked past the park. There were lights and people all over. My eyes narrowed as I tried to figure out what was going on.

'The orchestra concert, or whatever the hell it is, is on tonight,' Easton said. I caught the distant sound of instruments being warmed up. 'Bonnie's going, I think. Not quite your scene though, hey, bro? All that classical stuff.' He shook his head. 'How anyone sits through that kind of thing is beyond me.'

Bonnie. I hadn't seen or heard from her all week. She'd been gone from class for the past few days. It was . . . weird not to have seen her a few rows down. The room almost seemed empty with her gone. She hadn't texted me either. Not to meet up.

No more asking if I was okay.

I . . . I didn't like it.

'He a dick?' Easton asked as we walked into the bar.

I raised my eyebrow, confused. I'd been too busy concentrating on thoughts of Bonnie.

'The stepdad.'

We sat down. The barman nodded at us. 'Two Coronas,' Easton said, then thought for a second. 'And a couple of tequilas, Chris.'

Easton turned back to me, waiting for my answer. 'Don't know him well. Never made the effort. I'd moved out of home before she'd met him.' Easton nodded, but he looked at me like he was trying to figure something out. 'And your mama. You not get along either?' He shook his head. 'My mama wouldn't stand for that. She'd be marching into our dorm room and demanding that I talk to her.' He laughed. 'She can be quite the force to be reckoned with.'

'I used to get on with her.' I paused while the drinks arrived. I went for the tequila first. I knocked it back in one, forgetting the lime and salt. 'Not anymore.' I hated talking about my family. Hell, I hated *talking*, full stop.

'And what about your da—'

'What's wrong with Bonnie?' I cut Easton off before he could ask that question. My heart was still racing at even the thought of having to answer it.

He didn't seem to notice. He took a sip of Corona, then said, 'Flu. She went back to the folks' for the week so my mama could look after her.' He laughed. 'I'll tell her you care.'

'Don't bother,' I snapped. But inside something in me relaxed. She'd had the flu. Which meant she'd be coming back to school soon.

Easton's face lit up. 'I find it hilarious that my room-mate and my sister hate each other.' Bonnie hated me? I didn't realize I was frowning until he said, 'Don't tell me that hurt your feelings?' He slapped the table. 'Shit! We've found your kryptonite. A chick that doesn't like you is what pisses you the hell off.'

'Not at all.' I waited until he calmed down. Until *I'd* calmed down. Bonnie didn't like me . . . 'We have to work together for composition class. That's as far as it goes.' I wanted to change the subject. Quickly.

'Okay, okay. I'm just messing with you.' He leaned forward, arms on the table. He was watching me. No, studying me. 'I can see why y'all clash though.' He waved at the barman for more drinks.

'Are you going to explain, or just let that hang in the air?'

Easton smiled, shifting in his seat to get comfortable. 'Bonnie's always been a go-getter. Ever since we were kids, she would organize things. Events, stupid little games for the neighborhood kids.' He stared off into the distance for a second. 'I was always the one in trouble. The one who got under my folks' feet.'

'Nothing's changed there then.'

'True.' Easton clinked my Corona with his. He sighed. 'Then she fell in love with piano. And that was it.' He clicked his finger and thumb. 'She was hooked. Never went anywhere without her little keyboard.' He huffed a laugh. 'Gave me a headache for about two years before she got good enough that I could actually tolerate her playing. Then it was recital after recital.' His smile faded. He went quiet. Too quiet. The silence made me uneasy. 'She's good people. She's my sister. But she's more than that. She's my best friend. Damn, she's my moral compass. She keeps me in line.' He downed the rest of his Corona and shoved the empty bottle aside. 'She's the better of the two of us. Don't think anyone doubts that. I'd be lost without her.'

It went quiet. Then Easton looked up at me and smirked. 'You, however, are in a shitty mood twenty-four-seven. Never do anything on time. Hardly speak. Keep to yourself. And worse, you play EDM. My sister, who *loves* classical music and folk, has been paired with a dude that can't play nothing but his laptop and drum machine.'

He pissed himself laughing. I stared at my Corona, thinking how totally wrong he was about me. And he was wrong about Bonnie. She'd seen me. The real me. The one I was deep down inside.

And she didn't like me? I knew I'd been a dick at times. But she'd *seen* me. It wasn't sitting well that she didn't like me.

Because I was quickly realizing I kind of liked her.

The doors to the pub opened, ripping me from my thoughts, and a few girls walked through. Easton's eyes set on them straight away. 'Yes,' he said under his breath, light in his eyes. 'Alex is here.' On cue, a girl with red hair came up to the table and stood before Easton.

'Easton Farraday. Fancy seeing you here.' She smiled, and I took that as my cue to leave.

I downed the rest of my Corona, shot back the new tequila, and put the new beer bottle in the pocket of my ripped jeans. I put the discarded top back on so it didn't spill everywhere.

'You going?' Easton asked, one arm already around the redhead's waist. He nudged his head in the direction of her two friends. One of them, a blonde, was already watching me, sizing me up.

'I'm going outside.' I held up my cigarette packet.

Easton nodded then took the redhead to the bar. I didn't look at her friends as I stepped out into the street. I sparked up my smoke then just started walking. I wasn't going back in. I wasn't feeling the need for partying tonight.

I was confused. I didn't want to stay in, but I didn't want to go out. I wanted to climb out of my skin, just be someone else for a while.

I was sick of being me.

The street was getting busy, people out for dinner and drinks. I kept my head down as I passed some of the students from college.

Older people were walking toward the park. When I found myself on the edges of the park, I looked inside through the railings. Hundreds of people sat on the lawn, most on picnic blankets. I looked at what they were all facing. What looked like a fifty-piece orchestra was in the center of a stage. A burst of applause rang across the park. I squinted, trying to see through the trees blocking my view.

I could make out the conductor making his way onto the stage. My heart took off into a sprint as he brought his baton high and signaled the orchestra to prepare. Bows rested on strings, reeds were brought to mouths, and the pianist laid her hands on the keys.

A second later, they began, in perfect unison. Beethoven's Fifth Symphony started the show. I pressed closer to the railings. I knew I should leave. I *needed* to leave. But instead I saw myself walking to the entrance. A ticket booth was there, a 'Sold Out' sign hitched on the main gate.

Go home, Cromwell. I forced myself to cut through the path that ran alongside the park and back to campus. But with every new movement, the colors grew brighter and brighter in my mind. I stopped dead and squeezed my eyes shut. Leaning against the fence, I pressed the heels of my palms to my eyes. But the colors didn't go.

Reds danced into triangles, shimmering and gliding into forest greens. Bright yellows flicked and shifted into peach; long drawn-out sections of sunset oranges burst into the lightest of browns.

I dropped my hands, and my shoulders sagged in defeat. I turned and looked through the railings. The stage was in the distance now. I looked for security guards, but I didn't find any. There was no one in sight. I hooked my feet into the fence and pulled myself over the top. I jumped to the floor, the branches from the bushes and trees scratching at my skin.

The dark that was building kept me hidden as I waded my way to the main area of the park. I slid through a gap in the trees and began walking toward where the music was playing. With every step the colors got brighter, until I did what I hadn't done in three years, what I was too tired to fight anymore . . .

I let them free.

I tore off the leash that held them back, and let them fly.

My hands itched at my sides as I took in the music, eyes closed and just drinking it in.

When the fourth movement came to a close, I opened my eyes and walked to the edge of the audience. I saw a tree to my left and moved to sit at it. I looked out at the stage as the next piece began . . . and not a few feet in front of me was a familiar brunette. My heart stuttered. After a week of not seeing her, the pale pink and lavender colors surrounding her seemed brighter. More vivid.

I couldn't tear my eyes away.

Bonnie had a blanket wrapped around her shoulders, and she sat on another, alone. It made me think of the blanket she'd put on me as I slept that night in Brighton.

She'd covered me with a blanket, even though I'd been a complete tosser to her. My heart squeezed again. I rocked on my feet to chase the feeling away.

I was over feeling so much.

Bonnie's knees were bent, her arms resting on top.

Even from here I could see that her eyes were fixed on the musicians. She wasn't missing a single beat.

I stayed watching her as they switched to one of Bach's Brandenburg Concertos. My hands clenched at my sides. Then when she moved her hand and wiped a stray tear off her cheek, they relaxed and I found myself moving to where she sat. I slumped to the grass beside her.

I could feel her eyes on me the minute she could bear to tear them away from the orchestra. I sat forward, arms hanging over my legs. She was watching me, a surprised expression on her face.

My teeth ground together as my pulse started to race. I pulled my Corona from my pocket and took a sip. I could still feel her looking, so I met her gaze. 'Farraday.'

Bonnie blinked, then her eyes snapped back to the orchestra. When the Bach finished, the interval began. The orchestra left the stage, and people moved toward the food and drink trucks. I lay back on the grass, resting on my elbow. I had no idea what I was doing here. Easton had just told me Bonnie didn't even like me.

And I knew that was it. I shouldn't care that she didn't, should have encouraged it, in fact. But I couldn't get it from my head. She'd seen me. She knew that I could play.

I didn't have to pretend with her.

'I can't believe you're here.' Bonnie's voice shook. She was nervous. I could see it on her face. In her brown eyes. I couldn't believe I was here either. When I didn't answer her back, Bonnie busied herself by reaching into the basket she had beside her. She was wearing a pink jumper – or 'sweater,' as she would probably call it – and jeans. Her brown blanket now covered her legs. She pulled out a packet of sweets, opened them, and started chewing on a long piece of red licorice.

I brought a cigarette to my lips and went to light up. Her hand came down on my arm. 'Please don't, Cromwell.' I looked down at my arm. She was holding it in the same place as she'd held it that night in the music room. When she'd heard me. When she'd seen me playing the instruments.

When she'd seen me break.

I looked up at her. Her cheeks were flushed and her eyes were wide. I wondered if she was remembering the same thing. I kept her stare, trying to read whatever was in her eyes. But when I couldn't, I lowered my smoke and put it back in my pocket. Then she eventually breathed out. 'Thank you.' She rubbed her chest. I wondered if her heart was beating fast too.

I didn't know what to say around her. The last time I'd seen her, I'd cracked and amended her composition. I'd been short with her. Tried to push her from my head. But no matter how hard I tried, she would never go.

Bonnie looked everywhere but at me. 'You were ill,' I blurted. It sounded more like an accusation than a question.

She must have thought that too, as she stared at me, then smirked. That smirk did funny things to my stomach. Made it pull tight. 'I was ill.'

I sat up and looked out over the crowd, trying to push the feeling away.

'Did you miss me?'

I turned to Bonnie, firstly not knowing why the hell she asked that. And secondly, not knowing what the hell to say.

She was smiling. When I blinked, confused, she burst out laughing. She put her hand on my forearm. 'I'm only joking, Cromwell.' She waved her hand in a calming gesture. 'You can breathe now.'

I finished off my Corona, but all I kept hearing was her laugh. The pink of her laugh. That and the fact it'd been aimed at me. I never thought she'd smile at me that way. Then again, I never thought I'd be here tonight. My body was taut as I waited for her to bring up the music room. To ask me questions. To push me about our composition project. But she didn't.

'You want one?' Bonnie held out a piece of licorice. I shook my head. 'What? You don't like candy?'

'Not American candy, I don't.'

'What?' she said on a single laugh. I turned my head back to the stage, to look at the set-up. I always did. Bonnie pulled on my arm, forcing me to look at her. 'No, I have to hear this. You don't like American candy?'

I shook my head.

'Why?'

'It's shite,' I said honestly.

For a minute, Bonnie's expression didn't change from shocked. Until she dropped her mouth and burst out laughing. She pulled back the sweet box she was holding and held it to her chest.

That feeling was back in my stomach. Like a stab, which started moving to my chest until it had taken over my whole body. She wiped her eyes. When she could talk again, she asked, 'Okay then, what British candy is good?'

'Just about any of it.' I shook my head at the memory of the first time I'd tried US chocolate. It was bloody rank. I hadn't touched it since. I was waiting on a shipment of the good stuff from my mum.

Bonnie nodded. 'I have to say, I tried it when I was over there this past summer. And I agree, it's amazing.'

The orchestra started retaking their seats. People began rushing back to their spots on the grass. Bonnie watched the musicians with rapt attention, before shifting her gaze to me. 'So you really *do* like classical music?' I froze. 'I know we're not allowed to talk about it. About you. That night.' Sympathy spread on her face. 'And I have to respect that.' She shrugged. 'But you're here. At a classical concert.'

I was picking the label off the Corona, but I met her eyes. I didn't speak, because the answer to her question was obvious. I was here. That said everything.

She must have got that I didn't want to answer, as she pointed at the orchestra. 'They're incredible. I've seen them so many times.'

They were okay. Good at best.

'Well?' she said.

'What?'

Bonnie took in a deep breath. 'You like classical music, don't you? By now . . . after everything, you can admit that to me.' I heard the plea in her voice. A plea for me to just give her this.

Wagner's Ride of the Valkyries poured from the orchestra, the colors rushing through my head like the paint Easton had sloshed onto his canvas. I tried to push them from my head. But I found, sitting here with Bonnie, they weren't going anywhere. She made them fly freer somehow.

'Cromwell—'

'Yes,' I said, exasperated. I sat up straighter. 'I like it.' A long breath rushed out of me as I admitted it. 'I like it.' The second admission was more to myself than to her.

I looked up at the crowd watching the orchestra, at the musicians on the stage, and felt completely at home. It had been a long time since I'd felt this. And as I stared up at the conductor, I saw myself in his place. Remembered how it felt to be in a tux, hearing the orchestra play your work back to you.

It was like nothing else.

'I haven't been able to get your music from my head,' Bonnie said, pulling me from the orchestra and my thoughts. I met her eyes and felt my heart sink at the fact she was talking about this. 'The few bars you left on the table last week at Jefferson Coffee.' My stomach tightened.

'Cromwell,' she whispered. I was surprised I even heard her voice over the music. But I did. Of course I did.

It was violet blue.

My hands balled into fists. I should have just got up and walked away. Christ knows I'd done it enough before. But I didn't. I sat there and met her eyes. Bonnie swallowed. 'I know you don't want me mentioning this.' She shook her head. 'But it was . . .' She paused, struggling for words, just as the string section took the lead. I didn't give a shit about the violins, the cellos, and the double basses right now; I wanted to know what was going to come from her mouth. 'I liked it, Cromwell.' She smiled. 'More than liked it.' She shook her head. 'How did you . . . Did you just think of that right then on the spot?'

I swallowed and put my hand in my pocket for my cigarette. I pulled it out and lit up. I saw a flash of disappointment from Bonnie, but I was on my feet before she could say anything else to me.

I went to the tree and leaned against the trunk. I only half watched the orchestra. Bonnie held the rest of my attention. Her focus was back on the musicians, but her slim body was slumped. She was dejected. And it had been my reluctance to talk that had made her this way. She chewed on her licorice, but I could see she was no longer lost to the music.

I'd robbed her of that joy.

I thought of how she looked when I arrived. She'd been enthralled by the orchestra. I wondered if I'd ever been like that. Just so caught up in it all. Not caring about anything else. Not letting anything else even enter my head while the music played. And I knew I had. Once upon a time. Before it all went wrong and this classical shit became the one thing I wanted to despise.

But as I stood there, letting the nicotine I needed so badly fill my lungs, I knew deep down I never could. For three years I'd been fighting a losing battle.

It's what you were born to do, Cromwell. It's who you were born to be. You have more talent in your little finger than anyone I've ever known. Including myself.

My throat clogged as I heard my dad's voice in my head. When I looked down at my cigarette, my hand was shaking. I took one last drag, forcing myself to keep my shit together. But the usual stirring of red-hot anger and gutting devastation, so deep I couldn't breathe, swirled in my stomach, like it did whenever I thought of him. Whenever I heard this music. Whenever I was around Bonnie.

I didn't know what made her so different.

I threw my cigarette on the floor. I felt like hitting something as the pianist took the solo. But my feet were soldered to the ground. The sounds of the ivories made me listen. Made me watch. But all I saw was me on that stage. Me, performing the one piece I'll never be able to finish. That one piece that had haunted me for too long.

The one I could never see in my head. The colors muted and lost to the dark. The one that made me walk away from my biggest love.

'Cromwell?' Bonnie's voice cut over the roaring white noise that had filled my head, the piano that was bombarding my brain like the bombs that had rained down on my dad for most of his army life. I shut my eyes, palming my sockets again. A hand wrapped around my wrist. 'Cromwell?' Bonnie pulled my arms down. Her big brown eyes were fixed on mine. 'Are you okay?'

I needed to get away. I need to leave, to get gone, when—

The pianist took the floor again. Only this time it was . . . 'Piano Concerto No. 6,' Bonnie said. 'Mozart.'

I swallowed. *It's my favorite, son. That's my favorite thing you play that isn't yours.*

I looked from left to right, lost. Bonnie's hand tightened on my wrist. As I looked down at her fingers on my tattooed skin, I realized she hadn't let go. 'Come and sit down.' Her touch always seemed to cut through my darkness. And this time I let it happen. I didn't fight it. Didn't run away. I stayed. And I didn't let myself worry about it.

Bonnie led me back to where we'd been sitting. A bottle of water appeared in my hand. I drank it, not even thinking about anything else. When Bonnie took the empty bottle from my hand, she put a long piece of red licorice there instead. She smirked as I met her eyes. I lay back on the grass, resting on my elbow. The orchestra had moved on to Chopin's Nocturne in E-flat Major, the night coming to a close.

We sat in silence. But when I took a bite of the licorice, I chewed on the tasteless sweet and muttered, 'it still tastes like shite.'

Bonnie laughed.

And I could finally breathe.

10

Bonnie

I didn't know what to think as I sat beside Cromwell.

The way he'd looked as he'd smoked next to the tree. Like he was trapped in some kind of nightmare. He'd been shaking. His face was pale as he stared at the pianist like she was a ghost. It mirrored how he was the night in the music room. The flash of fear I'd seen in him as he looked at my work in the coffee shop. As though just the sound, sight, and reading of musical notes pulled him into some horror he didn't want to face.

It was at these times he acted the most cruel. The most harsh. But it was also when my heart cried out for him the most. Because I understood what fear could do to a person. I could see something held him in its thrall. But I just didn't know what. I didn't know how to help.

When the orchestra finished, I got to my feet and applauded with as much enthusiasm as I could muster. Cromwell stayed sitting on the grass. My heart beat loudly in my chest as I looked down at him. He was watching me. His blue eyes were fixed on me. His tattoos were like prized paintings on his bare arms. His piercings glittered in the stage lights. His muscular frame and tall height seemed to take up all of the grass and his presence to consume all the air in our vicinity.

I turned my head, focusing on the orchestra taking their bows. I could feel his eyes still on me. It made nervous shivers rattle down my spine. Because every time I saw Cromwell, every time we spoke, I heard the broken boy in his voice. And I saw him hunched over the piano, crying. And I heard the music he'd been playing so perfectly circling around my brain.

It was hard to dislike a person when you knew they were in pain.

When the orchestra left the stage, people began to disperse. I leaned down to pick up my things. I packed everything away into my basket and finally let myself look at Cromwell. He was staring straight forward, his arms around his bent knees. I thought he would have gone by now. That was his usual behavior. But then nothing about Cromwell was making sense to me anymore.

'You okay?' I asked, and he looked up at me, eyes still glazed and lost.

Cromwell nodded, then silently stood and fell into step beside me as we walked toward the exit. He reached over and took my basket from my hands. My heart melted a little at that.

I wrapped my arms around myself, feeling freezing cold. 'I thought you'd be out tonight. At the bar. Or the Barn. Playing your music.'

'No.' He didn't elaborate further.

When we reached the main gates, I heard the sound of a horn. I looked over the road to see my mama in her car. 'I'm over there,' I said, turning to Cromwell. His eyebrows were furrowed. 'It's my mama.' I ducked my head, cheeks on fire. 'I've been staying with them this week while I've been sick.' Damn. I sounded like a kid who had to run home to her mama at the littlest thing that was wrong.

I was nineteen. I knew what it looked like. I hated to think that Cromwell would think me pathetic. But by the way he was looking at me, I didn't think he did. In fact, the way he was looking at me made me breathless. It was intense, and open. Cromwell was always guarded, an island unto himself. But tonight there was a shift, where before I'd only seen glimpses.

There was one thing I was sure my heart couldn't take, and that was Cromwell Dean being sweet to me. I wasn't equipped for the kind of emotion it inspired.

I took the basket from his hands and rocked on my feet. 'Thank you Cromwell. For carrying the basket.'

Cromwell nodded, then looked over his shoulder as a group of people spilled out of Wood Knocks. I sighed. I knew that was where he'd be going after this. That was his life.

It wasn't mine. I'd do right to remember that before my head ran away with its thoughts.

'Night.' I turned and started walking to my mama's car.

'Are you going to be in class again this week?' I stopped dead. Cromwell Dean was asking me about class?

I looked over my shoulder at him. 'Should be,' I said, then couldn't help but ask, 'Why?'

Cromwell rubbed the back of his tattooed neck with his hand. His jaw clenched. 'Just asking.'

'We have that project to get started on, remember?' He nodded his head. It seemed as though he wanted to say something. But he didn't. He just stood there, switching between awkwardly watching me or watching the road. As

I roved my eyes over the people milling about, Cromwell stood out like a sore thumb. His tattoos, his piercings, his clothes, his dark hair and dark blue eyes.

'Should we meet Wednesday?' I said, and his shoulders stiffened.

Cromwell rolled his tongue ring in his mouth. I'd noticed he did that whenever he was faced with something he wasn't sure he should do. When he was conflicted, especially when it came to music. I watched him fight that simple question, before he met my eyes and gave me a single nod. 'Night, Cromwell,' I said again.

Cromwell didn't say it back. He turned away in the direction of the bar. I didn't go to my mama's car until he had pushed through the door, a blast of music escaping as it opened. I turned and got into the car.

My mama was watching the bar too. 'Who was that?' she asked as she pulled out onto the street.

'Cromwell Dean.'

My mama's eyes widened. 'Your brother's new room-mate?'

'Yeah. And my partner in composition class.' And the boy who was pretty much in every waking thought I'd had since I'd seen him in the music room. Since he'd amended my music in minutes into something breathless. And since he sat beside me at a classical concert and carried my basket.

Cromwell Dean was an enigma.

'Well . . .' my mama said. 'He's interesting.'

'Mmm-hmm.'

'So, how was the concert?'

'Amazing.' I took a deep breath. It was labored. I rubbed my chest.

'You okay?' Mama asked, concern on her face. 'You still feeling tired? You're not pushing too hard, are you?'

I smiled. 'I'm fine. Just tired. This week has been long.' Mama didn't say anything to that. She just put her hand in mine and squeezed it tight.

'Maybe you should stay at home next week too.'

I knew I should. But, 'I'll go back for Wednesday.' There wasn't a chance I was missing working with Cromwell. I was already further behind in school work than I'd ever been in my life. But the real reason was that I wanted to see if he would open up with his music any more. I was forever on a precipice, waiting to hear whatever glimpse of his genius he would offer.

'Okay, honey. But don't push yourself too hard.'

'I won't.'

Mama pulled into the driveway, and in ten minutes I was in my room. I was exhausted. My bed called my name, but I found myself sitting at my electric piano. The sheet of music Cromwell had amended was on the stand. I plugged in my headphones and placed my hands on the keys. And like I'd been doing all week, I followed the messily drawn notes. And like every time, my chest filled with the most amazing feeling of beauty. My hands danced over the keys as if they had no other choice but to put sound to the pen marks Cromwell had so easily jotted down.

Too soon the short burst of music was over. So I played it again. I played it six times before my tiredness became too much. I ran my hand over the manuscript paper. I couldn't help but shake my head. This had been so natural for Cromwell. He thought I hadn't seen him reworking my opening bars, but I had. I'd watched him war with himself over touching it.

His hands had twitched and his eyes had rocked back and forth from me to the sheet until some desperate need within him had won out. The same one I saw that night in the music room. An expression I couldn't explain came over his face as he scribbled. Then he threw the pen and sheet to the table as if they were a naked flame in his hand.

Taking off my headphones, I went to my bed. I replayed the orchestra's performance in my head. Then I thought of Cromwell next to me on the grass. I shook my head. It was surreal.

I replayed the look in his eyes as he had watched the pianist.

The shaking of his hand.

The foreign look of peace I'd seen on his face.

The revulsion over the Twizzler I'd put in his hand.

And I smiled.

'No coffee shop today?' Cromwell appeared confused as I led us to the music department practice rooms. It was time we started getting something done.

I swiped my ID and led us to the room I'd booked. Cromwell hovered near the door as I moved to the table in the center. A piano sat in the corner.

I pulled out my notepad, blank manuscript paper, and my pens, trying to ignore the ache in my head. I got a bottle of water from my bag and took a few huge mouthfuls.

Cromwell dropped into the chair beside me. By looking at him you would think he was in an execution chamber. He had his laptop with him. I pulled out the music he worked on at the coffee place last week. He took one look at it and sighed in frustration.

'I like it.' I ran my hand over it. I met Cromwell's eyes. 'It's beautiful. And it's only a few bars.' I didn't hide that I was in awe of his talent. He knew. My reaction to him a couple of weeks ago spoke that without words. It was a few bars scribbled down in a hurry. Yet it was breathtaking. I smiled, trying to cover the thoughts in my head. 'I think it's a great start.' Cromwell stared blankly at the table-top. 'What were you thinking of?' I asked, tapping the sheet. 'When you wrote these notes?'

'I wasn't,' he said. Back was the Cromwell from before, the one who struggled to open up. Though there was an approachability that had been gradually building since I heard him play.

'You just read my notes, and what?' I pushed.

He put his hands behind his head. 'I don't know.'

'You don't?' I asked. He shook his head, but I could see that he was lying.

'You look pale,' he said, completely off subject.

'I'm always pale.'

'No. Not like this.'

'I've been sick, Cromwell. Kinda comes with the territory.'

'Your composition was nothing new,' he blurted. It took me a second to catch up with his snap change in conversation. My mouth opened to speak, but the swift stab in my stomach prevented any words from slipping out. 'It lacked intensity.' He delivered the blows through gritted teeth, a soft voice making the harsh critique slightly easier to take. Like he wanted to be anywhere but here ripping my hard work to shreds. Like he didn't want to give me this assessment at all. 'The notes didn't complement each other as well as they could have.'

'So basically it was bad,' I said with a self-deprecating laugh. It was either that or show how upset I was.

'Not bad just . . . not special.' He winced as he said it.

I stared at him, trying to not be a total baby about his criticism. I was failing hard. I sucked in a breath. 'Okay.' I looked about me then got up. I needed a minute. I found myself at the piano. I sat down on the stool and lifted the lid.

My fingers dragged over the keys. I closed my eyes and played whatever came from my heart. The notes of the bars I'd created spilled out, drifting into my ears. When they ended, another set began.

Those that Cromwell wrote.

And I heard it. I heard it as clear as day. The difference. The comparison of quality. His were a vibrant dream. Mine, a mild nap in the afternoon. I sighed and closed my eyes. My hands fell from the piano.

'How do you do it?' I whispered, more to myself than to Cromwell. He was watching me, lazing back on his seat. I couldn't read the look in his eyes.

'You . . .' He paused, clearly struggling with how to explain what he wanted to say. 'You don't play with meaning.'

'What?' I hadn't expected him to say that.

Cromwell nudged his chin in the direction of the piano. 'The way you sit, you're too rigid. Your body is too uptight. It makes the playing uncomfortable. If it makes the playing uncomfortable, the *sound* will be uncomfortable.'

'I don't . . . I don't know how to play in any other way.' I hated the way my eyes filled with tears. Hated the way my voice shook. Hated the way my heart plummeted. My dream was to play the piano well. I'd settle for being a fraction as good as Cromwell was.

Cromwell was silent. I could hear the distant sound of people practicing their instruments in other rooms. I inhaled deeply, then exhaled. My eyes closed. Suddenly, I felt someone beside me. I darted my eyes open. Cromwell stood to my right.

'Budge over, Farraday.' My heart thumped like a drum in my chest as his tall frame towered over me. Because I wanted Cromwell sitting at this piano beside me. I wanted to see what he would do.

I didn't dare let myself hope that he would play.

My stomach flipped at his proximity. But I did as he said and shuffled over on the stool. Cromwell wavered. I wondered if he was having second thoughts, but a moment later he dropped beside me.

He smelled good. Of spice. And although I hated smoking, I couldn't deny that the linger of tobacco that clung to his clothes only made his scent more appealing. 'Your hands are too stiff.' Cromwell didn't look at me as he spoke. Ironically, his hands were rigid too. His posture was ramrod straight. 'You need to relax more.'

I laughed. 'You're not exactly the picture of relaxation, Buddha.' Cromwell glanced at me from the side of his eye. I thought I saw his lip twitch. But it was too quick to confirm if it'd actually happened.

Cromwell reached for my hands, shocking me half to hell. I held my breath as his hands took my fingers and laid them on the keys. His hands were warm, but his fingers were rough. I wondered if that was from his years of playing so many instruments. I didn't ask him. I knew I'd only lose this curious side of him if I did.

'Play,' he ordered.

I frowned. 'Play what?'

He looked at me like I'd spoken another language he didn't understand. 'Whatever you need to.'

'Need to?' My head shook. I was so confused.

'Play.' His eyebrows were furrowed. 'Just *play*.'

I closed my eyes and began. I swallowed when I realized I was playing the bars Cromwell had written. When I stopped, I took a deep breath then met his gaze. His black eyebrows were pulled down in confusion. Then it dawned on me . . . 'You just play what's in your heart, don't you? You don't need music? You simply just . . . play.'

His blank face told me everything. He had no clue that other people didn't do that. *Couldn't* do that. I felt dizzy. Dizzy from the knowledge that Cromwell must look at a piano and just play something that was his and his alone.

His hands ghosted over the keys. I watched his tattooed fingers. The inked skulls and the numbers were a stark contrast to the purity of the keys. Yet they meshed seamlessly like they were long-lost soulmates.

My chest was tight. Had been all the while I'd been sick and showed no sign of letting up. But it was nothing to the taut string that pulled in me as the most beautiful music poured from the instrument. I felt like I was listening from outside of myself. I remembered that night when I'd seen him play a piece so sad it brought me to tears. Now, I was watching him up close, experiencing this beside him. And it felt like a taste of the divine. There was no other way to put it.

I risked a glance at his face. His eyes were closed. That look . . . that look of pure peace was etched on his normally lined and pinched face. My heart stuttered. My eyes widened.

Cromwell Dean was so *beautiful*.

My stomach stirred, and flutters I couldn't explain swarmed in my chest. Panic set in. I wanted to rub my chest. Shift on my seat and run from what was working its way into my brain. *No, no, no, no . . . I couldn't . . . I couldn't let myself go there—*

Cromwell pulled my attention from my freaked-out thoughts with a swift change in tempo. His body swayed to the rhythm, and I knew he had no idea he was even doing it.

This – playing, creating – was as natural to him as breathing.

I didn't dare breathe in case I broke the spell he was under. If I could have, I would have chosen to sit here on this stool until Cromwell tired of playing completely. I only let myself exhale when his hands stopped playing, the piece I'd never heard before fading to nothing but an echo in the silent room.

When the final note hung in the air, Cromwell's eyes fluttered open. His jaw clenched a few moments later, and a thick wave of sadness eroded the happy serenity that had possessed him as he played. He was once again conscious that he was back in this room with me and not wherever his music had just taken him. Tormented again. The expression on his face seemed hurt.

This close, witnessing his playing, I realized it actually pained him to play.

'Cromwell . . .' I whispered, fighting the need to hold him in my arms. In this moment he looked so alone. So completely alone with his pain.

'That was . . . there are no words . . . How . . . ?'

'It was the concert,' he said, so low I could barely hear him.

'What?'

Cromwell ducked his head. He ran his fingers down his stubbled cheeks. 'I was thinking . . .' He sighed. I wasn't sure he was going to finish his sentence, but thankfully, he did. 'I was thinking of the concert.' His lips tightened like they were fighting back whatever it was he was trying to say . . . No. *Had* to say. 'Of that night . . . the music . . .' He focused on the bare white wall in front of us. 'Of . . .'

I swallowed hard when he didn't finish. *Me?* I wanted to ask. But that question would never come from my mouth. Especially now. Especially after *this*. I needed to end this session. I needed to get away from Cromwell. When I'd first met him and he was rude, when he was unfriendly in the first days of the semester, it had been easy not to see his good looks. It was easy to ignore the way his muscles flexed in his arms, turning his tattoos into living, breathing pieces of art.

But seeing the real him at the piano that night, his struggle with amending my work, and right now, trying to help me play better . . . Speaking to me so quietly, so vulnerably, his voice deep and husky, like another symphony he'd brought to life. The fingerprint of his perfectly created music still thick in the air around us, it was too easy to see the real him.

To see how handsome he truly was.

'I . . .' He cleared his throat. It was the push I needed to clear the Cromwell-induced fog that had clouded my mind. I looked at him from under my lashes, hoping they would offer a layer of protection from whatever I was feeling right now. But he paused when he met my eyes. His cheeks were bursting with red.

'You what?' I whispered. It sounded like a scream in the silent room.

'I've got more,' he admitted, as if it was the worst kind of confession.

'More?'

He pointed at the sheet at the piano. My stomach rolled in excitement. 'The composition?'

Cromwell nodded once, tightly.

'Can I hear it?' Cromwell looked to the side. His wide shoulders were stiff. I held my breath. I didn't dare breathe as he looked about the room, darting his eyes to everything but me, the piano, and the truth – that he was born to do this.

My eyes watered as I watched him. Because whatever it was that held him back from giving this to himself, from embracing who he was, was all-encompassing. It was smothering him.

It seemed like it was *destroying* him.

In that moment, I felt a kinship with him. He would never know, but he and I . . . we weren't so different.

It wasn't intentional. My hand lifted and landed on his bare shoulder, a familial crest painted in bright colors on his olive skin. It was instinctive. It was the need to help this closed-off boy and show him without words or explanation that I understood.

Cromwell froze under my touch. I kept my eyes on my hand. Goosebumps spread along his skin like wildfire. A red rose in the eye socket of a skull twitched under my fingers.

Cromwell closed his eyes and took a long inhale. I didn't move my hand, in case it was the energy he needed to show me this. To give himself this. His hands moved to the keys, fingers in position. He didn't need to see where he positioned them; he knew exactly where each key was, a comfort you only got from years and years of practice.

Cromwell exhaled, and the music began to play.

I was frozen. Trapped on the outside of his world, looking in but not able to penetrate the bubble. My chest rose and fell quickly, but I didn't make a sound. I wouldn't pollute the melody, wouldn't tarnish the beauty that spilled from his soul with the sound of my stuttered breathing.

I wanted to watch him. I wanted to drink in the vision that was Cromwell Dean at a piano. But my eyelids closed, giving me no other choice but to awaken my sense of hearing. And I smiled. I heard everything he was feeling. Sorrow in the slow notes. Flickers of joy in the quickness of the high notes, and the utter devastation in the low.

I remembered the first time I saw Cromwell. This summer, in the club, allowing his beats to wash over me this way. There was no comparison. I felt nothing but disappointment on that sticky, humid dancefloor. Now . . . I was awash with a rainbow of feelings. My erratically beating heart unable to keep any kind of rhythm, struggling to allow all that Cromwell was giving me into its weak walls.

And then something happened. The notes and the creation Cromwell was giving to me turned into something else. The piece changed, an abrupt change. My eyes rolled open, and I stared at his hands. They were moving so quickly, his body swaying and swept up in the music, that it was like he was on another plane. I kept still, watching as sweat broke out on his forehead. His eyes were pinched, but there was a brief flicker of a smile on his lips.

My heart jumped in my chest at the sight.

But then the smile fell and his lips pursed. I didn't know what to do, what to think. I was aware I was watching something happen before my very eyes. The music filling the room was like nothing I'd ever heard before.

I had never *felt* anything like it before.

A lump clogged my throat when I saw a tear start to fall down Cromwell's cheek. My lip quivered in sympathy. The music was beautiful, like the feeling of the sun on your face breaking through the harsh wind of winter and welcoming the spring.

Cromwell swayed more deeply, his body leaning back and forward as he became one with the piano. There was no beginning or end to him and the music.

I was sure I caught a glimpse of his soul.

My hand slipped from his shoulder when a tear splashed onto the keys. The loss of my hand caused Cromwell's eyes to snap open. It was instantaneous. His eyes opened and his hands froze, stopping dead on the keys. Cromwell launched back off the stool. I jumped to my feet before the stool crashed to the floor. I pressed myself against the piano for balance as Cromwell's eyes locked on mine. They were wide. The pupils were so blown that it engulfed any dark blue.

His neck was corded with veins, and his muscles were so tight they made him seem huge. I was breathing hard, light-headed from the sudden shock.

His gaze darted to the piano, then to his hands. His fingers rolled into fists and he shook with a sudden anger. Tears stained his cheeks, the evidence that whatever he was playing had caused his heart to break.

It had ruined him.

Cromwell rushed to the table and gathered his things. I watched him silently, having no clue what to say.

It was the second piece of music. The one he had switched to. Lost himself to. It had caused this change inside him. One that he was clearly fighting. My palm was still warm from his shoulder. Where I had been connected to him as he played his masterpiece. In my peripheral vision I saw that he had stilled, and I looked back at him. Cromwell was staring at my hand ... the hand that had supported him as he played.

I knew the look in his eye by now. He was going to run. As Cromwell started toward the door, I intercepted his path, placing myself before him. Cromwell stopped dead, his laptop clutched to his chest like a shield. 'Don't,' I begged, my voice broken with panic.

I didn't want this to end. I didn't want him to leave again. Not like this. I searched his confused face. His jaw was tight and his eyes were wide. His body was shaking.

I swallowed, feeling the temperature rise between us. I didn't know what was happening to me. I didn't even let myself think too much about it. I couldn't. Because reason was flying out of the window. Cromwell was a statue, the only movement from his rapidly flowing breath.

My hands trembled as I lifted them toward his face. Cromwell never broke my gaze. A sense of dizziness overcame me as my palms touched his cheeks. I rose to my tiptoes, trying to meet Cromwell's eyes. 'Don't run.' I heard the waver in my voice. I sounded as nervous as I felt. 'It's okay,' I whispered. He closed his eyes, and an almost silent choked sound came from his mouth. That simple sound destroyed me. It conveyed a glimpse at the agony he held inside his heart.

Suddenly, his eyes slammed open and he stepped forward, crowding me so completely that our chests touched and we breathed the same air.

His laptop dropped to the ground, shattering on the hard floor as his hands took my wrists. 'I can't do this, Bonnie,' he whispered, voice hoarse and accent thick. His cheeks were still flooded, his eyes red. 'I can't face it all. I can't deal with what you're making me feel. When you're near me. When you touch me.' His face contorted and he sucked in a tight breath. 'I can't cope with all the pain.'

I wanted to say something. I wanted to reassure him. Tell him I knew what that kind of haunted suffering felt like. But nothing like that came out. All that spilled from my lips was a tortured call. A wounded 'Cromwell . . .'

As his name slipped from my lips, he staggered back. He didn't even spare a glance at the shattered laptop on the floor. He just fled, leaving an air of desolation in his wake.

I slumped against the wall, trying to calm myself down from the tension of the moment. I rushed to my bag and pulled out my bottle of water. I drank and drank until my pulse had calmed and the sudden surge of dizziness left me.

What was Cromwell doing to me? I wasn't meant to

feel this way about anyone. I'd vowed not to let anyone get too close. But the way he played, how his deep blue eyes fixed to mine like they were silently crying for help . . . this broken boy was burrowing his way into my weak heart.

But a slither of doubt crept into me as I thought of him as he left. I now recognized that expression on his face when he ran. He was pushing me away. Like he'd done now numerous times.

I glanced down at my hand. I stared unseeing at my palm, and a realization hit me. He'd played with my hand on his shoulder. He'd been lost, wrapped up in his own creation with me touching him . . . until my hand slipped away and it had all broken into pieces.

I closed my hand into a ball and looked away. I had no idea what that meant.

But to have touched him like that . . . to have seen a flicker of his smile and heard the music he had created thinking about the concert . . .

'Cromwell,' I whispered to the silent room. Then I waited for my heart to calm down so I could push him from my mind.

It was dark before I left.

And like a forever-raging sea, my heart never calmed.

11

Bonnie

My eyes were heavy as they blinked awake. The dark room was only illuminated by the nightlight in the corner. My hand slapped at the nightstand as the sound of my cell pierced the quiet night.

I squinted at the screen. My stomach sank. 'Matt?'

'Bonnie,' he said, out of breath. 'You need to come. It's Easton.'

My legs were over the edge of my mattress before he'd even said my brother's name. 'What's wrong?'

'He's worse than ever.' Matt went quiet. I could hear him moving away from the sounds of music and laughter. 'You still there, Bonn?'

'Yeah.' I put the cell on speaker as I threw on my jeans.

'He's taken a swing at one of the frat brothers. He hit East back.'

I pulled on my sweater. 'Is he okay?'

'He's bloodied. But he's not letting anyone near him.' Matt paused. 'I've never seen him like this, Bonn. He's all over the place.'

'Where are you?' I grabbed my car keys. I briefly saw my face in the mirror. I looked awful. I threw my hair back in a bun and forced my tired feet to move from the room.

'The Barn.'

'What?' I asked as I made my way breathlessly to the

127

car. 'On a Wednesday?' I checked the time. 'It's three in the morning, Matt!'

'It was Cromwell. He wanted to spin. None of us were missing seeing him live. He came back to the dorms earlier tonight ready to party, drunk as hell. East sent out the word and we all came. It's been lit!' At the mention of Cromwell's name, my breathing stuttered. He'd gotten drunk again. No doubt on the whiskey I'd seen him consume over and over again. 'Bonn? You there?'

'I'll be there in fifteen.'

I pulled out of campus and onto the back road that led to the Barn. With every mile, I fought to stay awake. I was getting more and more tired of late. I realized I'd been asleep for all of ninety minutes before Matt called. *Cromwell . . . what has you so hurt?* I thought. I hadn't been able to get tonight out of my head. Now I had Easton to worry about.

Guilt assaulted me when I thought of my brother. Then dread, followed by absolute gutting pain. My hands tightened on the steering wheel. Tears clouded my eyes. I wiped them away before they could fall.

'Not now, Bonn,' I told myself. 'Keep it together for Easton.'

I shook my head and opened the window to let in the fresh air. As I drove I looked at the stars in the dark sky. They always made me feel better.

The lights of the Barn pulled me in. Drunk students piled out of the doors. Fast thudding music played, and I wondered if it was still Cromwell spinning.

Somebody waved their hands. In the glow of my headlights, I saw it was Matt. I pulled my car to a stop around the back, near an old silo. It was déjà vu as I got out of the car. I took a deep breath of air, ignoring the slight new strain it took to inhale. As I walked toward Matt and Sara, I saw a familiar pair of legs next to the silo.

I pushed past Matt to Easton on the grass. His eyes were rolling around in his head. I kneeled down. 'Easton?' I slapped his cheek. I looked back at Matt. 'What the hell has he taken?'

Matt shook his head. 'Don't know. Never saw him take shit but shots and beer.'

I ran my finger under the leather cuffs he always wore and over his scarred skin, searching for his pulse. It was beating fast, but not crazy.

His eyes opened. 'Bonn.' He smiled, his mouth bloodied. I assumed it was from the fight. Easton's face slipped from happy to torn in a matter of seconds. He pulled me closer. 'What's happening?'

'You're drunk and, I think, high, Easton.' I took hold of his hand.

'No.' He searched my eyes. It looked like there was a moment of clarity in his. 'I mean what's happening?' I stopped breathing for a second. He laughed once without mirth. 'I know it's something.' He cupped my head and brought me in close, touching my forehead to his. 'You're hiding something from me. I know it.'

Tears pricked my eyes as his rolled back again. Pain shot through me, and I wanted to scream. Instead, I turned to Matt. 'Can you help me, please? I need to get him back to his dorm.'

'Bonn?' Another voice came from behind me. Bryce was jogging over to us.

'Hi, Bryce.'

'Everything okay?'

Matt hoisted Easton to his feet, but my brother's weight was too much for him. Bryce helped prop Easton up. 'Where to?' Bryce asked.

'My car, please.' I led them to my car and opened the back door. Bryce slid Easton inside and shut the door. Hit with a sudden wave of dizziness, I leaned against the car and put my hand to my head. I was too hot. As much as I was fighting it, I knew this was getting too much.

'Bonn? You okay?'

I faked a smile. 'Yeah. Just tired.'

Bryce smiled at me and rubbed the back of his neck with his hand. 'I'll follow you back in my car. I didn't drink.'

I glanced at the Barn. 'Were you on the decks?'

'Yeah. But it doesn't matter. Party's over anyway.'

'You sure?' Bryce had a nice smile. I wondered what Cromwell's full smile would be like . . . I shook my head. I wouldn't think of him right now.

'Bonn?' Bryce tucked a piece of hair behind my ear. I tensed. 'Sorry,' he said, blushing. 'I shouldn't have . . . I . . .'

'It's okay.' I squeezed his hand. It wasn't calloused like Cromwell's. He didn't have tattoos on his knuckles.

I doubted he could create a masterpiece from nothing either.

I released Bryce's hand and opened my car. 'I'll see you back at his dorm.' I slipped into the car as Bryce jogged to his. I watched him go and felt an ache in my chest. I had never let him in. He'd been there all this time, on the sidelines. And I'd never let him in. I'd never let anyone in.

You can't, an inner voice said. *It wouldn't be fair.*

My traitorous brain brought Cromwell's image back to my head. And what it felt like sitting beside him. What it felt like to touch him. Listening to him. Him fighting a smile as we sat on the grass at the concert.

'Bonn?' Easton's slurred voice came from behind me.

'I'm here, Easton.'

'What's happening?'

'I'm driving you home.' I turned onto Main Street. 'Not long now.'

'No, with you. What's happening?'

My stomach fell again. It was the second time he'd asked it. A cloud of darkness seemed to settle over the car. I felt like I couldn't breathe as I looked in the rearview mirror. Easton's face was tormented. His hand landed on my shoulder. 'You'd tell me, Bonn, wouldn't you? The truth.'

'Easton.' A lump the size of Jupiter clogged my throat. 'I'm okay.' I hated myself the minute I said those words. 'Just rest.'

Easton smiled in relief, but I could see the lines of worry still printed on his forehead. He must have been thinking this for a while. My hands shook on the wheel as I drove the rest of the way home. I pulled into a parking spot in front of his place.

Bryce pulled in beside me. I turned off the engine and just sat in silence for a second. It was all getting too hard. It was all getting too much. I looked at the students staggering drunkenly back to their dorms and felt a gap form in my stomach. I had never experienced that. Would never know what it felt like.

I wasn't one to wallow. But right then, I let the grief for what I had to miss consume me.

A knock on my window snapped me out of my sadness. Bryce's face was there. 'Open the door. I'll get him out.'

I pushed out of the car, trying to ignore the fact that my legs felt like lead. Bryce threw Easton's arm around his neck. I led the way to the room. I pulled out my key, but I paused when I thought of how Cromwell had reacted before.

I knocked on the door. My heart worked overtime as I waited to see if he would answer. It was only hours since he'd walked out on me. Yet it felt like a lifetime ago. No one answered. He must have still been at the Barn.

I slid my key into the lock. As I did, the knob turned and the door opened. I lurched forward, righting myself at the last minute with my hand on the doorframe.

It took me a while to lift my head, but when I did, I was greeted with a hard wide chest, every inch of which was covered in tattoos. I sucked in a breath when I saw Cromwell standing before me in only black boxer briefs. His chest was rising and falling, and I realized he was out of breath.

His dark blue eyes were glazed from liquor and struggled to fix on me. 'What the fuck?' he growled.

'Cromwell, I'm sorry. It's Easton, he –' My voice cut off when I heard a mattress creak. My eyes immediately moved to Cromwell's bed, and my heart completely shattered in my chest. I didn't know that was possible. I didn't realize my heart was still able to function this way.

'Cromwell?' A voice I knew sailed from the bed. Kacey lay under the comforter, only her bra straps showing.

My face set on fire. My cheeks burned and I struggled to breathe. I looked up at Cromwell and found him still watching me. Only now his face had paled. His lips parted, like he was going to say something, but the only word whispered was 'Bonnie . . .' I heard something in his voice. Saw something in his eyes as he stared at me, something I couldn't explain. Guilt? Embarrassment?

I didn't know if that was just wishful thinking.

Ever the one to torture myself, I couldn't stop studying him further. His chest was red and glistening. His hair, which was, to be honest, always in some form of disarray, was even more messy and unkempt. And then I focused on his lips. I didn't know why, but seeing them red and swollen got to me most. When I'd got to my dorm tonight, I'd stupidly let myself wonder what it would be like to kiss them. To feel them against mine. To hear my name whispered from them as he held my hand . . .

I made myself focus on the here and now, and push that painful vision from my head. Cromwell was practically naked. As was Kacey. I quickly realized that Cromwell hadn't cared. What we had shared tonight hadn't meant anything to him. Not if he could, only hours later, go out and do this.

'Oh, hi, Bonnie.' Kacey sat up in the bed. Her eyes avoided mine. Her cheeks blazed with embarrassment.

'Hi,' I managed to force out. I turned, ignoring Cromwell. 'Um . . . I was bringing Easton home. He drank too much.' I walked back to where Bryce was glaring daggers at Cromwell. 'But he can stay in my room with me. I can see you're busy.'

I put my hand on Bryce's shoulder and ushered him back. I didn't want to turn around to see if Cromwell had shut the door or watched us go. But nothing seemed to be going my way tonight. A glutton for punishment, I glanced over my shoulder, only to see Cromwell standing in the doorway, his tattooed body taut as his hands gripped his black hair. But it was those deep blue eyes. Those eyes as dark as a summer's night that fixed on mine, drunken desperation shining in their depths, that utterly destroyed me.

With every step, I grew more and more confused. It was only when I missed the turning for my dorm room that I realized how shook up I actually was. There was a pit forming in my stomach.

I wanted to gouge out my eyes when all I kept seeing was Cromwell's flushed skin and pink cheeks. His chest coated in sweat from . . . from . . .

'Bonnie, it's this way.' Bryce was waiting for me at the door to my dorm.

I smiled and brought out my key. 'Sorry. I'm so tired.' I didn't know if Bryce bought it or not, but he dutifully followed me through my door and placed Easton on my bed.

Easton was fast asleep in seconds. I pulled the comforter over him and then faced Bryce. 'Thank you,' I said, finally making myself look at him.

'You okay?'

'Yeah.' I sighed. 'I need sleep. I . . . I still haven't been feeling too well.'

'Okay.' Bryce stood awkwardly on the spot, before he leaned down and pressed a kiss on my cheek. I sucked in a breath as his lips touched my skin. My chest didn't tingle with flutters, and my stomach didn't tighten the way it did around Cromwell, but it was sweet. Bryce was sweet.

And wasn't intent on self-destruction. On destroying me too.

'See you tomorrow, Bonn.' He walked out of the door. I rocked on my feet as I watched him go. I thought back to Cromwell and Kacey. The way he clearly didn't feel anything toward me like I'd thought. The music he shared with me meant nothing; it was simply a display of his talent. I laughed a mirthless laugh. I thought I'd somehow helped Cromwell play from his heart in some magic way. It turned out it was only true in my mind.

'Bryce?' I spoke before I'd even thought it through. But when Bryce turned, I ignored the blush that burst on my face and said, 'You know you always ask . . .' I shook my head, my voice wavering. I tipped my chin up and met his eyes. 'If you want, we could go out on Friday?' I glanced at the floor. 'I mean, if you want—'

'Yeah,' he said before I even got a chance to finish my words. He took a step closer to me. 'I'd love to take you out.'

I didn't get the fireworks I'd expected in my soul. But I got a happy bloom, and I supposed that was enough.

'Good.' I put my hands in my pockets, just for something to do.

'Good.' He smiled. 'I'll see you tomorrow, Bonn.'

I changed into my pajamas in the bathroom then lay on the small sofa bed that my mama put in my room when I moved in. I stared at the ceiling when sleep didn't find me. I willed my brain to turn off, because I didn't want to feel anymore. But it betrayed me. It didn't help me by allowing my body to rest, my limbs too heavy and aching. Instead it showed me this evening like a show reel. From the start to the finish.

When it ended, I found myself starved of breath. But I forced a deep inhale and refused to give in. I had fought for so long, never giving up. I was fighting still.

I wouldn't give up now.

As my eyes grew heavy, I failed at eradicating the image of Kacey in Cromwell's bed, cheeks flushed and eyes bright.

I stared at my hand, the one that had touched him earlier. And it quickly lost its shine. It seemed as though Cromwell would let anyone touch him but me.

And, I hated to admit to myself, that hurt.

'Bonnie.' Professor Lewis blew out a slow breath.

I met his gaze straight on. 'I can't . . .' I shook my head, feeling the palpitations like thumps in my chest. I rubbed at my sternum. 'Professor Lewis, I understand your position about dropping partners. I do. But working with Cromwell . . .' I sighed. 'Frankly, it's been the most trying academic thing I've ever done.'

Lewis studied my face. 'Ms Farraday—'

'Have you checked your emails today?' I glanced to the clock; it read eight thirty. I'd met Professor Lewis as he was unlocking his office ten minutes ago. I knew he probably hadn't.

He frowned. 'Why would that matter?'

'Please.' I swallowed the nerves that were beginning to rise. 'There'll be something from the dean.'

Professor Lewis kept the confused look on his face as he switched on his computer and read the email from the dean. I knew he had received it because I saw his face drop in sympathy – it was why I didn't tell anyone.

He opened his mouth to speak. I beat him to it. 'Working with Cromwell causes me more stress than I can cope with.' I gave him a smile. 'I love your class, Professor. It's my favorite.' He smiled back at that. But I hated the new way he was looking at me. Like I was damaged. Like I was a fragile doll that might break apart at any minute.

I looked around the office, at the pictures on his wall. At the painting of swirls of bright colors hanging above his desk. It reminded me of one of Easton's pieces. I stayed staring at the picture but said, 'I want to create music.' I huffed a laugh. 'In all honesty, I'm not that good at it.'

'You're a lyricist,' Professor Lewis said. He pointed at my file. 'I read it.'

'I am.' I took in a breath, feeling my cheeks heat. That was something else I didn't share. My love of words. Words that attached themselves to music until their meaning was only heard through song.

'I'm determined, Professor. To finish your class.' I sat straighter in my chair, hoping it would give me the confidence I was lacking at that moment.

'I plan to submit my composition at the end of the year with everyone else.'

'I'm sure you will,' he said encouragingly. It fueled the spark that forever sat within me and helped fill me with hope.

'But I can't do that with Cromwell Dean.' I shook my head. 'I'm sorry. I know you trusted me to help him. To push him to work for this assignment . . . but . . .'

'No need for further explanations, Ms Farraday. I am fully aware of Cromwell's attitude.' He scribbled something in my file then sat back in his seat. 'Very well. It's done.' He rubbed his hand over his stubbled chin. 'Are you okay working alone?'

'I'm better that way.' I shrugged. 'Years of practice have been forced on me.'

'Then, Ms Farraday, I look forward to hearing how your composition progresses.'

A heaviness I didn't know I carried lifted from my shoulders as Lewis granted me permission to break from Cromwell. It was quickly replaced by great fear. Fear that I would never be able to produce anything like Cromwell had played for me last night. But it didn't matter. The main victory was that I was free of him.

I ignored the dull underlying ache that simmered underneath the strong sense of relief. I got up, seeing that class was about to begin.

'I wish you luck, Ms Farraday. With everything.'

I gave Lewis a tight smile. 'Thank you.'

I left his office and walked down to the classroom. Bryce was already sitting in his usual seat. He flashed me a wide smile when I climbed the two steps to join him. My stomach flipped, but not in nervousness or excitement. I knew it was because I had agreed to go out with him, finally. I really shouldn't have. I was reacting to that night. To Cromwell and Kacey. But seeing Cromwell living life exactly on his terms made me determined to start doing things I had never experienced while I still could.

I simply couldn't let myself or Bryce get too invested.

'You look beautiful,' Bryce said shyly as I took my seat next to him.

'I look tired,' I said and laughed. The dark circles under my eyes were getting worse. No amount of sleep would help with that. But he didn't need to know it.

Bryce's attention went to the front of the class. His smile slipped from his mouth and his face flushed with red. I knew who had walked in just by Bryce's reaction. I kept my eyes on my notepad. I was doodling around the margins, meaningless swirls. When Cromwell passed me, I smelled the spice of his cologne or whatever it was that made him smell that way. My heart leaped to my throat when I realized he'd stopped. My breathing increased in rhythm and my hand worked faster on my meaningless drawings.

I didn't want to look up. I couldn't, then . . . 'Bonnie.'

I closed my eyes as Cromwell's voice hit my ears. His voice was laced with sadness again, like it had been so many times when he'd briefly let me inside a little. When some of his armor had cracked.

But right now, I couldn't let his rough voice in. Seeing him with Kacey had hurt. So I kept my eyes downcast. This, and the tiredness that was sapping me of my energy, was too much.

My shoulders were tense, cold shivers darting down my back. Finally, Cromwell walked up the remaining steps to his seat.

'Dick,' Bryce muttered under his breath. I pretended I didn't hear that either.

Lewis walked into the room. 'Turn to page two-hundred and ten. Today we learn about concerto form.'

I did as instructed and managed to block Cromwell out

completely. That was until Lewis called his name at the end of the class. 'Cromwell, I need to see you tomorrow at the end of day.'

I gathered my things and got out of the classroom as quickly as I could. I knew what that meeting was about. 'Bonnie!' Bryce caught up with me.

'Hey.'

'So tomorrow?' Bryce rubbed his neck again. I realized this was his nervous tell.

'Tomorrow,' I echoed.

'How's eight at Jefferson Coffee?'

'Perfect.' I relaxed a bit. I knew the coffee place inside out. It would make the date easier for me to go on. I would be there on Saturday too, but the Saturday crowd was never made up of students. Saturday was for the Barn around here. It made going to the coffee house two nights in a row more bearable. No one knew me.

He laid his hand on my arm and squeezed. 'See you then.'

'You too.' I watched him go. He was nice. Kind. And that's exactly what I needed to tick this experience off my list. Someone who didn't make me feel worse than I already did. Instead, they'd show me what a real date was.

I reached into my purse for my chewing gum. It wasn't until I looked up that I saw Cromwell leaning against the wall across the hall, outside Lewis's office. He was close enough that he would have heard me and Bryce talking.

He was glaring at me, a pinched, almost angered expression on his face. I didn't care. Because all I could see when I looked at him was Kacey half-naked in his bed, and his unkempt state as he answered the door.

Shoulders straight, I walked past him and into the fall air. The cool breeze was no comfort to my starved lungs. I wasn't sure there was any remedy for the way my body always reacted to Cromwell. Distance was the only thing that would help.

So I planned to keep far, far away. As I looked behind me, I saw him smoking beside the door, eyes locked on me. Only, in this light, I saw the sadness shining through like a beacon. It made me lose a breath.

So I put my head down and walked to my next class.

I didn't look back again.

12

Cromwell

'What?' I wasn't sure I'd heard that right.

'You'll be working alone from now on,' Lewis said. 'I've decided to separate you and Ms Farraday. The pairing wasn't working. You weren't producing anything that could be submitted.' He shrugged. 'Some people just aren't suited creatively. I made an executive decision to allow you to work on your compositions alone.'

I stared at Lewis, stunned. She didn't want to work with me anymore. My stomach fell and I shifted on my seat. Her face on Wednesday flashed in my mind. When she'd stood at the door and saw me, saw Kacey in my bed. I shifted in my seat again when a stab sliced through my chest.

Bonnie had been hurt. I saw it in her brown eyes.

I'd hurt her.

I'd sent Kacey home later that night. I hadn't even tried to get back into it. Back into what we'd been doing before the knock came. I couldn't. All I saw was Bonnie's face. Even drunk off my face, I knew I'd fucked up.

As I sat here now, my shoulder burned. Right over the exact spot she'd put her hand on me and I'd lost myself in the music. It had sucked me under to the point that I wasn't even aware of what I was playing. And I'd been playing that piece. The one I never wanted to touch again.

Bonnie had heard it.

No one ever had but me.

'Cromwell,' Lewis said, pulling me out of my own head.

'Fine. Whatever.' I left his office and stormed through the corridor. The few music students left knew to give me a wide berth. Bonnie was gone from my life. I should have been okay with it. It was what I wanted. I'd pushed her away like everyone else.

But my body was a live wire. And I couldn't let it go. I worked better alone. Always had. But the thought of her not being there . . .

I sparked up a smoke and walked home. But with every step I got more and more agitated. I knew Bonnie had done this somehow. She'd made Lewis drop me. I pushed through the door to my dorm. Easton was out. Good.

I sat at my desk and fired up my new laptop. I cracked the window so the fire alarm wouldn't go off when I lit up another cig. With my headphones over my ears, blocking out the world, I let the colors lead me in the beats.

I closed my eyes, and the pulsing shapes of vivid colors took form. I followed the patterns, let them control my fingers as I slammed the keys and drum machine, chasing the painting on the backdrop of the black canvas.

I worked and worked until my cigarettes ran out and my fingers ached. I'd drunk the last of the cans of beer and drained a two-liter bottle of Coke. But when I slipped off my headphones and saw that it was dark outside, nothing had changed inside me. It didn't matter that I'd mixed tunes that would have the clubs bowing down to me like I was a god.

I was still pissed off that I'd messed up. Anger running

through my veins, ready to burn like lit petrol. I tipped my head back and let out a loud groan of frustration.

She'd had me dropped because I'd hurt her.

I'd gotten drunk after I'd left her. So drunk that I just needed to spin, I needed to be busy. The next thing I knew we were at the Barn. I downed shot after shot of whiskey to forget Bonnie. So that I didn't rush back to where I'd left her and tell her it all. She was getting too close. And something happened to me when I was around her. My defenses fell.

I couldn't let them fall.

Kacey had been at the Barn, clinging to me like glue. When I couldn't get Bonnie from my head, I knew I needed to be with another girl. But when she was at my door, her brown eyes wide with hurt, I knew I'd fucked up.

It would never have worked. Bonnie Farraday was cemented into my brain.

How about eight at Jefferson Coffee? That wanker's words ran through my head at a million miles an hour. I looked at the clock. She'd be with him now. It was nine. The dark pit that started forming in my stomach at the thought of her with Bryce McCarthy grew and grew until, the next thing I knew, I was out of the door and pounding the pavement until I hit Main Street.

Her brown eyes filled my mind, urging me on. Her smile and my name coming off her lips. The imprint of her hand still burned on my skin and her palms I still felt on my cheeks. The scent of peach and vanilla from her neck was still in my nose.

It tasted of sweetness on my tongue.

I stopped dead outside the coffee shop. I kept my head

forward, telling myself to go the hell home and to not do this. But my feet didn't listen. The pit in my stomach didn't go. Bonnie was in there with Bryce.

And I hated it.

I gritted my teeth, then snapped my head to the side and looked through the window. Something resembling a stone in my chest dropped when I saw Bonnie at her usual table with Bryce. Her hair was down and curled, hanging halfway down her back. I'd never seen her hair down.

And she looked . . . I couldn't look away.

She was wearing the purple dress she'd been wearing in Brighton. Someone came out of the door holding a take-away espresso. He held the door for me. 'You want in?'

I didn't think it through; I just walked in the door, the scent of roasted coffee beans slamming into my face. When I saw Bryce leaning into Bonnie, Bonnie smiling, something seemed to snap within me.

I crossed the coffee shop and pulled out the chair at the table right next to theirs. I leaned back in the seat. Bonnie's brown eyes were wide as they latched onto me. Her lips parted. Slowly, a burst of red flared on her cheeks. It was like seeing the sound of a G-sharp note tattooed on her pale skin.

Sam, the barista who had served us before, came over. I flicked him an uninterested glance. He frowned and looked between me and Bonnie. 'Black coffee,' I said then looked over at Bonnie again.

She'd ducked her head away from me. But I had all of Bryce's attention. His face was fuming. Good.

He leaned closer to Bonnie and gave her a smile. My fingers dug into my palms when she smiled back. My coffee arrived, and I turned my head away. I needed to breathe. To keep it together. Because the sight of them together was driving me mad.

I listened in to their conversation, zoning everything else out. They talked of school. Of music. When Bryce talked about what he was creating for Lewis, I wanted to punch him. But when Bonnie told him she'd started composing her own, I froze.

She'd already started without me.

About five minutes later, Bryce got up and went toward the toilets. Bonnie turned her head to me, eyes tired. 'Cromwell, what are you doing here?'

I didn't like how sad her voice sounded. It was navy blue. 'I was thirsty.' Her shoulders sagged and she played with the handle of her cup.

Bonnie flicked her hair back from her shoulder, showing a big silver hoop in her ear. She had more makeup on than I'd ever seen her wear. I shifted in my seat when it hit me that I thought she looked beautiful.

She must have seen me staring. She leaned forward, voice low. 'Cromwell. Please,' she begged. 'Stop, whatever this is.' Her eyes fell. 'This constant back and forth . . . I can't do it anymore. You have your life and I have mine. And that's okay.'

'You had me dropped as your partner.' I said, and she blinked in shock.

She looked toward the toilets. When there was no sign of Bryce, she said, 'Lewis didn't think we were working. I agreed. He allowed us to do the project on our own.' She took a deep breath. 'It's for the best.'

You heard it, I wanted to say to her. *No one else has ever heard it, but you did. And you've walked away. You've let me push you away . . .*

'You've been given a gift, Cromwell. A beautiful gift. And when you let your walls down, it's pure and beautiful . . .' Her face filled with sympathy. 'But you fight so hard. Fight against letting anyone in.' She shook her head. 'You run, Cromwell. You run from music. And you ran from me because I heard it.' She took a sip from the glass of water beside her.

Bryce pushed through the door of the men's room, and she glanced at me from the side of her eye. 'Please leave, Cromwell.' She clutched onto her cup. 'I want to enjoy tonight.'

She turned her back to me, breathing labored. I stared at her, chest aching from what she'd said.

Bryce sat back down. His eyes narrowed as he looked at us. 'Everything okay, Bonnie?'

'Yeah.' I heard the fake smile in her voice. 'Cromwell was just leaving.'

Anger built inside me in an instant. I watched her with Bryce and let the fire consume me. I'd been a walking inferno for three years, and seeing her with him right now, Bonnie choosing Bryce over me, sparked the flame so hot I had no way to stop it. 'Nah, don't think I'll leave,' I said and settled back in my seat. Bonnie looked at me, confusion engulfing her face.

Sam came and refilled my coffee. Bryce and Bonnie started talking again in low tones. Reaching over to their table, I swiped the sugar bowl. My action cut off their conversation. Bonnie was beyond pissed off; I could see that much. 'Need sugar,' I said.

Bryce folded his arms across the table. I leaned closer and listened in. My hand absently played with the handle of the cup. 'It's based on the journey of an immigrant to America from Ireland,' Bryce was saying. 'We start with an Irish violin solo, then move in a flute, then more strings.' I huffed a laugh. Bet it sounded great.

Bryce shot me a glare. Then he covered her hand with his, and he turned his attention back to her. Bonnie tried to move her hand away, but Bryce threaded his fingers through hers and kept hold of the touch. Bonnie stared at the entwined fingers and frowned.

The wanker didn't see it. Two conflicting things happened within me. I felt a stupid amount of relief that she clearly didn't like him that way. But my blood turned to lava at the fact that he was touching her.

I downed my coffee, hoping the spike of caffeine and sugar would help. I winced. I bloody hated sugar in my coffee. When I put the empty cup back on the table, nothing had changed.

'You'll be happy you're working on your own now, yeah?'

He had no idea what the hell he was doing. I knew that much. Because if he knew I was this close to smashing my fist into his mouth, he'd keep it shut.

'Yeah,' Bonnie said. She had the sense not to say anything else.

'Some people just aren't meant for classical music, you know?' I raked my teeth over my bottom lip. But the arsehole didn't stop. 'Some people can throw together some beats on a laptop and call it music. They sail by, conning everyone into thinking they're something special. All the while, the real artists among us get overlooked.'

I laughed. 'Artist? You?' His lips tightened. I shook my head. 'You still sulking at the fact I came to Jefferson and pissed on your bonfire?'

'What the hell does that even mean?'

I folded my arms and leaned back on my chair. 'The Barn. The fact that I could out-mix you with no hearing and my eyes shut. You're pissed off that I got a free ride on the course and you didn't.' I got up and towered over where he sat. 'You're jealous that my piss hitting the toilet bowl would sound better than anything you could compose.' I curled my lip. 'You reek of mediocrity, bitterness, and jealousy.'

I sat back down and signaled for more coffee. It was silent behind me until I heard the scraping of a chair. I looked back to see Bryce on his feet. 'Sorry, Bonn. Can we reschedule?'

'You're leaving?' she whispered. I didn't like the swirling I felt in my stomach as I heard the embarrassed shake in her voice. I didn't like the pale gray I saw as her words hit my ears. My heart was still thudding. But as the red mist dropped from my eyes, and I turned and saw Bonnie's pale face, something like regret built there instead.

'Yeah. I . . . I'll call you, okay?'

I heard the door to the coffee shop close. Bonnie's eyes were hurt. 'Why?' she said under her breath. 'Why did you have to come here tonight?' She scrabbled in her purse and threw a handful of notes and coins onto the table. 'Just to get your revenge for the fact we're no longer partners?' She laughed without humor. 'Well done, Cromwell. You ruined it for me.'

She got up from the chair so quickly she seemed to lose her footing. Sam flew over and grabbed her arm to stop her from falling at the same time as I jumped from my seat. 'You okay?' he asked.

She put her hand on her head. 'I'm fine. Got up too quick.' Bonnie pulled back and rushed out of the door.

I glared at Sam, who was scowling at me. I threw a twenty on the table and got up. He grabbed my arm as I passed. 'Leave her alone.'

I stopped short at his order. I looked down at his hand wrapped around my bicep. 'You might want to remove that hand.'

Sam pulled it back, wide eyed, and I pushed past him and burst out of the door. I scanned Main Street, but I couldn't see her anywhere. As I crossed the road, I saw her in the distance, leaning against the wall of an antiques shop, under a street lamp. She had a denim jacket on over her dress, and brown ankle boots on her feet.

Bonnie lifted her head as I walked toward her. She looked tired and worn out. 'He's gone.' Her attention drifted down the dark road. When she turned back to face me, there were tears in her eyes. 'I just wanted this one night,' she whispered. 'After everything . . . I just wanted this one night to go right.'

The sound of her broken voice did something inside my chest. Cracked it somehow. She wiped away a tear that fell down her cheek. 'I've never let myself have anything like this. Have never been able to.' She choked on a hitched breath. She straightened her shoulders and looked me in the eye. 'But I wanted to know how it felt. I wanted to not have to think about it all for one damn night . . .'

I stared at her, having nothing to say. What the hell was she talking about? What did she want to forget about?

I ran my hand through my hair. Her tears came harder, until she stood off the wall and turned on me. The tears were there, but now so was something I recognized all too well – anger. 'Tonight you were cruel, Cromwell Dean. You were cold and cruel and unkind.'

She stepped closer. Her face was almost touching mine. 'Just leave me alone.' She lowered her eyes. 'Please.' She turned around and started to walk toward her car.

But hearing her hurt voice, seeing her walking away, snapped something inside me. My blood rushed so fast through my veins that my head became dizzy. I didn't think it through; I just acted on instinct. I reached out and grabbed her arm. As she turned, I pushed her back until her back hit the wall.

'Cromwell, what—?' she went to say. But before she could, my lips smashed onto hers. The minute I tasted her on my tongue, my heart started slamming in my chest. A surprised sound fell from her mouth and I swallowed it down. My chest flattened against her, and I felt the warmth of her body as it meshed with mine.

Then she started kissing me back. Her lips opened, and I pushed my tongue into her mouth. Bonnie sagged against me as I took her mouth. As I drank her in. Her hands clutched my arms, her nails digging into my bare skin.

We were a blazing fire against the wall. I couldn't stop. Bonnie's mouth didn't either, lips moving faster and stronger the longer we kissed. Until I broke away, stunned. Bonnie's eyes opened and met mine.

She stared at me for what felt like an age, then her eyes flooded with tears, completely breaking my heart. She didn't say anything. Her cheeks were flushed, her breathing erratic. Then she was off, rushing to her car. She started up the ignition in seconds and pulled out onto the street. I watched her tail lights disappear from view.

I stood on the side of the road, breathing deeply, until a noise from behind me snapped me out of whatever the hell fog I'd just found myself in. The wind blew across my face, and it immediately woke me up.

I forced my feet to move, one in front of the other, until I was heading back home. But with every step I remembered it. Tasted her peach scent on my tongue. I looked down and saw the nail marks from where she'd gripped me so tight. My chest was still warm from where she had been pressed up against me.

'Shit,' I muttered as I licked my lips, my tongue ring hot from her tongue against mine. I didn't notice anyone around me as I walked. I didn't even realize I'd arrived home until I came to a stop at our dorm's door.

As soon as I entered my room, I saw Easton on his painting stool, paint spilled all over his clothes, and a canvas covered in dark tones. I stared at the canvas. I was used to seeing his gaudy colors, not grays, browns, and dark reds.

Easton glanced over his shoulder. 'Cromwell.'

I flicked my chin at him. But that was all he was getting. My head was full. Full of his twin sister and the taste she'd left in my mouth. I dropped down to my bed and stared at the ceiling. Closing my eyes, I saw her in my head. Her long brown hair. Her purple dress and brown boots. I palmed my eyes, trying to rid myself of the image.

You were cruel tonight, Cromwell Dean. You were cold and cruel and unkind . . .

The words sank down deep, stabbing in my chest. But

the wounds were softened when I thought of her eyes after the kiss. Her swollen lips and flushed cheeks.

I opened my eyes. Easton was still sitting in the same spot, staring at the painting. 'East?' My voice seemed to snap him out of whatever he was thinking. He'd been acting weird lately. Keeping more to himself instead of inserting himself into my life, invited or not.

Easton turned. 'What?'

'I was calling your name.' Easton put down his brushes and paint palette. He ran a hand down his face. I looked at his painting. 'Deep.'

He glared at the canvas then pulled a huge smile on his face. Shrugging, he got up from the stool and sat on the end of my bed.

'You get paint on my covers and you're washing them.'

His eyebrows danced. 'After Kacey was here, you'll need to wash them anyway.'

Kacey . . . the memory left a sour taste in my mouth. I wanted to keep the memory of Bonnie there as long as I could. I wasn't sure I'd ever be able to let it go.

'Didn't shag her.'

'Not what Bonnie said.'

'She's wrong.' I found myself drawn to the painting again. 'Where's all the neon?'

Easton exhaled a deep breath. 'Not feeling it at the moment.' There was something different to his tone. I couldn't place it. But it was forest green in color. 'Where've you been?' he asked, changing the subject.

I shifted on the bed and pulled my laptop from my bedside table. I'd just uploaded more mixes. I checked the downloads – thousands. 'Went for a coffee.'

'You see Bonnie? She's always there weekends. The Barn's not her scene.'

I shook my head, not meeting his eyes. 'Nah. Didn't see her.'

'She'll have probably gone home. The open mic night's tomorrow.' He made the comment so casually that I almost missed it.

'Open mic?'

Easton peeled off his shirt and got into his bed. He got his tablet and loaded up the next episode of whatever box set he was watching.

'She goes and watches it?' I asked, bringing up my music.

'She plays there.' Easton lifted his headphones. 'I'm about to go dark.' I nodded as he put the headphones on and zoned out. I frowned, wondering what the hell Bonnie was doing at an open mic night. I thought her deal was classical composition? I started finishing off the mixes, but my head wasn't in it. I couldn't stop thinking of Bonnie. The kiss. Her eyes. The way I'd completely lost it when she'd told me to leave her alone with Bryce. And how she'd looked after the kiss. The way her brown eyes had locked on mine.

I closed my mixing program and brought up the coffee shop's website. Open mic night. Started at eight tomorrow.

I shut my laptop, closing my eyes. All I saw was Bonnie's pretty face, the sight making that tether inside me slacken.

'Cromwell?' Easton's voice woke me from almost-sleep.

I cracked one eye open. 'What?'

'Barn's on tomorrow. You good for the decks?'

I opened my mouth to say yes, but instead I paused, then said, 'Can't. Busy.'

'Hot date, huh?'

I blew out a slow breath. 'Just got somewhere to be.'

'Great. Stuck with Bryce again.' Easton returned to his tablet.

I lay awake until the sun rose.

I blamed it on the peach taste lingering on my lips.

13

Cromwell

The place was packed.

People spilled out onto the path to smoke or to move on to the bar across the street. I looked through the window, but I couldn't see a thing. I ducked my head and walked through the door. There was no sign of Bonnie. The lights were low, except for the spotlight shining on the stage.

As I squeezed through the mass of people toward the side of the room, a table in the dark became free. I slid onto the seat before anyone else could take it. It was ten minutes before the barista came to me to take my order. When Sam saw me, his face frosted over.

He looked behind him and then faced me again, looking panicked. 'I can't believe you'd—'

I held my hand up. 'I'm just here for coffee.'

Sam's face told me he doubted that, but he asked, 'the usual?' I nodded, and he disappeared. I wasn't sure if he'd tell Bonnie I was here or not. So I just sat and listened to three singers. One of them was good. I stared at the table-top the whole time, seeing colors as they played and sang. I rubbed my head. My temples throbbed, making me feel like I was in the middle of a migraine. My head ached and my neck was stiff. It was because I was fighting them – the colors, the emotions, the tastes. I was fighting them all, when all my body wanted to do was embrace them.

You can't stop them, my dad's voice echoed in my head. *It's part of who you are, son. Embrace them.* He smiled. *I wish I saw and felt them too. What a gift . . .*

I squeezed my eyes shut, about to just leave, when the manager of the place came to the mic. 'And now, a good friend of Jefferson Coffee – our hometown girl, Bonnie Farraday.'

I had a clear view of the stage from my seat. So I saw the minute Bonnie stepped onto the stage with the help of Sam. He passed up an acoustic guitar. It looked battered and worn. But she held it like it was an extension of her arm.

Bonnie didn't look up at the crowd. Not once. She kept her eyes on the guitar, on her stool when she sat down. She was dressed in skinny blue jeans and a white jumper that hung off one shoulder, showing her pale skin. Her hair was off her face in an intricate plait. She had pearl earrings in her ears, and some kind of charm bracelet hung on her wrist.

'Hey y'all. This one's called "Wings."'

Bonnie shut her eyes as her hand found the neck of the guitar. I held my breath as she started playing. Olive greens danced in my mind, the slow strumming of the strings. And then she opened her mouth, and the most vibrant violet blue I'd ever seen flashed like a firework in my head, making my breath catch in my throat. And then the lyrics hit my ears, and my chest ripped apart as the words registered and sliced right to my heart.

Some are not meant for this life for too long.
A fleeting glimpse, a silent birdsong.

Souls too pure, they burn out too bright,
Bodies so fragile, losing the fight.
Hearts lose their beats, rhythms too slow,
Angels they come, it's time to go.
Lift from this place, to the heavens and skies,
Smothered in peace, where nobody dies.
Hope left behind in the ones they have loved,
No longer caged, now wings of a dove.
Wings, white as snow, sprout from my heart.
Wings, spreading wide, now to depart.
Tears in my eyes, I give one last glance.
I lived, and I loved, and danced life's sweet dance . . .

I was frozen to the seat. My body locked at pale pinks and lilac purples. The violet blue kept a shimmering circle with every new bar. The triangles of tempo, switching and molding into different sizes and angles.

A lump formed in my throat as her voice sailed over the coffee shop. My stomach and chest strained so tightly they ached.

My father's face came into my head – his smiles, his applause . . . and the time I'd walked away . . .

A loud round of applause broke through my thoughts. The painting in my head faded, leaving only shadows of color as they gripped on to the darkness. I exhaled, feeling drained, like I'd been running for miles. I took a large gulp of my coffee.

The manager announced a small break. The minute the lights came on, Bonnie turned her head. It was like she had felt me sitting here. Watching.

Her face froze when her eyes met mine. She stumbled

off the stage. Sam caught her, and she managed to keep hold of her guitar before it fell. Bonnie said something to Sam then rushed from the stage and out to the back.

I was on my feet in seconds, pushing through the crowd. Sam stood in my path. 'No one's allowed back there.'

I gritted my teeth, prepared to knock this guy out if he didn't move out of my way. Then I looked out of the window and saw Bonnie crossing the street with her guitar in its case. I didn't overthink it. I just slammed through the crowd, the lights dimming as the manager came onstage and announced the next performer.

Bonnie disappeared into the park. I rushed over the road and followed her path. She was standing under a streetlight just before the pavilion in the middle of the grass.

My foot snapped a fallen twig, and Bonnie looked up, her brown eyes huge. Her shoulders sagged. She brought her guitar over her chest as if it would protect her. Protect her from me.

'Cromwell . . .' Her voice was tired and strained. It was because of me, because of last night. What I did. What I'd done too many times. I didn't like how sad I'd made her sound. 'Why did you come here tonight?'

I stared at her, not saying a word. I couldn't. Now that I was here, I couldn't say a thing. I just kept seeing the imprint of her colors in my mind. Heard those lyrics playing on loop, stabbing me in the chest.

How did I make her understand? I froze at that thought. Because I wanted her to understand.

Bonnie sighed loudly. She turned her back to me and started walking away. My pulse fired off. She was leaving.

My mind raced, my lips opened, and I shouted, 'Your bridge was weak.'

Bonnie froze mid-step. She turned to face me. I edged closer. Only a few feet. 'My bridge is weak?' Her voice was husky and exhausted . . . exasperated.

'Yes.' I put my hands in my pockets.

'Why, Cromwell? Why was it weak?' I could see she was expecting me to shut down. To not explain myself. To run.

'Because the bridge was navy blue.' My face set on fire.

'What?' Bonnie said. I looked around me. I couldn't believe that I'd even said those words. 'Cromwell, what—?'

'The bridge was navy blue. Navy blue tells me it's weak.' She was a statue in front of me. Her face was full of confusion. I fought the tightness in my chest and cleared my throat. 'The rest was olive green and pinks . . . all but the bridge.' I shook my head to get the image of the navy blue from it. I tapped my temple. 'It was navy blue. It didn't fit. Navy doesn't belong in good compositions.'

Her mouth dropped open, and the excitement I saw the night I played the piano with her next to me flared in her eyes. 'Synesthesia,' she whispered, and I heard the awe in her voice. 'You're a synesthete.' She didn't put it to me as a question. Bonnie stepped closer, and I wanted to run again. Because it was all on me this time. But I fought it. I refused to run from her again.

I blew out a breath. *I'd* told her. She hadn't forced me to say it. She'd just played, somehow got beneath my walls, and the truth came pouring out.

'Cromwell . . .' She looked at me in a way she never had before. I realized in this moment that she'd always

160

approached me with caution. Her face had always been somewhat closed around me.

But now it was open.

It was *wide* open.

'What type?' She stopped, and her feet met mine. She was so close. The smell of her peach and vanilla perfume drifted up my nose, and I tasted the sweet taste on my tongue. Everything was *more* around her. My senses were so overwhelmed that I almost couldn't breathe. I saw color and fireworks. Tasted sweetness, smelled her scent, and breathed in who she was. It was lines and shapes and tones and colors, metallic and mattes. It all slammed into me like a flood. And I let it in. Like a dam bursting, I let her in.

I gasped at the force of the emotions. 'Cromwell?' Bonnie took hold of my arm. I froze, looking down at her hand on me. She went to pull it back. But I reached out and covered her fingers with my own.

Bonnie stilled. Her eyes fell from my face to our hands. I waited for her to pull away, but she didn't. I heard her labored breathing. I saw her chest rise and fall. She blinked, her long black lashes hiding what I knew would be huge, shocked brown eyes.

I'd finally let her in.

'Chromesthesia,' I said. Bonnie looked up, her eyebrows drawn together in confusion. I inhaled through my nose and resigned myself to admitting it. 'The type of synesthesia I have. Mainly chromesthesia.'

'You see sound.' A small smile pulled on her lips. 'You see color when music plays.' I nodded. A quick breath left her mouth. 'What else?'

'Hmm?'

'You said it was mainly chromesthesia. What else happens to you? I didn't know you can have more than one type.'

'I don't know much about it all,' I admitted. 'I have it. Apart from what my da—' I swallowed and forced myself to keep going. 'Apart from what my dad told me when he researched it, that's all I know.' I shrugged. 'It's normal for me. It's everyday life.'

Bonnie was staring at me like she'd never seen me before. 'I've read so much about it,' she said. 'But I've never met anyone with it.' Her fingers tightened on mine. I'd forgotten I was even holding her hand. I looked at the entwined fingers. Something calmed in me. It always did around her. The constant anger inside me faded to almost nothing. It only ever happened with Bonnie. 'Your senses mix together, hearing and sight and taste.' She shook her head. 'It's incredible.'

'Yeah.'

'And my bridge was navy blue?' I nodded. 'Why?' she asked, sounding almost breathless, she was trying to talk so fast. 'How?'

'Come with me.' I started leading Bonnie by the hand through the park. She followed. I didn't know if she would. If she'd forgiven me for hurting her this past week.

'Where are we going?'

'You'll see.'

When she lagged behind, I slowed. She didn't move any faster. Her breath was coming in pants. I stared at her flushed face and damp forehead. Reaching over her, I took the guitar from her hand.

Red burst on her cheeks. 'You okay?' I asked. I had no idea why she was so out of breath.

She pushed some fallen hair from her face. 'Just unfit.' She laughed, but it sounded off to my ears. It wasn't pink. 'Need to start on some cardio.'

I kept a slow pace as Bonnie walked beside me. I kept waiting for her to pull her hand away, but she didn't. I liked holding her hand.

I was holding a girl's hand.

I kept holding on.

When we arrived at the music department, I could feel the air thicken around us. I paused at the door.

'What's wrong?' she asked.

I gripped the guitar tighter, then finally pulled my hand from hers so I could get out my ID to swipe us inside. My jaw was clenched when I pulled away. Bonnie's eyes were wide on mine, and I knew why I'd hesitated.

I hadn't wanted to let her go.

It sounded like there were a couple of people in the building. Lines of crimson red floated in front of my eyes as an oboe played in one of the rooms. Bonnie looked up at me, lips parted, about to say something.

'Crimson-red lines.'

Bonnie stopped dead. 'How did you know I was going to ask that?'

I stared down at her face. She had freckles on her nose and cheeks. I hadn't noticed them before. Her nose was small, but her eyes and lips were big. Her lashes were the longest I'd ever seen.

'Cromwell?' Bonnie's voice was hoarse. I realized I'd been staring. My pulse had kicked up a notch, and I could feel my heartbeat thumping in my chest. The beats brought me strobing flashes of sunset orange.

'You have freckles.'

Bonnie stared at me, not moving and not making a sound. But then her face reddened. I opened the door to the practice room and walked through. I turned on the light and put down her guitar.

Bonnie shut the door. The room was silent. I put my hands in my pockets. I didn't know what I was supposed to do now.

Bonnie came forward. I couldn't take my eyes from the shoulder that her white jumper hung off. At her pale skin. 'Why are we here, Cromwell?' Her voice was shaking. When I really looked at her, I could see she was nervous. I'd made her nervous around me. I hated myself for that.

I took her guitar from its case. I handed it to her and pointed at a stool. Bonnie hesitated, but she took the guitar from me and sat down. Her hands ran down the neck, just feeling it.

'Sing,' I said, my palms sliding over my jeans when I sat down opposite her.

Bonnie shook her head. 'I don't think I can.' Her hand tightened on her guitar's neck, and she licked her lips. She was nervous to sing.

'Sing. Play,' I said again. I shifted in my seat, feeling like a dick. But for the first time in years, I found myself actually wanting to help someone. In the only way I knew how.

Bonnie took a deep breath and strummed the opening notes. I closed my eyes. I could see the color better when I did. Like before, I saw olive greens. I saw the shapes and lines and tones. Only with her this close, they were . . . more.

They were brighter. They were more vivid.

My body twitched as it tried to slam up the walls to block them out. It had been my MO for three years. It was rote. My body trying to shut out the colors. It never really worked. Not once in three years had I been able to fully block them out. They only settled for being somewhat dulled.

But not right now. Right now they were so bright that they were almost too much to cope with. But as Bonnie started singing, the violet blue took over everything. The jagged line at the forefront, the color that refused to be dimmed.

My heart raced as I let my brain do what it had been born to do. Bring color to sound and spark like Guy Fawkes Night in my head. My muscles unwound and the music seeped into the fibers, giving every one of them life. With every barrier I let fall, my body relaxed, the tension I'd carried for so long fading away on Bonnie's voice.

My head nodded in time to the beat, until she changed the tune, and a jagged navy blue line, shaped like a lightning fork, sliced through the violet blue, greens and pinks.

'There.' I opened my eyes.

Bonnie stopped playing, hand frozen on the guitar's neck. I leaned forward, seeing the still photograph of the colors in my mind. Capturing the moment the canvas was ruined.

Bonnie was watching me, breath held. Her hands were tense on the guitar as if she didn't dare move. I edged forward, taking my stool with me, until I was in front of her. I couldn't get close enough to the guitar. So I moved forward even closer, Bonnie's legs between mine. She looked up at me. I could smell mint on her breath from the chewing gum she always chewed.

'Go back a few bars.' I never took my gaze from hers. Bonnie placed her fingers and played. I was frozen as the color washed over me like a shower. My chest felt so warm.

When the navy blue sliced through my brain, I stopped her hand with my palm. Eyes closed, I moved her hand on the neck of the guitar. I knew where I wanted her fingers to be and what notes she needed to play. 'Strum,' I ordered. Bonnie did. I moved her hand again. 'Again.' I moved to another chord. 'Again.' I did it again and again, following the color pattern in my mind. Painting the colors in advance and following their lead. I mentally painted the notes until they meshed back into the ones Bonnie had created.

My hands lifted off the guitar and Bonnie kept playing. I felt her breath as it moved past my ear, as her voice sang the words of the song so softly. I moved in closer, needing to see the violet blue dance before my eyes. I listened until the last note rang out and took the finished canvas in my mind with it.

Bonnie's breathing was shallow. It was shaking. I slowly opened my eyes. When I did, I realized just how close I'd gotten. My cheek was next to hers, the ends of my stubble touching her skin. My ear was near her mouth.

I'd moved closer to hear her sing.

To hear that perfect violet blue.

Bonnie's breath stuttered. I hung close, not wanting to move away. Slowly, I pulled my head back until I faced her, her nose only a centimeter away from mine. Her eyes were huge, and filled with something I hadn't seen in her before. And I wished I knew what it was.

'What . . .' I swallowed. My knee knocked against her thigh. 'What did you think?'

'Cromwell,' she whispered, a slight tremor of vibrato in her voice. 'I haven't . . . I couldn't ever write anything like that.' Her cheeks blushed. 'Not without you.'

My heart slammed against my ribcage. 'I just followed the colors.' I nudged my chin in her direction. 'Colors you created.'

Bonnie searched my eyes like she could see through them. Like she was trying to see inside of me. 'This is why he brought you here. He knew it still lived inside you. Lewis. It's what he saw in you.' Her brown eyebrows knitted together, a sympathetic expression on her pretty face. 'Why, Cromwell? Why do you fight it?'

Her words were like a bucket of ice poured over my head. I moved back, my defense mechanism to flee, to verbally knock her down kicking in. But Bonnie's hand moved off the guitar and lay on my cheek. I froze. Her touch kept me rooted to the spot.

I fought the need to run. The lump that choked my throat clawing up from my chest. But when I looked at her eyes, I didn't move. Instead, my lips opened and I said, 'Because I don't want it anymore.'

Her hand was warm on my face. Her fingers soft. 'Why?' Tears filled her eyes when I didn't answer. I wondered if she'd seen something in my face. I wondered if she'd heard something in my voice.

But I couldn't answer her.

Bonnie's hand slipped from mine, and I felt like I'd been plunged back into the middle of an English winter. Everything was suddenly cold and dull, stripped of warmth. Bonnie smiled. She put her hand back on the guitar. Lines wrinkled on her forehead. 'I can't remember the new chords.'

I lifted off the stool and moved behind her. 'Budge forward.' Bonnie looked over her shoulder at me. Her pupils dilated, but she did as I asked. I sat behind her. She wasn't close enough, so I threaded my arms around her waist and moved her back. Bonnie let out a surprised sigh as her back moved flush against my chest.

My arms wrapped around her, shadowing hers. The tattoos on my bare arms stood out like lights in the dark against her white sleeves. My chin came just above her shoulder. I caught her sharp inhale.

It was a burst of russet in my mind.

'Hands ready,' I said. I glanced down at her bare shoulder beneath my mouth. Her skin bumped, her ears turned red, and I saw her lips part. I felt the corner of my mouth hook up into a smile.

'Play. When we get to the bridge, I'll step in and help.' So she did. Bonnie's words washed over me. But the lyrics were again like a dagger to the heart. The sadness in them as she sang. The violet-blue line of her voice that ran through me like a heart monitor swelled with her emotion. With the words that resonated with her the most.

As the bridge came up, I put my hands over hers. I felt her shudder against me. But I kept going, letting her strum as I placed her hands on the chords that were in sync with the rest of the song. We played it three more times before her hands fell from the strings.

'You got it?' I asked, my voice sounding husky even to my ears. It was being this close to her. Her small body fitting against mine like a piece of a jigsaw.

'Yeah, I think so.'

But neither of us moved. I didn't know why. But I sat there on the stool with Bonnie Farraday leaning against me. Until . . . 'Cromwell?' Bonnie's voice cut through the silent comfort. 'You can play anything, can't you? Without lessons or practice. You can just see the music, and you have the skill to play whatever you want.' Her head turned, her lips almost brushing past mine. Her eyes studied me. 'The colors show you the way.'

I thought back to the first time I picked up and instrument. It had felt as natural to me as breathing. The colors that danced before my eyes were like a path. I just had to follow them and I could play. I found myself nodding my head. Bonnie sighed. 'Can you . . . could you play my song?'

'Yes.'

Without taking her eyes off me, Bonnie found my hands that were resting over the guitar and moved them into position. She settled back against my chest. 'Please play for me.'

She seemed tired, her body leaning against me and her voice quiet. My fingers flexed. The guitar wasn't an instrument I usually picked up. But that didn't matter. She was right. I could just play it.

My hands simply understood its language.

Closing my eyes, I started playing the chords. No words accompanied the piece this time. Bonnie stayed silent as she listened. She didn't move a muscle as the music she'd created poured from my fingers. On the instrument she clearly loved.

When the song finished, the silence broke into the room. I felt Bonnie against me. I smelled her peach scent and I saw her bared skin. I hadn't even realized my fingers had started moving again until the colors showed me the way. And I let them. No fighting it this time. No hiding it from Bonnie. I just thought of her and us and right now, and used the guitar she loved so much to tell her without words what I was feeling.

Like muscle memory, my body reacted to being able to create. Real, pure instruments in my hands. Not laptop keys and synthetic beats, but wood and string and the colors that led. Peach and vanilla, milk-colored skin and brown hair pushing me on, inspiring notes.

I wasn't sure how long I played for. It could have been two minutes or two hours. I let my fingers loose, let them free from the shackles I'd forced on them three years ago. And with every note played, a part of the anger I fueled each day with my refusal to play, to compose, fell away until it was nothing but vapor, flying away with all of my reluctance to finally feel this.

This addictive, soaring feeling that only music could give. My body reacted like it had taken a deep breath after years of shutting down my lungs. I breathed. My heart beat. My blood pumped through my veins. And I composed music. It was part of me, not something I did. Part of my makeup.

And after this, I wasn't sure I'd ever be able to go back.

My hands came to a stop. My fingers felt numb from playing. But it was a good kind of numbness. Addicting. I blinked, clearing my eyes, and saw the piano looking at me from across the room. The violin. The cello. The drums. Adrenaline rushed through me, urging me to play them all. Now I'd had a hit, I was like a junkie. Needing more and more.

'Cromwell . . .' Bonnie's voice sliced through my thoughts. Her hand came up to my cheek, and she turned her head. She had tear tracks down her cheeks. Her lashes were clumped together from the wetness, and her lips were red. Bonnie always had the most peculiar color of lips. Such a deep red that they almost looked unnatural.

Her hand was a damn furnace on my skin. I turned into her palm, and a quick gasp of breath escaped Bonnie's mouth. 'That was beautiful,' she said and dropped her hand. It ran over my fingers that lay on the guitar's neck.

'These hands,' she said. I could only see her cheeks move from this angle, but I knew she was smiling. 'The music they can create.' She sighed. 'I've never seen anything like it.'

My chest expanded, something inside of it swelling at her words. Her finger ran over and over my hand until she finally pulled it away. She yawned, and I could see her eyes were getting small from tiredness. 'I'm exhausted, Cromwell. I need to go home.'

I didn't. For the first time in I didn't know how long, I didn't want to move. I wanted to stay in this music room. Because I wasn't sure what would happen when we left it. I wasn't sure if the anger would return. The need to run from all of this.

I didn't know if Bonnie would walk away. After the way I'd treated her, I thought she might.

'Cromwell?' Bonnie pushed. I couldn't hold on to this

moment any longer. I pulled my hands back from the guitar. I needed to get off the stool. I moved my legs, but before I got up, I moved my mouth to her ear.

'I like your song, Farraday,' I whispered and caught her quick exhale.

I closed my eyes and breathed in the peach and vanilla. Bonnie arched into my chest. I dropped my head, running my nose down her neck until my mouth was at her bare shoulder. I brushed my lips over the pale soft skin, then I kissed it once and moved back off the stool.

I got the guitar case off the floor and took the guitar from Bonnie's hands. She hadn't moved off the stool. When the guitar was packed, I finally looked down at her. She'd been watching me the whole time. I could tell by the embarrassed expression on her face. 'I'll walk you back,' I said.

Bonnie got up. Her feet faltered. She pushed her arm out. I grabbed hold of her, pulling her to my side to keep her steady. She was out of breath and seemed too hot.

'You okay?'

'Yeah,' she said nervously. She tried to push away from me.

I kept my arm around her. 'I might just keep you here to make sure you don't fall.'

Bonnie smiled a little and sank back into my side. I walked her back to her dorm. The night was quiet. I didn't know what time it was. But it must have been three or four in the morning.

Bonnie didn't say a thing. Not until she stopped dead and looked up at me. 'I wish I knew,' she said, voice strained. She needed to get home. She needed to sleep.

'Knew what?'

'What it's like for you to see them.' She gazed off to the distance, lost in thought. 'To hear colors.'

'I . . . I don't know how to explain it,' I said. 'It's normal to me. I don't know what it would be like to *not* see them.' I shrugged. 'It'd be weird.'

'It'd be dull.' Bonnie fell back into step beside me. 'Believe me, Cromwell. It would be a dream of mine to step into your world for just a brief moment. To see what you hear . . . a dream.'

We arrived at Bonnie's dorm. 'You have a room on your own?'

Bonnie's head ducked, but she nodded. 'Yeah.'

'Lucky you.'

She smiled. 'You don't like my twin?'

My lip twitched. 'He's okay.'

Bonnie took her guitar from me. She stood in the doorway, head down and nervous. 'Thank you,' she said, looking up at me through her long lashes. 'Thank you for tonight . . .' I nodded. I tried to get myself to move. My feet had other plans. 'I guess I'll see you in class on Monday.' She turned to go inside, but before she could, I leaned in and kissed her cheek. Bonnie sucked in a sharp breath.

'Night, Farraday.'

I had only walked a few feet before she said, 'Cromwell?' I turned. 'What's your favorite? Your favorite color to see?'

I didn't even think before I spoke the words. 'Violet blue.'

She smiled and went into her dorm. I watched her go, dumbstruck at what I'd just said.

Violet blue.

I didn't go home. I kept walking. I walked until I arrived at the spot by the lake that Easton showed me. I sat down on the grass and watched as the sun began to rise.

Birds sang and brought flickers of bright orange to my head. Cars passed, bringing scarlet reds. The same canoe-ist I always saw paddled in the distance, and I breathed in deeply. I tasted the freshness of the air and the green of the grass. It was keeping the walls from climbing back up. I tipped my head forward and pushed my fingers through my hair. I didn't like how shaky I felt. Too many emotions were rushing through me, mixing the colors until I wasn't able to tell them apart . . .

'I don't want it anymore,' I snapped at my dad as he stood next to the stage.

I pulled on my bow tie and stormed past him. 'I missed my footie match with my mates today.' I started pacing. 'Instead I had to be here.' I pointed at the hall that was packed with people. All of them older than me by at least twenty years.

'Cromwell, I know you're pissed off. But, son, the chance this is giving you. The music . . . You're so talented. I can't say it enough times.'

'I know you can't! It's all you ever talk about. This is all I ever do!' I balled my hands into fists. 'I'm starting to hate music.' I hit my head with my hand. 'I fucking hate these colors. I wish I never had them at all!'

My dad put his hands in the air. 'I get it, son. I do. But I'm just looking out for your future. I don't think you see your own potential—'

'And Tyler Lewis? Why is he here now? Why has he been trying to work with me?'

'Because he can help you, son. I'm an officer in the British Army. I have no idea how to foster your talent. How to help you realize your

potential.' He shook his head. 'I don't see the colors like you. I can't even play "Chopsticks" on the piano. I'm out of my league.' He sighed. 'Lewis can help you be the best you can be. I promise . . . I love you, son. Everything I do is only ever for you . . .'

I blinked away the memory and felt my stomach sink. I sat for two hours just watching the lake. I grabbed a breakfast burrito on the way home, but then stopped at the music building. My emotions warred inside me. I wanted so badly to accept all this again – the music, the love of playing, the passion of composing. But the darkness I'd had for three years always lurked near, ready to bring the anger and snatch it all away. But then Bonnie's face flashed in my head, and a sense of calmness washed through me. I let myself inside and saw the light on in Lewis's office.

My jaw clenched as I raised my hand to knock. I stopped for a second and just breathed. *What the hell are you doing, Dean?* I asked myself. But then I thought of Farraday's smile, and my knuckles hit wood.

'Come in?' The permission to enter was a cross between a question and command. I pushed the door open. Lewis stood behind his desk, sheets of music spread on the tabletop. He was wearing glasses. I'd never seen him wear them before.

'Cromwell?' he said in surprise. His stuff was all over the place. He looked like he hadn't been to sleep at all.
Join the club.

'Lewis.' I sat down on the seat opposite him. He watched me warily. He sat down, gathering his sheets of music.

I caught sight of them as he did. He stopped and turned them to face me. 'What do you think?' I could tell by his tone that he didn't think I'd answer. But when I saw his scribbled notes on the manuscript paper, I couldn't look away. He had parts for almost a full orchestra. My eyes ran over the notes, the colored pattern of the music playing in my head. I looked at them all, synergizing them into the symphony it was being written to be.

'It's good.' I was putting it mildly. It was beyond good. And by the look on Lewis's face, he knew it.

'Still in its infancy, but so far, I'm happy with it.'

I looked at that picture of him in the Royal Albert Hall. I always did when I came in here. It held so many memories for me. 'What's it for?' I pointed at the music Lewis was putting into piles.

'The National Philharmonic is playing a huge gala concert in Charleston in a few months, celebrating new music. They've asked me to conduct. And I've agreed.'

I frowned. 'I thought you didn't conduct your music anymore.'

'I don't.' He laughed and shook his head. 'I've been in a better place in recent years . . .' He didn't finish that sentence, but I knew it was in relation to his drug and alcohol problems. 'I thought I'd give it a go.' He leaned forward and put his folded arms on the table. 'It's Sunday morning, Cromwell. And you look like you've been up all night too. How can I help you?'

I stared down at my hands in my lap. My blood was rushing through my veins so fast I could hear it in my ears. Lewis waited for me to speak. I didn't know how the hell to explain. I almost got up and left, but Bonnie's face came into my head and had me rooted to the seat.

I played with my tongue ring, then blurted, 'I have synesthesia.'

Lewis's eyebrows rose.

He nodded. And by the lack of shock on his face, I knew. 'My dad . . .' I shook my head. I even let out a single laugh. 'He told you, didn't he?'

Lewis was wearing an expression I didn't recognize. Pity maybe? Sympathy? 'Yeah, I knew,' he said. 'Your father . . .' He watched me closely. I didn't blame him. I'd almost torn his throat out the last time he'd mentioned him. When he saw I was keeping my shit together, he added, 'He contacted me when I was in England on one of my tours.'

'The Albert Hall.' I pointed at the picture on his wall. 'He brought me to meet you. We all came. Me, Mum, and Dad. He was on leave from the army.'

Lewis gave me a tight smile. 'Yeah. I invited you to the show. But I wasn't—' He sighed. 'I wasn't in a good place then. I'd been using for years by that point.' He looked up at the picture. 'I almost died that night. Took so much heroin that my agent found me on a hotel floor.' His face paled. 'I was minutes from death.' He faced me again. 'It was a turning point for me.'

'What's that got to do with me?'

'I remembered you. I have no memory of that night at all, yet I remembered meeting you. The boy with synesthesia and the ability to play anything he picked up.' He pointed at me with his hands steepled. 'The boy who, by ten years old, could compose masterpieces.'

Icy coldness ran through me.

'I failed your father, Cromwell. It was years before I was in a better place to help. I contacted him. I even came to England, but you were already falling out of love with composition.' He met my eyes. 'When I heard of his death . . . I wanted to honor the agreement I made with him years ago. To help you. To help you with your talent.'

My chest was tight. It always was when I thought of my dad. 'I kept in touch with your mother. We talked, and I told her about my teaching here in Jefferson. That's when I offered you the place.' Lewis ran his hand through his hair again. 'I knew you had synesthesia.' He raised an eyebrow. 'And I knew you now fought classical music. I wondered when it would all finally get the better of you.' He gave me an accepting smile. 'You can't fight the colors you were born to see.'

I wasn't ready to talk about all that yet. I was here for another reason. 'I want to be able to explain it to someone. What I see when I hear music. I want to explain. But I have no idea how.'

Lewis's eyes narrowed. For a second I thought he was going to ask me who. But the guy knew to keep out of my business. 'It's hard if you don't have it. It's hard to explain if you do. How do you know how to explain the absence of something you've always lived with?'

I rolled my eyes. 'That's why I'm here. Wanted to know if you had any suggestions. You're a music teacher, after all. You've surely heard of it before. No doubt studied it or some shit.'

He smirked. 'Or some shit.'

Lewis got up and took a leaflet out of a rack on his wall. He put it in front of me. It was for a museum just outside of town. 'You're in luck, Mr Dean.' I scanned the leaflet. It was advertising an exhibition on synesthesia.

'You have to be kidding me. There's an exhibition on it?'

'Not yet. But it's almost done.' He sat back down. 'It's a complete sensory experience, created by an artist friend of mine. It's really quite something.'

'But it's not open.' I blew out a frustrated breath.

'I can get you an early viewing if you'd like.' Lewis shrugged. 'He might like more feedback from another synesthete. It could benefit everyone.'

'When?' I asked, pulse starting to race.

'Next weekend should be fine. I'll ask him.'

I took the leaflet and put it in my pocket. I got to my feet. 'You sure it's good? That it'll explain what I see and hear?'

'It might be different. Synesthetes often see things slightly differently to each other; there are no rules, after all. The exhibition may not show the exact colors you see for certain notes.'

'Then how do you know it's any good?'

He smiled. 'Because it's based on me.'

My feet were cemented to the ground as what he said sank into my sleep-deprived brain. My eyes widened and drifted to the picture above his desk, the one with all the colors. 'You too?'

Lewis nodded. 'It was why I wanted to meet you all those years ago. I've met other synesthetes in my life, but none that shared such a similar type to me.'

I stared at Lewis. I didn't know if it was because of the shared synesthesia, but I suddenly saw him differently. Not as the professor that kept poking his nose into my business, or the infamous composer who gave it all up for drugs. But as a fellow musician. Someone who followed colors like me. I stared at the composition on his desk and wondered what color story he saw.

'Er . . . thanks.' I turned for the door. Just before I left, I asked, 'What color is D?'

Lewis smiled. 'Azure.'

I huffed a laugh. 'Ruby red.'

Lewis nodded. I closed the door and made my way back to the dorm. A synesthesia exhibition. Perfect. Now I only had to find a way to get Bonnie to come with me.

She wanted to know what I saw when I heard music.

The thought of letting someone else in that close still rubbed me the wrong way, and the walls began to build once more. But then I remembered her song, and her face when she found out the truth about me. And I pushed them down. Keeping her face in my head.

And I fell asleep smelling peach and vanilla, and tasting sugar-sweetness on my tongue.

14

Bonnie

I didn't know why I was looking in the mirror. I didn't know why I cared what I looked like. I was fully aware that Saturday night was just a fluke. That Cromwell Dean would be his usual self today.

Yet here I was, checking my hair in the mirror. My hair was down and pulled to one side. I wore my jeans and a pink sweater. I had my silver hoops in my ears. I rolled my eyes at my pathetic-ness. Then my stomach fell.

You shouldn't be doing this to either yourself or him.

I closed my eyes and counted to ten. Then I ducked out of my room. The sky was bright, the sun shining and not a cloud to be seen. Students milled about the quad. 'Bonn!' Easton came up behind me and wrapped his arm around my shoulder.

'Where've you been?' I asked. 'You weren't in the cafeteria this morning.' I stopped and looked at my brother, using his appearance as my excuse to pause. Truth was, I was out of breath from just a few steps.

Easton shrugged. 'Wasn't in my room last night, Bonn. Let's just save you the details about all that.'

'Thank you,' I said sarcastically, and he smiled. 'I feel like I never see you lately.' I really looked at my brother. He had dark circles under his eyes. I put my hand on his bicep. 'You okay?'

He winked. 'Always, Bonn.' He started walking, guiding me with his arm around my shoulders. 'I'll walk you to class.'

My breathing became labored again after only a few feet. I held back the sudden onslaught of tears that threatened to fill my eyes. It was too soon. It was all happening too fast.

I hadn't expected things to progress so quickly.

I tipped my head up and looked at the treetops. At the birds flying among them and the rustling of the turning leaves. Like summer was changing to fall, I too was losing my sun. A fated leaf, destined to fall.

Easton brought me to the music building. 'Catch you later in the cafeteria, yeah?'

I smiled and kissed him on the cheek. 'Yeah.' It was our standing date. Our chance each day to see each other. To catch up. If I went a day without Easton, life didn't seem right. Easton ruffled my carefully styled hair. 'East!' I admonished and rolled my eyes as he ran away, laughing. Students passed by me, entering the music building. But I watched him go. Running to a girl I didn't know and giving her his usual bright smile and god-awful pick-up lines.

My heart seemed to crack down the center. I had no idea how to tell him. I would never be able to find the words. Because I knew it would break him too. I'd held off for months. Telling myself every day that today would be the day. That I would muster up the strength. But the day never came.

And I knew it wouldn't be long until the choice was taken from me.

He would know soon enough.

Darkness loomed over me as I thought about Easton. He was bold and larger than life on the outside, but I knew him differently. I knew the fragility that resided within him. I knew of his demons. Of the blackness that threatened to consume him.

Finding out about me . . . it would destroy him.

Easton's loud laughter sailed on the wind to my ears. The hairs on the back of my neck pricked up at the sound, but I couldn't help but smile. His energy, when good, could light up the sky.

The quad was almost empty when I finally slipped inside the door. I took my usual seat in Lewis's class. From the minute I sat down, the butterflies swarmed in my stomach as I cast a glance back at where Cromwell usually sat. He wasn't in class yet.

I played with the edge of my notepad as I waited. My heart bounced around in my chest, an uneven beat. I rubbed my hand over my sternum. I inhaled a long breath, focusing on my breathing the way I knew helped. On my fourth exhale, my eyes darted to the doorway. It was as though I sensed he was there.

Cromwell Dean walked into the room, wearing ripped jeans and a fitted white shirt, his tattoos framing his muscled arms and his piercings gleaming against his olive skin and messy dark hair.

He was clutching a notepad in his hand. A pen rested behind his ear. I tried to look away from him as he walked across the room toward the stairs that led him to his seat. But I couldn't. Images of Saturday night were technicolor flashbacks in my mind. The music room. Him, sitting behind me, hard chest against my back. His lips on my shoulder, kissing my bare skin. If I concentrated hard enough, I could still feel the softness of his lips.

My lips parted as I remembered it. I knew my face was flushed. Cromwell Dean did that to me. It was as big of a blessing as it was a fear.

As if hearing the thoughts in my head, Cromwell looked up. His eyes fixed straight on me. Every part of me tensed, apprehensive about what he would do. So when his lip hooked up at the corner, a hint of a smile aimed right at me, my pulse kicked into an erratic kind of sprint.

Infected by his smirk, I gave him the ghost of a smile back, ignoring the way the girls in the room looked at him like he was their source of warmth on a cold day. Because his attention was aimed at me. The British boy with a permanent chip on his shoulder was looking at *me*.

I steeled my nerves when he began walking up the stairs. His long legs ate up the path to me in no time. I expected him to walk by me, leaving me breathless in his wake. I didn't expect him to come and sit beside me, slumping down on the seat that Bryce normally sat in.

I stared at him. He lounged back in the seat like he didn't have a care in the world. 'Farraday,' he said, lazily, his accent wrapping like melting butter around my last name.

'Dean,' I whispered back. I could see other students looking our way. I shifted nervously in my seat under their attention. I turned to see him watching me. There was a light in his eyes that I hadn't seen before. An air of peace that showed in his relaxed shoulders.

The tapping of his hand on his desk pulled my attention. The skull and numerical tattoos danced with the movement. I couldn't take my eyes off those fingers, because I knew what they were capable of. I had seen them play the piano. And play on my guitar.

I looked up at the sound of someone clearing their throat. Bryce was standing beside us. His face was pissed, his eyes boring into Cromwell in his seat. 'I sit there,' Bryce said. I hadn't spoken to him after Friday night. I was ashamed to say that my head had been too full with Cromwell.

'Yeah? Well I'm here now,' Cromwell said, dismissing him completely. I closed my eyes, hating the confrontation.

'Why're you such a dick?' Bryce spat.

Cromwell kept his face forward, completely ignoring him.

Bryce let out a single humorless laugh then walked past us. 'Bryce,' I said, but he either ignored me or didn't hear me. I wasn't sure which.

'Cromwell,' I said. His stubborn expression said it all. He wasn't moving anywhere.

Lewis came into the room. Cromwell's leg brushed up against mine. He didn't move it. Lewis looked around the room, and his eyebrows lifted slightly when he saw Cromwell beside me. Cromwell shifted in his seat. But then Lewis addressed the students, and class began.

Bryce was out of the classroom the minute Lewis dismissed us. I sighed as I watched him go. There was clearly no love lost between him and Cromwell.

I stood. 'Bye, Cromwell.'

He got off his seat and followed me out into the quad. I thought his body would be tense and his face would be pinched. But he seemed relaxed. I'd never seen this from Cromwell before, and it confused me more than anything. He nudged his chin at me when I left to go to my next class. I shook my head as I watched him leave, wondering what all that was about. He hadn't spoken to me apart from greeting me when he sat down. But he'd pressed his leg against mine, causing shivers to break out all over my skin. And he'd leaned in to me, his arm occasionally brushing mine. My emotions were going haywire. I had no idea what was going on with us. With him. The fact that he wasn't glaring at me felt strange. The fact that he was almost being warm and kind . . . I couldn't bring myself to believe it.

Yet I couldn't deny being on the receiving end of his small smile made my heart sing.

After my morning classes, I went to the cafeteria. Easton was at our usual table. I grabbed a salad and made my way over. Easton, as always, was eating enough to feed a small army.

'You got enough there, East?' I joked.

He scrunched up his nose. 'Nah. Was thinking of going back for more.' Easton looked over my shoulder. 'What the hell?' he said, a smirk on his mouth. I followed his gaze, and my mouth parted at what I saw.

Cromwell stood in the doorway, scanning his eyes around the room. When they fell on us, he walked right in our direction. For once, my heartbeat found a rhythm – and it was exactly in sync with Cromwell's footsteps.

He sat beside us. He pulled a few unfamiliar candy bars from his pockets, opened one, and started eating. Easton looked at me, then back at Cromwell. 'You lost, Dean?'

Cromwell finished off one candy bar and opened the

next. He looked at Easton then spared a flicker of a glance to me. 'No.'

Easton carried on eating, looking at Cromwell like he was some science experiment. 'You know you're in the cafeteria, yeah?' Cromwell raised one eyebrow at Easton. Easton laughed and pointed at his candy bars. 'And that they serve food here.'

Cromwell sat back. He glanced around the cafeteria. 'I'm good with these.' He opened his last candy bar.

I pushed my salad around my plate. 'So,' Easton said. 'How's your project coming along?'

Only silence met him. 'It's not,' I finally said. 'We're no longer partners.' I wasn't an overly shy person. Wasn't easily intimidated. But the images of Saturday night clogged my mind and made me lose the ability to speak around Cromwell.

Why was he here in the cafeteria? Why had he sat next to me in class, yet spoken zero words but my name?

Easton glared at Cromwell. 'What did you do?' Cromwell stared back at my brother. Easton always joked with people. He was always happy. But he had a side to him that people didn't know. Especially when it came to me.

Cromwell's jaw was clenched. I covered Easton's hand with my own. 'Nothing happened, East. Lewis saw that our work wasn't as good together as it was apart, so he allowed us to work alone. That's all.'

Easton narrowed his eyes, first on me, then on Cromwell. 'You sure?'

'Yes,' I replied.

A wide smile decorated his face. 'Then that's okay.' He flicked his chin at me. 'Weren't feeling the EDM, sis?'

I laughed. 'Not so much.'

'She just doesn't understand it.'

I turned to face Cromwell. He finally looked at me.

'I just don't rate it as a music genre.'

'You should,' he argued, but his voice was calm. 'You just need to be shown its merits.'

His voice might have been calm, but his blue eyes were dancing with light. 'I've heard your music,' I challenged.

I saw his lips pull up at the corner. Warmth burst in my chest. 'Not properly.' I frowned at his cryptic answer.

'I need cake.' Easton rose from his seat. He eyed us both weirdly, like he was on the outside of some joke only we were in on. 'Don't kill each other while I'm gone, yeah, kids?'

'We'll try,' I said.

The silence stretched on. Cromwell kept his gaze on the view outside the window. I glanced down at his empty candy wrappers. 'Package from your mama came in, huh?'

Cromwell nodded then held out a square of chocolate from the bar he was currently demolishing. 'I . . . I don't eat fatty foods.' I felt my face flame. I knew the excuse sounded lame.

Cromwell ate the square. 'You should learn to live a little, Farraday.'

I gave him a weak smile. 'I'm trying.'

I couldn't tell what he was reading in my face. I wanted to ask him. Wanted him to talk to me. At least mention Saturday night. But when Easton sat back down, chocolate cake on his plate, Cromwell got up. 'I'm out.'

I followed him with my eyes out of the door, where he stopped near the window and pulled out a cigarette. Girl after girl looked at him as they came in for lunch. I could barely take my eyes off him myself.

Easton cleared his throat, causing me to put my focus back on my twin. He was still giving me a weird look. 'There something I should know?' His voice was filled with concern.

'No.'

He clearly didn't believe me. 'Cromwell has fucked no less than ten girls since he got here, Bonn.'

An ache pulled in my chest at that information. 'So?'

Easton shrugged. 'Just thought you should know, is all. Cromwell's a screw-them-and-leave-them kind of deal.'

I flicked my hair over my shoulder. 'I really don't care, East.' Easton ate his cake. 'I thought you liked him, anyway?'

'I do,' East said with a mouthful of cake. He swallowed then met my eyes. 'I just don't want him anywhere near you.' His hand covered mine and his voice lowered. 'You've been through enough, Bonn. A guy like that would chew you up and spit you out. And after everything you've been through . . .' He shook his head. 'You deserve more.'

I nearly cried. Tears pricked my eyes, not just because of his words, or his protective nature. But because if he knew . . . if he knew what was happening to me . . .

'You're my best friend, Bonn. Don't know what I'd do without you.' Easton's smile faltered. 'You're the only one who has ever understood me.' He blew out a long breath. 'Who gets me.'

I squeezed his hand and never wanted to let go. Grief and panic stole my breath, overwhelming me. 'I love you, East,' I whispered.

He smiled. 'Back at you, Bonn.'

It was on the tip of my tongue to tell him. But when I looked into his blue eyes, at the pain I saw lurking underneath, I didn't dare. Easton released my hand. He threw on his usual smile. 'Gotta get to class.' He got to his feet. A few people came over to him, and he laughed and joked with them like always.

I'd never felt more worry for a person in my life than I did for him.

Not even myself.

I picked up my tray and cast one last glance out of the window.

Cromwell was gone. So I went to my class, wondering how everything had gotten so messed up.

'. . . and let the darkness fade . . .'

I finished my most recent song, put down my guitar, and scribbled the new lyric and chords down on the staff paper. I closed my eyes, replaying it in my head to make sure it was perfect, when there was a knock at my door. I looked up at my clock. It was nine p.m.

I looked down at myself. I was dressed in black leggings, a black top, and a white cardigan. My hair was thrown back in a messy bun. Basically, I wasn't suited for company this late on a Friday night.

My legs ached as I walked to the door. My ankles were heavy from too much walking. I cast a quick glance around my room. The boxes were stashed in my closet. If it was Easton, I didn't want him to see. Slapping my cheeks to bring more life to my skin, I eventually turned the knob. I opened the door just a fraction and looked out into the hallway.

Cromwell Dean was leaning against the opposite wall, hands in his black jean pockets. He was wearing a black knitted sweater, sleeves rolled up to his elbows. 'Farraday,' he greeted casually.

'Cromwell?'

He pushed off the wall and came to stand in front of me. He smirked. 'You decent?' He pointed at the partially open door.

I flushed then opened the door the rest of the way. I wrapped my cardigan tightly around me. 'Yes.' I looked down both sides of the hallway. It was empty. 'What are you doing here, Cromwell?'

He had a cigarette tucked behind his ear and a chain hanging from the waistband of his jeans. 'I've come for you.'

'What?'

'I'm taking you somewhere.'

After hours of laziness, my tired heart kicked to life. 'You're what?'

'Get some shoes on, Farraday. You're coming with me.'

My skin broke into betraying bumps as excitement soared through me. 'And where are you taking me?'

If I wasn't mistaken, Cromwell blushed.

'Farraday, just get your shoes on and your arse out of this door.'

'I'm not dressed right.' My hand ran over my bun. 'My hair's a mess. I'm not wearing makeup.'

'You look good,' he said, and I stopped breathing. He

must have seen. But he didn't move his eyes off mine. 'We're losing time, Farraday. Let's get going.'

I should have stayed. It wasn't wise to let him do this. But, despite what I knew was right, what was fair, I couldn't help it.

I had to go.

I sat down and pulled on my boots. Cromwell leaned against the doorframe, his arm stretched above his head. The black sweater clung to his arm muscles, and the hem lifted, exposing a couple of inches of his tattooed stomach. My cheeks set on fire. I averted my eyes and concentrated on fastening the laces of my boots. But when I stood and saw the flicker of a smirk on his lips, I knew he'd seen me looking.

'Let's go.' He walked out to the hallway. I let him lead the way outside and to a matte-black truck, a vintage Ford pickup.

'Is this yours?' I ran my hand over the paintwork. 'It's beautiful.'

'Yeah.'

'You just get it?' He nodded. 'It must have cost you a pretty penny,' I said as we pulled out of campus.

A dimple I hadn't even known he had popped in his left cheek. I'd almost gotten a smile. Almost. 'I do all right,' he said cryptically.

'With your music?'

'I don't spin for free, Farraday.' I knew he was the most streamed EDM DJ in Europe – hell, maybe the US too for all I knew. I hadn't really thought of him like that. I'd forgotten he was Cromwell Dean, up-and-coming EDM star. It seemed crazy to me.

Especially when I knew what he could create in classical.

Cromwell had sat with Easton and me every lunchtime this week. He'd sat beside me in all the classes we shared. He had hardly spoken, but he'd been there. I didn't know what to make of it.

I certainly didn't know what to make of right now.

'So, any clues to where we're going?'

Cromwell shook his head. 'You'll just have to wait and see.' I couldn't help it; I laughed.

'You're not at the bar tonight, or at the Barn? Won't all your adoring fans – and by fans, I mean girls – miss you?'

'I'm sure they'll survive,' he said dryly. It only made me smile wider.

Cromwell pulled out onto the freeway. I frowned, wondering where we were going. 'Can I put your radio on?' I asked.

Cromwell nodded his head. When I switched it on, I wasn't surprised to hear fast tempos, pounding crescendos, and slamming beats. EDM. I sighed. 'I guess this comes with the territory, huh? If I'm in your car?'

'What do you have against EDM?' he asked. He kept glancing between me and the road.

'Nothing, really. I just don't know how you could pick this over all the other genres.'

'You like folk.'

'I like acoustic folk. I write the music and the lyrics.'

'I create the beats, the rhythms, and the tempos.' He turned up the current track. 'This is one of my most recent.' He looked at me. 'Close your eyes.' I raised my eyebrow. 'Just shut them, Farraday.' I did as he asked. 'Listen to the breakdown. *Really* listen. Hear the beat and how it carries the base of the song. Hear the layers. How the tempo changes with each sound, the keyboard, how they overlap until I have five or six layers that all work seamlessly.' I did. I let myself use all my senses to drink it in, shedding each layer one by one until I heard all of the composition. My shoulders moved to the beat, the tempo controlling my movements. And I felt myself smile. I built back the layers in my head, until they were a fusion of sounds and rhythms and beats.

'I hear it,' I said, so quietly I didn't know if he could hear me over his music. When I opened my eyes, Cromwell turned down the volume. I sighed in defeat. 'I heard it,' I said again.

Cromwell glanced at me from the side of his eye. 'I think you're a music snob, Farraday.'

'What?'

He nodded. 'Classical, folk, country, any other genre, really. All but EDM. Computer-created sounds.' He shook his head. 'You're a snob.' I didn't know why, but being called a snob in an English accent made it feel so much worse.

'I'm not at all. I . . . I . . .'

'I what?' he said, and I could hear the smile in his voice.

'I really don't like you at times,' I said, fully understanding that I sounded like a two-year-old.

'I know you don't,' he said, but there was no belief in his tone. Because as much as I hadn't liked Cromwell Dean, I was beginning to. That was a lie. I already liked him.

And that's what terrified me.

Cromwell pulled into the road that led to the Jefferson Museum. I sat in confusion as he pulled us to a stop at the nearly deserted parking lot. 'I think it's closed,' I said as Cromwell got out of the truck. He opened my door and held out his hand. 'Come on.'

I slid my hand in his, trying to keep it from shaking. I thought he'd let go of my hand as we made our way down the path to the entrance. But he didn't. He kept tight hold. I tried to keep up with him, but I couldn't. Cromwell stopped. 'You okay? You're limping.'

'I twisted my ankle,' I said, feeling the tinny taste of lies on my tongue.

'Can you walk?' The truth was, it was becoming more and more difficult. But I wouldn't give up.

I was determined to fight.

'I can walk if we go slow.' Cromwell walked slowly beside me. 'Do I get any clue yet as to what we're doing here at the museum after hours?' I pulled on his arm. 'You're not gonna break us in, are you?'

Cromwell's dimple popped again. A single dimple on his left cheek. The sight pulled at my heart. 'It's the tattoos, isn't it?' he said.

I fought a laugh. 'The piercings, really.' As if on cue, Cromwell rolled his tongue and his tongue ring came between his teeth. My face set on fire when I remembered how it had danced so close to mine. I hadn't kissed him enough yet to feel its full effect.

I couldn't let that happen at all.

'Don't worry, Sandra Dee, I've got permission to be here.'

The security guard must have expected us, because he let us straight through. 'Second floor,' he said.

'I've been here this week already.' Cromwell led us toward the stairs. He quickly looked back at me, then took us to the elevator. I melted a little.

As the elevator doors closed, Cromwell stayed right by my side. 'Any clue yet?' I asked, when the proximity and strained silence got too much.

'Patience, Farraday.'

We got out of the elevator and stopped in front of a closed door. Cromwell ran his hand through his hair. 'You said you wanted to know what it felt like.' He opened the door and led me inside a dark room. He pulled me by the hand to the center then moved to the side. I squinted, trying to see what he was doing, but I could barely see in front of me.

Then Mozart's Requiem in D Minor flooded through speakers hidden somewhere in the walls. I smiled as the music filled the room.

And then I sucked in a quick breath. Lines of color started dancing along the black walls. Reds and pinks and blues and greens. I stood, mesmerized, as with each note another color burst against the walls. Shapes formed on one wall, triangles, circles, squares. And I let it wash over me. As the music poured into my ears, colors flared in my eyes.

I drank it all in. This was synesthesia. It had to be. Cromwell had brought me here to show me what he saw. When the piece ended and the walls faded to black, Cromwell came over to me. I turned to him, wide eyed and filled with so much awe it was overwhelming.

'Cromwell,' I said, and a line of bright yellow splashed along the walls. I threw my hand over my mouth, laughing when it happened again.

Cromwell brought a couple of beanbags over from the side of the room. He placed them side by side and said, 'Sit.'

A flash of pale blue darted across the walls as he spoke. I did as he said, grateful for the reprise. I stared up at the ceiling; it too was painted black. I turned to Cromwell, his face already watching mine. He was so close to me. Our arms already touching. 'It's what you see, isn't it?'

He looked at the lines of color that flickered in tune with our words. 'It's like it.' He studied the blue that came when he spoke. 'It's based on someone else. My colors are different.' He tapped his ear. 'I hear Requiem differently. My colors aren't in tune with this one.'

I tilted my head to the side. 'So y'all hear colors differently?'

'Mmm-hmm.'

Cromwell lay back on the beanbag. They were put here, I guessed, for this reason. So you could lie back and see the colors colliding with the music. A full sensory experience. I watched Cromwell. Watched as he caught the dying embers of the colored lines. This was how he lived. This was his norm.

'You said before that you didn't just see colors when music played . . .' I left the sentence hanging there.

Cromwell put his arms behind his head. He rolled his head to me. 'No.' He became lost in thought. 'I can taste it too. It's not strong. Certain sounds or scents leave tastes in my mouth. Not really specific, but sweet or sour.

Bitterness. Metallic.' He laid one hand on his chest. 'Music . . . it makes me feel things. Certain types of music make my emotions more heightened.' His voice was clipped as he said the last part, and I knew without asking that there was something more behind that.

Then I wondered if it was classical that made his emotions heightened. Maybe too heightened to cope with. Or if it somehow reminded him of something painful. I wondered if that's why he ran from it.

Cromwell rolled over to face me. I lost my breath as he studied me. I had just opened my mouth to ask him what he was thinking when he said, 'Sing.'

'What?' My heart began its unmelodic beat.

'Sing.' He pointed up at the ceiling, at the black walls, at small microphones planted in the ceiling's crevices. 'The song you sang at the coffee house.'

I felt my face light with fire. Because the last time we sang, Cromwell had been behind me, his chest to my back. 'Sing,' he said again.

'I don't have my guitar.'

'You don't need it.'

I stared into Cromwell's eyes and saw the pleading there. I had no idea why he wanted me to sing it. I had sung as much as I could of late. It was getting harder and harder, my breathing robbing me of my greatest joy. My voice had lost strength, yet I hadn't lost passion.

'Sing,' he said again. There was a desperation on his face. One that made me melt. In this moment, begging me to sing, he looked beautiful.

Even though I was scared, I pushed through. It was the way I lived. I always tried to face my fears head-on.

Closing my eyes, needing to escape Cromwell's stare, I opened my mouth and let the song free. I heard my voice, weakened and strained, sail out around the room. I heard Cromwell's breathing beside me. And I felt him when he moved closer to my side.

'Open your eyes,' he whispered into my ear. 'See your song.'

I let go and just let Cromwell lead. I opened my eyes and lost my rhythm when I was bathed in a cocoon of pinks and purples. Cromwell's fingers ran across mine. 'Keep going.'

With my eyes locked on the ceiling, I sang. Tears sprang to my eyes as my words brought forth colors so beautiful I felt them down to my soul. As my voice sang the final word, I blinked the tears away. I watched the final line of pink fade to white, then nothing.

The silence in the aftermath was thick. My breathing was labored. It was labored as I felt the heavy stare of Cromwell's blue eyes on me. I took three deep breaths then turned his way.

I didn't get time to look into his eyes. I didn't get time to see his dimple in his left cheek. I didn't get time to ask him if he saw the pinks and purples of my voice, because the second I turned, his hands cupped my face and his lips pressed to mine. A shocked cry sounded in my throat when I felt him against my mouth. His hands were hot against my face. His chest was pressed flush against mine. But as his lips started to move, I melted into him. Cromwell's taste of mint, chocolate, and tobacco slipped into my mouth. My hands reached out and clutched his sweater. His musky scent filled my nose, and I let his soft lips work against mine.

Cromwell kissed me. He kissed me and kissed me in soft, slow kisses, until his tongue pushed against the seams and slid into my mouth. He groaned as his tongue met mine. He was everywhere. I felt him everywhere, my body and senses swept away by the hurricane that was Cromwell Dean.

I moved my tongue with his. Then I felt the cold metal of his tongue ring and sank into him further. Cromwell Dean kissed like he played music – completely and with every ounce of his soul.

He kissed me and kissed me until I had no breath left in my body. I broke away, gasping. But Cromwell wasn't finished. As I searched for air, for any way to fill my lungs and calm my pounding heart, he moved down my neck. My eyes fluttered closed, and I held onto his sweater like it was my lifeline from being swept away by everything that was Cromwell. His warm breath drifted down my neck and caused goose-bumps to spread over my skin.

I looked up, and I saw bright greens and lilac purples dancing around us – the color of our kisses.

But it was too much. My chest tightened at the exertion, at the all too encompassing heaviness that was this kiss. I moved my head to tell him so, to break away, but in a second, Cromwell's lips were back on mine. The minute I felt them, I was his. I sank back into the soft cushion beneath me and let him take my mouth. Cromwell's tongue met mine and he shifted his body until it lay over me. My hands moved to his back. His sweater had ridden up as he moved over me. My palms met warm skin, the feel of it heightening every sense I had.

'Cromwell,' I whispered. Orange flashed over the ceiling.

'Cromwell,' I repeated, smiling when the same color returned. But that smile faded when I realized what we were doing. That I shouldn't be here. Shouldn't have let him kiss me. I should have walked away when I still had the chance.

I squeezed my eyes shut and hung on to him like I would never let him go. I deepened the kiss. I kissed him so I would never forget. I kissed him until he was imprinted on my soul.

I eventually pulled back, moving my hands up Cromwell's body until my hands shadowed his and I cupped his cheeks. His lips were swollen from the kiss, and his stubbled cheeks were warm.

'I can't.' My heart cracked in two at the confession. 'We can't do this.'

Cromwell searched my face. 'Why?'

'I need to get home.'

Cromwell's eyebrows pulled down in confusion. 'Bonn—'

'Please.'

'Okay.'

He got up from the beanbag and moved silently across the room to the lights. I flinched at the invading brightness. In the light, the walls were just black. The magic had gone.

I watched Cromwell move around the room making sure everything was switched off. He came toward me, and as his eyes fell upon me, I couldn't believe how someone could be so handsome. When he stopped, his feet at mine, he dropped a single long kiss on my forehead.

The room shimmered, and I felt a tear escape my eye. He went to move away, but I grabbed his wrists, savoring him just a little more. Cromwell looked down, a serious expression on his face. I never moved my eyes away. I kept my eyes on him as I moved in, shifting to my tiptoes. I didn't let myself think this time; I just followed my heart and pressed my lips to his. It was the first time I'd ever initiated a kiss in my life. I would never have believed it would be with Cromwell Dean. But now we were here, like this, suspended in this most perfect of moments, I knew it would never have been anyone but him.

As I pulled away, I let my forehead fall to his. I breathed him in, committing every second to memory. I lifted my head and met his eyes. A burning question was in my mind. 'What did it look like to you?' I asked. 'My song. The colors.'

Cromwell breathed in, then, eyes bright, said, 'It illuminated the room.'

I sagged against him, resting my head on his chest, my arms around his waist. *It illuminated the room.*

Cromwell led me out of the museum and into his truck. No music played as we made our way home. We didn't talk either. But it was a comfortable silence. I couldn't speak. I had a million questions I wanted to ask him. But I didn't. I had to leave this night exactly where it belonged. In the past. As a memory I'd keep to help me through the journey ahead.

It illuminated the room . . .

Cromwell pulled up in front of my dorm. I looked at the entrance with a sense of dread. When I was through that door, this would all end. Whatever this was. I still wasn't sure myself.

Cromwell sat in his seat, his eyes on me. I could feel it.

And I didn't want to look his way. Because I knew that when I did, I had to end it.

'Cromwell,' I whispered, hands in my lap.

'Farraday.' I wished he hadn't just said that. I liked the way he had always called me that. Only now when he said it, it was breathtaking to me. Just like his music.

'I can't.' My voice sounded too loud in the old truck's cabin. Cromwell didn't ask what I couldn't do. He knew what I meant. When I finally looked up at him, he was staring straight out of the window and his jaw was clenched. In that moment, he was the Cromwell I knew from the first days of school.

I squeezed my eyes shut, hating to see him this way. I didn't want to hurt him. I had no idea what he thought of me, but by the way he'd acted this past week, what he did for me after the coffee house performance, and what he showed me tonight . . . I knew it had to be something real. And that kiss . . . 'I . . . I can't explain . . .'

'I like you,' he said, and as the sweetly accented words hit my ear, I wanted to move across the seat and wrap my arms around him. I didn't know Cromwell well, but I knew he didn't say those words easily. He lived behind high walls, yet with me, they had started to lower.

I didn't want to be the cause of them growing back high. In my heart I wanted to be the one to smash them until he was free. But I couldn't. It just wasn't fair.

A sudden wave of anger hit me. At the unfairness. That I couldn't just be here right now, enjoying the moment, falling into his arms.

'Bonnie?' I wanted to sob when my name left his lips. He'd never called me Bonnie before.

'I like you too.' I looked into his blue eyes. I owed him that much. 'But it's more complicated than that. I shouldn't have let it get this far. It isn't fair. I'm so sorry . . .'

The feel of his hand slipping into mine silenced me. 'Come with me to Charleston tomorrow night.'

'What?'

'I'm playing at a club.' He held my hand tighter. 'I want you to come.'

'Why?'

'To see . . .' He sighed. 'To see me play my new mixes. To stand beside me and see how it is. To make you understand. It's only an hour away.'

'Cromwell, I—'

'East is coming.' Disappointment dripped off him in waves. 'It doesn't have to be anything you don't want it to be.'

I wasn't sure I could be around East either. When Sunday came, I would have to tell him. And Cromwell would no doubt find out too.

I thought of one night. One last night where I got to be free. Surrounded by music and Cromwell. My brother and us, sharing laughs. 'Okay,' I said. 'I'll come. But I have to come back here afterward.'

Cromwell's lips pursed, the promise of a small smile. 'Good,' he said. 'Let's get you into bed, Farraday.'

Cromwell got out of the truck and held my door open like before. And like before, he held out his hand for me. He held my hand until he brought me to the door of the dorm. My heart flip-flopped in my chest when he faced me. He put his hands on my face and pressed a single, soft kiss to my lips. 'Night.'

He turned and walked off. I wasn't sure I could move. Then, just before he got into his truck, I said, 'Cromwell?' He looked up. I could feel my cheeks burning before I even spoke. 'What color is my voice?'

Cromwell stared at me, eyes full of some kind of light I couldn't decipher. That small, beautiful smile pulled on his lips again, and he said, 'Violet blue.'

I tried to breathe. I really did. I tried to move. *Violet blue*. Cromwell got in his truck and pulled away. A memory from last week came to my mind.

'Cromwell?' I asked, and he turned my way. 'What's your favorite? Your favorite color to see?'

'Violet blue,' he said in an instant.

Violet blue. His favorite color to see . . . and also the sound of my voice.

If my failing heart hadn't let him in before, it did just then.

15

Cromwell

'This is gonna be fucking lit!' Easton bounced around on the seat of my truck. I eyed him, wondering what the hell was into him tonight.

'Easton.' Bonnie put her hand on his arm. 'Calm down.'

'Calm down? My boy is playing at Chandelier and you're telling me to calm down? No way, Bonn. The Barn is one thing, but seeing Cromwell spin tonight at a real venue is gonna be sick. You know how many people are coming to see him? A few thousand at least!'

I drove us toward Charleston, listening to Easton losing his mind over tonight. Easton hadn't even been concerned over why his sister was coming. I thought he'd give me shit. He'd been asking about Bonnie and me the past week. I thought he suspected something, but ever since we got up this morning, he'd been all over the place, high as a damn kite. The daft bugger had even woken me up at four a.m. asking me to go for food. I'd only gone to bed half an hour before. I'd created a mix just for tonight.

I couldn't wait to play it.

It took just under an hour to get to the venue. The security at Chandelier told me to pull my truck around the back. A couple of guys tried to take my new laptop from me. Not a chance. No one ever touched my laptop. Easton walked on one side of me. Bonnie was on the other. I'd lost my mind, I had to have, because I wanted to reach out and hold her hand.

And I couldn't get last night from my head. Couldn't get the taste of her lips off my tongue. But more than that, I couldn't get my head around the fact that she said we couldn't happen.

I didn't do girlfriends. Never had. I was a use-them-and-move-on kind of guy. But from day one Bonnie Farraday had gotten under my skin. And sod's law, the one girl I was chasing as more than a quick shag wasn't having any of it.

I had no idea why. We'd both been into it last night. I'd felt her against me. Her hands hadn't left me. Even afterward, she'd clung to my hand like she never wanted to let go.

But I was learning Bonnie Farraday was a complex girl.

Even though she'd pushed me away, I couldn't let her go. I'd wanted her here tonight. I didn't know why, but I needed her here. I wanted her to see me in a real setting. I wanted her to hear my new mixes.

One I'd made just for her.

The manager was up my arse the second I walked in the place. Apparently it was a sellout. I'd go on at midnight. It wasn't far off.

'I'm gonna get shots,' Easton said, flashing his fake ID at Bonnie and me before leaving us alone in the ridiculous-sized dressing room. Couches, a TV – even a bed sat in the corner. It was a good venue. I didn't feel nervous about playing; I never did. But I was nervous about having Bonnie beside me on the podium.

Nervous about what she'd think of the new mix I'd made for her.

Bonnie sat down on the couch and rubbed her hand over her face. She was pale. But she looked good. She was wearing black flowery high-waisted trousers and a white long-sleeved top that showed off every inch of her curves. Her hair was in a high ponytail, and I wanted nothing more than to wrap it around my hand and pull her to my mouth.

I was making sure I had everything lined up on my laptop. The sound of the opening DJs came from outside. Colors, as always, danced before my eyes. But I blocked them out and concentrated on my own set.

'You ready?' Bonnie said eventually. We'd had no time alone since we'd got in the truck.

'Always.' I stared at her. Her hands were fidgeting in her lap. She looked so damn cute. 'Farraday.' She looked over. 'Get your arse over here.'

Bonnie looked as if she'd refuse, but then she got up off the couch and came to my seat. I shifted over, making enough room for her to sit down too. She hesitated. I groaned and pulled her down by her arm. 'For Christ's sake, Farraday, I had my tongue down your throat twenty-four hours ago. I think you can sit down beside me. It's not like there isn't room. You must weigh all of eight stone.'

'What?' she asked, brown eyebrows pulled down. 'Eight stone?'

I threaded my arm around her waist, making her yelp. 'It means you weigh nothing. Now.' I shifted her close enough that she was pressed against me and my hand could still use my laptop.

'Cromwell.' She sighed. 'This isn't wise.'

'No one ever said I was.' I pointed to my laptop. 'My

set,' I said. Bonnie's love for music overrode any complaint she had about being next to me. She stared at the program.

'So these are your tracks?' I nodded. 'Then how do you mix them?'

I shrugged. 'I judge the crowd. Decide when I'm up there what to play next. See how far I can push them.' I tried to picture the crowd in my mind. 'I just do what feels right.'

'You follow the emotion,' she said knowingly. 'What you told me last night.'

'Yeah.' I closed my laptop and looked up at Bonnie. Her eyes were already on me. Then they dropped to my lips. 'Farraday.' I inched closer and pressed my forehead to hers. 'If you don't want me to take your mouth right now, I'd stop looking at me like that.'

'Like what?' she whispered, cheeks flushed.

'Like you want to feel my tongue ring in your mouth again.'

She laughed, the sound causing the violet blue circle I normally saw to spike and pulse with pale pink. 'You're a regular Romeo,' she said jokingly. 'Feel your tongue ring again?'

I felt my damn chest expand and my lip hook up at the corner. I pulled her closer and ran my nose down her cheek. Her breathing was shallow and stuttered. My lips nipped her earlobe. 'Never claimed to be,' I said into her ear. I moved back, my lips running over her cheeks and to her lips. My eyes were open, wide open, as hers locked on mine. She was breathing hard.

I closed in, forgetting that she told me we could never

happen. Just as I pressed my lips to hers, a knock sounded on the door. 'Cromwell?' a voice said. 'Five minutes.'

I sighed, my head dropping to her shoulder. Bonnie's hand fell into my hair. 'We'd better go.'

I sat up, then before she could argue, I crushed my mouth to hers. She sighed into my mouth, but I pulled away quickly, grabbing my laptop. I held my hand out for hers, and this time, Easton or not, I was going to hold her hand.

Bonnie didn't resist.

We walked the corridor to the main stage. Some of the workers said hello. I nodded at them. But with every step, I got myself more and more in the game. When we arrived beside the podium, I could hear the crowd. I could hear the shouts and calls. Bonnie's hand squeezed mine. Her eyes were wide. I kissed the back of her hand and leaned in close. 'Sit to the side of the stage. I asked them to put a chair there for you.'

Her eyes melted at that. I had no idea why. I let go of her hand and threw my headphones around my neck. The stage manager waved me on. I took one last look at Bonnie then walked onto the podium. A wave of screams and shouts came crashing at me.

I put the laptop on the decks and opened it up. Like always, I risked one glance at the crowd and drank in the moment. It was like slow motion. The crowd waiting for me to start. I scanned my eyes over the thousands of faces. All looking up at me as if I were a young god. Then I looked to the side. Bonnie was still offstage.

I pointed at the stool that was waiting for her. Bonnie swallowed, her eyes huge. She was so friggin' cute as she took her first step up onto the podium. I reached down for her hand when she looked unsteady.

She sat down and looked around at the crowd. If her eyes were wide before, now they took up her entire face. I gave her a spare set of headphones, signaling for her to put them on. I wanted her to hear every beat I threw out. I wanted her to soak up the tempos, drink the rhythm, and live the bass.

When she looked back to me, breath held, I lined up the first track, let my hand hover in the air . . . then with a slam of a finger, ripped the fucking roof off the place.

The crowd played right into my hands, all falling for the mix. I moved to the decks and the drum machine and let the colors lead me. It was minutes before I looked at Bonnie. She was watching me so closely, watching my hands create every beat, every track. I didn't need to look at the laptop, the decks. Instead I met her eyes. When her attention was fully on me, I started mouthing the colors. *Peach. Turquoise. Black. Gray. Amber. Scarlet.* Tune after tune, I told her what I saw. And she was in it with me. She never moved her eyes away from me, a smile on her lips as I let her see my colors.

Let her see me.

Then, *Violet blue*, I mouthed. Bonnie's eyes widened. I glanced down at my laptop and lined up the track I wanted her to hear. The one I couldn't get out of my head last night. The one that played so loudly in my mind I'd had to get it down.

The words of which she'd had no idea I'd recorded.

Some are not meant for this life for too long. I threaded the opening verse over the beats. The volume was quiet, a crescendo building the second verse. *A fleeting glimpse, a silent birdsong*. Drums built, violins soft in the background. Then, the drum beat in double time, her voice gaining volume, until I smashed it, bringing the song to its maximum beat, Bonnie's soft voice pushed to the highest volume, her violet-blue words coating every inch of the room . . .

Some are not meant for this life for too long.
A fleeting glimpse, a silent birdsong.
Souls too pure, they burn out too bright,
Bodies so fragile, losing the fight.
Hearts lose their beats, rhythms too slow,
Angels they come, it's time to go.
Lift from this place, to the heavens and skies,
Smothered in peace, where nobody dies.
Hope left behind in the ones they have loved,
No longer caged, now wings of a dove.
Wings, white as snow, sprout from my heart.
Wings, spreading wide, now to depart.
Tears in my eyes, I give one last glance.
I lived, and I loved, and danced life's sweet dance . . .

I layered acoustic guitar chords I'd had stored for years but never used over the top. And Bonnie's voice sang loud and clear. I mixed it three times, until the next track pushed through the background, replacing the violet blue with lime green.

When the next mix pumped from the speakers, I looked up at Bonnie. Her hand was over her mouth, tears streaming down her cheeks. My stomach cramped. Until she looked into my eyes and her hands fell away. A smile so wide it seemed to hit the damn ceiling spread on her lips. She got off her stool and walked to me. I pushed her back out of sight of the crowd, and let her smash her mouth to mine to a background of gold and magnolia and chocolate browns. I tasted the tears on her lips and the mint on her tongue.

Her chest pressed against mine as my mixes controlled the crowd, making them sway and jump and dance. When Bonnie pulled back, I wasn't ready. I cupped her cheeks and took her mouth again. Now she'd given me her lips, I never wanted to give them back. The colors shifted to blue, heading for navy. I pulled away and walked back to the podium. The crowd went insane. I glanced down and saw Easton at the front, eyes closed, some girl hanging off his arm. He had two bottles of beer in his hands, just feeling the beat.

I slowed it right down. The lighting technician took my cue and brought the flashing lasers to a soft white glow, dimming the brightness. The smoke that had been pumped out all night hovered in the air, suffocating the dormant white beams. I held my hand in the air, the crowd waiting for my call. The slow beats calmed their slamming hearts; the long low notes brought their pulses to normal. I heard my breath echo in my ears. I felt the heat from their bodies slam into mine, felt their readiness to be brought back to the high only I could give them.

My fingers waited; the technician waited for his cue. I looked at Bonnie to see her on the edge of her seat, waiting for me too. I smiled to myself, feeling so full from the music. Then, when they were ready, when they had taken as much pause as they could possibly take, I slammed my hand down and brought the rain.

The lights dropped, and strobing lasers bathed them in green. The beats drugged them, slaves to my hand. I heard a laugh from beside me and turned to see Bonnie scanning the jumping crowd, their bodies moving as one unit to the heavy bass I gave them like a drug.

I smirked, and gave them more, gave her more, and her hands went in the air and her eyes closed. I paused and just looked at her.

Something settled in my chest that I hadn't felt in years. Something I never thought I'd find ever again. Silver. I choked at the sight.

Happiness.

My hand slipped from my laptop, waking me the hell up. I refocused on the set, but that silver never left me. It was branded on my brain. Its color as strong as if it'd been gilded, like a crest, onto my mind.

The whole time I played, Bonnie sat, a smile on her face, and watched me. And all the time violet blue and silver warred for dominance in my mind. I flicked my hand off the laptop, the final beat glittering on a sphere until it faded into nothing toward the back of the room.

The house DJ took over. I picked up my laptop, holding my hand up for the screaming crowd. Sweat beaded on my forehead, but adrenaline surged through my veins. I turned to Bonnie. Her face was flushed and, despite the time, her eyes were bright. I slipped the headphones off her head, tucked my laptop under my arm, then lifted Bonnie off the stool. Her hands came down on my biceps as I dragged her down my chest until her feet hit the floor. I took her hand and led her off the podium and into the corridor. I didn't care if anyone was around. I didn't give a damn if anyone saw. I walked Bonnie up to the wall. The minute her back was against the brick, I smashed my mouth to hers. Bonnie was just as eager as me. Her hands threaded into my hair, yanking on the strands to get me even closer. My blood sang with the music I'd poured from my body for the past three hours.

Bonnie gasped against my mouth, but I needed to taste the sweetness that always burst on my tongue whenever we kissed. I traced my tongue down her neck. 'Cromwell,' she whispered. The sound of my name from her lips only spurred me on.

Bonnie grabbed my head and brought me back to her mouth. I wasn't sure how long we kissed, but she broke away again, struggling to breathe. My hand flattened against the wall. Hers were on my chest. She breathed and breathed, and I let her catch her breath. When she'd calmed, she spoke only two words: 'My song.'

'Your song.' I'd never put lyrics to my mixes before. Never felt the need . . . until her.

The sound of the door opening was like thunder in the corridor. I stepped back from Bonnie just as Easton stumbled through. 'Fucking Cromwell Dean!' A girl trailed behind him. Easton wrapped his arms around me. 'That set!' He looked at Bonnie. 'Bonn . . . your song.'

She smiled at her brother. 'It was amazing.'

I patted Easton on the back. 'Let's go.'

Easton shook his head and threw his arm around the girl standing behind us. 'Going back with Emma. She goes to the college here.'

'How are you going to get back?' Bonnie asked.

'Bonn, it's an hour back home. I'll get the bus tomorrow

215

sometime.' He looked at the blonde in his arms. 'Or maybe Monday.' He shrugged. 'Just gotta see what happens.'

Easton backtracked the way he came, back into the club. Bonnie watched after him, concern on her face. 'He'll be okay,' I said and took her hand in mine.

Bonnie gave me a tight smile, but she let me lead her back toward the dressing room. We grabbed our stuff then made our way to my truck. As soon as we were inside, the air in the cabin thickened.

'Well?' I turned to Bonnie. She was already watching me, an unreadable expression on her face. 'What?'

'I get it now.' She wrapped her arms around her waist.

'You cold?'

'A little.' I reached for my black jumper and handed it to her. She smiled and slipped it on. It drowned her small frame. She closed her eyes and smelled the collar. 'It smells like you.' She opened her eyes. I waited for what else she would say. I turned the engine on and let the heater heat up the car.

'How?' Bonnie's voice cut through the white noise as I pulled onto the road. I glanced at her, eyebrow raised. 'How did you get my song?'

'The museum,' I said. 'When you sang, I recorded it on my phone.'

She frowned. 'Last night?' I nodded. 'But how did you get it on a track?'

'I stayed up all night to do it.'

She sighed. 'You've complicated things for me, Cromwell Dean. You were never meant to complicate things.'

I laughed a single laugh. 'I *am* complicated. I've been told that enough times.'

Bonnie didn't laugh though. Instead she shifted beside me and laid her head on my shoulder. I wasn't sure if she was asleep, but when I looked at her in my rearview mirror, she was staring straight forward. I narrowed my eyes, wondering what the hell was wrong. But then she wrapped her arm around mine and held on.

I wanted her to talk. I wanted her to say something, but she didn't. I thought on what she'd said. How I complicated things. I knew I was messed up. I knew I was a moody bastard, that I blew hot and cold. But I had a feeling that wasn't what she meant.

An hour later, we pulled onto the campus, and I headed in the direction of her dorm. I'd barely made it a few yards when she whispered, 'No.'

'What?'

Bonnie paused. 'Go to your dorm.'

Confused, I looked at her in the rearview mirror. Her brown eyes were already on mine.

'Go to your dorm, Cromwell.' There was a shake to her voice. Her cheeks blazed and she held my arm tighter. 'If . . . if you want to.'

It took me a second to catch on.

'Bonnie,' I said and felt her hold her breath. I read her face and saw the fear in her eyes. But not fear of what she was asking. Fear of me saying no.

That was never going to happen.

'You sure?' I asked.

'I want to,' she whispered. 'I want *you*.'

My hands were tight on the steering wheel all the way to my parking spot outside my dorm. When I killed the engine, Bonnie didn't move. I put my hand under her chin

217

and forced her to look up. I cupped her cheeks. 'You don't have to do this,' I said. A small shy smile pulled on her lips. Tears filled her eyes.

'I want it, Cromwell. I want this.' She laughed. 'I never want this night to end.' She lowered her eyes. 'Please don't make me beg.'

'You don't need to beg.' I shook my head. 'I want it too. So bad.'

I got out of the car. I came around to the passenger side for Bonnie. I held out my hand, and, like she always did, she held on tightly as I guided her out. We walked slowly back to the dorm. Bonnie was walking slower than normal.

'You good?' I said, checking that she was okay, that she still wanted to do this.

She smiled at me, her hand tight in mine. 'More than good.'

The dorm was silent as we entered. When I closed the door of my room behind us, the air felt thick. Bonnie stood in front of me, my jumper practically to her knees. I stepped closer and took her face in my hands. Her brown eyes were huge as she looked up at me.

I lowered my mouth to hers and kissed her. Bonnie sighed into my mouth, and her tense body relaxed. I kissed and kissed her, then broke away.

'Bonnie—'

'I want this,' she said again. Bonnie walked to the light switch and flicked it off. The room was plunged into darkness, all except the light from my desktop computer. Her face was shadowed, but when she turned toward me, I could see her eyes in the blue light.

I let her take the lead. She took my hand and led me to my

bed. She sat on the edge then shuffled up until she lay on my pillow. I stopped and stared. The sight of her looking so small and nervous on my bed hit me like a ton of bricks. Her lips were parted, her ponytail splayed on my pillow.

Bonnie slowly held out her hand. Her fingers were shaking. I took hold of her hand and crawled over where she lay. I pushed her hair from her face. In the dark, it was hard to make her out. But her eyes were visible. That was all I needed.

I moved my head down and kissed her. Bonnie's hand was still in mine. She didn't let go. She just held on. I kissed her lips. I kissed her until she needed breath. Then I kissed down her throat. I kissed over her shoulder, where my jumper had slipped down her arm.

When I ran out of skin, I lifted my head and met Bonnie's eyes. 'I've . . . I've never done this before,' she confessed.

I swallowed. 'Never?'

She shook her head. 'I've never . . .' She raised her chin. 'I've never done anything . . . but kiss before.'

I dragged in a breath and stared down at her. Her eyes were watching me, waiting for my reaction. 'Bonnie, I'm not sure I'm the one—'

'You are.' Her shaking hand landed on my face. 'You're the only one who *could* have this.' Her eyes watered, and the tears tracked down her cheeks. 'I tried to fight it, but you never left. And my heart didn't let me turn away.' Her fingers traveled over my chest and lingered over my heart. Her eyes closed briefly, like she was counting its beat. When she opened her eyes, she sat up, and I got to my knees. She pulled my jumper over her head and let it fall to the floor. Then her hands were on my shirt. She lifted the hem and started pulling it over my head.

I pulled it off the rest of the way, throwing it to join the jumper on the floor. Bonnie swallowed as she lifted her hands and ran them over every one of my tattoos. Over the swirls of color that swarmed over my chest. And over the two swords, lion, and crown that made up the British Army crest. She tipped her head back and her eyes met mine.

I pulled out the band that kept her hair from her face. Her long hair fell down her back. I ran my hands through the strands, and as I did, she leaned in, kissing my skin. My jaw clenched at the feel of her tentative mouth on my stomach. She kissed me again, this time over the tribute I'd had tattooed to my dad. Seeing Bonnie kiss the crest that had meant so much to the man who was my best friend did something to me.

My hands threaded into Bonnie's hair. I pulled her to my lips. And I kissed her. I was pretty sure I could kiss her all day and never grow sick of it.

'Cromwell,' she whispered against my lips. I broke away, only enough for her to speak. 'I need you,' she said, shredding my heart. 'I need you so much.'

'What do you want?' I asked, running my lips along her cheek. I was unable to move away from her. I needed to touch her.

'Make love to me,' she said, and my eyes closed. 'Show me how it could be.'

My heart thudded in double time at her request. I laid her back down and kissed her again. But as I kissed her, I moved my hands down to her trousers and untied the waist. Breaking from her mouth, I pulled them down her legs. I sat back and looked at her. Her body was mostly shaded in darkness. But I could see enough of her to make out her silhouette. She was perfect. Every part of her was perfect. And I realized just how much I wanted this. Wanted her. I ran my hands up her legs, slowly. With every inch, Bonnie gasped, her back starting to arch.

The sound hit my ears, and deep red squares fluttered in my eyes. My hand touched her skin below her top. It was so warm, so pale. I never wanted to take my hand away. I shifted the material up and over a camisole underneath. Bonnie's breathing was like a song in my ear, strings commanding me to move. To touch her, feel her, taste her. I slipped the top over her head, watching as her skin turned pink and her eyes grew leaden. I wondered what she was thinking. But when her eyes met mine, I didn't need words. Her pretty face told me how much she wanted this too. My hand next moved to her camisole. I pushed the material up, exposing her stomach. I paused, just looking at my tattooed tanned skin against her white.

I'd never seen anything so perfect.

'Please leave it on.' Bonnie's voice made me look up. She pulled her camisole back down. Lowering my head, I kissed her lips just to chase away the momentary flash of worry in her eyes. I didn't know what that worry was for. But I didn't need to have her naked. She was beautiful enough, just like this.

I kissed her, licking along her lips. Her breath was warm on my face, and I could smell the vanilla of her shampoo. My fingers traced along the softness of her arm. Her body moved against mine, showing me how much she liked it.

My chest swelled. I'd never had this in bed before. Never felt this much for a girl before.

All those before had meant nothing to me. Their faces were all a mass blur. Even my first time was a drunken, meaningless mess. But this felt different. Being with Bonnie, like this, felt different. Bigger somehow. Bonnie's gaze locked with mine and we just stared into one another's eyes for a few seconds. It felt like a lifetime before her hand moved down to the fly of my jeans. Her face was filled with nervousness, her brown eyes wide. I laid my hand on top of hers and took the lead. Leaning down, I kissed along her cheek, her forehead, and finally her lips, as my jeans came off.

I pulled the covers over us. I thought it might make her feel better. Bonnie smiled at the action, and I crawled on top of her, covering her body with my own. I met her eyes and ran my hand down her cheek. 'You're beautiful.' Because she was. She so bloody was.

A tear slipped from the side of her eye. 'So are you,' she said and smiled. I pressed my lips to hers. And as I did, I ran my hands down her waist, over her stomach, and down to her legs. 'Touch me,' she whispered, and I shut my eyes, taking a second to breathe.

Violet-blue lines flashed across my mind every time she spoke, bringing me a kind of peace I couldn't describe. Silver was the backdrop, the color never fading, still bright from tonight at the club.

Bonnie's back arched as my hand moved. She whimpered and fought for breath. I watched her face in the blue light, trying to soak in every noise and every move. I kissed her shoulder, the same one I'd kissed in the music room. Sweetness burst on my tongue when her peach and vanilla scent drifted into my nose.

'Cromwell,' she whispered. I reached into my drawer and pulled out a condom. When I was ready, Bonnie, now wearing nothing but her cami, held out her arms.

I settled above her, pushing her hair from her face. 'You sure?'

'More than sure.'

I never took my eyes off her face. Bonnie's hands were on my back, holding on tight. I was as gentle as I could be. I didn't want to hurt her. My breathing echoed in my ears. Bonnie's eyes were locked on mine. She never looked away. As I built up speed, when her breaths became short and shallow, she never once looked away.

And the way she looked at me . . .

Her hands ran through my hair, slowly and softly. I lowered down and kissed her. Kissed her lips, and kissed her cheeks. I kissed every part of her face. When I lifted my head, tears were falling down her cheeks. I worried that she was in pain, but when I stilled, Bonnie put her hand on my cheek. 'Please don't stop,' she whispered, her throat tight.

So I kept going, my teeth gritted together at how good it felt. At how good she felt beneath me. But not because I was inside her. But because it *was* her, looking up at me like this. Brown eyes watering and lips shaking.

Wanting me.

Needing me.

She was my silver.

'Cromwell,' she murmured and held on tighter to my arms. I built up speed, feeling her body warm and her lips part. I couldn't look away as her head tipped back and her eyes fluttered to a close.

Her hands were gripping me so tight. As she caught her lost breath, she turned her head and kissed my forearm. I stilled, going over with her as a multicolored burst of light shone behind my eyes. Illuminated like the crescendo of a symphony, my soul at peace with the quiet hum of happiness. Tucking my neck into the crook of her shoulder, I breathed as I slowed to a stop.

I breathed in her peach and vanilla scent and just lay there in the darkness. My chest didn't feel as tight as it usually was. The anger that bubbled like a dormant volcano in my stomach had calmed, so much that I could barely feel it.

I breathed easier.

Bonnie's hands traced lazy lines up and down my bare back. Her body was warm beneath me. Her breath drifted past my ear. She was still breathing fast.

Finally, I lifted my head and met her gaze. Bonnie's eyes shone, the tears still falling down her cheeks. I smoothed them away with my thumbs, then kissed her wet skin. Her finger ran down my face. Her bottom lip trembled as she whispered, 'Thank you.'

I kissed her in response. Slowly. Softly.

I wrapped my arms around her and pulled her to me. Bonnie held me back. I felt her tears on my shoulder. But I didn't ask her why she was crying. She wasn't sad.

She was *moved*.

I rolled us to the side, and she faced me on the pillow. 'You have the prettiest eyes,' she said, circling my right eye with her fingertip. She smiled and just about blew apart my heart. 'You're handsome, Cromwell Dean. So handsome.'

I took hold of her hand and kissed each one of her fingers. Bonnie watched me do it. I could feel a sadness in her that I couldn't explain. As another tear fell, I asked, 'You okay?'

She smiled at me. It was a real smile. 'More than.' She took my hand in hers and played with my fingers. 'I never thought I'd ever have this moment.' She smiled sadly. 'And with someone who understands.'

'Understands what?'

'What it's like to have been born with a song in our hearts.' I swallowed, my stomach rolling at her words. Her grip tightened on my hand, and a nervous expression flashed across her face.

'What?'

Bonnie looked up at me, then said so quietly I almost didn't hear her, 'I saw you. When you were younger.'

I frowned. 'I don't understand.'

Bonnie kissed my finger. 'My music teacher showed me a video of you in concert. Conducting music you composed. The BBC Proms Young Composer of the Year.' I swallowed, my chest hollowing out in shock. 'I never forgot your name after that day. I listened out for you.' She lifted up onto her elbow. Her hand ran through my hair. 'You went quiet. And I always wondered what happened to you. Until I heard of you again. Only this time the classical symphonies had gone, and in their place was electronic dance.'

I wanted to speak, but I couldn't get my head around the fact that she'd seen me as a kid. Performing. 'That's why you saw me when you were in England.'

She nodded. 'I wanted to see you in person.'

Something stabbed in my stomach. 'That's why you said my music had no soul.'

Bonnie lost her smile. 'I believe that music should tell a story. I believe that in the notes and melodies there should be some kind of meaning. Music should take you on a journey, crafted by the creator's heart.' She kissed my lips. 'Your music that night . . . there was no story to me. No meaning.' My stomach fell, but it rose again when she said, 'I don't think that anymore. I've seen you play. Heard the music you can create. It's *all* soul, Cromwell. The things I've heard you play on the piano, they were full of meaning. So much so that it made my heart cry.' Her eyes shimmered. 'Never doubt your talent, Cromwell. I see it clearly now.'

'It's you,' I admitted. Bonnie stilled. 'You were right. I'd lost my way. My music . . . it didn't have purpose. There was no story. They were just the colors that made me feel the least.' I wanted to tell her why. But even now, I couldn't bring myself to say it. I rubbed a strand of her hair between my fingers. 'Since you . . . it's felt different. Music. It's you, Farraday. You've made it different.' I laughed to myself. What I was going to say was cheesy as hell. But it was true. 'I'm inspired.' She sucked in a breath. 'You inspire me.'

'Cromwell.' She shook her head. 'I can't inspire you.'

'You have and you do.' I put her hand on my chest. 'Since I met you, music I'd kept away has been filling my head. I've played, when for years, I hadn't picked up any instrument but my laptop.'

Bonnie dropped her head to my chest, and I held her there. We didn't speak after that. I heard Bonnie's breathing even out and knew she'd fallen asleep.

I stayed awake until the sun started to rise. I stroked her

hair and just held her to me. There was a pit in my stomach again. And my hands itched to create. They always did when something big happened in my life.

And having her with me like this, right now, I knew it was big. Bonnie Farraday had stormed into my life like a hurricane.

It was the first time in a long time that I fell asleep with a smile on my lips.

I woke to the sound of people out in the corridor of my dorm. I blinked in the room, clearing the sleep from my eyes. I felt cold. When I looked to my right, I expected to see Bonnie. But she wasn't there. 'Bonnie?' I called. There was nothing.

I sat up. Her clothes were gone. A sinking feeling dropped within me. I threw the duvet back and picked my jeans and jumper off the floor. The jumper smelled of her.

Where the hell has she gone?

My shoes were on in seconds and I was out the door. The cool breeze whipped at my face as I took the path that led me to the other dorms. I had no idea what time it was, but it must have been late morning or early afternoon. Students milled about, some eating in the quad, some just chilling out.

When I arrived at Bonnie's dorm, a student was just coming out. I caught the door and walked down the corridor until I arrived at her room. As I went to knock on the door, I noticed it was slightly ajar. I pushed it open to reveal her room.

Boxes were all over the floor. Everything had been packed away. Her bed was stripped, and the walls were bare. I stepped into the room and saw Bonnie sitting on the chair at her desk, her eyes lost as she stared at the box beside her. She was dressed in leggings and a long jumper, all black, and her hair was thrown back in a bun. She was holding a notepad in her hand.

She looked up, and her face drained of color. She didn't say anything as she met my eyes.

My eyebrows were drawn down in confusion. 'I'm moving out,' she said, clearly reading my mind. I was a statue, glued to the spot. Bonnie tried to smile, but then her lip trembled and her eyes filled with tears. 'I wasn't meant to fall for you,' she said quietly. Brokenly. She laughed, but it held no humor. 'We didn't see eye to eye. And it was meant to stay that way.' She tucked some of her loose hair behind her ear. My heart thundered in my chest, beating a million miles an hour.

'But then I heard you play in the music room that night. Saw how it seemed to hurt you, impact you.' She shook her head. 'And it did something to me ... something I couldn't seem to move on from.'

A tear fell down her cheek. I watched it travel down her skin until it hit a box at her feet. 'I tried to tell you, Cromwell. I tried to tell you we couldn't be together. It isn't fair. Nothing about this is fair.'

'You're not making sense,' I said, a sense of dread eating at every part of me.

She stared at me for a few strained seconds. 'I have a broken heart.'

My confusion didn't lift. Then anger quickly took me. She liked someone else? She'd kissed me. She slept with me, and all the time she'd liked someone else. 'You ... Bryce?' I asked, my words curt and tone harsh.

Bonnie shook her head sadly. She stepped forward until she was in front of me. She took my hand and brought it to her chest, right over where her heart was. 'Cromwell, my heart is *literally* broken.' Her wet lashes left marks on the top of her cheeks as she closed her eyes. 'I have heart failure, Cromwell.' She smiled sadly. Devastatingly. 'My heart is dying.'

It was as if a strong wind blew into the room. I couldn't breathe. My chest pulled tight, so tight that I felt it ripping at my muscles.

My heart is dying . . .

'No,' I said, my voice sounding hoarse and graveled. 'No . . .' I gripped Bonnie's hand and pulled her to me.

'I've tried everything, Cromwell. I've had surgeries. Valve replacements.' She sighed, breathing out a slow controlled breath. I wondered if it was to stop herself falling apart. 'I even saw the best doctor in the world for it, to see if there was anything they could do. In London, this summer.' The reason why she'd been in the UK suddenly became clear.

'Bonnie . . .'

'But there's not. My heart is too weak to keep going.' She sniffed and wiped at her cheeks with her free hand. 'I didn't plan for you.' Her trembling hand fell on my cheek. Her hand was cold. 'I knew I could never get close to someone. It wouldn't be fair. To either of us.' She smiled at me, a devastated watery smile. 'But your music made me see you, Cromwell. It called me to *you*. The boy who hears color.'

Her head fell to my chest. 'I'm so sorry. I should've had the strength to walk away. But with you . . . I just couldn't.'

Bonnie's legs seemed to falter. I caught her and helped

her back to her seat. 'You okay?' I asked, then felt stupid. Of course she wasn't.

Her heart was dying.

'It's getting worse.' She looked at the boxes around her. Her college life all packed up in cardboard. 'I'm fading fast. We knew it was a possibility. But I didn't think it would be this quick. My breathing is getting worse. My hands and limbs are getting weak.' When she looked into my eyes, hers were haunted. 'Soon I won't be able to play or sing.' Her face contorted, and I dropped to my knees and pulled her to my chest. 'Music, Cromwell. I won't be able to sing.' She drew back and said, 'I have to move home now. Things have gotten too hard to be here on my own.' She sucked in a breath. 'Then, it'll be the hospital.'

'No.' I shook my head. 'There's got to be something they can do.'

Bonnie ran her hand through my hair. It was becoming my favorite thing she did. 'I'm on the transplant list, Cromwell. That's all there is left to do. Right now I'm nowhere near the top.' A steely determination set in her brown eyes. 'But I'm determined to get that heart. I've fought for years. And I am not giving up now.' She took my hand in hers and held on tightly. Her bottom lip shook. 'I don't want to die, Cromwell. I have too much to live for.'

I couldn't breathe as those words slipped from her lips. I felt my eyes fill and I closed them, trying to chase the tears away. Bonnie just held on tighter. When I opened my eyes, she was watching me. 'I would have lived my whole life trying to achieve even a tenth of the talent you have, Cromwell. It's why I was so hard on you. Because of the gift you have.' Her eyes dropped. 'And I think I would have spent my whole life waiting for a boy to treat me as you have recently.' She swallowed. 'Last night . . . it was everything I could have wished for.'

'Bonnie,' I whispered.

'But you can't be with me for this next part, Cromwell.' I shook my head. 'Shh,' Bonnie said. 'I should never have let it get that far. But even though it is failing, losing strength, my heart latched itself to yours, and I had to know what it was like. To be with you.' She sniffed and a tear fell. 'You made me feel so cherished.'

I needed to get up. To take Bonnie with me and to fucking run from whatever this shit was. But we couldn't run when the very thing we were trying to escape from, the thing that was dying, was the thing that still kept her alive.

'I'm sorry.' Bonnie put her hands on my face and kissed me. 'I'm so sorry, Cromwell.'

'No,' I argued, head shaking. 'Don't.'

'I'm sorry,' she said again. 'But I can't do it to you.' She stood, leaning on her chair for support. My mind reeled when I thought of her lately. How slow she would walk. The times she would stop and catch her breath, disguising her reason for stopping as something else. The dark circles under her eyes. The need for so much sleep. The camisole she didn't want to take off last night. If she'd had surgeries before . . . it had covered her scars.

'I don't want to go anywhere,' I said.

'Please, Cromwell. Please just leave it be.' Her hand was tight on the chair. 'I have to fight. But if I lose . . . if that fight is over before I have a chance to try . . .' She shook her head. 'I couldn't do that to you. I couldn't hurt you in that way.'

'Bonnie—'

The sound of footsteps came into the room, cutting me off. A woman, with brown hair and Bonnie's eyes, walked into the room. Her eyes widened when she saw me. 'Oh, I'm sorry. I didn't realize you had company.'

'He was just leaving, Mama,' Bonnie said. Her voice was still thick with tears.

'Bonnie—'

She leaned in and kissed my cheek. 'Thank you,' she said and sat back down on her seat. My mind was reeling.

'No,' I argued.

'Please,' she said, breaking into a cry. I reached forward, but a hand on my back stopped me. I turned to see her mum.

'Please, son,' she said, her accent just as strong as her daughter's. I didn't want to leave Bonnie. I didn't want to go. But I didn't want to see Bonnie cry. I stepped out into the corridor with her mum. I ran my hands through my hair in frustration. My head was a jumble. Bonnie . . . dying . . . heart failure . . . transplant . . . It wouldn't sink in. It wouldn't . . .

Her mum was watching me closely. Her eyes were shining too. 'Give her a chance to get settled at home. Give her a chance to adjust. This is all hitting her hard.'

I stared at her, wondering how the hell she was holding it together. But then I saw her lip shake and realized she wasn't. She'd just got good at hiding it.

'Please, son,' she said. 'We just want to make this as stress-free for Bonnie as possible.' Her façade faltered. 'We have to do whatever we can to help her keep up the fight.'

I stared at Bonnie's door. Then I backed away from the door, toward outside. My head was pounding, my mind trying to take it all in. This couldn't be happening.

Not now I had her.

Not after I'd let her in.

I burst through the door and into the cool air. My feet stopped dead and my eyes closed. I couldn't get my head around what had just happened.

I opened my eyes, and my gaze fell on the quad. On the students laughing and joking, not a damn care in the world.

I wanted to scream.

I stared at the dorm and thought of Bonnie inside. I had to do something. My hands pushed through my hair. And like it did every time I thought of her, music played in my head. Notes danced, all to Bonnie's pretty face.

I took off at a sprint.

I didn't know what to do.

She wanted me to go . . .

. . . but I wasn't sure that was something I could do.

16

Bonnie

'Bonnie?' My mama pushed open the door to my room. The second I saw her, I crumpled where I sat. Tears streaked down my face. My shoulders shook as I remembered the look on Cromwell's face as I told him about me. It was devastation, pure and simple.

And when he wouldn't go . . . when he wanted to stay by my side . . .

Arms wrapped around me. I sank into my mama and cried like I'd never let myself cry before. She ran her hand down my back, letting me have this moment. Letting me exorcise this pain. I cried and cried until my tears ran dry. My throat and chest ached with the purge. Mama lifted my chin and I looked into her eyes.

She had been crying with me.

'Baby,' she whispered. She ran her hand along my cheek. 'I never knew you liked him.' I nodded and looked out of my window. At the students going about their everyday life, not a care in the world. Not living in the pain of hurting someone they'd grown to care deeply for. Feeling the void in my room since Cromwell had left.

'It's not fair.' I sighed and felt the palpitation flutter in my chest. The feeling no longer surprised me. It was part of my life. 'Why did God put him in my path now? When it's too late? When I might not make it?' I looked at my mama. 'Why would He be so cruel?'

Mama sat on the end of my bed. 'Maybe he was brought into your life to help make it better. Have you ever thought of that? Maybe he was brought in at exactly the right time. When you will need people you love around you most.'

If my heart could have raced, it would have right then. But I shook my head. 'Mama . . .' A cave formed in my stomach. 'What if they don't find me a heart?' I saw her flinch just at the thought. Seeing those I loved ripped into pieces by my illness was the worst thing of all. The sight of them falling apart was the cruelest kind of torture. And I'd let Cromwell slip through. 'What if I let him in completely, and then I don't make it? How could I do that to him? How could I hurt him that way?'

Mama held my hand. 'Don't you think that should be his choice, sweetheart? You've already got so much weighing on your soul. Don't add making decisions for him to the list.'

I imagined letting him in. I thought of the weeks and months ahead, not fought alone, but having him by my side.

The suffocating darkness of fear was drowned out by the light.

'Your papa will be here now, sweetheart. Let's get your things and go home.'

I rested on the bed as my mama and papa took care of my things. Mama waited in her car as I shut my dorm room and walked outside. My papa was driving my car home.

'I've called Easton,' Mama said. I took a deep breath.

She squeezed my hand. 'We have to tell him, Bonnie. There's no more holding it off.'

I ran my hand over my sternum. 'I don't think I can . . . it will break his heart.'

Mama said nothing. Because she knew it too. But it had to be done. She pulled away from the campus and drove toward home.

As we turned into our driveway, I looked up at the white house with its wrap-around porch. Mama's hand squeezed mine. 'You okay, Bonnie?'

'Yeah.' I got out of the car and walked slowly to the front door. I went to go up to my room, but my mama put her hand on my arm. 'We've made up the office as your room now, sweetheart.' I shook my head. I remembered now. Stairs were causing me too much of a problem. And as things got worse, equipment would have to be brought to the home. My room needed to be accessible.

Mama led me to what was once my papa's office. I smiled on seeing my electric piano in the corner. I absently noticed the lilac color of the walls and the carpet at the end of the bed. But I was moving to my piano and sitting on its stool before I'd even blinked.

I lifted the lid and started playing. I felt all the tension leave me as the music filled the room. I didn't even know what I was playing at first; I just played whatever was in my heart. My fingers were clumsy, the agility in them fading. But I kept playing. I wouldn't stop until I had no choice.

As the last note faded out, I smiled. Opening my eyes, I noticed my mama standing in the doorway. 'What was that? It was beautiful.'

I felt my cheeks burning. 'It was something Cromwell

wrote.' I had memorized the few bars he had composed in the coffee house. It was my new favorite.

'Cromwell composed that?'

'He's a genius, Mama. And I'm not just saying that or exaggerating. He can pretty much play any instrument. It's why he's at Jefferson. Lewis invited him and gave him a scholarship. He was something of a child prodigy. Some say he's a modern-day Mozart.'

'Then now I see it.' She joined me on the stool.

'What?'

'Why you've fallen for him.' Her arm linked in mine. 'The way you love music. You were always going to find someone who loves it too.'

A smile crept on my lips, but it quickly fell. 'He's kinda damaged, Mama. He has all this talent, but he doesn't like to play or compose. Something holds him back.'

'Then maybe you should help him find the love he's lost.'

I blew out a breath. 'I can't believe you're approving of him.' I thought of his tattoos and piercings, his permanently dour expression. 'He's not exactly the typical boy next door most mamas want for their baby girl.'

'No, he's not.' She bumped my arm. 'But the way he was fighting for you, didn't want to leave you, tells me everything I need to know. Obstacles in life sometimes make you look at the world in ways you never did before.'

'And what did it tell you?'

'That he's fallen for you.'

I stared at my mama and shook my head. 'I'm not sure that's quite true. He can be cold and rude, even cruel at times . . .' But then I thought of how he held me last night.

How he was so gentle. How he checked I was okay. And I wondered . . .

'Yet despite it all, you've fallen for him.' Mama got up and kissed me on the head, leaving me sitting in silence on the piano stool. 'Your papa is bringing your things in now.'

'Okay,' I said, as if by rote.

'Bonnie?' Mama asked. I looked up. 'Do you want me to tell Easton?'

Fear of telling him left me paralyzed. But I shook my head, knowing it had to come from my lips. 'I'll tell him,' I said and felt the weight of the world bear down on me. Because the thought of Easton's reaction scared me more than the heart failure itself.

'Bonn?' Easton walked into the office that was now my bedroom with a look of confusion on his face. He saw my piano and my bed. The walls, the carpet. He stopped dead. He was still wearing his clothes from last night. He must have come straight from Charleston. 'What's going on?'

I could tell by the look of apprehension on his face that he already had an idea. 'Come and sit by me,' I said, patting the bed.

'No,' he said, his voice tight. He started breathing deeply. 'Just tell me, Bonn. Please . . .' The fear in his voice almost destroyed me.

I stared at him. At his long blond hair and bright blue eyes. 'I wasn't in England this summer for a music seminar, East.' He stood still and listened. 'I was there seeing a team of doctors about my heart.' His nose flared. I needed to just tell him quickly. 'There's nothing more to be done, East.' I inhaled, forcing myself not to break. 'My heart is failing.'

It was slow, but second by strained second, Easton's face contorted into one that was racked with pain. 'No,' Easton said.

'I'm on the transplant list. But I've had to move home. My body is getting weak, East. I'm deteriorating fast. It made sense to come home so I'm safe.' I didn't add the list of possible threats that came with heart failure. He knew them as well as I did. Both of us were too terrified to say them aloud.

'How long?' he asked, voice hoarse, thick with emotion.

'I don't know. The doctors don't give a specific time-frame, but—'

'How long?' he asked, more panicked.

'Maybe three months. Two at the least, four if I'm lucky. Though it could be sooner.' I got off the bed. Easton stayed where he was, like he was soldered to the floor. I stood before my twin, my best friend, and put my hands on his arms. 'But a heart might turn up, East. We have to pray that one comes.'

Easton stared down at me, but his stare was vacant. 'East.' I tried to put my hand on his face. Easton moved back, and back again, until he ran out of my room. I tried to chase after him but he was too quick. He burst through the front door and out into his waiting truck.

'East,' I tried to shout as I watched him pull away, tires screeching, onto the road, but tiredness stole my voice. My mama was behind me, a worried expression on her face. But I didn't say anything. I was too tired.

No matter how much sleep I had of late, no amount would ever make me feel replenished. And after last night, after staying up with Cromwell, and telling both him and Easton today, I was wiped.

I climbed under my comforter and laid my head down on my pillow. I closed my eyes and blocked everything out but the will to sleep.

It wasn't a surprise that the image of Cromwell's face managed to sneak through. *I don't want to go,* I heard his voice say.

It made me smile. Because as much as I prayed I'd be strong enough for the battle ahead, having Cromwell along with me made the task that much less daunting.

I felt like I was in a waking dream when he held my hand. When his soft lips brushed against mine and I heard him play the piano so perfectly beside me. In such a short time, the memories he had given me had become the most treasured in my weak heart.

And it would be these memories, and the ghost of his lips against mine, that would inspire me to fight that much harder.

17

Cromwell

I banged on the door of Lewis's office, rocking on my feet as adrenaline rushed through me. Last night I hadn't slept for shit. I wanted to text Bonnie. Call her and hear her voice, but I had left her alone. I wanted her; I knew she wanted me. But I had to find a way to make her realize she *needed* me. Because as I'd lain there awake, staring at the ceiling, I knew I wasn't giving her up.

I was a selfish prick. Always had been. But this time I wasn't going anywhere, and it wasn't just for me. Bonnie needed me too. I knew she did. I heard it in her voice and I saw it in her face.

I banged harder. 'Lewis!'

I was running on no sleep. Easton hadn't come home last night either. He hadn't said a thing about Bonnie all this time. But his warning not to hurt her weeks and weeks ago now made sense. I assumed he'd gone to their home to be with her. And that just made me so jealous I couldn't see straight.

I should be there with her too.

I *had* to be. The claws digging into my heart told me so.

I wouldn't let her go through this alone. Because she had to get through it. There was no other choice.

'LEWIS!' I kicked the door in anger.

'That won't get me to appear any sooner, Mr Dean.' I

spun around and saw Lewis approaching, carrying his briefcase.

'I need to speak with you.' I moved aside as he opened the door to his office. I pushed past him and went inside. Lewis came in afterwards, closing the door shut as I paced along his office floor. Lewis sat on the edge of his desk, putting his briefcase down beside him. 'You have to put me and Bonnie back together.'

Lewis raised an eyebrow. 'I'm not sure it'll work, Cromwell.'

'Don't!' I snapped. 'Don't give me your professor shit about it.' I stopped in front of him. The anger that was pulsing through me, the desperation, faded. 'She's sick.' Lewis didn't say anything. Sympathy filled his face. *Knowing* sympathy. 'You knew,' I said through gritted teeth. He nodded. 'How long?'

'I found out just a couple of weeks ago.'

I sank down to the guest seat at his desk. 'That's why she stopped working with me?'

'That's up to Bonnie to tell you, Cromwell.'

The blood drained from my face. 'Because I was giving her shit. Not helping with the composition . . . Because she knew she was running out of time, and I . . . I . . .' I shook my head and pressed my palms into my eyes. 'No,' I hissed.

Lewis moved to the coffee machine in the corner. 'You want one?' he offered. I stared at him, almost saying no. But then I realized I had nowhere to go. I had no one else to talk to.

'Yes. Black, no sugar.'

Lewis busied himself with the coffee, and I looked at all

his pictures and paintings. I stared at the one above his desk. The colors, like synesthesia. 'She loved the exhibit,' I said.

Lewis turned to me and smiled. 'Did she?'

'She's fascinated by it all.' I thought of her sitting with me on the stool, singing her song as I played her guitar. 'She just loves music, full stop. Wants to be so good at it that it's all she thinks about.'

'And you?' he asked, putting my coffee before me. He took his own and sat down behind his desk.

I stared at the picture that always pulled my attention. The one of Lewis at the Royal Albert Hall. 'I never realized how much I loved it too.' I shook my head. 'No, I did. That's a lie.' But I wasn't going to say anything else on it. I wasn't ready to think of the reason I stopped playing yet. On top of Bonnie, it was all too bloody much.

Lewis sat forward, arms on his desk. 'Forgive me for prying, but it seems you and Ms Farraday have grown closer of late.'

I stared down at the blackness of my coffee. 'Yeah.'

Lewis sighed. 'I'm sorry, Cromwell. It's got to be hard. To grow closer, and then . . . *this* . . .'

'Not as hard as it is for her.'

'No,' Lewis said. 'You're right.'

'She wants to pass this class so bad.' I looked at him. 'She wants to complete the composition for the end of the year so much.'

Lewis nodded. The realization of her situation hit me so hard it almost winded me. 'She won't get to do it, will she?' My throat closed until I felt like I was being choked. I stared down at my hands. 'I looked it up. Everyone says don't Google things, but I couldn't help it.' I swallowed back the lump. 'She'll struggle to walk until she's bedridden. Her hands and feet will become painful to use, filling with fluid.' I rubbed my chest, my voice growing more and more hoarse the more I spoke. 'She'll struggle to breathe, her lungs growing weaker. Her kidneys and liver will start to fail.' I squeezed my eyes shut, my nose flaring as I tried to keep my shit together. I tried to imagine Bonnie like that. I tried to imagine her in hospital, confined to a bed, her spirit strong but her body failing her day by day, and I couldn't fucking cope.

'And you want to help her?'

I stared Lewis straight in the eyes. 'I want to give her music. *Have* to.' I tapped my head. 'Already, it's building up in me, like my heart knows what it has to do for her. It has to give her what she needs so she can fight – hope.' Nervous energy swirled inside, making it impossible to sit still. I started pacing in front of his desk. 'I keep hearing melodies. Keep hearing the different sections – string, woodwind, brass – playing the same music, showing me their color pattern. Mapping out the way for me in my head. It's pressing at my brain. I need to get it out.'

Lewis was watching me, his coffee abandoned on his desk. 'I know what that's like.'

'You do?'

He pointed to the photo of him conducting. 'That piece, my most famous, was born from losing someone I loved. From being robbed of a life that should've been mine.' He walked to the photo and stared up at himself. 'I lost the one I loved through my own stupidity. All that was left was the music that never quieted. I had to write.

The notes and melodies haunted me until I did.' He huffed a laugh. 'Then, once it was done and out in the world, the symphony haunted me for the rest of my life. Still does.' He ran his hand through his hair. 'I can't play that piece of music. Even now. All these years later. Because it reminds me of what I could have had, who I could have loved, the life I could have lived if I hadn't been so messed up.' Lewis came beside me and tentatively laid his hand on my shoulder. 'Don't let her go if she means that much to you, Cromwell. Bonnie needs you now, more than ever.' He stared vacantly at the wall. 'This could be something special that only you can give her. Music, Cromwell. It can be both a healer and a comfort. If you care for her, like I'm assuming you do, you have the gifts to make this time truly memorable for her. And I can't say that about anyone else but you.' Lewis checked the time. 'We have a class, Mr Dean.'

I got up from my seat and headed for the door. 'Thanks.'

Lewis gave me a tight smile. 'If you need me, Cromwell, I'm here.'

I headed to the classroom and stopped dead in the doorway. Bonnie sat in her seat, staring at her notepad. I looked right at her, just drinking her in. I didn't care who saw me. She was dressed in jeans, as always, this time with a pink jumper, and her hair was in a messy bun. In this moment, I didn't think I'd ever seen anyone more beautiful.

The clearing of a throat snapped me back to the moment. Lewis was behind me. I took a deep breath and walked into the classroom. Bonnie lifted her head, and her face paled. Her eyes watched me as I walked up the stairs. They were shining. She was worried about what I'd do, I could see that. I could see the guilt on her face, in the tensing of her slight frame.

I stopped at her seat. Not giving one shit about the other students in the class, I leaned down and pressed my lips to hers. Bonnie didn't even try to pull away. She just melted into me like she knew where she belonged.

I broke the kiss and sat beside her, taking her hand and pulling it onto my lap. I faced Lewis at the front of the class. A small smile appeared on his face, before he turned and wrote something on the board. I brought my gaze back to Bonnie and the flush on her cheeks. Students were talking in whispers and looking our way.

They could damn well look.

Bonnie ducked her head then glanced at me from the corner of her eye. 'Farraday,' I said. Her eyes filled with tears. The sight was a damn crowbar to my chest.

Then she smashed it wide open when she whispered, 'Dean.'

I gripped her hand tighter as Lewis started the class. I never let her go through the whole lesson. I made no notes, but I didn't care. Holding Bonnie was more important than anything right now.

When class was done, I released Bonnie only long enough for her to get her things. Taking her hand again, I led her slowly down the stairs and out into the corridor. She let me lead her through the building and toward the practice rooms.

Her feet faltered, and I held her tightly. Now that I was aware of what she was going through, I picked up on things that I hadn't before. She walked heavily; the beat of her foot hitting wood sounded like a drum in my ears. Her short breaths were sharp bursts of irregular rhythm that felt out of sync with the brightness she exuded.

The sounds were dark colors in my head. Colors I didn't like to see. Especially on Bonnie.

I brought us into a practice room and sat her down on a chair, pressing my lips to hers before dragging over the piano stool and sitting before her.

Her huge brown eyes were on me. She was nervous. I could tell by her fidgeting hands.

I couldn't take my eyes off her face. It was as if ever since I found about her heart, I couldn't stop noticing just how beautiful she was. I must have stared longer than I realized, because she tucked some loose hair behind her ear and whispered, 'Cromwell.'

I blinked, ripping myself from my thoughts. Bonnie wore a worried expression. I reached out for her hand. Her focus dropped to our fingers. 'We're going to work together again,' I said, and her head snapped up. 'On Lewis's composition.'

'Cromwell.' She shook her head sadly.

I ran my free hand over the thigh of my jeans. 'I want to play again.' I closed my eyes and could see the colors sparking back to life, growing more vibrant as I allowed that truth to hit home. Bonnie squeezed my hand. I opened my eyes. 'I want to play because of you.'

'Me?'

I got on my knees, on the floor, my eyes level with hers. I cupped her face and felt my lip hook up. 'Because you, with your questions and tenacity, made damn sure that I faced some shit I didn't want to face. You pushed and pushed until

I couldn't turn away from it anymore. You pushed until I found myself in here, in the practice rooms, picking up instruments I hadn't touched in three years.'

I kissed her forehead. 'I fought against it. Fought against you. But when I saw you at that coffee house, singing, just you and your voice and your acoustic guitar, I finally saw something in you I hadn't seen before – kinship. You loved music as much as I did. But unlike me, you weren't afraid to show the world.' My stomach clenched. 'Now I know . . . everything . . . my need to play again is just . . . more.'

Bonnie shook her head, ready to argue. I cut her off before she could. 'You make me want to make music again, Farraday. Let me do this with you.'

Her eyes dropped. 'Cromwell,' she said softly. 'Things will get worse.' I held my breath. 'A lot worse. You have a life. You have a chance to create something great alone.' She swallowed and looked dead into my eyes. 'I will only hold you down. You don't need to do this for me.' She smiled a self-deprecating smile. 'I won't be able to compose anything that is worthy of your time. I'm driftwood to your tall ship.'

I knew she was talking about more than the music right now. She was talking about her. She was talking about me. About us.

'Then lucky for you I'm a musical genius and can take the lead.' My lip hooked in humor. Bonnie's smile turned from sad to amused. I kissed her nose, just because I could and it was there. 'I'm not going anywhere. If you haven't learned by now, I'm stubborn and pretty much do whatever the hell I like.' I moved to the piano, taking the stool with me. I nudged my head to the space I'd left on the stool. 'Get your arse here, Farraday.'

I could see her debating what to do. I never looked away from her. She took a deep breath then got to her feet. My blood pumped faster around my body when she sat down beside me.

'Well, you had better be as good as you've said. You've kinda built yourself up, Dean,' she joked, and I laughed out loud. Bonnie froze, shock engulfing her pretty face.

My humor dropped. 'What's wrong?'

'You laughed.' A wide smile pulled on her lips. 'Cromwell brooder-of-the-century Dean actually laughed.' She closed her eyes, making my heart fucking melt. 'And it was bright yellow.' She opened her eyes. 'Like the sun.'

'You got synesthesia now?'

'No. But I don't need it. When you laughed . . .' She nudged my arm. 'It illuminated the room.'

I smirked and put my hands on the keys. The minute I felt the ivories under my fingertips, it was like coming home. My hands played a few scales, warming up for the music we were about to create. 'We need a theme.'

'I know we do. I've been trying to get you to agree to one for an age now.'

I nodded, guilt tightening my chest. 'I'm here now.'

Bonnie rested her head on my shoulder. 'You're here now.' She still sounded dubious. Like she didn't think I should be. But she knew by now that I was stubborn.

The room was silent as Bonnie thought. 'It should be personal.' I nodded. I waited for her to finish her thoughts. 'What about my journey?' She looked up nervously through her lashes and laid her hand over her heart. 'With my heart.' She gave me a watery smile. 'And wherever it may go from here. The fight. The uncertainty. The joy . . . or . . .' She didn't finish that sentence. I didn't need her to.

'Yeah,' I rasped. 'That's good.' Already, my head was racing with ideas, notes forming as she spoke. Distant violins played in the background, trumpets and flutes chasing the melody.

'And for your side?'

I stared at her. 'What do you mean?'

'What can we thread into the piece for you? So you're represented too.'

My hands balled into fists. 'I've got nothing.' That pit that had lived in my stomach for so long threatened to erupt. Bonnie's disappointment was broadcast on her pretty face. But, unlike all the other times, she didn't push me. Her silence screamed her sadness at my response. But, like always, my shutters went up.

'I loved the piece you played that night. The one you didn't finish.'

I squeezed my eyes shut. 'No.' I was being a dick. I knew it. But I just . . . couldn't . . .

Bonnie laid her head on my arm again. It was funny. She was acting no differently to all the other times, but now I could see how tired she was getting. Or maybe she was just letting me see her as she truly was. She didn't have to pretend anymore.

Unlike me.

My fingers started moving, her words circling like vultures in my head. *I loved the piece you played that night. The one you didn't finish . . .*

My lips moved to her head, a soft kiss pressed into her

hair. But my hands followed the music that was coming from within. A short rhythmic singular note. A heartbeat. Then another. People. Lots of people all with beating hearts. More. More and more hearts beating in unison . . . then –

'Mine,' Bonnie said, eyes closed, understanding the musical story I was telling. A single delicate note, out of sync and standing on its own. Bonnie's smile lifted as a melody came next, light and bright.

Violet blue in my mind.

Bonnie listened, arms clutching mine as I played, my idea jotted down on the keys. 'There,' she would say. 'Keep that.' I'd play. 'Add strings,' she'd add. 'Violins and violas taking the top notes.'

I played, and Bonnie wrote down the parts we were keeping on manuscript paper. Hours passed. I looked down at Bonnie resting against my arm and realized she was asleep. I moved my hands from the keys and just stared at her peaceful face.

A slam of pain crowbarred into my stomach as I did. A rush of anger seemed to singe the bones in my body. Because Bonnie Farraday was perfect.

Perfection with an imperfect heart.

I stared down at the piano. As the keys stared back at me, the familiar pain of loss cut through me, making me lose my breath. The emotions I kept trapped inside threatened to break free. But I couldn't face them *and* this. I inhaled Bonnie's scent and tried to keep from falling apart.

I had to think of Bonnie. Nothing else.

We'd talked some. She'd told me a little of what the doctors said. She'd wanted to stay in school for as long as she could. I could tell by her eyes that she was determined.

But I could tell by how tired she was, by how she struggled with such simple tasks, that she wouldn't be attending classes for long.

I wrapped my arm around her and hugged her close. I stared at the blank wall in front of me and just let her sleep. It was strange. I'd never been one for closeness and affection before, but Bonnie Farraday in my arms, sleeping and clawing back the strength that was trying to escape, felt like the most natural thing in the world.

I'd pushed too hard today. I made a note to not work us so hard from now on. It was another half hour before Bonnie stirred. When she blinked herself out of sleep, she looked up at me, a moment of confusion taking hold before her cheeks blazed.

'Cromwell . . . I'm so sorry.'

I took her chin between my thumb and finger. 'Look at me, Bonn.' She looked anywhere but at me. Until she eventually lifted her eyes. 'You needed sleep. It's fine.'

'Sorry.' I could hear the embarrassment in her voice, see the glistening of her eyes.

It just about broke my heart. I leaned forward and kissed her lips. She kissed me back. I laid my forehead to hers and said, 'let's make a deal right now. You ever need to rest while you're at school, you come to me. You need anything at all, you come to me. And you don't get embarrassed. Deal?'

Bonnie hesitated but then said, 'deal.'

'I'll take you home.' I helped her stand and took her out to my truck. The minute I got in the driver's side, she laid her head on me and fell back to sleep. As I drove away from campus, I felt too many emotions at once. Overcome that Bonnie felt comfortable enough to fall asleep against me. But scared shitless at how tired she was. A few hours in the music room and a couple of classes had exhausted her body.

I heard the opening notes of the piece we had begun, the mass of heartbeats with one single outlier. And nothing could be more true. Since the second I arrived in Jefferson, everybody had been the same. All except one, a girl called Bonnie Farraday.

The single exception to the rule.

I pulled to a stop at Bonnie's house. She was still fast asleep. I allowed myself a short glance at her face before I took her in my arms and carried her to the house. The door opened before I even had to knock. Bonnie's mum showed me the way to her room. I laid her on the bed, Bonnie not even waking once.

I kissed her head and whispered into her ear, 'I'll see you soon, Farraday.' I stood, wanting to move, but my legs wouldn't let me leave. It took me a further five minutes to turn and head for the door. Bonnie's mum was watching from the doorway.

She shut the door behind me. I ran my hand through my hair. 'She fell asleep in the music room when we were practicing. Then she fell asleep again in my truck.'

I wasn't sure I'd seen pain reflected in someone's stare before. But as I looked at Mrs Farraday, I saw it clear as day. She was losing Bonnie. She was losing her daughter. Her child. And she had to stand back and watch it happen, helpless to do anything about it.

I couldn't breathe at that thought.

'She's getting weaker,' she said, a strength in her voice

that I didn't expect. I looked at the closed door as if I could see Bonnie through it. My stomach fell at Mrs Farraday's words. Her hand came on my arm. 'She wants to stay at school for a while longer, but I'm not sure it's feasible. I'd say she has three weeks at most before she becomes too weak. It's her breathing mainly. Her lungs.'

'That fast?' My voice was gravel as the question slipped from my lips.

'She's not in a good way, son.' Her voice hitched, her bravery faltering for a second. She fixed her hair then smiled. 'But she's strong, Cromwell. She's determined to get a heart. We're praying every day for that miracle. It will happen. I know it will.'

'I want to be here,' I said, my chest constricting. 'When she can't be at school, I want to be able to still see her.'

'I know my daughter, Cromwell. And she'll want you to be here too.' She reached out and held my hand. 'Maybe you're the guardian angel that has arrived to get her through all this.'

A wave of emotion hit me, so overwhelming it stole my ability to speak.

'We'll be away for a few days in Charleston,' she said. 'Specialists, you see. I'm sure Bonnie will let you know when we're back.'

I nearly demanded she let me come. Insisted that they take me too. But one look at the slumped shoulders on Bonnie's mum, and I couldn't. I tensely nodded my head then left the house. Just as I stepped onto the path, Mrs Farraday said, 'if you see Easton, will you please tell him to come home?' She dropped her head. 'His sister needs her best friend.'

I nodded and got into my truck. Easton was already in the room when I got back. I shut the door, about to face him, when he flew at me, his hands flattening on my chest as he smashed me against the door. 'What the hell are you doing with my sister?' he spat. His face was beetroot red. I pushed him back, but Easton was a brick wall.

I yanked his arms off me and shoved him against the wall. But he wasn't finished. 'She's not one of your easy fucks!' he hissed. His fist came out and punched me across my face. I tasted blood on my lip. I tightened my hands into his shirt and held him still, anger fueling my words.

'I know she's not, you prick.' Easton tried to strike me again. I pushed my forearm over his neck, stopping him from moving. 'I *know* she's not!' I pushed harder, cutting off his breath. 'You think I don't know that? She's . . .' The truth made me pause. But when I looked into Easton's eyes, I said, 'she's everything, East. Fucking everything!'

Easton stilled. I dropped my arm and backed up. Easton was breathing heavily, chest rising and falling. His cheeks were red, but the rest of his skin was pale. His eyes were tiny and rimmed with red. Blood from my lip dripped down my chin.

Easton sagged against the wall, and I looked at him. Really looked at him. Where the colors around him were once bright, a rainbow of neon, now there were only blacks and grays and navy blues.

'She's gonna die,' he said quietly, and his face contorted in sadness. I could feel the waves of fear pulsing from his body. His eyes fell on me, but I could tell he wasn't really seeing me. 'She's fought it for so long. But it's finally giving up. Her heart.' He met my eyes. 'She's gonna die.'

'They might get a heart for her.'

Easton laughed, no humor in his tone. 'You know how rare it is for one to become available? The exact match?' I clenched my jaw when I realized I didn't. Beyond an internet search, I didn't know anything. Easton slumped down the wall, completely dejected. 'Almost never happens.' I sat on the floor too, leaning against my bed. I licked at my lip, tasting nothing but blood.

'Her body will give up soon,' Easton whispered. His eyes were haunted; it was the only way to describe them. He leaned his head against the wall. 'She's had so many surgeries throughout the years.' He shook his head. 'I thought she was getting better. I thought . . .'

'The valve started to fail,' I said, telling him what he no doubt already knew.

'What the hell is the world without Bonnie?' My stomach tensed. Because I wouldn't even let myself think it. A world without Farraday would be . . .

I shook my head. 'She's strong.' Easton nodded, but I could see he didn't believe it. 'She is.'

'Bonnie's strong. But her heart isn't.' His eyes lost focus. The colors around him deepened even further into darkness. It reminded me of his latest paintings. 'She can only be as strong as her heart lets her be.' He sighed and ran his hands down his face. 'I knew there was something wrong.' I looked at the unfinished painting on his easel. 'I could feel that she was lying. Hiding the truth.' He tapped his head. 'Twins.'

'She wanted to be as normal as she could.'

Easton's eyes narrowed on me. 'You hated each other.'

'No. Not really.'

He shook his head. 'She's too fragile.' The spark of anger that always waited, ready to strike, in my stomach flared to life at his words. Because I knew this was him warning me off her. But it was too late. He didn't understand me, and he sure as hell didn't understand me and Bonnie. What we shared. 'She doesn't have the strength to deal with your shit.'

'She needs me. Wants me.'

Easton shut his eyes and just breathed.

'She needs you,' I said, and he tensed. Every muscle in his body pulled tight. 'She needs you more than ever.'

'I know,' he said after several strained seconds. I leaned back against my bed. A huge, crushing weight seemed to lie on my shoulders. Easton sat in silence for so long I didn't think he would speak again. Until he whispered, 'she can't die.'

I looked up at Easton, only to see tears fall down his cheeks. My gut clenched, and I felt the same lump I'd been fighting since yesterday block my throat. Easton's face crumpled. It was one of the first times I'd ever seen him serious. Right now, he was as serious as death.

'She's my sister. My twin.' He shook his head. 'I can't, Crom. I can't be without her.'

My eyes blurred, but I got up and sat beside him. Easton's head fell forward and his body shook as he cried. I clenched my jaw, not knowing what the hell to do. It felt like my stomach was ripping open when I let Easton's words sink in. *She can't die . . .*

I pushed my tongue against my teeth to keep from falling apart too. Easton's sobs grew louder, my friend losing it as he sat against the wall. I lifted my arm, letting it hover

over him, until I laid it around his shoulder and pulled him to my chest. Easton fell against me. I stared across the room at his unfinished painting. At the black swirls and the turbulent paintbrush strokes.

It was this moment. It was exactly what he was feeling now. He'd known. Known something was wrong with Bonnie, but he hadn't dared ask. As I stared at the painting, as Easton cried for his twin, I couldn't help but see Bonnie's face in my head. Her dark eyes and dark hair. Her pretty face. And her sitting up on that stage, guitar in her hands, violet blue pouring from her mouth. I gasped for breath when pure fear stole all the air in my lungs. Fear that I'd lose her before I truly got the chance to know her. My favorite color ripped from my life. Bonnie taken away before she could leave her fingerprint on the window of the world.

I shook my head, ignoring the damn tear that fell from the corner of my eye. 'She won't die,' I said, gripping Easton tighter. 'She won't die.'

My father's face flashed into my mind, and with it came the reminder of the void his absence had brought, never to be refilled.

Until Bonnie Farraday walked into my life on a beach in Brighton and started bringing me something I didn't even know I needed – silver.

Happiness.

Her.

'She won't die,' I repeated one last time, letting the conviction of those words settle inside me.

Easton lifted his head ten minutes later. He wiped his eyes with his forearm and stared across at his painting. 'I need to go see her.' I nodded, and Easton got to his feet.

I moved away from the door and sat on my bed. Easton rocked awkwardly on his feet. He scratched the back of his head. 'If you're in, you gotta be all in.' He took a deep breath. 'It's gonna be rough, and she's gonna need those who love her around her.' Easton's eyes bored right into mine, a clear challenge. Then his face softened. 'She acts tough. She fights hard. But deep down, Bonn is terrified.' He swallowed, and I felt the lump in my throat thicken. 'She doesn't wanna die, Crom. She has so much fucking life in her that if she were to be taken away now . . .'

When he looked at me again, there was only conviction in his face. 'She's the best of us both. I've always known that.' He looked as if he wanted to say something else, but instead he left the room, leaving the shadow of his blacks and navy blues behind. I wasn't sure anything else would color this room until Bonnie got the heart she needed.

I lay, staring at the ceiling, for an hour, before getting up and taking a shower. As the water fell over my head, running down my body and hitting the tiles at my feet, Bonnie's question wouldn't leave my head. The one about the unfinished piece I had accidently played that night. The one I hadn't touched in three years. I laid my forehead against the wall and closed my eyes. But the water from the shower, like rain on the window, like the sound of the tears that fell all those nights ago, brought that piece to my mind.

Easton's dark colors danced in my eyes as the piece grew in volume. And I couldn't shut it off. Like a flood, it stormed the dam, demolishing the walls.

The shower room was silent, empty but for me this late at night. And I was glad. I was glad as my hands slapped at the tiles when my legs became weak, the music playing in my head, the opening bars crushing my heart. Only now, instead of just my father's face in my mind, Bonnie's was there too. I shook my head, trying to get them all to leave me alone. I couldn't cope with the emotions they brought. The emotions that were too much, too bloody much for me to take.

Colors burst like fireworks in my head. My stomach tightened, my heart pulled, and my legs gave way. I dropped to the floor, the hot water turning cold as it battered my head in rhythmic beats. And then the tears fell. The water and the tears were a blur as they collided and crashed to the floor. Though neither felt cleansing.

Nothing but the 'gift' I'd been given would take these feelings from me. I sat back on my knees and stared down at my hands. They were shaking. They curled into fists, and I wanted to smash them against the tiles. But I didn't. Because the need to create governed my choices right now. My hands were my tools. They were the only things that could take these emotions away.

Some saw synesthesia as a God-given gift. Some parts were; that I couldn't deny. But this part, the part that made my emotions so strong I couldn't take it, was a curse. I could see them. Feel them. Taste them. And it was too much. As I thought of Bonnie, as I pictured my father that last time I saw him ... I bent over, the pain in my stomach becoming too much to bear. It was like someone had taken a bat to my ribs, my heart carrying so much sadness it couldn't cope.

I took a deep breath and got to my feet. Still wet, I threw my clothes on. And I ran. I ran across the quad to the music building, bursting through the door and into the closest music room. I didn't even bother with the light.

I just sat at the piano and lifted the lid. The moon shone in through the high window, bathing the ivory and black keys in a silver glow.

Silver.

It was as if my father was watching over me. Showing me the way back to happiness. This – music – my greatest lost love, only found again thanks to one girl in a purple dress.

She was my God-given gift. The girl that brought me back to life.

My hands splayed on the piano. And, closing my eyes, I started to play. The piece that had inspired my change to dance music flowed out of me as though a prisoner locked inside a cell for too many years to count had been freed. I was lost to the notes. Lost as I replayed my mum walking into my room telling me he was gone. The army officer showing up on our doorstep with a set of dog tags in his hand. And the night I learned he'd gone missing, my heart shattering with regret and pain. The music filled every inch of space, leaving nothing but this piece for me to breathe in. My hands ached as I played and played it again. The new bars of notes pouring from me like they had always been. My hands never faltered even though my heart stuttered. Memories like grenades were thrown at my feet. But my fingers were ready and fought through the minefield.

Then, when the piece had ended, the sound of gunshots in my head, a goodbye to a fallen soldier, a war hero . . . *my* hero . . . my hands stilled. My eyes opened, feeling swollen and beaten . . . but I could breathe.

The colored pattern was imprinted in my mind. A tribute to my dad. Peter Dean.

'Dad,' I whispered, the word echoing in the room. I leaned my head on the piano and knew, without a doubt, that it was the greatest piece I'd ever composed. Half the heaviness had lifted from inside me. And when I lifted my head, wiping the silent tears from my face, I knew there was someone who needed to hear it.

I had to play it one more time.

When she was back, she'd hear it.

I needed her to hear it.

I just needed her, full stop.

18

Bonnie

I was on my bed, listening to my music, when Easton walked in. I sat up, swallowing back the sadness that infused me when I looked at his face.

I slipped my headphones off and held out my hand. 'East,' I whispered, my voice hoarse. I tried to breathe, take full inhales of air, but my lungs would no longer let me. I shifted where I sat, gritting my teeth at the effort it took me to move.

But when Easton's hand slipped into mine, I found strength in his touch. He sat on the edge of the bed. His eyes were red and his face was pale.

'I'm okay,' I said and tried to grip his hand tighter.

Easton gave me a weak smile. 'You don't lie to me, Bonn. Don't start now.'

This time it was me who gave a weak smile. 'I'm determined to be,' I said instead.

'I know.' He moved beside me and we rested our backs against the headboard. I didn't let go of his hand. Ever since we were kids, holding his hand had given me strength.

'It's been ten years,' he said, his voice graveled. I nodded. Ten years since the problems in my heart had been found. Easton's eyes shone with . . . pride? 'You've fought hard, Bonn.'

I couldn't stop my eyes filling with water. 'You have too.'

Easton gave me a mocking laugh. But I meant it. 'Not like you,' he said. He sighed and tapped his head. 'I'm convinced that my issues up here are directly linked to your heart.' My stomach fell. 'I think when we were created, I was linked to you somehow. When your heart started failing, so did my brain.'

I moved until I sat in front of him. I put my hands on his cheeks. 'They're not linked, East. You're doing well.' I dropped my hand to the leather cuff he always wore. I pushed it down his arm until his scar became visible. Easton clenched his jaw when I ran my fingers over the raised flesh.

A flash of pain burst in my chest. 'You have to promise me, East.' I stared into his blue eyes. 'Promise me that you'll stay strong. No matter what. Don't give in to the demons that threaten to take over.' I pulled on his hand when he looked away. 'Promise you'll talk to your therapist. To Mama, Papa, Cromwell. Just someone.'

'Cromwell doesn't know anything about it. Only you guys do.'

'Then talk to us.' I stared at my brother, and worry stabbed at my brain. 'How are you now?'

'Sad,' he said, completely demolishing what was left of my useless heart. 'Because of you. *For* you. Not because of my head.'

Relief was a balm to the chest pain that never left. 'You promise?' Easton smiled, making my skin warm, and held out his pinky finger. I hooked my pinky in his. 'I promise.'

I smiled and moved back against the bed. My eyelids felt heavy. 'It'll be like last time.' I rolled my head on the pillow to face Easton. He raised an eyebrow. 'This upcoming surgery.' I didn't mention that the surgery may never happen. Or that a heart may never be found. I never let myself utter those words aloud. I wouldn't let them loose in the universe that way.

I watched the pain of that distant hope wash over Easton's face. But I smiled and said, 'I'll wake up and you'll be beside me. You, Mama, Papa, and . . .'

'And Cromwell,' Easton finished.

I stared into my brother's eyes and, mustering courage I didn't know I had, said, 'and Cromwell.'

Something in his expression changed. 'I think he loves you,' Easton said, knocking the wind right from my sails. My heart bounced in my chest like a basketball that was slowly deflating. I heard its dull thud and unrhythmic beat. My voice had left me. Easton held up his fist, his knuckles red. 'I hit him tonight.'

'No,' I whispered. I didn't have the strength to say more.

'I saw you guys in Charleston. I saw him kiss you.' Redness bloomed on my cheeks. 'And I see the way you look at him.' He sighed, defeated. 'And the way he looks at you.'

'How?'

'Like you're his air. Like you're the water to whatever hellfire lives inside him.'

'East,' I hushed out, my body warming with happiness at his words.

'I had to make sure he wasn't gonna hurt you.' Easton pushed his cuff back up his wrist, his scar hidden once again. 'I had to be sure he wasn't gonna mess around with you.' He paused, then said sadly, 'especially now.'

I smiled, even though my lips wobbled. 'Always looking after me.'

'Always, Bonn. I'll always look after you.' He smiled, and it was like seeing the sun burst through a gray cloud. 'I'm your big brother, remember?'

I rolled my eyes. 'By a whole four minutes.'

He dropped his smile. 'It doesn't matter. I'm your big brother. I had to be sure he wouldn't hurt you.'

'He won't.' I'd answered without thinking. But then a peace settled over me at my response. Because I knew it was true. I knew Cromwell wouldn't hurt me. I thought of his blue eyes, deep like the night. I thought of his messy black hair and olive skin. Of the tattoos that covered his skin. The piercings that shone when they hit the light. And my lazy heart lobbed back into its form of a steady beat.

Cromwell Dean inspired my heart to try.

'You like him a lot too, huh?' Easton said. When I met his eyes, my face set on fire. He'd been watching me as I thought of Cromwell.

'He's not what everyone thinks.' I traced the rose pattern on my bedspread with my finger. 'He's moody and curt. He was awful to me when we first met.' But then I caught the echo of his music in my head, and my body felt weightless with light. 'But he's not like that with me now.'

'No?'

I shook my head. 'He's . . . he shows me he cares in many ways. He holds my hand and refuses to let go. He wants to be with me, even if all we do is sit in silence. And best yet, he shows me he cares in the only way he knows how.' I stared at my piano, and I could see him sitting there in my mind's eye, his fingers at home on the ivory keys. 'He brings music to my silent world, East.' I smiled, feeling my chest shimmer. 'He plays music for me that says more to my heart than his words ever could.'

I searched for the words to express what I meant. I wasn't sure I'd ever be able to convey completely what being with Cromwell had done to me. 'Cromwell doesn't speak much with his voice, but he screams what he feels with melodies and notes and the change of keys.' I took a deep breath. It barely inflated my lazy lungs, but it gave me enough air to say, 'I know I'm being selfish, but I can't seem to make him leave me, East.' I met my brother's gaze. It was filled with tears. 'I know what lies ahead. And I know how hard it will be.' I gathered my strength and said, 'I feel stronger when he's beside me.' I pictured myself sitting next to him on the piano stool, my head lying on his muscled bicep as he played. As he told me the story of us with eighth notes and perfect fifths. 'It may sound crazy. It may sound rushed and impossible . . . but he speaks to my soul. Cromwell is damaged and dark. I know it. And he has yet to let me in. But from the minute we met, his music has made it impossible for us to be apart.' I shook my head in disbelief. 'He says I'm the one who inspires him to play. I'm the one who's brought something inside him back to life.'

'Well then,' East said, lying down next to me. 'I'd better not hit him again.'

I couldn't help it. I had to laugh. Easton smiled, showing me a glimpse of the happy brother I loved. 'He's a good guy. He's turned out to be a good friend.' Easton lowered his eyes. 'I kind of lost it tonight, Bonn. About you.'

'East . . .' I said softly, devastation stealing any other words I could offer as a comfort.

'But he was there for me. He sat beside me and let me get it all out. He never moved, instead he sat by my side and told me how strong you were and how it was all gonna be all right.'

'He did?'

Easton nodded. 'And he meant it, Bonn. I saw it on his face.' He stared at me, and I couldn't read his expression. 'He loves you.' It was the second time he'd uttered those words, and my heart still gave the same response. Miraculously, it raced. 'I always worried about you, sis. You never had a social life. Never had a boyfriend. Christ, I didn't even think you'd ever been kissed. Too busy fighting to stay alive.' I blushed. 'But I'm glad you've found him now.' He held my hand, and he held on tight. 'When it's hardest. He'll help you get through it.'

'You all will,' I said. 'You, Mama, Papa and Cromwell.' I brushed my hair from my face. 'I feel like I can do it. I can hold on until a new heart saves me.' I didn't let myself mention the chance of heart rejection or the million other things that could go wrong even if I was given a heart. I couldn't think of that, or I wasn't sure I could keep up the fight.

Tiredness crept over me like a lulling wave. 'Are you coming to the hospital with me tomorrow?'

'Of course,' Easton said. My eyes began to close. But I still felt my brother beside me. He wouldn't leave my side. As sleep took me, hope hung heavy in the air. It sounded like a cello and a violin. I wondered what Cromwell would see.

Me, I hoped. I prayed that Cromwell would think of hope and see my face.

Because I thought of him. Cromwell Dean brought with him hope. And right now, it was the most important thing in my world.

'Accelerated failure . . .' The doctor's voice faded in and out of my ears as he put the scan pictures from yesterday on a board for my parents to see.

My attention drifted out of the window to the birds in the sky. I wondered where they were flying to. I wondered what it was like to fly. To soar through the sky, the air under your wings.

'Bonnie?' Doctor Brennan's voice cut through my musings. I rolled my head on the pillow to face him. I saw the sadness in my mama's and papa's faces. Easton stood, leaning against the wall, his arms crossed across his chest, his eyes lost as they stared at the floor.

'Bonnie?' Doctor Brennan said. 'Do you have any questions?'

'How long before I can't play music anymore?'

I heard my mama's soft cry, but I held the doctor's stare. He had the answers.

'It won't be long, Bonnie. Your limb function is already compromised.' I looked down to my fingers and saw the swelling that had started to creep in weeks ago but was now here, inhibiting my ability to play. I breathed, my inhales and exhales choppy.

About a month, I had heard Doctor Brennan say. *Six weeks at most.*

It was strange, getting a timeframe on your life. To no

longer count it in years, but in weeks, in days, and even hours.

'Sweetheart?' Mama ran her hand over my head. I looked up at her. 'They're gonna be bringing some things to the house for you. Things to help you breathe and be more comfortable.'

'Can we go home now?' I said, not even acknowledging what she'd said. I didn't want to.

'Yes.' My mama went to the closet to get my clothes. I dressed, and I sat in the wheelchair as they pushed me out of the hospital. I closed my eyes as the sun hit my face, feeling its rays on my skin.

I wasn't in it long enough before we were in the car and on the way home. The car was silent as we left Charleston and made our way back to Jefferson. I looked at my papa, his hands tightly holding the wheel. I glanced at my mama in front of me; she was looking out of the window.

Easton was next to me. His eyes were downcast and every muscle was tight. I sighed, closing my eyes. I hated how this affected everyone I loved.

Accelerated failure . . .

The words spun around my head like bullets, but I was numb to their hits. I laid my hand over my chest and felt my heart against my palm. As always, it beat to its own drum, one of tiredness and exhaustion. One of trying to hold on when all it wanted to do was let go.

But I couldn't let go . . .

When we pulled up to the house, my papa helped me out, and I walked slowly to the path. As I looked at the paved driveway, at the path I'd walked along since I was a child, it suddenly seemed like a green mile. I took a deep breath, ready to walk, when I saw Easton beside me.

I looked at my brother, and I saw that he was losing it. 'Easton,' I said quietly.

'I need to get back to the dorm.' He kissed my cheek and backed away to his truck that was parked on the driveway.

'East?' He turned, mid-step. I swallowed. 'You're okay, yeah?'

He threw on a smile that I wasn't sure was entirely real. 'I am, Bonn. I swear. I just gotta get to school. I need . . .'

'I get it.' He needed space. Easton smiled then got into his truck. I watched him drive away. He had sworn to me he was taking his meds. I had made him promise to tell me if it all – me, my illness – got too much.

'You think he's okay?' I asked my papa as we started walking slowly up the path.

'I check in with him several times a day, Bonn. He's doing the best he can. His therapist is happy with his progress.' My father's voice grew husky as he said, 'It's just you, you know? He wants to fix you. And he can't.' My papa pulled me close. 'It's hard for your brother, and your papa, to deal with. The fact that we can't protect you. Can't heal you.'

'Papa . . .' I whispered, my throat thickening with sadness.

'Let's get you to bed, sweetheart. It's been a long day.' My father led me down the path, each step like a marathon to my quickly tiring legs. I knew he couldn't talk to me right then. And I didn't know what to say in return.

I slept for hours. When I woke, it was dark outside, the rain slashing off the windows. It was nearly midnight. Realizing I hadn't texted Cromwell to let him know I was back, I sent him a quick message that I would see him tomorrow and went back to sleep.

It felt like I'd barely closed my eyes when I heard a knock at my window. I squinted in the dark, trying to get my bearings. When the knock sounded again, I got up from my bed, using the frame to keep me steady. The clock on the side table said it was two thirty in the morning.

I pulled back the curtains. At the window, drenched, black clothes slick to his body, was Cromwell. At just the sight of him, my heart seemed to try to leap from my chest as if it could break free and reside next to his. I reached up and flicked the lock. Before I'd even had a chance to lift the window, Cromwell had it open and was climbing inside.

I stepped back as his tall frame came into my bedroom. I was breathless when he looked up. His intense blue eyes were on me, and his black hair was messy, strands sticking to his face. I went to speak, but before I could, Cromwell had stepped forward and taken me in his arms.

His mouth took mine, a sigh slipping from my lips. He was wet, soaked through to the bone, but I didn't care as his lips moved against mine, soft yet demanding. Rough, yet so caring it almost made me cry. He knew I was struggling to breathe lately, and he pulled back, leaving his hands framing my face.

'I've missed you.'

His words were a fire to a chill I didn't even know I felt. His eyes never left mine, his stare intense.

'I missed you too,' I whispered and watched his tense shoulders relax. His eyes ran down my pajamas.

'You're tired?'

I laughed, the sound weak. 'I'm always tired.'

Cromwell swallowed then scooped me up in his arms. The arms of his black sweater – the sweater I'd once worn – were wet, but I didn't care. I would face the cold if it meant being in his arms like this.

Cromwell laid me on the bed and sat down on the edge. His tattooed hand pushed back my hair before skimming softly down my cheek. I caught it in my hand before he pulled it away. I pressed it against my face and closed my eyes. I could smell the rain. I could smell *him*.

But when I opened my eyes, I truly looked at his face. 'Cromwell?' I asked, concern taking me in its grip. 'What's wrong?'

Cromwell's eyes looked haunted, his olive skin pale. He had dark circles under his eyes. He looked . . . sad.

But before I could ask any more, Cromwell got to his feet and moved to the piano. For a few moments, I didn't dare move, watching as he pulled out my piano stool and slowly sat down. His back was ramrod straight, his head hanging low.

I could hear my short breaths echoing in my ears, only faintly catching the sound of the piano lid being opened and the volume being turned to its lowest setting. I sat up, wondering what Cromwell was doing. I hugged my pillow, keeping the chill from my now wet pajamas from me, and Cromwell started to play.

I froze, every part of me captured in shock, as the piece he had once partially played drifted across the room. The time the touch of my hand on his shoulder had helped him to play. My eyes widened and my bottom lip trembled as the most beautiful composition I'd ever had the pleasure of hearing graced my ears. The notes sank into the marrow of my bones and spread throughout my body. They filled every part of me, until they filled my heart, infusing it with life.

I sat mesmerized as Cromwell passed the point at which he'd once stopped, and blessed me with more. Notes I'd never heard so beautifully, perfectly placed together poured from him, his body moving to the rhythm like he was part of the song. Cromwell was the music he created. I was sure I was seeing through the walls he kept so high. I was seeing the darkness he kept hidden deep finally fleeing its prison.

My shaking hand came to my mouth. I forgot to breathe, the power of the piece like a weight in my chest. Because it spoke of sorrow and loss. It spoke of anger and regret.

It spoke of love.

I recognized every feeling, because I had felt them too. Was feeling them now. Cromwell's hands danced over the keys, perfectly, gracefully, and with such beauty that I was sure that if my heart gave out at that moment, it would be at peace after hearing this.

Music so heavenly it almost didn't feel real.

I knew I was crying. I could feel the tears drenching my face. But there were no wracking sobs. No shuddering breaths, just a serenity that came with pure happiness. From being moved so profoundly that something shifted inside you. Something that made you understand what perfection truly looked like.

As Cromwell brought the music to a close, I moved off my bed. I didn't even know why; I just let my defective heart take the lead. And of course, it led me to Cromwell. It seemed I had been led to Cromwell since this summer in Brighton.

Cromwell was still, his hands braced on the keys, on the final chords. And as I walked beside him, he looked up. His cheeks were wet, and I knew without asking that something had just broken within him.

And he'd let me see it.

Open.

Vulnerable.

Him.

I stared at Cromwell's beautiful face, at a genius so tortured that he pushed everyone away, had tried to push me . . . but his music had spoken to my soul. My voice his siren call.

Cromwell's eyes squeezed shut, and his head fell against me. I wrapped my arms around his head, keeping him close. I didn't know what this piece of music was about. And I didn't know what pain he harbored, but I knew I could be here for him right now.

I thought of my journey ahead, and how in a matter of days, weeks if I was lucky, my ability to move and breathe would be taken from me. And I knew. I knew, as sure as I knew Cromwell was the most perfect musician I'd ever heard, that I wanted him.

While I could.

For us both.

I steered Cromwell's head back and cupped his cheeks. Cromwell looked up at me. I took a moment to savor him.

To leave a photograph in my soul of the moment his walls fell down and he led me, hands grasped and fingers entwined, inside his heart. Where I would never leave.

Where I forever wanted to stay.

Leaning down, I pressed my lips to his. I tasted the salt from his tears and the cold left by the rain. Taking his hand, I guided him off the stool and toward the bed.

No words were needed. I wouldn't tarnish the perfect melody that still lingered in the air. Right now there was just me and him and silence. Right now there was nothing but healing and *this*.

My hands shook as I stepped toward Cromwell and lifted his sweater. I pulled the hem over his stomach, baring a beautiful canvas of ink. I brought it over his chest, thankful for Cromwell's help as he lifted it the rest of the way and discarded it on the floor. His chest rose and fell as my hands flattened to his cold tanned skin. The expression in his eyes made my legs weak.

Adoration.

I leaned forward and pressed a kiss to his skin, hearing the hitch of his breath. He let me lead. My British boy who had just shown me his impenetrable heart.

I moved my hands to the shirt of my pajamas. I started unbuttoning it, but my fingers were already too weak. Cromwell stepped closer to me and gently took hold of my hands. He brought them to his lips and kissed each finger. My bottom lip trembled at the sight. At the action. Then he placed my hands on his waist as he leaned in and took my mouth. He kissed me softly, so softly it felt like our lips barely touched. And I felt his hands undoing my buttons.

I held on to his waist, feeling his skin go from cold to warm under my touch. I traced the swirls of quarter notes dancing on a curved bar. The shield that took pride of place on his torso, 'Dad' written on a red ribbon underneath.

My heart clenched at the sight, then as my shirt fell to my elbows, I breathed in and out, knowing what he'd be seeing. I had nothing underneath my shirt, nothing but my skin and my scar and my true self.

I held my breath as Cromwell saw the result of years of fighting. I worried it would disgust him. I worried it would be too ugly. I worried that —

A quiet sob slipped from my throat when he leaned forward and pressed his lips over the raised skin. He kissed the scar from the tip to the bottom. Every inch that told the world I had a broken heart. My entire body shook.

Cromwell took my face in his hands. My shirt fell to the floor, leaving us both exposed. 'You're beautiful,' he whispered, those words, and his voice, like a symphony to my ears.

I smiled. It was the only response I could give, Words were absent, taken away by the gentle touch of his soft kiss. Cromwell kissed me as the rest of our clothes fell away. He kissed me as we crawled into the bed and he moved over me.

Cromwell kissed and kissed me, making me feel so cherished that I didn't think I ever wanted this night to end. And as we made love, his eyes locked on mine and his kisses so sweet, he felt heaven-sent. Sent into my life exactly when I needed him. When the true fight would begin, when I would need an ally by my side.

I pushed the dark hair from his face, our breathing

labored. My hands trailed down his cheek, only for him to catch my fingers and kiss them again. Like he was worshipping me. Like he was thanking me. For what, I didn't know. But I wanted him to feel so cherished too.

We hadn't been together long, but when your time is finite, love is felt stronger, faster, deeper. My eyes widened when that thought hit me. Because . . . 'I'm falling in love with you,' I whispered, letting my soul take the lead and speak its truth unguarded. Cromwell stilled, and his blue eyes fixed on me. My hand lay on his cheek. I swallowed. 'I'm falling in love with you, Cromwell Dean. So very deeply in love.'

Cromwell crushed his mouth to mine, my eyes closing as he told me without speaking how much he needed those words. I smiled against his lips when I felt his heart beating next to mine. It was a strong beat, one that my heart tried desperately to chase.

Cromwell pressed his forehead to mine. 'I'm falling in love with you too,' he said, his deep voice broken and hoarse. Broken or not, my heart absorbed those words like a flower drinking in the rays of the sun. It expanded in my chest and beat with wild abandon.

'Cromwell . . .' I kissed him again. I kissed and kissed him as we built up speed and then broke apart into a million tiny pieces.

Cromwell moved beside me and pulled me to him. I watched him from my pillow and wondered how he had fallen so perfectly into my life. How I'd been so lucky. How God had heard my whispered prayers.

Cromwell took my hand. But when his grip tightened and his eyes closed, I knew he was going to speak.

'All he ever wanted for me was to play music. He knew that I loved it. Needed it . . . but I let him down.' Cromwell's face crumpled. 'And I shattered his heart.' I shifted closer, holding him tighter. Cromwell looked up at me. 'Then he never came home.'

19

Cromwell

My voice hung in the air, the confession like feathers stuck to tar. I held on to Bonnie like she was my lifeline, keeping me from falling apart.

I swallowed. 'My . . . dad.' Just the mention of that word caused ice to cut down my spine and my stomach to fall.

Bonnie didn't say anything, She just let the silence keep me calm. I stared over her shoulder at the piano across the room. It made me think of the old wooden piano he'd gotten for me on my twelfth birthday.

'Keep your eyes closed, Crom,' he said as he led me along the hallway in our home.

'What is it?' Excitement zipped through me like the electric pylons outside our house.

My dad's hands covered my eyes. When we came to a stop, he stepped away from me and dropped his hands. 'Okay, son. You can look.'

I gasped when my eyes fell on the wooden piano across from the table in our dining room. I ran over and stopped just before it. I swallowed and ran my hand over the wood. It was chipped and marked, but I didn't care.

'It's not much, Cromwell. I know that.' I looked back at my dad and saw his face flushing red. My mum stood in the doorway, tears in her eyes. I turned back to the piano. 'It's old and secondhand, but it's in good working condition. I had it checked over.'

I didn't know what he was talking about, because to me, it was the prettiest thing I'd ever seen. I looked back at my dad. He nodded, seeing the silent question in my eyes. 'Play, son. See how she feels.'

My heart beat in a weird rhythm, racing and flipping as I sat on the creaky old stool. I stared down at the keys, and I could just read them, like a book. Colors attached themselves to the notes the keys would produce, and all I had to do was follow their lead.

I laid my fingers on the keys and started to play. Colors, so bright they almost burned my eyes, danced before me. Rainbows and spectrums took over my mind. Reds and blues and greens, all running ahead for me to chase.

I smiled as the music filled the room. As something happened in my chest. Something I couldn't explain. When the path the colors led me down ended, I moved my hands back from the keys. I looked up to see my mum and dad watching me. Mum had her hand over her mouth, tears running down her face. But my dad wore a different expression. One of pride.

My stomach squeezed. He was . . . proud of me.

'How did that feel, son?' my dad asked.

I stared down at the keys and wondered how to put what I thought into words. It was funny; I could just look at music and play what I felt. The colors showed me the way. The emotions that took over me told me what to play. I could speak with my music.

I wasn't so good with words.

I tried to think of something similar. When I looked up at the wall of pictures my mum had had hanging for years, I knew. I looked back at my dad. 'Like when you come home.'

My dad seemed to stop breathing. He followed my eyes to the picture of him on the wall. The one where he was wearing his officer's uniform. 'Cromwell,' he rasped and put his hand on my shoulder.

'Like when you come home . . .'

My voice shook as I looked at Bonnie and said, 'He took me everywhere after that day. He tried to get the right people to see me. People who, like me, could play.' I laughed. 'He tried to play once. I tried to teach him.'

'How the hell do you do this?' He shook his head. 'My boy, the child musical genius. And his dad, a tone-deaf fool.'

'I played and played. Composers in Brighton took me under their wing. When he went away on tours, I would practice and practice until he came home. Symphonies and pieces poured out of me month by month. And every time he came home, he would try harder. Try to help me reach my dream . . .' I closed my eyes.

'What is it, Cromwell?' Bonnie leaned in to kiss my cheek.

Taking a deep breath, I continued. 'I was young. When I look back now, I see that I didn't have much of a childhood. I toured the country, composing and conducting music I'd created. At twelve, fifteen, and finally at sixteen.' I stared off into the distance as my mind brought me to that day. 'I was sick and tired.' I shook my head. 'I was sixteen, and I'd spent most of my life creating music instead of going out with my mates. Playing every instrument known to man instead of dating girls. One night, I'd had enough.' A lump clogged my throat. 'A night before my dad left on another tour to Afghanistan. The British Army was withdrawing, only a few companies left to keep an eye on things.'

I stopped speaking, unsure if I could say anymore. But when I looked up into Bonnie's eyes, big brown eyes that were starting to fade in light, I knew I had to. She had to know this about me. And I had to tell it. It was like a cancer within me, eating away at me until there was nothing left.

I didn't want to be dark and empty inside anymore.

I no longer wanted the anger.

I wanted to live.

'I was at another concert,' I said, instantly reliving the past. 'I had just walked offstage . . . and I flipped . . .'

'Son! That was amazing!' My dad came around the corner of the wings. The audience was still applauding in the theater, but all I felt was anger. Redhot anger ripping through my veins. I ripped off my bow tie and threw it to the ground. My mobile vibrated in my pocket.

NICK: Can't believe you bailed again. Missed a great night.

'Son?' my dad said. I closed my eyes and counted to ten.

'I'm done,' I said when the anger didn't go.

'What?'

I pushed past him and headed to the dressing room. I slammed the door open and reached for my bag. I needed out of this tux before it strangled me.

'Cromwell.' My dad shut the door, keeping out the world. Because that's all he ever did, kept me locked away creating music. No childhood, hardly any friends, and no fucking life.

'I'm done.' I threw my jacket on the floor. I put on my t-shirt and jeans. My dad watched me, a confused look on his face.

'I . . . I don't understand.'. His voice shook. It almost made me stop, but I couldn't. I knew Lewis had been out there tonight. The composer he'd tried to convince to take me under his wing. But I was done. I was so fucking done.

I spread my arms. 'I don't have a life, Dad!' I shouted. 'I have no close friends, no hobbies but music, and nothing to do but write symphonies. Play music. Classical music.' I shook my head, and I knew that now I'd started I wouldn't be able to stop. 'You've shopped me around to as many concert halls as you could. Enrolled me in more orchestras than I could count and whored me out to any composer that thought he could teach me something. But none of them could.' I laughed, almost faltering when my dad's face paled. 'This is so easy to me, Dad. The music I create just pours from me. And once upon a time I loved it. Lived for it. But now?' I pushed my hands through my hair. 'Now I hate it.' I pointed in his face. 'You have made me hate it. Pushing me. Always pushing me.' I laughed. 'I'm not a damn soldier, Dad. Not one of your squaddies you can bark orders at and I'll fall in line.' I shook my head. 'You've taken the one thing I loved from me by taking away my fun. My passion. You've ruined it for me. You've ruined me!'

The room was thick with tension as I tried to calm down. I eventually lifted my head to see my dad looking at me. He was stricken. Tears were in his eyes. My heart cracked at seeing my dad, my hero, so hurt by my words. But I couldn't take them back. Anger had me in its hold.

'I . . . I was just trying to help you, Cromwell,' he said, voice cracking. He stared at the tux discarded on the floor. 'I could see your potential, and I just wanted to help.' He shook his head and loosened his tie. My father was always dressed to perfection. Not a thing out of place. 'I have no talent, son. I . . . I can't understand what lives within you. The colors. The music.' He swallowed. 'I was just trying to help.'

'Well you didn't.' I threw my bag over my shoulder. 'You ruined it. You ruined it all.' I pushed past him and threw open the door.

I had just stepped into the corridor when he said, 'I love you, Cromwell. I'm sorry.' But I kept walking, not saying anything in return. I never went home that night, for once getting drunk and staying out with my friends . . .

'He was gone the next day when I came home. Left for the next tour that would last nine months.' A dagger stabbed in my stomach.

284

'Cromwell. You don't have to—'

'It was only four days later when they took him,' I blurted. Now I was talking, I was unable to stop. 'They took him and his men.' I remembered my mum coming in to tell me. I remembered my heart pounding in my chest, so loud I could hear it in my ears. I remembered my legs shaking so much I didn't think I'd be able to walk. And remember my lungs becoming so heavy that I couldn't breathe. And all I could see was my dad's face in the dressing room. When I'd struck him in the heart with my words.

'It was months before they were found.' Bonnie shifted closer and pulled my head to her chest. I wrapped my arms around her waist. I held on, distantly noting the odd sound of her heart underneath my ear. 'There was a knock at the door one day. When my mum answered, it was a man from the army. Mum sent me to my room. But the minute she walked in the door, I knew. I knew the minute I saw my father's dog tags in her hand.'

'Cromwell,' Bonnie said. I heard the sadness in her voice.

'They killed him. They killed them all. And they left them to rot. My dad . . .' I choked on my voice. 'My hero . . . was killed like an animal and left to rot.' I shook my head, holding tighter to Bonnie's warmth. 'And he died thinking I hated him. Hated him for doing all that he could to make my dreams come true.'

'He knew you loved him,' Bonnie said, and I lost it in her arms. 'He knew,' she whispered into my hair, before kissing my head. I fucking fell apart. And Bonnie stayed with me right through it.

When I could breathe again, I said softly, 'I played that night, when we were told. I played that piece . . . the one you just heard.' The pain of that night was still as fresh as three years ago, the colors just as vivid. 'Then I never played again. Classical, that is.'

Bonnie's hand stroked through my hair. 'And the EDM?'

I sighed, feeling the rawness of my chest from the confession. 'I had to play.' I laughed without humor. 'I had no choice. My dad had been right, I needed music like I needed air. But after Dad . . . I couldn't touch another instrument. I couldn't hear classical, never mind play it. Compose. So I turned to EDM.'

I lifted my head and met Bonnie's watery eyes. She ran her finger down my cheek.

'I like EDM because the colors are so bright.' I tried to make her understand. 'It gave me the outlet I needed, a chance to play. But the emotions aren't as strong.' I took Bonnie's hand and placed it over my heart. 'The other music, the classical, it makes my emotions too strong. It consumes me. But it fuels me too. After Dad, I was numb. So numb that I never wanted to feel again. With EDM the process was less . . . everything. I love it. It's music after all. I like it because it doesn't make me feel.'

I smirked. 'Until this summer, when with one insult, you cut that numbness wide open. *Your music has no soul.*'

Bonnie winced. 'I'm sorry. I would never have said that if I'd known.'

I shook my head. 'No. It was the push I needed. I didn't realize it at the time, but it was the start.'

'The start of what?'

'Of the music coming back to me.' I thought back to my mother. 'My mum remarried earlier this year, and it destroyed me. I got lost in the nightclub scene, the girls and the drink.' I felt Bonnie tense. But it was the truth. 'Then Lewis took the job here and contacted me again.'

'Your dad contacted Lewis about you years ago?'

I nodded.

'He loved you.' Bonnie smiled and kissed my hand. 'He loved you so much.'

My vision blurred with tears. 'Yeah.'

Bonnie moved closer still until she lay on the same pillow as me. 'You honor him by being here, Cromwell. By finishing that piece. By playing any instrument you had given up on three years ago.'

'But the way I left things . . .' I tucked my face into Bonnie's neck.

'He sees you now.' I froze. Bonnie wore such conviction on her face. 'I believe that, Cromwell. I believe that with everything I am.'

I kissed her again. Bonnie's lips had started to change in color. A tinge of purple to the previous red. But they were no less beautiful. 'What happened at the hospital?' I asked. Bonnie's face fell. It took my stomach plummeting with it. 'Bonnie?'

'I'm in accelerated failure.' Her words were like bullets to my chest. I opened my mouth to ask her to explain, but she beat me to it. 'It means I have only a short time left until my heart can't take it anymore.' I was frozen, unable to move as I stared into her eyes. Her eyes that held more strength than I'd ever seen in anyone before. 'I won't be able to attend college anymore. In a short while, I'll be too weak to leave this room.' I could hear what she said, but my pulse was slamming in my neck, the blood rushing around my body.

'You gave me back music,' I said. Bonnie blinked at the sudden change in conversation. Then her face melted. I took a deep inhale. 'It was you, Farraday. You gave me back what I'd lost.' I ran my thumb over her bottom lip as her eyes glistened. 'It was you who brought the music back to my heart.' I paused, trying to find the words to say what I meant. I had to settle for, 'You helped my music rediscover its soul.'

'Cromwell,' she murmured and kissed my lips. I could feel her lips tremble. Then her eyes closed and she confessed, 'I'm scared.' My stomach fell and my chest ripped in two. 'I'm scared, Cromwell. I thought I had more time.' Her tears tumbled from her eyes and tracked down her cheeks.

My hand fell over her chest where her heart was. I felt its erratic and too-slow beat under my palm. The feel and sound was a pulsing circle of auburn in my mind. She stilled as I touched her. Then she covered my hand. 'How is it possible, Cromwell?' She took in a shallow wheezy breath. 'How can a heart be so damaged, yet feel so impossibly full? How can a heart be failing when it's filled with so much life?'

'I don't know,' I whispered, devastation sweeping through me until it was all that I could feel.

'And how can I live with the sadness of knowing that I won't get to compose with you? That I won't finish what we started?'

'We will finish it.' I held her tighter. 'I don't care if you're bed-bound. But we'll finish.'

Her eyes closed. 'You promise?'

'I swear it,' I said firmly. 'And when you get your heart,

288

we'll hear it performed by the school's orchestra at the end of the year.'

'I won't be able to play anything as we compose,' she said, humiliation lacing her words.

'Then I'll play.'

'I won't be able to write.'

'Then I'll write it for us.'

'Us.' Bonnie smiled. This time there was no sadness in her eyes. 'Us,' she repeated. 'I like the sound of that.' She closed her eyes. 'It sounds like a song.'

'You're the lyricist.'

She nodded. 'It's my dream. To put words to music. To bring them to life. I'm not much of a performer.' I wanted to argue that fact. The night I'd seen her at the coffee house, that's when everything changed. 'But my dream would be to write for others.' She looked to me. 'What's yours?'

'To just make music.' I sighed. 'Music that means something.'

'Wouldn't it be something if our two dreams collided?' I smiled, because I saw it in my head. Saw Bonnie by my side, writing lyrics as I composed the music. Her by my side, bringing life to my notes.

'It would be something,' I echoed. Bonnie yawned. As her eyes began to drift closed, I heard her song, 'Wings,' that I'd layered over my mix. And I smiled.

Us.

'Cromwell?' Bonnie sat up, putting on her pajamas. I watched her. I didn't think I'd ever be able to take my eyes off her again. She lay down, her eyes pulling shut. 'Put your clothes on, Cromwell. Before my papa comes down in the morning and shoots you.'

Despite feeling the rawness in my chest, and despite the fucking ten-ton weight of fear I felt knowing that Bonnie didn't have long until her heart couldn't take anymore, I laughed. Bonnie smiled, eyes still closed, and I dressed. But I lay back on the bed, not even giving one shit about my damp clothes, or the fact that her parents could find us like this in the morning. I pulled her to me as she lay under the comforter, vowing to never let her go.

'Crom?' Bonnie said, her voice laced with sleep. I smiled at the nickname that had just slipped from her lips.

'Mmm?'

'I love you,' she whispered and obliterated what was left of my heart.

'I love you too.'

Music filled my head as I thought of her fight. As I heard her wheezing breath and saw her lips deepening in color through the lack of blood from her heart. It was a melody just for her. To keep her strong. To inspire her to fight.

I knew I'd record it as soon as I went home.

Because she had to survive.

I couldn't take another loss. But the loss of what could be, that was what scared me most. Because I was sure we could be something special.

She just had to survive.

20

Cromwell

Two weeks later . . .

I walked back into the dorm room to darkness. I went over to the curtains and pulled them back. Easton was in bed again. He threw the duvet over his head. 'What the hell, Crom?'

I stood beside his bed and pulled the covers back. Easton whipped around. He stank of alcohol. I'd just got back from sleeping over at Bonnie's, but I knew he'd only just got in.

'Get up. I need your help,' I said, crossing my arms over my chest. I looked at the painting on the easel. Another dark, messed-up piece. I got it. Christ knew I got it. I could see the pain he was in every day as he walked around, lost.

He saw Bonnie, and when he did he was all smiles. Even as she started to fade. As her days at college became less and less frequent. As her legs grew weak and she was forced into a wheelchair, and when her breathing got so bad she needed oxygen through her nose every day. A piece of me died each time I saw her body giving up. And I wanted to scream when I saw the fight in her eyes. As she held my hand, gripping on as hard as she could . . . the once hard grip now as light as a feather.

Easton was getting worse. But Bonnie needed him. Hell, I needed him. He was the only other person who understood all this.

But when he was back here, he was thrashing canvases with black paint or out getting hammered.

'I need you to help me load up my truck.' Easton cracked his eye open. I rubbed the back of my head, my chest pulled tight. At every moment, I felt I was only ever one step from falling the hell apart. 'I'm taking the instruments to her.'

Easton's face fell, and I heard him inhale deeply. He knew what it meant. Bonnie was no longer able to come to college. She was no longer able to do much of anything.

'Please, East.' I knew he would have heard the telltale rasp in my voice. Easton got dressed and followed me to the music building. Lewis had given me permission to work with Bonnie at home. We'd gotten far. But now Bonnie could only lie in her bed and listen. If she tried to pick up a violin her arms would fail. If she tried to play the keys of a piano, her fingers would become too numb for her to move. And, the worst part, if she tried to play the guitar she loved so much, her hands couldn't find the strength to strum.

And her voice. The violet blue. Her passion. Her words . . . they would fade to a whisper, her short breath making it impossible for her to sing. That was the worst of all. Each day she sang. I would lie with her on her bed, and she would sing. And every day the violet blue grew weaker and weaker, fading until it was a diluted sort of lilac. Until there was no pigment left at all.

When the truck was loaded, we made our way to Bonnie's home. Easton didn't talk any more. He hardly smiled. I glanced over at him. He was staring out of the window. I had nothing to say to him. What the hell *did* I say? We all waited, every day, for the call. The call that a heart had been found.

Palliative, Bonnie's mum had explained to me recently. Bonnie was now officially in palliative care. A nurse would come around every day. And I could see the humiliation in Bonnie's eyes as she was cared for. The longing to lift off the bed and walk. To sing and to play.

Just to be well.

We pulled to a stop outside the Farradays' house. Easton didn't move his eyes from the window. 'You okay?' I asked.

Easton turned to me, a vacant look in his eyes. 'Let's get the instruments in to my sister.' He stepped out and began unloading. I followed, carrying a violin, a flute, and a clarinet. As soon as I entered the house, the smell of antiseptic hit me. The entire house now smelled like a hospital.

When I entered Bonnie's room, it didn't matter to me that she was lying on the bed, a plastic tube flowing oxygen into her body through her nose, she was still the most perfect thing I'd ever seen. Mrs Farraday was sitting beside her. Easton put down the drum he was carrying and moved to the bed to kiss Bonnie's forehead.

Bonnie smiled, and the sight of it split my heart wide open. A drip hung from her arm, fluids to help keep her strong now that she couldn't eat or drink very well. She'd lost weight. She'd always been slim, but now she was fading before my eyes.

I suddenly couldn't breathe, tears pricking at my eyes. I turned and went back to the truck to get more instruments. The minute the cool air hit me, I stopped and just breathed it in. Easton came beside me and stopped too. Neither of us said anything. But when he exhaled, his breath shaking, he may as well screamed it from the rooftops.

Bonnie was dying, and there was fuck all we could do.

When I could move again, I took the cello and sax to the bedroom. This time Bonnie was waiting for me, her eyes fixed on the door. As I caught her eyes, a smile so bloody big it lit up the sky pulled on her sallow cheeks.

'Crom . . . well . . .' she stuttered, her voice barely there. I had only left a few hours ago, but when your time was limited, every minute apart was an eternity.

'Farraday,' I said and moved beside her. Her mum was gone, and I'd seen her nurse, Clara, in the kitchen as I'd passed. I brushed back Bonnie's hair. When her eyes looked around the room, they filled with tears. Her purple lips parted and a wheezy exhale slipped from her mouth. 'You . . . brought . . . me . . .' She sucked in a quick breath. Her eyes closed as she fought to simply breathe. 'Music,' she said, her chest rising and falling at double speed as she managed to push out the final word.

'We're getting it done.' I leaned over to kiss her lips. 'I made you a promise.'

Easton appeared on the other side of her bed. He sat down and took her hand in his. I could see the torment in his eyes. And I saw the dark shadow that hung around him like a cloak. The navy blue and graphite evidence of how seeing his sister in this bed was his version of hell.

'I'll leave you to the music.' He looked up at me. 'Cromwell's got you now, okay?' He kissed her hand. 'I'll see you, Bonn.' Easton's voice cut off. The lump in my throat was getting bigger and bigger each day, shutting off my ability to swallow. And right now, seeing Bonnie shed a tear, watching as it rolled down her pale cheek, made it swell so big I couldn't breathe.

Bonnie tried to hold onto him tightly. But I could see she was struggling to move her fingers. Easton stood and kissed her forehead. He looked at me. 'Cromwell.'

'See you, East,' I said, and he left the room.

A sob came from Bonnie, and I was on the bed in two seconds flat, lifting her into my arms. I felt the tears on my neck. She weighed nothing in my arms. 'Don't want . . .' she whispered. I held still while she finished the rest. 'To make him sad.'

My eyes squeezed shut and my jaw clenched. I held her tighter. The piano I played at most days stared at me. I moved my mouth to her ear. 'I wrote something for you.'

I laid Bonnie back on her bed, wiping her tears away with my thumb. 'You have?' she said.

I nodded then kissed her quickly. All our kisses were quick now. But I didn't care. They were no less special. I ran my hand over her hair. 'You are the bravest person I've ever met.' Bonnie blinked, her eyes closing a fraction too long as my words sank in. Her skin was clammy, so I pushed back the long brown hair that framed her face. 'You're going to win, Bonnie. I'm never giving up hope. I wanted to create something to remind you of it, the fight you told me you'd put up. I wrote something for you to play when you lose hope.'

Excitement flared in her eyes. It always did when I played. She reminded me of my dad in those moments. Another person I loved who believed in me so much. Whose greatest joy in life was listening to me play. The loss I felt in these moments were extreme. Because if my dad had met Bonnie . . . he would have loved her.

And she would have loved him.

'You ready?' I said hoarsely, those thoughts stealing away my voice.

Bonnie nodded. She didn't release my hand until I got off the bed to walk across the room. I sat down at the piano and closed my eyes.

My hands started to play the colors that I had committed to memory. The pattern that poured from my soul and whose music filled up the room. A small smile pulled on my lips as I let the images that had inspired this piece spring to mind. Of Bonnie walking ahead of me, holding my hand. Of her smile and pink lips. Her pale skin flushed with color under the weight of the heavy South Carolinian sun. And her, sitting down in the grass with me, overlooking the lake. Canoeists and rowers moving slowly along the water, no urgency or rush. The breeze would flow through her hair and I'd notice the freckles the sun had brought out on her nose and cheeks.

She'd move above me to kiss me. I'd hold her waist, feeling the fabric of her summer dress. And she'd breathe easily as I took her mouth. Her body would be strong. And when I laid my palm over her heart, it would beat a steady, normal rhythm.

Her lungs would breathe in the fresh air.

And she would laugh and run just like everyone else.

Then we'd sit together, in the music room. Her, next to me on the piano. I'd play, and her voice would fill the room with the most vivid violet blue I'd ever seen.

I'd hold her in bed at night, and she'd fall asleep with her head on my arm . . . happy.

My fingers lifted off the piano. I took three deep breaths before I turned around. Bonnie was watching me, a floored look on her face. 'Perfect,' she whispered, shattering my heart. I sat down on the edge of the bed. I took her phone off her bedside table and loaded the piece onto it. 'When you're lonely, when you're feeling down. When you're losing hope. You play this, and get back that strength you've shown me since I first met you in Brighton.'

Bonnie nodded her head. Her finger clumsily pressed play. The piece I'd just played drifted between us. Bonnie closed her eyes and smiled. 'It's like . . .' She worked on her breathing. 'Being on the lake.'

'You like to be on the lake?'

Her eyes opened. And she smiled, ruining me. 'Yes . . . especially in summer.' I nodded my head. 'In a . . . boat.'

I held her hand. 'When you're better, we'll do it.'

She smiled wider. 'Yes.'

Bonnie's eyes closed, and with my music still playing beside her, on repeat, she fell asleep. I stayed beside her until night fell. When Bonnie still didn't wake, I kissed her cheek. 'I'll be back soon.' I got off the bed and walked to the door.

Bonnie's mum stood by the doorway. She smiled at me. 'That was beautiful, Cromwell. The music you played for her.'

I ran my hand around the back of my head. 'Thank you.' I didn't want to ask. I couldn't take it if it was bad, but I asked anyway. 'How long have we got?'

Mrs Farraday stared at her daughter on her bed, listening to the music I'd composed for her. 'I was just speaking to Clara. She thinks it'll only be a few more weeks, maybe a month, before she'll have to be in the hospital.' Mrs Farraday's eyes watered. 'After that . . .' She didn't finish that sentence. I didn't need her to. Because after that, the time we had was only as long as Bonnie's heart could hold out.

'She'll get one,' I said, and Mrs Farraday nodded.

'She'll get one.'

I drove toward home, but I found myself driving in the direction of the clearing Easton had taken me to. I came here most days. Sometimes Easton came too. I pulled my truck to a stop and sat on the grass overlooking the lake. The same canoeist I saw every time was here. The one I believed didn't sleep at night either. Needed physical exercise to exorcise his demons. And at the dock to the right sat a small boat. *It's like being on the lake . . .*

I stared at the moon and its reflection on the water. And I found myself doing something I'd never done before. I prayed. I prayed to a God I'd never spoken to before. But one I was sure had brought Bonnie into my life for a reason. And I had to believe that it wasn't to help me through this, through my rejection of music, only to lose her at the end, knowing she owned my heart as much as the failure owned hers. Completely and irreversibly.

I sat watching the canoeist in the distance until he rowed out of sight into the dark distance beyond. I got to my feet and drove back to the dorms. The place was quiet as I walked to our door. The room was dark inside. I flicked on the light and stopped dead as the smell of paint smacked me in the face.

Black and gray paint had been smeared on all the walls. Easton's posters had been ripped down, the remnants lying on the bed. I stepped further into the room. What the hell had happened?

And then I saw a pair of feet around the side of the wardrobe. I stepped closer, a deep thud starting to slam into my chest.

Then I saw blood.

I moved quickly around the corner. The wind was knocked from my chest and the blood drained from my face as I saw Easton sitting on the floor, slumped against the wall, blood seeping from slashes in his wrists.

'Shit!' I dropped to the floor and covered his wrists with my hand. Warm blood coated my palms. I looked about the room, not knowing what to do. I ran to my bed and pulled off the sheet. I ripped it into strips and tied them around Easton's cuts.

I fumbled for my phone and called 911. 'Ambulance,' I said, my words rushed and panicked. 'My friend has slit his wrists.'

'Is he breathing?' I saw he wasn't unconscious yet. His chest was moving up and down. His eyes rolled around.

I moved my hand to his neck. 'He has a weak pulse.' I gave them the address and dropped my phone. I held Easton in my arms, wrists held up in my hands. 'Easton, what the fuck?' I whispered in his ear. My voice was hoarse with devastation. He lost consciousness just as I heard the ambulance sirens outside.

The paramedics burst into the room and took him from me. I stood and watched, feeling like I was seeing the scene from outside of my body as they got him on a gurney and rushed him from the room. I didn't think; I just ran with them. I rode in the back of the ambulance as they worked on him. And when they burst into the emergency room and through a set of doors I wasn't allowed to go through, I stood in the waiting room, with dozens of eyes set on me.

My hands shook. I looked down; I had blood all over my hands and shirt. I walked out of the doors and into the night air. My hands were still shaking as I took my phone from my pocket, shaking even harder when I brought up Mrs Farraday's name and pressed call.

'Cromwell?' Her surprised, tired voice greeted me. She must have been in bed. It was late.

'It's Easton,' I said, my voice raw. Mrs Farraday went silent on the other end. 'He's in hospital.' I squeezed my eyes shut. 'I don't know if he's going to be okay. There was so much blood . . .' I didn't know what the hell else to say. He'd gone white in the ambulance. He wouldn't wake up.

'We're on our way,' Mrs Farraday's voice hushed out, panicked fear lacing her every word. Then my phone went silent.

I wandered back into the waiting room. I didn't remember anything else until Mrs Farraday came rushing through the door. She darted to the desk, then her eyes fell on me. I got to my feet. Right now I was numb. But I knew what would come next. The emotions would come and smother me, making it impossible for me to breathe.

Mrs Farraday grabbed my arms. Her eyes were huge and rimmed with red. 'Cromwell, where is he?'

I swallowed and looked toward the closed doors. 'They took him through there.' I followed her gaze as it fell to the blood on my hands.

'He slit his wrists,' I said, my voice coming out whether I wanted it to or not. 'I found him in our room. He sliced them open with a knife.'

A choked sound came from behind Mrs Farraday. When I lifted my head, Mr Farraday was there . . . and in a wheelchair in front of him, oxygen mask on her face and IV in her arm, was Bonnie. My heart pounded in my chest, the numbness falling away as I laid eyes on her face. Tears dropped in freefall down her cheeks, and her brown eyes were wide, looking almost too big for her face. Her frail hands shook as they lay in her lap.

'Bonnie.' I stepped closer to her. With every step, more tears fell from Bonnie's eyes. I stopped and looked down at myself. At the blood. Her twin's blood. 'Bonnie,' I whispered. Her mouth opened, but nothing came out.

'Are the parents of Easton Farraday here?' a voice asked from behind us.

The Farradays rushed to the doctor. He led them through the doors I wasn't able to go through. I watched the door close, keeping me out. And then I heard them. The sounds of doors closing, bringing orange to my mind. The sounds of pencils being scratched on paper. The dings of the speakers. The sniffles of crying friends and family members in the waiting room.

I started pacing, trying to push them from my mind. And the numbness that had begun to fall away when I saw

Bonnie shed to the floor in strips of scarlet red. I sat down, hands on my head, as the rush of emotions I knew I'd feel came barreling at me like a freight train.

The sight of Easton on the floor, covered in blood, smashed into my head. I could smell his blood, the tinny scent of metal bursting on my tongue. Pain split into shards in my chest, the spiked fragments blistering my skin. Easton's eyes. The blood pooled on the floor. The black paint. Easton's eyes. Mrs Farraday's voice . . . then . . .

'Bonnie,' I whispered, the memory of her face as she looked at me, as she cowered away from me, was a hammer to my ribs.

I fidgeted on the seat, not knowing where to go or what to do. I didn't know how much time had passed when someone sat beside me. I glanced over, raking my hands through my hair. Mr Farraday was sitting next to me.

I froze, waiting for what he would say. Then his hand came down on my shoulder. 'You saved my son's life.' Relief like nothing I'd ever felt surged through me. But it only heightened the already elevated emotions. I needed to leave. I needed . . . needed . . . I needed music. I needed to get these emotions out of me in the only way I knew how. 'You saved him, son,' Mr Farraday repeated.

I choked on the lump in my throat. I nodded and looked at Mr Farraday. He looked destroyed. He had two kids. One was dying of heart failure. The other had just tried to take his own life.

I couldn't take being here. My heart felt like it was trying to rip from behind my ribs. My skin felt itchy. I needed to leave, but . . .

'Bonnie will be a while yet.' Behind the pain, there was a look of understanding in Mr Farraday's eyes.

'I can't leave her,' I said softly. Because even though I felt like I was coming out of my skin, I wanted to see her. To be sure she didn't blame me somehow. I wanted to hold her hand. It was always cold now. It only ever warmed when I held it.

'Go and get changed. Freshen up. She'll see you soon enough.'

I wanted to burst through the doors that led me to her. I wanted to screw what anyone said and run to Bonnie. Make sure she was okay after her twin tried to kill himself, as all the while she was fighting to stay alive. How the hell did she wrap her head around that?

'Please, Cromwell,' Mr Farraday said. I glanced at him. He was broken. My father's face flashed through my mind. Of how he looked the last night I ever saw him. When I lashed him with my words and ripped apart his soul.

I jumped from the chair and ran out of the door. I drove to the nearest liquor store and bought my old friend, Jack Daniels. I hadn't drunk it in weeks.

I didn't give a shit about the look the cashier gave me as I slammed my fake ID and cash on the counter, covered in blood.

I ripped through Main Street, fighting the emotions that were threatening to consume me. My head pounded, and pressure built behind my eyes. I blasted a mix that beat in time with my heart. Loud bass notes blasted the cabin of the truck. They usually helped me block it all out. All of the fucked-up thoughts of Easton that were rushing in my head. But it didn't help. It didn't drown out the emotions, the feelings that were building in me so strongly that I needed to squash them with alcohol.

I slammed my truck into park. I ignored the stares and the whispers of the students as I stormed up the path to the music room, Jack in hand. I ripped the cap off and took a long sweet swig, waiting for the burn to take the emotions away. To numb them until I could breathe.

I shouldered the door to the building and staggered down the corridor until I entered the music room I usually used. I stood still as the instruments looked back at me. Mocking me. Crying out for me to use them. But anger took hold. Anger and frustration. I was just so damn sick and tired of it all. I took another swig of Jack then flew at the drum kit, knocking the whole thing over with one furious kick.

But it didn't help. A cymbal crashed to the floor, but the emotions were still there, bright and vivid in my head. The neon colors almost blinding, the metallic taste of the pain, of the suffering, the helplessness, leaving the taste of burning acid on my tongue.

I shot out of the door and found myself at Lewis's office. I didn't think; everything in me was just too consuming to think. I pounded on the door, hot tears seeping from the corners of my eyes, scalding my skin. I slammed my fist on the heavy wood, the thuds building in both volume and tempo. Throbbing yellows filled my head. My breath echoed in my ears – olive green. My heart pounded in my chest – tan brown.

I hit the door harder, every sound, every emotion, every taste an assault on the senses. No, not an assault; a damn near air strike, obliterating everything in its path.

The door flew open and I fell into the room. Lewis was suddenly before me, eyes wide and staring at me in horror. 'Christ, Cromwell! What happened?' I pushed him off and started to pace the room. I downed some more Jack, half the bottle gone. But this time the emotions were too strong for me to fend off.

I threw the bottle against the wall, hearing the glass smash and shatter. Tarnished gold spots sailed through my mind. I gripped my hair, pulling at the strands. I hit at my head until Lewis pulled my wrists away. He held them tight and made me look into his eyes.

'Cromwell.' His voice was harsh and strict. 'Calm down.'

The fight drained from me, leaving only the florescent print of everything I was fighting in my mind. My tongue ring rolled in my mouth, trying to rid it of the bitterness.

'Cromwell!' Lewis shook me, and my shoulders sagged.

'I can't take them,' I said, my voice breaking. Lewis's eyes saddened. I stared down at the blood still on my hands. I hadn't even washed off Easton's blood. 'He tried to kill himself.' My voice was shaking. I squeezed my eyes shut. 'She's dying.' I palmed my eyes, trying to take away the navy blue pigment that washed over any other color in my mind. A navy canvas, blotting out everything else.

I fucking hated navy blue.

'She's waiting on a heart. But I don't think it's coming.' Lewis's hold slackened, but he didn't let me go. I stared at the painting of brightly colored swirls on his wall. 'She's getting weaker and weaker every day.' I shook my head, seeing Bonnie at the hospital. Being wheeled toward me, eyes sunken and huge. She looked so weak.

She looked like she was losing the fight.

'She's going to die,' I whispered again. Pain so strong and blue so dark drilled themselves into my every cell, knocking the air from my lungs. 'She made me want to play again.' I smacked my fist over my chest . . . over my still-working heart. 'She made me listen to the music inside me again. She made me play. She inspired me . . . She made me *me* again.' I swallowed the lump that I was sick of feeling. 'She can't die.' All the fight drained from my body. 'I love her. She's my silver.'

The emotions rose higher again, like a tsunami ready to demolish an unsuspecting shore. Then Lewis was leading me somewhere, his hand on my arm. I didn't even register where we were going until I blinked and we were in a music studio. Only this was better than any I'd seen since I'd gotten here. I looked around the polished room, at the instruments perfectly laid out and ready to play. They were all new and high spec. And then my eyes drifted to a grand piano in the corner. The glossy black finish was like a magnet to me. My feet were moving across the light wooden floor. I felt I was gliding as I arrived at the piano I'd played on numerous times in concert as a kid. As packed theaters heard me play . . . as my dad stood in the wings and watched his synesthete son share the colors of his soul.

'You must play,' Lewis said. He was standing in the center of the room, watching me. In this moment, he looked like the composer I'd watched all those years ago in the Albert Hall.

Tyler Lewis.

I winced as the emotions took their hold. My head felt like it was in a vice, pounding, throbbing. 'Release them,' he said. I let his voice hit my ears.

His voice was burgundy.

I liked burgundy.

My hands spread on the keys. The minute I felt the cold of the ivories under my fingertips, everything calmed. I kept my eyes closed as everything from tonight morphed from images into colors. Into shapes that danced and shimmered, stabbed and flexed.

And I followed them, just like my heart told me to. With every key, with every chord played, the emotions lessened. I played and played until I no longer thought. I let the music lead me, eyes closed, into the dark. I breathed, my chest relaxing. My muscles became one with the piano, the tension seeping from the fibers into the melody. And with the sonata that was materializing in this music room, the emotions were appeased. My head lost its ache as the notes danced and scattered into the air, lifting their burden from my body.

I played and I played until the music chose to end, and I was replete.

I breathed. I inhaled and exhaled, in and out, until my hands chose to fall to my side. I blinked my eyes open and stared at the black and white keys. Despite tonight, despite the pain and sadness that I knew was only going to get worse, I smiled.

Bonnie would have loved that smile.

When I looked up, Lewis was still standing where he had been when I started playing. Only his expression was something else entirely. And his eyes were wet.

'That, Cromwell,' he said, voice hoarse, 'was why I wanted you here, at this school.' He took a step closer. 'I've never heard anything like that, son. Not in all my years of composing and conducting have I heard anything as raw, as *real,* as I just witnessed.'

He came to the piano and leaned on its top. He was silent. I stared down at the piano, running my hands over the black gloss.

'I want this,' I whispered, and felt the final string that tightly bound my passion for chords and melodies, rhapsodies and symphonies, break free. The lump that had been clogging my throat all but disappeared. I breathed, and I felt my lungs truly exhale for the first time in years – maybe even since before I lost my dad – because this was my choice.

The music had been screaming at me to compose from the minute I was born . . . and now I was ready to listen. 'I want this,' I said louder, with a conviction I hadn't ever had before. I looked up at Lewis. 'I need to do this.' I needed to create. Compose.

Then I thought of tonight, and the story this Steinway had just told. I felt the sadness well up inside me, clawing its way to the surface. My finger dropped to a single key, and I pressed on the E. E, I always liked. It was mint green.

'He slit his wrists.' I moved on to the G. 'Bonnie's brother, Easton. He tried to kill himself tonight.' A scale started as I walked my way up the keys. 'I found him.' My voice sounded like razor blades.

'Is he . . . ?'

'He's stable. That's what his dad said.' Scale after scale tapped its way along the piano. I put my free hand on my chest. 'The emotions . . .' I shook my head, not knowing how to explain it.

'They consumed you,' Lewis said. 'Broke you.'

My hand froze on the keys. I met his eyes. 'Yeah.' I drowned in confusion. He'd understood.

Lewis pulled an orchestra chair beside me. His fingers found their way to the keys too. I watched as his hands moved as if of their own accord. I saw the colors in my mind. So I started playing similar colors that meshed. I played a harmony. Lewis's lip hooked into a smirk. I followed his cues. Spectrums refracted in my mind. And I chased them until Lewis pulled his hands back and dropped them to his lap.

He sighed. 'It's how I started drinking. Taking the drugs.' He tapped his head, then his chest. 'The emotions. The colors I would feel when things went wrong.' He shook his head. 'I couldn't cope. I used alcohol to numb the pain. And my life spiraled from there.'

'Your emotions get heightened too?' I stared at him, floored.

Lewis nodded. 'I taste it too. And see colors.'

'I didn't think synesthetes ever had such similar symptoms.' Lewis nodded. I felt a lightness in my chest I couldn't describe. Because someone else knew. He understood. All of it. All of what sometimes buried me in so many sensations that I shut down. Built high walls to fortress the feelings. Who I really was.

Lewis closed his eyes, inhaled, then took something from his jacket's inner pocket. He placed a silver hip flask on the top of the piano.

'It's whiskey,' he said, staring at the hip flask. 'I've been sober three years.'

I just listened.

'When I was asked to compose for the gala in a couple of months, I thought I could do it. I thought I'd mastered my demons.' He flicked his chin in the direction of the liquor. 'I thought I had a grip on the emotions that rose in me when I played. When the colors came.' He laughed without humor. 'When I opened up my soul.'

His gaze dropped to the piano keys. He played a single F note, the sound and bright pink hexagon vibrating in the air. 'But I have too many regrets, Cromwell. Too many ghosts in my past that I'll never escape from. The ones that always come and find me whenever I compose. Because they are what lives within me. My music wouldn't be honest if I didn't leave everything on the sheets of music.' He ran his finger down the filigree pattern on the flask. 'But I can't handle the emotions that come because of my synesthesia. I was stupid to think they wouldn't resurface.'

'Have you drunk any?'

'Not yet.' He laughed again, but it sounded more like he was choking. 'I just carry it around with me. To prove to myself that I can resist it.' Before I could say anything, he said, 'I'm not composing at The National Philharmonic's Gala.'

I frowned. Then Lewis turned to me. 'I told them I had someone else who could debut instead.' As mentally exhausted as I was, it took me a few seconds to realize what he was getting at. A dormant heat that lived in my blood sparked to life as his words sank in. Shivers broke out along my skin and I felt my pulse race. 'The way you just played . . .' He shook his head. 'It's up to you, Cromwell. But if you want it, the place is yours. The program director remembered you from your youth. They now want you more than me. The musical genius who just one day stopped playing, making his big return.'

My heart slammed in my chest. 'There's not enough time. It's too soon. And I'd have to compose an entire symphony. I –'

'I'll help you.'

I looked at him curiously. 'Why do you want to help me so much? It can't all be to repay my father.'

Lewis glanced away, then facing me again, said, 'Let's just say that I have a lot of errors I need to amend. It's one of my twelve steps.' He went quiet, and I wondered what he was thinking. 'But it's also because I want to, Cromwell. I want to help you compose.'

Adrenaline pulsed through me at the thought of being back on a stage, an orchestra surrounding me, giving life to my creations. But then ice cooled that excitement. 'Bonnie . . . I don't know what's going to happen. I don't . . .' My jaw clenched when I pictured her on her bed. Then in the wheelchair, and her face when she saw Easton's blood on me. 'I don't know if I can.'

Lewis's hand came down on my shoulder. 'You don't have to make decisions now.' He shook his head, and his hand slipped away. 'I shouldn't have asked you right now. It was insensitive.'

'No,' I argued. 'It wasn't . . . I just . . .'

'Take your time. They'll hold the place open for a while longer.' I nodded. Then I looked down at myself. I was covered in blood. My hands . . .

'The keys,' I said, not knowing what the hell else to say. I had left some blood on the keys. On a Steinway. I grabbed my shirt and started rubbing at them to get them clean. But the blood on the shirt only made it worse. Lewis put his hand on my arm and stopped me.

I was shaking again. I closed my eyes and took a deep breath, pulling myself together.

'I'll fix it, Cromwell. Get yourself home and cleaned up.'

I opened my eyes and walked to the door. Just as I was about to leave, I turned to Lewis, who was staring at the flask. 'It was good,' I said gruffly. 'To talk to someone who understands.'

He smiled. 'Or just anyone at all.' I nodded as Lewis stared back at the flask. 'Your mother was always that person for me.'

My eyebrows pulled down. 'My mum?'

'Yeah. She never told you I knew her?' His face paled a little. Like he'd just shared something he shouldn't have. I shook my head. I had no clue what he was talking about. 'We went to college together. That's how she knew me. How your father knew to contact me.'

'She never said.' I wondered why she hadn't. Then again, I had never asked her. Just assumed she'd heard of him from the world I was in. But there was no space in my mind to wonder any more about that tonight.

'Night, Professor.' I left him in the room with his demons and temptation. I walked back to the dorm, my feet feeling like heavy weights. When I got back to the room, it had been cleaned, I assumed by the college's cleaning staff. Only faint stains remained on the wooden floor where Easton's blood had pooled. The debris he'd thrown around the room had been swept up. I showered then sat on the edge of the bed and looked at the black paint he'd thrown on the walls. At the swirling eyes that he'd drawn every few feet. Eyes that watched every move you made.

Exhaustion wrapped around me, and I lay down in my bed. I pulled out my phone, brought up Bonnie's name, and sent her a simple message:

I love you.

Simple. Yet, to me, it meant the world.

I blinked awake to the sound of knocking at my door. I rubbed my eyes and threw back the cover. Light from the sun sliced into the room around the edges of the thick curtains. Birds were singing.

I opened the door, and I stilled. Bonnie sat in her chair, looking at me. I swallowed. 'Farraday,' I rasped. At the end of the corridor, Mr Farraday was walking away. He gave me a tight smile.

A hand slid into mine. Bonnie was looking up at me, her eyes tired, her lips shaking. 'Bonnie,' I whispered and held her hand tight. I only let go so I could move to the back of her chair and push her into the room. As I shut the door, I heard a tiny gasp slip from Bonnie's mouth.

My stomach sank. Bonnie's hand moved to her mouth as she stared at the black-smeared wall. I tried to move around her to stop her from looking to the right. But I didn't make it in time. Silent tears tracked down Bonnie's cheeks when she saw the bloodstained floor.

I grabbed the blanket off my bed and covered the floor. I bent down to Bonnie and lifted her chin with my finger. Her gaze finally ripped away from that corner. 'You don't need to see that.'

Bonnie nodded her head. But when it fell forward and

she buried it into my neck, she unloaded everything. The sobs, the pain . . . everything.

I held her tight, feeling the rising emotions I could never fight off. She cried so much that she suddenly struggled to breathe. I cupped her face and pulled her back from me. Her cheeks were mottled and her skin was turning white from too little air. 'Breathe, baby,' I said. Panic swelled inside me, but I kept it under control as Bonnie started trying to take deep breaths.

It took minutes for her to calm enough for her breathing to return to what now passed as normal.

'You okay?' I asked. Bonnie nodded. Her eyes were dull with exhaustion. 'Come to bed.' I made sure the chair was close enough to the bed so that her IV and oxygen would be okay, then I picked her up. Her arms draped weakly around my neck. I paused, just drinking in her face. How pretty she was. Bonnie turned her face to me and gave me a small smile. She killed me then. Killed me with one simple smile.

Leaning in, I kissed her, lingering as long as I could before she needed to breathe. When I pulled back, I saw her lips tremble. 'I got you,' I said, hoping she knew that I meant more than just right now.

I laid Bonnie down on the bed and crawled beside her. She was wearing leggings and a sweater, and her hair was in a plait down her back. She couldn't have looked more beautiful if she tried.

I wanted to say something as her brown eyes stared into mine. But I didn't know what to say. My heart beat at a million miles an hour. Then she whispered, 'Thank you.'

Bonnie moved her tired arm to my chest and shuffled closer to me. 'You . . . saved him.' My eyes closed. 'No,' she said, more firmly than I'd heard her speak in a while. I opened my eyes. Her hand lifted to my cheek. 'I love to see your eyes.'

'Bonnie.' I shook my head. 'Is he okay?'

Bonnie's expression changed. She stared over my shoulder. 'East is bipolar.' I stopped breathing, everything stilling. My lips parted, and Bonnie continued. 'He has always found life . . . hard. But . . . he'd been better lately.'

'Bipolar.' I thought of his bright painting when I first arrived. The shouting over the mic in the Barn. The late nights. The drinking. The crazy behavior . . . then the darkness. The way the color around him changed from purples and greens to blacks and grays. His paintings. Him unable to get out of bed.

'He's good at pretending he's okay.' I faced Bonnie again and thought of his wide smiles around her, but his moods when he was here. Bonnie's eyes dropped. I threaded my fingers through hers. She stared at the entwined hands. 'He's tried before.'

I froze. Bonnie held it together, showing the strength she had inside her, even if her eyes screamed out their pain. 'His leather cuffs.'

Realization dawned. 'He'd slit his wrists before?'

Bonnie nodded. 'He gets moments of extreme highs and horrific lows. When the lows hit, it's the worst. He's been up and down for years. But he's been doing so much better lately.' Her shallow inhale was labored. 'He's admitted to being off his meds. He said he found them stifling, creatively. But he's back on them now. He needs them to keep his moods even.'

We sat in silence for five minutes while she took a

break. While she fought harder to breathe. I held her the whole time, just memorizing this moment. What she felt like beside me. Here, right now.

Everything that was her.

'He's stable.' I relaxed as she spoke those words. Then Bonnie was looking into my eyes. Her lips trembled and her eyes glistened. 'You were sent to me.' She smiled, purple lips spread wide. 'To get me through this.' My vision blurred at her words. 'Or to have shown me . . . how this felt.' I stilled. 'Love . . . before it is too late.'

'No.' I pulled her closer. I wanted to pull her so close that the strength of my heart could breathe life into hers. 'You're going to get a heart, Bonnie. I refuse to think otherwise.'

Bonnie's sad smile ripped my chest in half. 'It is . . . getting harder.' She closed her eyes and breathed. Her chest rattled, and the movements were erratic. When her eyes opened again, she said, 'I am fighting. I will keep on fighting . . . But if I have to, I can go . . . knowing how this felt.' She stroked my face, ran her finger over my lips. 'What it felt like to love you. To know you . . . to hear your soul through your music.'

I shook my head, not wanting to hear it. 'I won't lose you,' I said and kissed her forehead. I inhaled her peach and vanilla scent. I tasted her addictive sweetness on my tongue. 'I can't live without you.'

'Cromwell . . .' I met Bonnie's eyes. She swallowed. 'Even if I get a heart . . . it is not always the answer.'

'What do you mean?'

'My body could reject it.' I shook my head, refusing to believe it. 'Then there's how long I can live beyond the surgery. Some people only live a year . . . some can live between five and ten.' She lifted her chin. 'And . . . some can live for twenty-five years or more.' She lowered her eyes. 'We won't know until we know.'

'Then you'll live beyond twenty-five years. You'll do it, Bonnie. You'll sing again. You'll breathe and run and play your guitar.'

Bonnie tucked her head into me, and I heard her soft cries. So I held her tight. After a while the quiet hum of the oxygen machine and her starved breaths were the soundtrack to the moment. Until her breaths evened out, and she fell asleep in my arms.

But I didn't sleep.

An opening sonata started playing in my head, keeping me awake. I closed my eyes and listened to the music telling me the story of us. Watched the colors dance like fireworks on the fifth of November. With Bonnie's scent in my nose and her taste on my tongue, I let the symphony wash over me. I let it keep me warm.

We stayed that way for hours, until sleep claimed me too.

When I woke, it was with Bonnie in my arms . . . exactly where she was forever meant to be.

21

Bonnie

Two weeks later . . .

'I like it . . .' I said as Cromwell played the violin at the end of the bed. I watched his bow work, mesmerized at how somebody could play such an array of instruments so well.

My stomach tensed as I tried to breathe through my tight chest. But it didn't help. Cromwell closed his eyes and played the passage we had just written again. I said 'we,' but in reality it was all him. I couldn't fool myself when it came to composing with someone like Cromwell. He took the lead. How could he not, when all he had to do was follow his heart?

And I was tired. I was so tired. In the last ten days, I hadn't left my bed once. I glanced down to my legs. They were thin on the bed. I was unable to move. Yet Cromwell came every day. He kissed me as much as he could, held me against him when I was cold.

I sometimes wondered if my heart felt it too. Felt what my soul felt when he whispered in my ear how much he loved me. How much he adored me. And how I was going to get through this.

I wanted to believe that. I did. But I'd never realized I would get this tired. I'd never realized I would feel so much pain. But when I looked into Cromwell's eyes, my mama's and papa's eyes, and when I thought of Easton, I knew I had to hold on.

I couldn't lose them.

The sound of a car door opening came from outside. Cromwell paused in jotting down notes on our sheet music. My fingers tingled, knowing who it would be. Easton was coming home today. He had been at a rehab center just outside of Charleston that his therapist recommended. One that could help him get back to a safe place. One that could equip him with the tools he needed to battle his darker thoughts. And I'd missed him. I hadn't seen him except that first night at the hospital.

Cromwell stood when the front door opened. My heart seemed to pound in my chest, but it must have been a phantom beat. I knew it didn't have that kind of strength.

Cromwell sat beside me on my bed, holding my hand as the door to my room opened. Easton's head was bowed, and his wrists were bound in bandages. But he was my brother. And he looked just the same as always.

Tears fell down my cheeks as he stood awkwardly in the doorway. He didn't look up. Cromwell released my hand and crossed the room. Easton flicked his gaze up at him, and Cromwell pulled him into his arms. I couldn't help it then. Seeing the two of them there, the victim and his savior, I fell apart. Easton's back shook as Cromwell held him close.

They stayed that way for a few minutes, until Easton lifted his head and his eyes collided with mine. 'Bonn,' he whispered, and his face contorted seeing me in the bed. It was like he couldn't move. So I lifted my hand and held it out for him to take. He wavered, until Cromwell put a hand on his shoulder.

'She's missed you, East,' Cromwell said. I loved that boy so much. So impossibly much.

Easton came slowly, but when he sank to the edge of the bed and took my hand, I pulled him close. Easton hugged me, and I held on, just having him back in my arms. In my world.

'I love you, East.'

'Love you, Bonn.'

I held him for as long as I could. Then my IV beeped and Clara came back into the room. She gave Easton a smile and quickly changed my IV bag. I had to get fluids. But on top of that, I also now had a PICC line in my arm. I could no longer eat, so I needed to get nutrition this way. Easton watched, his eyes still sad. When Clara left, Easton sat on the seat beside my bed. And like he did every day, brazen as he was, Cromwell climbed on my bed beside me and took hold of my hand.

'How are you?' I asked, a lump in my throat.

Easton's eyes shone. His head dropped. 'I'm sorry.' He looked at Cromwell. 'Sorry, Crom.'

I went to speak, but Easton said, 'I just couldn't do it anymore.' He sucked in a breath. I would have taken one in too if I could. 'I'd stopped taking my meds. And it all got on top of me . . .'

I held out my other hand and he took it. 'I . . . I need you,' I whispered.

Easton met my eyes and finally nodded his head. 'I know you do, Bonn.' He gave me a weak smile. 'I'll be here. I promise.'

I exhaled and tried to read his face. He seemed tired, withdrawn. But he was here. Easton leaned forward. 'How are you?' His eyes scanned the machines that had been brought into my room.

'Holding on,' I said, and his face fell. Cromwell kissed my shoulder, his hand gripping mine tighter.

I cast my eyes out of the window. 'What's it like . . . out there?' I never knew a person could miss the sun so much. Miss the wind, and even the rain.

'Nice,' Easton said. I smiled to myself at my brother's one-word answer. I would never have described it that way. I wanted to know what color the leaves on the trees were. If it was cooler than ten days ago. What the lake looked like in the evening now the nights were growing darker.

'Nice,' I said, and Easton smirked.

'So?' Easton asked, a hint of my happy brother shining through his voice. 'What have you been composing?' I didn't think he actually cared, but I loved him for trying.

Cromwell reached into his pocket and pulled out his audio recorder. He always recorded what we played and then transferred it to my cell so I could listen to it. He played the parts we'd created, and even the rough mixes of how all the instrument sections would flow together.

Easton's mouth hung open. 'Was that you playing all those instruments?' he asked Cromwell.

Cromwell's face burst into flames. 'Yes,' I answered for him.

Easton frowned. 'Who wrote the music?'

'Both—'

'Cromwell,' I interrupted. Cromwell looked at me, eyes

narrowed. I couldn't help but smile. 'It's true . . .' This was his work. This was all him.

Easton sat back in his seat and shook his head. 'So the EDM star *is* into classical music.'

Cromwell's mouth twitched. 'It's all right.'

Easton laughed, taking Cromwell's lips from hooked to a full smile. The sound and sight of the happiness lit up my world.

It wasn't long before I fell asleep. When I woke, it was to Clara checking my heartbeat with her stethoscope. 'Still beating?' I asked, our usual joke slipping from my lips.

Clara smiled. 'Still holding on.'

Cromwell and Easton sat across the room. They were talking in low voices, heads close together. Cromwell turned, as if he'd sensed I was awake.

He came over and kissed me. Clara laughed and left the room. He sat on the edge of the bed. 'How are you feeling, baby?'

Baby. He'd just started calling me that. I loved it about as much as I loved him.

'Okay.' I rubbed my hand across my chest.

Cromwell lifted the stethoscope from the side table. 'Can I listen?'

I nodded. Cromwell put the cold stethoscope against my chest and closed his eyes. I watched as they flickered underneath his closed lids. I wondered what he was seeing. What colors and shapes. Then he reached into his pocket and put the small microphone attached to the recorder under the edge of the stethoscope. He stayed that way for a few minutes, then he opened his eyes, moving his head back. Without my having to ask, he played the recording.

I breathed in through my nose, taking in a deep lungful of oxygen as the stuttered, labored sound of my failing heart echoed around the room.

It was practically singing that it was giving up.

'Do Easton's,' I said. Cromwell looked confused, but he did as I asked. The beat was strong. I knew it would be.

'Now yours. I want to hear yours.'

Cromwell put the stethoscope over his heart, but this time he gave me the earbuds. The sound of his beating heart pounded into my ears. And I smiled.

This was the music of his heart.

'Beautiful,' I said.

I could have listened to it all day.

Three days later . . .

'Where are we going?' I asked as Cromwell helped me into my wheelchair. Clara had come into my room an hour ago and had taken me off my food bag from my PICC line. She had attached the small oxygen tank onto my pipe and helped me get dressed.

Cromwell pushed me to the door. My pulse seemed to build up speed as I passed my mama and papa. 'Not too long, okay?' Mama told Cromwell.

'I know. I won't push it.'

'What's happening?'

Cromwell bent down in front of me and laid his palm softly on my cheek. 'We're getting you some fresh air.'

My lips parted as the door opened, revealing a sunny day. I was wrapped up in Cromwell's thick black sweater, a coat, and blankets. But I didn't care if I looked ridiculous. I was going outside. I didn't care where.

I was going *outside*.

Cromwell pushed me out onto the path. He paused. I wondered if he knew I just wanted to feel the light breeze on my face. That I wanted to hear the birds singing in the trees.

His mouth came to my ear. 'You ready?'

'Mmm.'

Cromwell led me to his truck and settled me into the passenger seat. As his face moved past mine, he paused and pressed a single gentle kiss to my lips.

They tingled as he shut the door and got into the driver's seat. He threaded his hand through mine. He never let go as he drove slowly out of my street and onto the country roads.

I stared out of the window, watching the world pass us by. I loved this world. I loved my life. I wasn't sure many people thought that on a day-to-day basis. But it was often my most poignant thought.

I wanted to live. I wanted the possibilities that lay ahead. I wanted to see the countries I'd only ever dreamed of visiting. Cromwell squeezed my hand. I closed my eyes and took in a deep breath. I wanted to hear the music Cromwell would create. I wanted to be beside him, seeing his work come to life.

Cromwell took a right down a country road. The lake was this way. As his truck entered the parking area, I saw a small wooden boat, two oars ready at its side, waiting at the end of the wooden dock.

My blood warmed with affection. I turned to Cromwell. 'A boat . . .'

Cromwell nodded, putting his hooded leather jacket on over his thick black sweater. He looked so handsome like this. 'You said you like to be on the lake.' Half of me melted at the sweetness this gesture held. But the other stilled. Cromwell had said we would do this after my heart came. When I was better.

I wasn't a fool. And nor was he.

The days kept passing. And with every fading minute, I grew weaker and weaker.

The heart may never come. Which meant that this ride would never come. My lip trembled as he looked at me, a sudden rush of fear taking me in its grip.

Cromwell quickly leaned in and pressed his forehead to mine. 'I still believe you'll get the heart, baby. I just wanted to give you this now. Get you out of the house. I'm not giving up.'

The tension in me drained away on hearing the sincerity in his voice. 'Okay,' I whispered back. Cromwell kissed me again and got out of the truck. I was sure I'd never get sick of his kisses. When he opened my door and the cool breeze drifted through, I closed my eyes and just breathed. I could smell the green of the leaves. The freshness of the lake.

And of course I could smell Cromwell. His leather jacket. The musk of the cologne he wore, and the faint smell of cigarette smoke.

'You ready?'

I smiled and nodded my head. Cromwell lifted me out of the truck and picked up my oxygen tank. As we walked slowly down the dock, I neglected looking at the lake for just a few minutes. Instead I stared at Cromwell. At his olive skin. At the stubble on his cheeks. At the blue of his eyes and the long black lashes that framed their unique color.

Despite its weakness, in this moment my heart felt strong. And I was sure that if you were to look into its depths, Cromwell was who you would see. Cromwell must have felt me looking, as he peeked down at me. I wasn't even embarrassed about it. 'You're so handsome . . .' I said, my voice swept away by the breeze.

Cromwell stopped dead. His eyes closed for a moment. Then he leaned down and kissed me again. Butterfly wings fluttered in my chest. When he pulled back, I slipped my hand from around his neck and placed it on his cheek. Telling him without words how I felt.

After all, love was beyond words.

Cromwell stepped into the boat. It rocked slightly as he lowered me onto the seat. I leaned back and took a deep breath. Cromwell laid a blanket around me then took the oars in his hands. 'Do . . . do you know what you're doing?' I asked.

His wide smile took away the small amount of breath I had in my lungs. 'Just thought I'd wing it.' We pulled off onto the lake, and Cromwell quickly got the hang of using the oars. I smiled as we glided along the still water, the oars rippling the water around us. Cromwell met my eyes and winked. I couldn't help but laugh. The sound came out as a wheeze, but even that didn't stop me from cherishing the moment.

I decided I liked this side of Cromwell best. The one where he was free. Where he was funny, no walls guarding his heart. He looked off to the side of the lake, where the trees were thicker, as if they were cocooning us into a private world just for us. And I was struck. Struck that this boy from England, the prince of EDM, was here with me right now. The boy who was born with a melody in his heart and a symphony in his soul was on this, my favorite lake, rowing us along the water like it was the most natural thing in the world.

I hadn't wanted anyone else in my life for fear of what would happen if I lost this fight. But now I was here, with Cromwell, him becoming *my* oar, helping me sail down this lake, I knew it could never have been any other way.

We moved in silence, just the birds singing and the rustling of the leaves as our soundtrack. As a bird sang, I looked up and then at Cromwell. 'Mustard yellow,' he said. I smiled, then looked at the rustling leaves almost touching the lake from an overhanging branch. 'Bronze.'

I pulled the blanket higher over me when a chill started building at my toes. I closed my eyes and listened to the mustard-yellow and bronze notes.

I opened my eyes when I heard the sound of Mozart's Fourth Symphony. Cromwell had stopped rowing and had placed his cell next to him.

I was transported back to our first meeting. When I'd left the club and walked down to the beach in Brighton. I'd always loved the water, and there was something so majestic about the thrashing waves of the sea in Britain. Even in summer it was turbulent and cold.

The calm of Mozart's Clarinet Concerto in A Major had been playing beside me, a stark contrast to what I'd been watching. Then, as turbulent as the waves, Cromwell Dean had staggered down to the beach, Jack Daniels in hand. His troubled eyes had snapped to mine as he heard the music from my phone.

And now, 'Mozart?' I asked and smiled. He must have remembered that meeting too.

'Amadeus and I have reached an understanding.'

'Yeah?'

He nodded. 'We're friends again.'

'Good,' I said in response. But there was more to that word. Because Cromwell was in love with classical music again. He was playing again. I tipped my head to the side as he sat back in his seat. I waited until there was a dip in the symphony to ask, 'What do you want to do with your life, Crom?'

Cromwell sat forward and took my hand. It was as if it gave him strength. A man in a vintage canoe paddled past. Cromwell watched him. 'I always see him here,' he said absently. He shrugged. 'I want it all.' He squeezed my hand tighter. 'I want to create music. That's all I've ever wanted to do.' He smirked. 'I don't have any other talent.'

I wished I had the ability to speak more than a few breathless words. Because I would have told him that he needed no other talent. Because how he created music, his ability, was like nothing I'd ever seen or heard. It was above sheer talent. It was divine. And it was exactly what he was meant to do.

'I like EDM, but I need to compose classical too.' He rubbed his lips together. 'I just want to play. Create. For whoever, wherever, as long as I have music in my life. I love EDM, but I suppose nothing quite gives me the same feeling as classical.' He nodded his head in my direction. 'You were right. Through classical, you tell a story without words. Move people. Inspire them.' He sighed like he had found a glimmer of peace in his tortured soul. 'When I play classical, when I compose . . . it means something. It gives meaning to my life.' He looked at me and paused, as if stopping himself from saying something.

'What?' I tugged on his hand.

He searched my eyes, then said, 'Lewis has offered me his place in the show that's coming to Charleston soon. To compose and show my work.' My eyes widened. If my heart could have raced, it would have kicked into a sprint. Cromwell ducked his head, like he was embarrassed. 'A symphony.' He inhaled, and I saw the weight of what he had carried for three years, with his father, shine in his eyes. 'I wouldn't have long. To compose. But . . .' He could do it. I was sure he already had a symphony in his heart just waiting to burst out.

'You need to do it.' I thought back on all the videos I had seen of him playing as a child. The music that had come to him as naturally as breathing then. What was an even stronger need now. 'You must do it.' I used the little energy I had to lean forward and cup his cheek.

Cromwell looked at me. 'I don't want to leave you.' *In case this is all the time we'll ever have.* I saw the words in his head as vibrantly as he saw color when he heard a simple noise. I thought of the gala – to me, so far away. And I knew that if a heart didn't come, I wouldn't be there to see it.

It was funny. My heart was dying, yet I never felt any pain from it alone. But in that moment, I was sure it was crying at the fact that it might not see Cromwell Dean in his element, on the stage he was born to stand on.

'You . . . you must do it.' Because if I didn't make it,

329

then I would be looking down from the heavens, beside his father, watching as the boy we loved captivated the hearts and minds of everyone in the room.

Cromwell looked at the canoeist. The man nodded his head and silently passed us by. Cromwell watched him go. 'And you?' he asked. 'What do you want to do with your life?'

Cromwell moved my hair from my face. I thought it was just an excuse to touch me, and that brought warmth to my chilly bones. 'Writing is my passion ... I always thought I would perhaps do something with that.' I exhaled a difficult breath. 'Hear my words sung back to me.' It wasn't an overly complex dream. And it had already come true. I held his hands tighter. 'You have already given me that.'

But I had a greater dream in my mind, and it was only now I understood just how unreachable it was. Some might think it simple, or nothing of great importance, but to me, it was the world.

'Bonnie?'

'To be ... married,' I said. 'To have children.' My bottom lip wavered. Because even if a heart came, it could be difficult to have a family. Carrying babies post-surgery brought even more risks, but I knew I would chance it. I felt my lashes grow wet. 'To be forever in love ... and to be forever loved.' I gave a watery smile. 'That is now my dream.' When the threat of death hung over you, you realized that your true dreams weren't so grand. And they all came down to one thing – love. Material possessions and idealistic goals faded away like a dying star. Love was what remained. Life's purpose was to love.

Cromwell brought me to his lap. I melted into his chest, and we drifted that way for a while. 'Crom.'

'Yeah?'

'You have to play the gala.'

Cromwell tensed. It was a few moments before he said, 'I'll do it, if you make me a promise in return.' I looked up into his eyes. Cromwell was waiting for me. 'If you promise you'll be there, watching.' I didn't want to promise that, because the chances of it being possible were slim. And it terrified me to think of it. But when I thought back to Cromwell, slumped at the piano all those weeks ago, tortured over his father, needing to play the music in his heart, but pushing it away so it didn't hurt, I knew I couldn't do it to him.

'I promise,' I said, voice shaking. Cromwell blew out a breath I didn't even know he was holding. 'I promise.' He took my fingers and kissed each one. He brought his lips to my mouth, then my cheeks, my forehead, my nose. He held on to me, as if I'd slip through his hands and drift down the stream if he didn't.

'Cromwell?' I asked when a bird sang again. 'Who has synesthesia? Your mama or your papa?'

Cromwell's dark eyebrows pinched. 'What do you mean?'

'It's genetic . . . isn't it?'

Surprise washed over Cromwell's face. He shook his head. 'It can't be.' He glanced away to the water. 'Mum hasn't got it, and Dad definitely didn't.'

I frowned, suddenly feeling off. 'I must have gotten it wrong.' I was sure I hadn't, but in that case I had no idea how to explain Cromwell.

Cromwell didn't say much after that. He appeared deep in thought. I stayed in his arms, listening to Mozart and picturing him up on that stage. I rubbed at my chest when a pain started to build there. Cromwell put me back on the seat and started making our way back to the dock. But with every stroke of the oars, I felt less and less okay.

Panic rushed through me when my left arm started to go numb. 'Bonnie?' Cromwell said as we reached the dock. He threw the rope around the post on the dock just as pain, so great it winded me, seized control of my left side. I reached over to hold my arm as the ability to breathe was ripped away.

'Bonnie!' Cromwell's voice filtered into my ears as the world tipped on its side. My eyes snapped up, and I saw the sun spearing through the gaps in the trees. The sound of the rustling leaves grew louder, and the birds singing sounded like an opera. Then Cromwell was over me, his blue eyes wide and panicked. 'Bonnie! Baby!'

'Cromwell,' I tried to say. But my energy drained from my body, the world fading into muted tones of gray. Then worst of all, everything went quiet; the music of Cromwell's voice and the living world plunged into silence. I wanted to speak, I wanted to tell him that I loved him. But my world faded to black before I could.

And then a heavy silence took me in its hold.

22

Cromwell

'Bonnie! Bonnie!' I shouted as she slumped in her seat. Her right hand clutched her left arm, and her eyes started to close. Panic rushed through me like a river.

Bonnie's eyes fell on mine, and all I saw was fear staring back at me. Then her eyes shut. 'No! NO!' I shouted and moved over her. My hand searched for her pulse. It wasn't there. I didn't think. I just let instinct rule my actions. I took Bonnie in my arms and carried her to the dock as quickly as I could. I laid her down and started resuscitations, something my dad had made me learn years ago. 'Come on, Bonnie,' I whispered, my blood running cold when her pulse didn't come back.

I kept going, breathing into her mouth, pushing at her chest, when suddenly someone came beside me. I looked up to see the canoeist. 'Call 911!' I shouted, not daring to take my hands off Bonnie. Because she had to live. She couldn't die. 'Tell them she has heart failure. And to hurry!'

It was all a fog. I kept going and going until someone pulled me aside. I fought them to get back to Bonnie. But when arms held me down, stopping me, I looked up. The EMTs were here. 'She's got heart failure,' I said, watching them take Bonnie from the dock and onto a gurney. I sprinted after them and climbed into the back of the ambulance and stayed frozen against the side as the para-medics worked on Bonnie.

Her hand had fallen over the gurney. And that was all I could see. Her limp hand, one that only a short while ago was holding mine. The doors to the ambulance started to close. When I looked up, the man in the canoe was gone.

The ambulance pulled out, and the whole time I stared at Bonnie's hand. I called her parents. I didn't even remember the conversation. I followed the gurney through the hos-pital, as doctors and nurses swarmed around Bonnie like bees. I heard the beeps and whirrs of the machines keeping her alive. And I heard the pounding of my heart in my ears. The colors flew at me like shrapnel, hitting me with every strike. Emotions buried me until I felt like I couldn't breathe. I stayed against the wall, watching Bonnie's hand that still hung over the gurney. I wanted to hold it. Wanted her to know I was here, waiting for her to wake up.

'No!' Bonnie's mother's voice rang out behind me. I turned to see her father and brother coming in behind. Bonnie's mum tried to run to the bed, but Mr Farraday held her back. Easton stood in the doorway, his eyes fixed on his sister, a scarily calm look on his face. Like he wasn't even there. Like he wasn't watching his sister fight for her life.

Tubes and machines were all over Bonnie, drowning her dark hair and slim body. And all the time, I was buried further and further under colors and noises and shapes and feelings. Feelings I didn't want.

I stood there, watching the girl that had brought back my heart fight to save hers. I stood there until I was led away. Mrs Farraday steered me into a room. I blinked when the noises stopped and we were plunged into silence.

A doctor came into the room. I glanced up. Easton was beside me. But his eyes were vacant. His face pale.

Everything seemed to move in slow motion as the doctor started to speak. Only certain words made it through to my brain. *Cardiac arrest . . . terminal . . . no more than a couple of weeks . . . no going home . . . top of the list . . . medical help . . . machines . . .*

The doctor left the room. Bonnie's mother fell into her husband's chest. Crimson red filled my head as her cries filled the room. Mr Farraday reached out for Easton. Easton was pulled into their arms, but he didn't hold them back. He just stood there, eyes vacant, his body eerily still.

Bonnie was dying.

Bonnie was *dying*.

I staggered to the wall, and finally my feet gave out. I hit the floor and felt the shield of numbness drain out of me . . . only to lower my defenses so much that the emotions assaulted me, blanket-bombing me with images of Bonnie slumping in the boat, holding her arm, calling my name . . .

My head fell forward, and the tears I had held back came pouring out. I fucking fell apart on the floor until a pair of arms came around me. I knew it was Mrs Farraday, but I couldn't stop. She was her mother. Getting told her daughter would only have a couple of weeks . . . but I couldn't help it.

Bonnie was it for me. The only one who understood me. I loved her.

And I was going to lose her.

'She's gonna be all right,' Mrs Farraday kept whispering into my ear. But her words were navy blue.

Navy blue. Motherfucking navy blue.

She's gonna be all right.

Navy blue.

My feet were leaden as I walked into the room. The rhythmic beating of the life support machine was deafening. Mrs Farraday's hand squeezed my shoulder as she passed me, shutting the door and leaving us alone. The room stank of chemicals.

I closed my eyes, took a deep breath, and opened them again. My feet edged closer to the bed, and I almost fell down again when I saw Bonnie in the bed. Tubes and machines surrounded her, her eyes closed, depriving me of her light. A chair waited next to her, but I pushed it aside and carefully sat down on the edge of the bed. I took Bonnie's hand in mine.

It was cold.

I pushed her hair from her face. I knew she liked it when I did that. 'Hi, Farraday,' I said, my voice sounding like a scream in the quiet room. I squeezed her hand then leaned over her, careful of the tubes, and kissed her forehead. Her skin was ice cold. My eyes watered. Moving my mouth to her ear, I said, 'You made me a promise, Farraday, and I'm not letting you get out of it.' I squeezed my eyes shut. 'I love you.' My voice cracked on the last word. 'I love you, and I refuse to let you leave me here without you.' I swallowed. 'Just fight, baby. I know your heart is tired. I know you're tired too, but you have to keep fighting.' I paused, pulling myself together. 'The doctor said you're at the top of the list now. You're going to get a heart.' Of course I knew that wasn't guaranteed, but I had to say it. More for myself than for her.

I glanced down at Bonnie's chest. A machine made it rise and fall. It was a perfect rhythm. I kissed Bonnie on the cheek then sat on the chair beside her. I kept tight hold of her hand. Even when I closed my eyes, I didn't let go.

'Son?' A hand on my shoulder woke me up. I blinked, dimmed lights shining above me. Confusion clouded my head, until those clouds dispersed. I found Bonnie on the bed, eyes closed and machines loud. Then I looked down at my fingers still linked through hers.

'It's late, Cromwell.' Mr Farraday nudged his head. 'She's in an induced coma, son. She won't be waking up for a while yet. A few days at least. Her body needs time to get stronger.' I stared at her pretty face, pale and covered in tubes. I wanted to push them all away, but I knew they were keeping her here.

'Go home, son. Get some sleep. Something to eat. You've been here for hours.'

'I don't . . .' I cleared my hoarse throat. 'I don't want to go.'

'I know you don't. But there's nothing we can do now. It's all in God's hands.' He waved his hand for me to follow. I stood and kissed Bonnie on the cheek.

'I love you,' I whispered into her ear. 'I'll be back soon.' I followed Mr Farraday out into the hallway. 'I'm coming back in the morning.' This time I wasn't asking permission. They weren't keeping me away.

Mr Farraday nodded. 'Cromwell, you kept my baby alive until the paramedics got there. I'm not making you go anywhere.'

'My dad was in the army. He taught me.' I didn't know why I said that. It just came out.

I saw the sympathy in Mr Farraday's eyes. And I knew he knew about my dad. 'Then he was a good man.' He squeezed my shoulder again. 'Go. Sleep. And come back tomorrow.'

I turned and headed for the main doors. I wasn't thinking, just letting my feet lead the way. As I stepped into the cool night, I saw someone on a bench in a small garden across the road. As soon as I saw the blond hair, I knew who it was.

I dropped beside Easton on the bench. He didn't say anything as we stared at the statue of an angel in the center of the garden. It was minutes before he rasped, 'She has a couple of weeks, Crom. That's it.'

My stomach tightened, so much that it made me feel sick. 'She'll be good,' I said. But I didn't even convince myself. 'She's at the top of the list now. She'll get a heart.' Easton was silent. I turned to him. 'How are you?'

Easton laughed without humor. 'Still here.'

'She needs you,' I said, worried by his words. 'When she wakes, when they bring her around from the coma, she'll need you.'

Easton nodded. 'Yeah. I know.' He got to his feet. 'I'm going back in.'

'I'll see you tomorrow.'

I watched Easton walk back into the hospital. I stayed staring at the angel. Tonight ran though my head at a million miles an hour. Then one part kept coming back. *Who has synesthesia?* I pulled out my phone and typed the question into my browser. My stomach fell when what Bonnie said was mostly true. I told myself I must be one of the exceptions, but a little voice started whispering in the back of my brain.

You don't look anything like your dad . . . Your mum has blond hair. You have black hair . . . You're tall. Your mum and dad are short . . .

My heart fired like a canon in my chest. Adrenaline rushed through me, and thoughts and memories bombarded my mind. My feet moved to the taxi rank, and I grabbed a cab back to the lake. I went to my truck, not even looking at the lake, where Bonnie had collapsed in front of me. Instead I drove. I drove and drove until my body was exhausted. But my mind wouldn't shut off. Bonnie was dying. She needed a heart. Easton was falling apart, and yet . . . that question . . . that bloody question still stuck in my head.

I slammed my truck to a stop outside my dorm and looked in the rearview mirror.

My eyes were my mum's. My lips were my mum's.

But my hair . . .

'Why are you pushing him on me so much?' I asked my dad.

'Because he understands, son. He understands what it's like to be like you.' He sighed. 'Just give him a chance. I think you'll like him if you get to know him. You should know him, son.'

No. It couldn't be true. It wasn't true. It *couldn't* be.

Hands shaking, I reached into my pocket and pulled out my phone. Everything was too much. Everything, my life, falling apart. I pressed the contact and waited until it connected. 'Cromwell! Baby, are you okay?' My mum's faint South Carolinian accent drifted into my ears.

'Was Dad my real dad?' I blurted.

My mum paused on the other end of the phone. I heard her struggling for words. 'Cromwell . . . what . . . ?'

'Was Dad my real dad? Just answer the question!'

But she didn't. She was silent.

It said everything.

I slammed my hand down to end the call. My pulse was sprinting, and before I knew it I was out of the car. I started running, and I didn't stop until I got to his house on campus.

My fist pounded on the door until it opened. Lewis stood there, dressing gown on, wiping the sleep from his eyes. 'Cromwell?' he said groggily. 'What—?'

'Who had synesthesia, your mum or dad?'

It took him a while for the question to sink in. 'Um . . . my mama had it.' And then he looked at me. He saw me glaring. And I watched the arsehole's face pale.

'How well did you know my mum?' I asked, voice strained.

I didn't think Lewis was going to answer, but then he said, 'Well.' He swallowed. 'Very well.'

I closed my eyes. When I opened them again. I noticed Lewis's black hair. His build. His height. And I knew. I backed away from the door, pain and shock and Bonnie being in a coma all melting into one fucked-up pot.

'Cromwell . . .' Lewis stepped forward.

He was my father. My phone rang in my pocket. I took it out to see my mum's name. He must have seen it too. 'Cromwell, please, I can explain. *We* can explain.'

'Get the hell away from me,' I said, backing over his garden. But he kept coming, and my feet ground to a halt. 'Get away,' I warned again, and I felt something in my chest rip open when I thought of my dad. Of him trying to understand me. My music. The colors . . .

And I wasn't even his.

Lewis kept coming. He came closer and closer, until he was right in front of me. 'Cromwell, please—'

But before he could say any more, I sent my fist flying across his face. His head snapped back. When he turned around, his lip was busted. 'You're nothing,' I spat. 'You're nothing compared to him.' I rushed out of his garden before he could say anything else. I ran and ran, until I found myself back at the lake. But the minute I was back there, all I saw was Bonnie, and whatever was left of my heart shredded into fragments.

I sank down to the dock and hung my feet off the end. My head dropped, and I let everything come out. I couldn't hold it together.

Bonnie.

My dad.

Lewis . . .

Tipping my head back, I stared at the stars in the sky and had never felt so insignificant in my life. I couldn't be here. But I had nowhere else to go.

No. That was a lie.

I drove back to the hospital. When I walked into the waiting room, the Farradays all looked up at me. They hadn't left.

'I'm not leaving her,' I said, voice broken and raw. I knew I must have looked a sight. I knew because Mrs

Farraday stood and took my hand, bringing me back to a seat beside her. Easton came and sat beside me too. The window on the other side of the room showed Bonnie, lying in the bed. So I focused on her. Wishing on the stars I'd just seen that she would pull through.

I needed her, and I wasn't sure what the hell I'd do if I didn't have her in my life. So I would wait. I'd wait for her to wake. And we'd pray for a heart.

Or I was pretty sure I'd lose the beat in mine.

23

Bonnie

Five days later . . .

An incessant beep filled my brain. Its rhythm was unwavering. I wanted to go back to sleep, but when I tried to turn over, my body ached. Everywhere ached. I winced and felt something tickling my nose. I tried to move my hand to scratch it, but something was in my hand. It was warm, and I didn't want it to go. So I tried to hold on.

'Bonnie?' A deeply accented voice drifted into my ears. It made me think of Mozart. My eyes felt gritty as I forced them open. Bright light made me flinch. I blinked until my eyes got used to the light. Things started to become clear. White ceiling. Light in the center of the room. I glanced down. I was in a bed, a pink blanket covering my legs. Then I saw my hand, and the hand it was wrapped in.

I lifted my eyes, confusion thick in my head. But then my gaze collided with a set of blue eyes that immediately stole my breath. 'Cromwell,' I said. No noise left my mouth. I tried to clear my throat, but it hurt to swallow. My free hand tried to lift to my throat, but my arm was weak and I could barely move it.

Panic flared inside me. Cromwell moved to sit on the edge of the bed. I stilled, captivated by him as always, as he brought my hand to his lips. His other hand cupped my

343

face. I wanted to cover it with mine. But I couldn't and I didn't know why.

'Farraday,' he breathed, relief thick in his voice. It made my heart flutter in my chest.

'Cromwell.' My eyes shimmered as I looked around the room. Then I saw my hand on the bed. Wires were coming from it. Panic took me in its hold.

'Shh.' Cromwell brought his lips to my forehead. I immediately stilled, trying my best to calm down. When he pulled back, I studied his face. For some reason I felt like it had been a lifetime since I'd seen him. I searched my mind for the last time he'd been with me, but everything was muddled and unclear.

But as I surveyed him, I knew last time his eyes had been brighter. I knew he hadn't had that much dark stubble on his cheeks, and I knew that his hair, although always messy, had never been this unkempt. He had dark circles under his eyes, and he seemed pale. He was dressed as always in a black knitted sweater and ripped black jeans. I couldn't see his feet, but I knew that heavy black boots would be on them.

And his tattoos and piercings were as prominent as they'd ever been. And I knew one thing above everything else: that I loved him. I was convinced I could have forgotten everything about him but that. That I loved him with all my heart.

Cromwell stroked back my hair. I smiled, the movement familiar. He swallowed. 'We were on the boat, baby. Do you remember?' I searched my head for the memory. Fuzzy images of the lake came back to me. Birds singing and rustling leaves. Cromwell held my hand tighter. 'You had an episode.' Cromwell looked behind him. 'Maybe I should get a doctor. To explain it better. Your parents . . .'

He went to pull away, but I held on. 'You,' I whispered. Cromwell sighed and moved his hand over my heart. He clenched his jaw. 'You had a heart attack, baby.' His broken-voiced words swam around my head on repeat. *Heart attack . . . heart attack . . . heart attack . . .*

Fear and shock quickly took me in their thrall, their heavy weights pressing down, suffocating me. I wanted to climb from the bed and escape the heavy, confusing darkness I felt looming over me. But I couldn't move, so I clung to Cromwell for safety. His finger stroking down my cheek was like water to the fire of fear that blazed inside me. 'You made it through, baby. The doctors kept you going.' He gestured to the machines that hissed and beeped around me. 'You were in an induced coma while you got better. You've been under for five days.' His lip shook. 'We've all been waiting for you to wake up.'

I closed my eyes, trying to stave off the fear that I refused to let take me over. I breathed, feeling the oxygen tube in my nose. When I opened my eyes again, when I saw the dark circles under his eyes, I asked, 'You . . . stayed . . . here?'

I thought I saw Cromwell's eyes shimmer. He leaned in, until it seemed he was everywhere. Blue eyes fixed on mine, showing me in a simple gaze how much he cared. 'Where else would I be?' He gave me a flicker of a smile. 'I've decided that from this day on I go wherever you go.'

Cromwell kissed my lips, and the darkness that had been pressing down on me disappeared. His light chased it away. A tear fell from the corner of my eyes. He wiped it away with his thumb. 'I'd better go and tell the doctor and your parents you're awake.'

He kissed my hand again before walking out of the room. The minute he left, I felt a flash of coldness that I never felt when he was beside me. Cromwell Dean was my warmth. The blazing soul that kept mine tethered to this life.

My eyes drifted around the room. And my heart stuttered when my gaze fell on my guitar in the corner. The keyboard that stood against the wall. The violin that lay on the sofa. This time it wasn't just a simple tear that tracked down my cheek; it was a torrent.

'He played for you every day.' My eyes moved to the doorway. My stomach fell when I saw Easton. His hair was a mess, and I could see the anxiety on his face. 'Easton,' I mouthed, emotion stealing whatever voice I had managed to salvage since I'd awoken.

Easton walked into the room, his fingers brushing over the keyboard. His eyes were shining. 'He hasn't been to school. Just brought these the day after you were brought in. And he played for you all day every day. Papa had to force him to eat and sleep. Then when he had, he was back here, playing for you.' He shook his head. 'I've never seen anything like it, Bonn.' Easton ran his hand down his face. He looked tired. So tired. Guilt assaulted me. 'He's talented, sis. I'll give him that.' He stared at the instruments, lost in thought. 'There was this one piece he kept playing on the keyboard . . .' He huffed a laugh. 'Kept making Mama cry.'

My fight song.

I knew it without any further explanation. I knew that even unconscious, my heart would have heard it too.

Easton came to stand beside me. His gaze dropped, but after a few seconds, his hand threaded into mine. It crushed me to see him so hurt. His bandages were still on his wrists, and I wanted nothing more than to leap from the bed and tell him I was cured. 'Hey, sis,' he whispered, voice broken.

'Hey, you.'

My hand shook. So did his. Easton sat down on the bed. My face crumbled when I saw tears flooding his face. 'Thought I'd lost you, Bonn,' he said hoarsely. I held on to him as tightly as I could.

'Not yet . . .' I said and offered what smile I could. Easton stared out the window. 'I'm gonna make it,' I forced out. Easton nodded, and I ran my finger over his bandage. 'I'll live for us both . . .'

Easton ducked his head, his long blond hair hiding his face. I held him tight as he just sat there with me. Footsteps hurried down the hallway, then my mama burst into the room, my papa following behind. They both hugged me as best they could. When they moved back, I saw Cromwell in the doorway, and despite the fact that my parents were speaking to me, he was all I could see.

He was *my* violet blue.

My favorite-ever note.

The doctor came and checked on me. My heart cracked just that little bit more when he told me I was here to stay. That there would be no going home. And that I was now on the top of the heart donor list. It inspired in me both terror and hope. Hope that I may actually get a heart. And terror as my life was now on a countdown, an hourglass quickly losing sand. But I didn't ask how long I had. I

347

didn't want to know from the doctor. I didn't want to hear things like that delivered from his clinical mouth.

I wanted to hear it from someone I loved.

For a day I fought with tiredness, the residual effects of the induced coma. I thought I was dreaming. My eyes were shut, and I could hear the most beautiful music playing. In fact, I could've been fooled into thinking I was in heaven. But then I opened my eyes and saw the source of the music. Cromwell sat at the keyboard, his hands hypnotizing as he played my song. I listened, my heart listened, as the notes I'd inspired floated into the air and blanketed me in a cocoon. I listened until he played the very last note.

And when he turned, I simply held out my hand. Cromwell smiled, and I melted into the bed. He had rolled his sweater up to his forearms, showing off his tattoos. Today, his knitted sweater was white. He looked beautiful. Cromwell went to sit on the chair beside me. But I shook my head. He slipped his hand in mine and perched on the edge of the bed. But that wasn't enough either. I shifted my body, gritting my teeth at the pain it caused.

'Baby, no,' he said, but I smiled when I saw there was now enough room for him to lie down. He shook his head, but I could see the hint of a smile on his lips too.

'Lie down . . . please.' Cromwell lay on the bed. The doors of my room were shut, and frankly, even if they weren't I wouldn't have cared.

Cromwell's large body felt so perfect next to mine. And for the first time since I'd woken up, I felt warm. I felt safe. Beside Cromwell, I was complete.

'My song,' I managed to whisper, my throat still sore from the ventilator's tube.

Cromwell laid his head on the pillow beside me. 'Your song.' For a brief moment I felt a sense of utter peace. Until I fought to breathe, and I realized I couldn't keep up the feeling for long.

I leaned closer to Cromwell, using his scent and frame for courage. When I met his eyes, I found him already watching me. I swallowed. 'How long?' The minute the question was out, I thought I felt my heart pounding.

Cromwell paled as the words left my mouth. 'Baby.' He shook his head. I held his hand tighter.

'Please . . . I have to know.'

Cromwell shut his eyes. 'No more than a week,' he whispered. I'd thought his words would wound me. I'd thought if the answer was only a short amount of time, it would cripple me. Instead, a strange sense of calm beset me. *A week* . . .

I nodded my head. Cromwell's hand, this time, tightened in mine. It was he who needed the support. Not me. 'They'll get you a heart.' He closed his eyes and kissed my hand. 'I know it.'

But I knew different.

It was funny. After years of praying a heart would come, after wish after wish that I would be healed, now I was here. At the end. Days away from my tired heart being unable to beat once more, it felt freeing to just accept it. To stop the prayers. To stop the wishes. And to embrace the time I had left with the people I loved.

I took a deep breath. 'You must look after Easton for me.'

Cromwell stilled. He shook his head, fighting where I was taking the conversation. 'Don't, baby. Don't talk like this.'

349

'Promise me . . .' I was breathless, the short request taking so much out of me that I already felt exhausted. Cromwell's jaw clenched and he looked away. 'He is fragile . . . but he is stronger . . . than he knows.'

Cromwell's nose flared. He refused to look at me. I lifted my hand and steered his face toward mine.

'Don't,' he whispered brokenly. His lashes grew wet with the start of tears. 'I can't . . . I can't lose you too.'

I rolled my lips to stop myself from falling apart. 'You . . . you won't lose me.' I laid my hand on his heart. 'Not in here.' Cromwell ducked his head. 'Just like your father isn't gone either.' I believed that now. I believed that when someone was so imbedded in your heart, your soul, they never truly left.

A strange look passed over Cromwell's face, then he tucked his head into my neck. I felt the tears pour. So I wrapped my arm around his back and held him close. I stared at the keyboard and violin and knew that he would create music that would change the world. I was as sure of it as I was sure the sun would rise each day. It was the biggest sadness I held. That I wouldn't be beside him to hear it. To watch him perform at sold-out theaters. To see him on podiums, bringing people to their feet.

When Cromwell raised his head, I whispered, 'Promise me . . . Look after him.'

Cromwell, red eyed and cheeks flushed, nodded his head. A weight I didn't know I carried lifted from my shoulders. 'And compose.' Cromwell stilled. I tapped my hand on his chest. 'Don't lose your passion again.'

'You brought it back to me.'

His words were heaven to my ears. I smiled, and I saw

the love in Cromwell's eyes. 'My bag . . .' His eyebrows pulled down in confusion. 'A notebook . . . in my bag.'

Cromwell found the notebook. He went to hand it to me, but I pushed it back at him. 'For you.'

He looked even more confused. I motioned for him to lie back down. He did, settling beside me. 'My words . . .' I said. Realization spread on his face.

'Your songs?'

I nodded. 'The one at the end.' Cromwell ran his eyes over the book filled with my thoughts and dreams and wishes. And I just watched him. I realized I could have watched him for an eternity and never grown tired of it.

I knew when he had reached the last page. I saw his eyes raking first over the words, and then the notes. He didn't say anything, but the shine in his eyes and the words that never came told me enough.

'For . . . us,' I explained and kissed the back of his hand. Cromwell watched every single thing I did, as if he didn't want to miss a single movement I made. A gesture I gave. A word I spoke. I pointed at my old guitar. 'I wanted to sing it for you . . . but I lost my breath before I could.' It was my biggest regret, that I hadn't written this sooner. Clara had helped me. She had written down the words, and I had shown her how to draw the notes.

I wanted to sing this for him someday when I was better. But now . . . at least he had it now.

'Bonnie.' He ran his fingers down the page as though he had been handed the original score of Beethoven's Fifth Symphony to keep.

'You can imagine the music in your head,' I said,

pointing to the simple notes that made up its composition. Nothing fancy. Nothing hard. Just my words and the chords that made me think of him.

'"A Wish For Us,"' he said, reading the title aloud. 'Mmm.'

Cromwell got off the bed and reached for my guitar. My heart kicked to life when he brought it to the edge of the bed. He placed my notebook on the side table and placed his fingers on the neck of the guitar.

I held my breath for a second, waiting for him to play. And when he did, I knew it would sing to my soul like his playing always did. I knew he would play the music as well as anyone ever could.

But I never expected his voice. I never expected the pitch-perfect graveled tone of his singing voice to bring life to my words. I tried to breathe, but the beauty of his voice held any air I could have taken in captive. As I stared at this tattooed and pierced boy with a heart of gold, I wondered how I had been so lucky to have gotten this, at the end. I had made many wishes in my life, but Cromwell had been the wish that I never made. The granted wish that, in the end, was the one I cherished most.

Heart cold and alone, until it heard your song,
No symphony, no choir, not all notes, just one.
With a beat so loud, you brought rhythm to life,
With love so pure you turned dark into light.
For every breath I lost, I gained a smile,
I gave it all, just to sit with you awhile.
As the end grows near, I savor each kiss,
I pray for time, close my eyes and wish.

I wish to have a life with you,
And do the things I dreamed we'd do.
Chase the music, from dawn until dusk,
A wish for me, for you, for us.

You'd take my hand so tightly in yours,
We'd run over hills, over valleys and moors.
You'd kiss me by lakes, by trees and by skies,
I'd breathe you in, words, laughs, loving sighs.
Your fingers in mine would never let go,
I'd love you more than you'd possibly know.
You'd carry me home under stars and the moon,
And lay me down, in your arms, in our room.

I wish to have a life with you,
And do the things I dreamed we'd do.
Chase the music, from dawn until dusk,
A wish for me, for you, for us.

A whispered chance is what I hold dear,
My single last breath grows so very near.
I wish and I wish with all that I am,
And hold onto you for as long as I can.
I never dared hope for a love such as you,
With colors in your soul that you let me see too.
Now that you're here, I vow to hold on,
For the life we dreamed, a life full of song.

I wish to have a life with you,
And do the things I dreamed we'd do.
Chase the music, from dawn until dusk,

A wish for me, for you, for us.
A wish for me, for you, for us.

I listened as the words washed over me. The lyrics that were me and him. That were us. I listened as Cromwell never played a note wrong, his voice expressing more in my lyrics than I could have done.

And I listened as Cromwell Dean, the boy I had seen on a grainy video all those years ago, reached my soul with his voice. As the music stopped, and the moment came to its natural close, I waited until Cromwell looked at me and said, 'You've given me my dream again.' I smiled and replayed his performance in my mind. 'I've heard my words played back to me. The most perfect of songs.'

Cromwell put my guitar down and crawled into bed beside me. He wrapped his arms around me as though he could protect me. As though his hold could fend off the inevitable. I wanted to stay this way forever. 'There's not a part that I regret.' I felt Cromwell still. His body was tense as his lips brushed over my head. 'You . . . Cromwell . . . there's not a part of us that I regret. Not the beginning . . . not the middle . . . and certainly not the end . . .'

I fell asleep like that, waking in his arms too. And I decided it was how I wanted to say goodbye, how I wanted it to be when the day finally came.

Because it was perfect.

He was perfect.

Like this, life was perfect.

And it was how heaven would finally greet me.

24

Cromwell

I walked down the corridor, each step heavier than the one before. And with every breath I took, the more my heart shattered apart. I saw the door closed and heard the low murmur of voices beyond it.

The call had come twenty minutes ago. I had left the hospital to grab a shower. The doctor had been coming to see her, so I said I'd be back soon.

The call told me that the moment I'd been dreading had arrived.

'Son . . .' Mr Farraday had said on the other end of the phone. 'The doctor has just been in . . . It's time.'

I'd known it was soon. Bonnie was weaker than I'd ever seen anyone in my life. The color had disappeared from her face, but for her deep-purple lips.

I knew I was losing her . . . but I just couldn't bring myself to let go.

My hair was wet and I had a lump in my throat that wouldn't go. My feet led me to the room, but I didn't want to arrive. Because if I arrived, it meant this was the end. And I refused to believe it was the end.

My hand hovered over the doorknob. My fingers shook as the knob turned. The room was quiet as I entered, Mr and Mrs Farraday sitting beside Bonnie, her hands in theirs. She was asleep, her pretty face perfect in slumber. I swallowed, my vision blurring with tears as I stared at her.

I couldn't picture her gone.

I didn't know what my life looked like without her, now that she was in it.

I couldn't . . . I couldn't . . .

Mrs Farraday held out her hand. I wasn't sure if my legs would move, but they did. I slipped my hand in hers. She didn't say anything. Tears streamed down her face as her daughter slept peacefully.

As her daughter lay dying.

As the love of my life slipped further from my grasp.

She could already have passed for an angel.

Mr Farraday was on his cell. He shook his head, worry etched across his features. 'He's not answering. I can't get hold of him.'

'Easton?' I asked.

'I told him to come back immediately. He said he was on his way. But he hasn't come and I can't get through to him.' Mr Farraday ran his hand over his face, panic and stress evident in his eyes. 'He went home for a shower. I should have gone with him. I –'

'I'll go find him,' I offered. Then I looked back at Bonnie. 'Is there enough time?' I rasped.

Mrs Farraday's hand clasped mine tighter. 'There's time.'

I ran to my truck. I tried Easton's mobile, but it kept ringing out. I rushed to their house, but he was nowhere to be seen. I jumped back in my truck and flew to the campus. He wasn't in our dorm room, and I tore across the campus, checking the quad, the library, the cafeteria. I couldn't find him anywhere.

'Cromwell!' Matt's voice stopped me in my tracks.

'Have you seen Easton?' I asked before he'd even had a chance to say anything else.

He shook his head. His eyes were downcast. 'How's Bonnie? Is she . . . ?' Sara and Kacey came up behind him. Bryce brought up the rear. I pushed my hand through my hair. 'I need to find Easton,' I said, not knowing where the hell else to look for him, then . . .

I turned and ran when one last place came to my head. I made it to the hidden spot beside the lake in less than five minutes. But as I pulled up, my stomach fell to the ground. It was like I was seeing it from outside my body as I jumped from my truck and followed the flashing blue lights through the trees. I ran and ran, my breath echoing in my ears. My feet faltered when I passed Easton's truck, and when I rounded the corner, only for a policewoman to stop me dead, I saw paramedics wheeling a gurney into an ambulance. My pulse thundered so fast in my head that I struggled to make sense of what was happening. And then I saw the rope dangling from the tree . . .

'No.' Dread washed over me as the ambulance pulled away. 'NO!' I screamed and ran back to my truck. Fear like nothing I'd never known thrashed in my blood. I gripped the steering wheel, my knuckles turning white as I got stopped at every friggin' red light along the way.

I burst through the doors of the hospital and ran and ran until I got to Bonnie's room . . . only to see a police officer talking to Mr and Mrs Farraday outside. My heart was in my mouth as I waited, a statue on the ground, for what would happen next.

Mrs Farraday's hand flew to her mouth, and her knees

gave out. Mr Farraday shook his head, 'No' slipping from his lips as he followed his wife to the floor. My body shook at what I was seeing, at what was sinking into my head.

'Easton . . .' I whispered, dread cutting deep. 'No.' My head shook, and my stomach felt like it had been hit with a lead pole. Mr and Mrs Farraday were ushered to a private room. Mrs Farraday looked at me as they passed, excruciating grief shining in her eyes.

As if by a magnet, my eyes were pulled to the door of Bonnie's room. She was alone. She needed me. I wiped my face and walked numbly to her door. She looked so small on the bed. Tears that I couldn't help but shed spilled over my eyes and crashed to the floor. I moved to Bonnie's bed and took hold of her hand. She stirred, her brown eyes opening and flicking to mine. 'Cromwell,' she said, no voice to her words. 'You're here.'

'Yeah, baby.' I pressed a gentle kiss to her mouth. Her weak hand lifted to my cheek. She must have felt the wetness.

'Don't . . . cry . . .' I leaned into her hand and kissed her palm. 'Stay with me . . .'

'Always,' I replied and sat beside her on the bed. I pulled her close to me and held her in my arms. It wasn't long before Mr and Mrs Farraday walked through the door. They were walking ghosts. I swallowed, and I couldn't fight back the tears. Because in that second I knew.

He hadn't made it.

A doctor followed behind. Bonnie opened her eyes as the doctor addressed her. 'Bonnie, we have a heart.' Bonnie trembled in my arms as the doctor told her what was going to happen. But none of it registered as the truth hit me like a boulder.

Easton . . . it was Easton's heart.

With one glance up at her parents, I saw the truth staring back at me. After that was a rush of activity. A team of doctors came in and started prepping Bonnie. When I could, I held her hand. Her eyes were swirling seas of confusion and fear. Her mum and dad moved to her and gripped her other hand.

'Easton?' I heard her ask, and my heart splintered apart into millions of pieces.

'He's on his way,' her dad said, the lie so needed right now. We all knew Bonnie had to fight. She couldn't know the truth.

'Need . . . him . . .' Bonnie whispered.

'He'll be with you soon,' her mum told her, and I closed my eyes. Because he would be with her soon. More than she knew.

'Cromwell.' I opened my eyes. Mrs Farraday was looking at me, her eyes haunted and broken. She moved aside to clear the path to Bonnie.

Bonnie held her hand out. I moved across the room and took it. Her fingers were so cold. Bonnie smiled at me, and it destroyed my soul. 'A heart . . .' Her smile stretched as wide as it could, her purple lips showing the well of hope that was springing inside her.

'I know, baby,' I said, forcing my smile.

'I'll survive,' she said, more determination in her slight whisper than any shout could boast. 'For us . . .' I closed my eyes and dropped my head to her chest. I heard the labored beat of her heart and remembered the recording of Easton's. Which soon would beat in her chest. I raised my head and stared into her brown eyes. And I knew that that new heart would destroy her when she learned the truth.

The doctors came in. I cupped her face in my hands and kissed her lips one last time. 'I love you, baby,' I whispered as she was wheeled away.

'I love you too,' came her faint reply. Bonnie's parents walked with her as far as they could go. When Bonnie had disappeared though the double doors, I watched, emotions ripping me in two, as Bonnie's parents fell apart for the son they'd just lost.

The son whose heart might just save their daughter's life.

I dropped to the floor, the cold of the wall supporting my back. And I waited. I waited, with hope in my heart, for Bonnie to pull through. Then dread followed, because I wasn't sure how she would ever get over this.

One twin died so one would survive.

My best friend, gone.

The girl who held my heart, fighting for her life.

And me, helpless to do anything to fix it.

25

Cromwell

I stood, staring at her through the glass window. She had a ventilator in again, and chest drains that took the fluid from her body. But I had hope again in my heart.

Because she'd survived the operation. And so far, the doctor told us it was a success. But as I stared at her face, her closed eyes that today the doctor told us should open, I knew it wasn't that easy. Because today she had to wake up and be told that the heart that had so seamlessly melded to her body was that of her best friend, her twin . . . Easton.

I ran my hands down my face and turned to see Bonnie's parents on the sofa. They were holding hands, but their faces were vacant and destroyed. Everything had happened so quickly. Too quickly, so everything was just hitting them now. They'd cried when they'd seen Bonnie brought back from surgery, but they hadn't spoken much.

I had no idea what to say.

I looked at the spot beside me. Where Easton normally stood. My chest constricted as I thought of him. As I thought back to the first day, when Easton had taken me under his wing. As he paraded us through campus, larger than life. His vibrant paintings that had over time dimmed to darkness. And the colors that surrounded him, the bright colors that muted to grays and blacks.

Guilt swam strong in my veins. Because I'd seen the colors fade. But I thought it was because of his sister.

The police had come by today. They had ruled Easton's death a suicide, which we knew. And they'd brought a letter. A letter they had found in his truck, addressed to Bonnie. Mrs Farraday was clutching that letter as if it would somehow bring her son back.

I walked out of the hospital and pulled out my smokes. As I brought one to my mouth, I suddenly stopped. I glanced up at the sunny sky, at the birds singing mustard yellow and the leaves rustling bronze, and threw the cigarette to the ground. In fact, I walked to the bin and threw the whole pack away.

I slumped on a nearby bench, and everything hit me. Emotions built so high within me that they choked me. I wanted to run to the music room and pour it all out. But that made me think of Lewis, and I had to push that anger back down or it would destroy me too.

Patterns of music appeared in my head when I thought back to the first time I played the piano, when the colors showed me the way. I heard violins play pizzicato, heard a flute come in next. Then the piano would lead, telling the story of a musician born. Of a father sitting beside him, spurring him on. I saw my father fade in a solo cello. I squeezed my eyes shut. Then the story continued.

A hand squeezed my shoulder. I started and looked up. 'She's awake,' Mr Farraday said.

I swallowed. 'Does she know?'

He shook his head. 'She comes off the ventilator tonight.' He nodded, showing a strength I admired. 'She'll know soon enough.'

I got to my feet and followed Mr Farraday down the corridor to Bonnie's room in intensive care. I washed my hands and stepped through the door. Bonnie's brown eyes landed on mine. She had a tube down her throat, hiding her lips, but I saw the smile in her eyes.

She'd kept her promise. She'd made it.

'Hey, baby.' Taking hold of her fingers, I leaned close and kissed her forehead. My lips shook, hating that I had knowledge of something that would destroy her. Bonnie's hands tightened in mine. I closed my eyes and fought back the tears that threatened to fall. 'You were so brave, baby,' I said and sat beside her. A tear fell from the corner of her eye.

Her eyes started to close. Tiredness pulling her under. I stayed beside her as long as I could. I waited in the waiting room as her mum and dad visited with her too. Then, when night fell, the doctor made us all wait outside as they took her off the ventilator. When the doctor came back through to get us, I felt a damn canon explode in my chest. I followed her parents to the room. Bonnie's mum ran over to her and gently held her in her arms. Her father followed, and I hung back.

When they moved aside, Bonnie smiled at me. She was covered in machines again, but her smile was huge. I came close, then kissed her on the mouth. Her breathing hitched. 'I love you,' I whispered.

Bonnie mouthed it back. Her eyes lifted to the room again. My heart plummeted. I knew who she was looking for. Her eyebrows pulled down and she blinked, the question clear in her eyes.

Where is Easton?

Her dad stepped forward. 'He couldn't be here,

sweetheart.' He was trying to shield his sadness from her, but it wasn't working. Bonnie watched him like a hawk. Mr Farraday stroked her hair back from her face. But Bonnie looked at her mum slowly falling apart on the chair beside her. Then she looked to me, and her bottom lip trembled. My hands clenched into fists at my side. I felt useless, unable to stop her feeling what I knew she was about to feel.

'Easton?' she said, her voice croaky from the tube. Water brimmed in her eyes. 'Where . . . is he?' I dropped my eyes, unable to watch this unfold. I tried to breathe, but the boulder in my chest wouldn't let me. 'Hurt?' she managed to ask.

Her mum sobbed, unable to keep it held back. Then I looked up and saw that Bonnie was looking at me. I had to go to her. My legs carried me forward and I took her hand.

Mr Farraday stood. 'There was an accident, sweetheart.' His voice broke on the last part.

Her hand shook in mine. 'No.' The tears that had been brimming in her eyes tipped over her lashes and fell down her cheeks. And I watched, as her free hand slid from her mum's and painstakingly slowly made its way to her chest. She closed her eyes over her new heart, and her entire body started to shake. Tear after tear fled down her cheeks and onto her pillow.

I bent down and pressed my forehead to hers. It only made her worse. Wracking sobs fell from her mouth. Mr Farraday had said Easton had had an accident, but I was pretty sure that Bonnie knew the truth.

Easton, for whatever reason, felt displaced in this world. No one knew this better than his twin.

'Bonnie,' I whispered. I closed my eyes and just held

her. Held her as she fell apart. The moment that was meant to be a celebration had turned into a tragedy in her eyes. In all of ours.

I held her that way as she cried so hard I worried something would go wrong. She'd just woken up from major surgery, but I was sure nothing but finding this had all been a nightmare would take away her pain.

Bonnie cried until she fell asleep. I didn't go anywhere. I held her hand, just in case she woke up. Her parents went to the waiting room. They had things to handle with the police and the hospital. I couldn't imagine having to cope with all of this at once. How did you celebrate one child being spared from death only to lose the other in such a devastating way?

Right now I felt numb. But I knew what would come. I couldn't have all of these emotions warring within me and them not bubble to the surface. But for now, I pushed them down as far as I could.

I must have fallen asleep, because I woke to the feel of fingers in my hair. I blinked my eyes open and looked up.

Bonnie was looking at me. But just as before, her eyes were wet and her skin was pale and patchy from crying. 'He took his life . . . didn't he?' Her words were bullets to my heart.

I nodded. There was no point in lying to her. She'd known it from the minute she'd woken up. Bonnie held on to my hand. Even now, only a couple of days after surgery, her grip was stronger.

She was stronger.

I was sure, somewhere, Easton had a flicker of a smile on his face at that fact.

Bonnie breathed in deeply, her lungs filling with such a large amount of air that color immediately sprouted on her cheeks. Her hand took mine with it as it went to her chest. I heard the new heartbeat. The strong and rhythmic heartbeat under my palm.

It was magenta.

When I'd listened to Easton's heart under the stethoscope, it had been magenta.

'I have his heart, don't I?' Bonnie's eyes were closed when she said it. But then they opened and her gaze fixed on me.

'Yes.'

Her face contorted with pain. Something seemed to change in Bonnie at that instant. It was as if I watched her happiness and her soul flee from her body. The color that surrounded her switched from purples and pinks into browns and grays. Even her hand, that had been holding mine so tightly, slackened and pulled away. I tried to take it back, but Bonnie shut down like the gate of a fort.

Impenetrable.

I stayed in her room for two more days. And with every passing second, the Bonnie I knew and loved pulled further and further away. I wanted to cry when I played some Mozart on my phone and she turned to me, eyes vacant, and said, 'Could you please turn that off?'

Bonnie was healing, but her mind was broken. One night, I thought she'd come back to me. She'd awoken at three in the morning, put her hand in mine, and rolled to face me. 'Bonnie . . . ?' I'd whispered.

Her bottom lip shook, her exhausted eyes barely open. 'How can my heart be fixed, but already be broken?' I moved beside her and held her close. Just holding her while she fell apart. It was such a small thing, but in that moment, I'd never felt more useful to anyone in my life.

But the next morning she pulled away from me again. Back to the Bonnie that was trapped in her head, in her pain. The Bonnie that was shutting everyone out. Physically getting stronger, but emotionally falling apart.

The nurses gave me big smiles as I passed by their station on Bonnie's new ward. So far, her body wasn't rejecting the heart and she was doing well, well enough to leave intensive care. I took a deep breath as I approached her new room. Only when I got there, Mr Farraday was standing outside. 'Hi,' I said and moved to open the door.

He stepped into my path. I frowned. His face was pale and sad, filled with regret. 'She's refusing to see anyone, Cromwell.' I heard the words, but they didn't sink in. I tried to move past her dad again. But he only blocked my path once more.

'Let me through.' My voice was low and threatening. I knew it. But I didn't care. I just had to get in there to her.

Mr Farraday shook his head. 'I'm sorry, son. But she's . . . she's finding life real hard at the minute. She doesn't want to see you. Any of us.' I saw the agony on his face. 'I'm just trying to make things better for her, son. Any way I can.'

My jaw clenched and my hands started to shake. They curled into fists. 'Bonnie!' I called, my voice loud enough to draw the attention of everyone in the ward. 'Bonnie!' I screamed. Mr Farraday tried to usher me back. 'BONNIE!' I dodged Mr Farraday and burst through the door to her room.

Bonnie was sitting in bed, her back propped up against

pillows. She was staring out of the window. Then she turned to me. 'Bonnie,' I said and took a step forward. But I froze mid-step when Bonnie looked away. When she turned her back on me completely.

And then they came. The floodgates opened, and all the emotions of the past few weeks came hurtling forward like the heavy crescendo of a bass drum.

I stepped back and back again as I pictured Easton with his wrists slit. Bonnie having a heart attack in my arms. Easton on the gurney, the rope hanging from the tree. Then Bonnie . . . finding out Easton had gone, that his heart now beat as hers.

And I couldn't do it. I couldn't fucking cope. I turned just as two security guards came toward me. I held up my hands. 'I'm going. I'm going!' I risked a glance back at Bonnie, but her back was still to me. I started jogging down the corridor, but before I'd even made it out of the hospital I was at a full sprint. I made it to my truck, all the colors and emotions melding into one. My brain pulsed like a drum. My head ached, pressure behind my eyes so strong I could barely see.

Neon colors were fireworks in my brain, lighting up until I couldn't take it. I slammed my truck into park and practically jumped from the car. I burst through the music building, no plan ahead, just following my feet. My fist pounded on a door.

The door flew open, and Lewis's face was all I could see. I grabbed my head, then, not caring if anyone heard, said, 'I want to do the gala.'

Lewis's mouth fell open, and I saw the shock on his face. I brushed past him and entered his office. 'Bonnie got the heart.' I squeezed my eyes shut. 'Easton killed himself . . .' My voice broke, and sadness crashed over me like a tidal wave. I choked on the memory of the rope, the gurney . . . of Bonnie.

'Cromwell.' Lewis stepped closer.

I pushed out my hand. 'No.' He stopped dead. 'I came to you because no one else understands.' I hit my head with the heel of my hand. 'You see what I see, feel what I feel.' I sucked in a breath. 'I need help.' My hands fell away from me, my body starting to lose energy. 'I need your help with the music. It's building up. The colors. The patterns.' I shook my head. 'The music is too much, too much at once, the colors too bright.'

Lewis came closer again. Just as he reached me, as he held out his hand, I stepped back. I saw his face. I saw the desperation. I saw the need to talk. Then my eyes tracked their way to the hipflask on his desk. The liquor. The dark circles under his eyes. 'I'm not here for anything else.' He froze, then he pushed his hand through his hair. Just like I did. That was another crowbar to my gut. I choked on my voice, but managed, 'I'm here for the music. I don't want to talk about anything else. Just please . . .' My eyes dripped with tears. Bonnie's rejection was spurring me on. If she heard my music, if I played the gala, she'd hear the music was for her. She'd see that I loved her. She'd see she had a life to live for.

With me.

Beside me.

Forever.

I lifted my eyes to Lewis. 'Please . . . help me . . .' I tapped my head. 'Help me put this down in music. Just . . . help me.'

'Okay.' Lewis ran his hand through his hair again. 'But Cromwell, let me explain. Please, just hear me out –'

'I can't,' I choked. 'Not yet.' I shook my head, a cave tunneling in my chest. I tried to breathe, but it felt too hard. 'I can't cope with that too . . . not yet.'

Lewis looked like he wanted to reach for me. His hand was raised, but I couldn't go there. Not yet. 'Okay.' He met my eyes. 'We have little to no time, Cromwell. You ready for this? It'll be days and nights, *endless* days and nights, to get this where it needs to be.'

A sense of purpose so strong settled the storm within me. 'I'm ready.' I sucked in a breath, and this time I could breathe. 'I have it inside me, Professor. I always have.' I closed my eyes, thought of my dad, Bonnie, and the music that had tried to claw its way from my soul for too long. 'I'm ready to compose.' A sudden shift in me seemed to calm my mind, my emotions. 'I'm done with pushing it all away.'

'Then follow me.' Lewis led me to the music room he'd taken me to the night I'd found Easton, wrists slit, in our room. I moved straight to the piano and sat down. My fingers found their place on the keys, and I opened my soul and let the colors fly.

Reds and blues, purples and pinks swarmed around me, engulfing me in a cloud. And I let them fall where they lay, my fingers showing me the way.

Azure.

Peach.

Ochre.

And violet blue.

I would forever chase the violet blue.

26

Bonnie

I stared at the letter in my hand. The letter I hadn't been able to open for days now. My hands shook as I lifted the envelope to my nose. I inhaled the spiced scent that still clung to the paper. Easton. The familiar smell was a dagger to my heart.

His heart.

I pressed the letter to my chest and closed my eyes. The lump that had clogged my throat since I'd woken up swelled as I thought of Easton. His smile. His laugh. The way people were drawn to him like a magnet. Then that Easton washed away, leaving the sad version of my brother that sometimes took him over. The one who was bathed in black and gray paint, forlorn and so down not even the sunniest of days could raise his spirits.

'Easton,' I whispered as I ran my hand over my name on the envelope.

I glanced down at my black dress and black tights. I appealed to my soul to help me make it through, knowing what lay before me today. My first outing into the real world after my surgery.

The final goodbye to the brother who had saved my life. Who had been my life for so long, I wasn't sure how to breathe without him. Music came from the nurses station beyond the door, and I heard the high-pitched notes of laughter.

I wanted to smile at the happiness in their voices. But when I looked down at the envelope, I didn't know if I would ever be able to feel happy again.

I stayed that way for over an hour, just staring at the letter. Finally, when I had mustered up enough courage, I flipped it open and unveiled the letter inside.

My hands shook so hard I wasn't sure I'd be able to read it. But I turned it over and opened it. The letter wasn't long. And before I'd even read a single word, my vision blurred with tears.

I squeezed my eyes shut and tried to breathe. My new heart beat like a drum in my chest. The feeling still shocked me. I wasn't used to hearing such a rhythmic beat. But the beat was strong and loud, and it should have made me feel full of life.

Instead I felt empty.

I took a deep breath and looked down at the words written just for me . . .

Bonnie,

As I write this, I'm looking at the lake we love so much. Have you ever realized how blue it is in the sun? How peaceful? I don't think I've ever looked at the Earth much and saw its beauty.

I'm writing this as you lie in your hospital bed. Papa has just called to let me know that you don't have long left. I don't know if you will ever get this letter. I don't know if you'll make it. And if that's the case, then I'm sure we're together somewhere, somewhere that isn't this world. Somewhere better. Somewhere where there's no pain.

But if by some miracle you get a heart at the last minute, then I wanted to write you this note. And I wanted you to know why I just couldn't do it anymore.

I want you to know that it wasn't because of you. I know you've blamed yourself for so many years, but none of this has ever been about you.

I want to explain how I feel, but I'm not you. I don't have a way with words like you. I never lit up a room like you did. Instead, I always felt like I was on the outside looking in. Looking at everyone else happy and excited for life. But for me, it was the opposite.

I found life hard, Bonnie. Every day, when I took a breath, I felt like I was breathing in tar. Every step I took was like walking in quicksand. I had to keep moving or I would be pulled under.

I fought it. But the truth was, I wanted to sink. I wanted to close my eyes and disappear and stop the fight. The fight to want to live, when for as long as I could remember, all I've wanted is to let go.

When you got sick, it only made me realize the truth – that I just wanted to go. I wanted to fall asleep and never wake up. Because, Bonnie, what is a world if you aren't in it? And if you got your heart, if someone saved your life by giving you what they could no longer use, then know that I'm happy. You might be angry at me. In fact, I know you are. You're my twin. I feel what you feel. But I can't do it anymore. Even as I sit here now, knowing I have only minutes left, I want to go. I've lost the fight to be here anymore.

And I refuse to say goodbye to you, Bonnie. I want to leave it this way. With me at our favorite place, knowing that I'll see you again soon. After you've lived for us both. Lived a life I never could.

Some of us just weren't meant for this world, Bonnie. And I'm one of them. I know you'll mourn me, and if you survive, I'll miss you every day until I see you again.

Because I will see you again, Bonnie. Look up, and I'll always be there with you.

But I have to go now.

Keep strong, sis. Live a life that you love. And when it's your time, I'll be the one to come get you. You know I will.

I love you, Bonn.

Easton.

Wracking sobs tore at my chest, teardrops falling to the letter and smudging the writing. I quickly brushed it with my hand, needing to save every part of this letter. I pulled it closer to my chest, and I was sure, in that minute, that I felt Easton in my heart. Felt him smiling at me, trying to comfort me. I felt him *smile* at me. Smiling because, unknown to him, he became my miracle. He'd taken himself from this world and, unknowingly, had kept me in it.

I held his letter close to my chest until I had no tears left to cry. When my mama and papa came to get me for the funeral, as they wheeled me from the hospital, I kept his letter in my pocket. Close to me. I needed his strength to help me get through today.

The next hour was a blur. Being pushed into a car. Us following the car that held my brother's casket. Lilies spelling out his name in white. When we arrived at the church, my eyes watched the casket as it was pulled from the car. Papa and my uncles surrounded it. And then I saw one person I hadn't seen in days upon days.

Even numb, my heart managed to skip a beat when I caught sight of Cromwell. Cromwell, dressed in a black suit and black tie, his messy hair jet black in the sun. I tried to pull my eyes away from him, but I found that I couldn't. He walked forward and shook my papa's hand. I frowned, wondering where he was going. Then he took one point of the casket, lifting my brother onto his shoulders, taking the burden Easton couldn't carry onto him.

A hand slipped into mine as they started carrying Easton into the church. My mama pushed me behind the procession. I saw people from college in the pews. Bryce, Matt, Sara, Kacey. But I couldn't manage to acknowledge them. I was too busy staring at Cromwell. He walked with such purpose that it broke my heart.

Because I'd pushed him away.

Kept him from me when all he wanted to do was show me how much he loved me.

Loved Easton.

As the service started, I stared blankly at the altar, at the cross hanging on the wall. The pastor spoke, but I didn't listen. Instead, I stared at the casket and replayed Easton's letter in my head. But I did listen when the pastor said, 'And now, we have some music.' I had no idea what was happening, but then Cromwell got up from his seat on the opposite side of the church.

My heart was in my throat as he moved to the piano. I held my breath as his hands splayed on the keys. And then he crushed my heart when the pastor introduced the piece he was going to play . . . 'Wings'.

A familiar melody fluttered out into the cavernous church. I closed my eyes as Cromwell's version of my song began, angelic, and perfect in this moment. Unsung lyrics circled my head, so perfect next to Cromwell's genius:

Some are not meant for this life for too long . . . . Angels they come, it's time to go . . .

No longer caged, now wings of a dove . . .

Tears in my eyes, I give one last glance . . . I lived, and I loved, and danced life's sweet dance . . .

As the music played, a strange kind of contentment flowed through me. Cromwell's complicated passages and chords brought Easton to my heart, letting me know he was at peace now. That he was finally free from the chains that held him captive in this life.

That he was finally happy, and no longer in pain.

When Cromwell stopped playing, I heard the whispers in the church, the shock that Cromwell Dean could play like he just did. Perfectly. And without error.

He played just like he loved.

As Cromwell made his way back to his seat, he caught my eyes, and in that brief clash of gazes, I saw everything he was feeling. I saw it, because seeing him made me feel it too.

He missed me. He was in pain.

My mama reached over and took my hand. I held hers tightly as the service came to a close. The cars took us to the grave, and I let tears track down my cheeks as Easton was lowered into the ground.

I could hardly remember the rest. I knew I was taken back to our house, where the wake was held. But I spent most of it in my room, reading Easton's letter. I stared out at the darkening night and thought of Cromwell. He hadn't come back to the house. I'd wanted him to. But when he didn't come, I felt myself sinking deeper and deeper into despair. I needed the light Cromwell brought to my soul. I needed the color he brought to my world.

'Bonnie?' My mama stood in the doorway. She gave me a small smile. 'You okay?'

I tried to smile back. But the tears betrayed me. I

dropped my head into my hands and cried for it all – Easton, Cromwell . . . everything.

My mama hugged me. 'Cromwell played?' I said. It was a question. A question of how.

'He asked us last week if he could.' Mama's breathing hitched. 'It was beautiful. If Easton had heard it—'

'He heard it,' I said. Mama smiled through her tears. 'He was there today, watching us say goodbye.'

She stroked my hair. 'We need to get you back to the hospital, kiddo.' My heart fell. But I knew it was true. I couldn't be out long. I put on my jacket and let my mama push me to the car. But when she pulled out of the drive-way, I had one place I needed to be. Something was calling me back. And I knew what.

My heart wanted to pay one last visit to its old home. 'Mama?' I asked. 'Could you go past the cemetery first?'

Mama smiled at me and nodded. She understood what it was like for me to be a twin. We were inseparable. Even death would never change it.

When we arrived at the cemetery, my mama pushed me to Easton. As we drew closer, I saw a figure sitting beside the tree that sheltered his grave. Rustling leaves, and birds singing in the branches.

Mustard yellow and bronze.

Cromwell lifted his head when he heard us approach. He jumped to his feet, his hands in his pockets. 'I'm sorry.' I closed my eyes on hearing his voice. His deep, accented rasp instantly warmed my chilled body. I opened my eyes just as he passed me. I didn't think it through. I didn't have a plan. Instead, I let my heart guide me, and I slipped my hand in his.

Cromwell stopped dead. He took a deep breath then looked down at my hand in his. 'Don't go,' I whispered. His shoulders relaxed at my words.

'I'll leave you alone,' Mama said. 'I'll be in the car. Let me know when you want to go to the hospital.'

'I can take her.'

Mama looked to me, a question in her eyes.

I cleared my throat. 'He can take me.'

Cromwell exhaled a long breath. Mama kissed my head, then left us alone. Cromwell kept hold of my hand but stared straight ahead. 'I've missed you,' he whispered, his graveled voice traveling all the way through to my bones.

I inhaled, the cool air bursting in my chest. 'I've missed you too.'

Cromwell looked down at me and tightened his grip. 'You're talking better.' I smiled and nodded. 'I've missed your voice too.'

He kneeled before me, and I met his gaze to see the prettiest of blues staring back at me. His hand cupped my cheek. 'You're so beautiful,' he said. He pointed at the tree. 'Do you want to sit with me?' I nodded, and I held my breath when he scooped me into his arms. He sat down, placing me beside him. The birds sang above us, the branches cradling the spot where Easton lay.

I stared at the flowers that had been laid and the fresh soil that had been poured on top of his coffin. This was the perfect place for him to be.

It was beautiful, just like he had been.

'I'm going to put a bench right here,' I said. 'So that I can always come and see him.' Cromwell turned to look at me, his eyes glistening. 'The way you played for him today . . .' I shook my head. 'It was perfect.'

'It was your song.'

I sighed and looked out over the horizon, at the moon starting to rise. 'I haven't been able to listen to music since he left. It makes me feel too much.' The lump bobbed in my throat. 'I've lost the enjoyment it once brought me.'

Cromwell just listened. Exactly what I needed him to do. Then, 'Lewis is my father.'

I whipped my head to him so quickly that I felt it in my neck. Shock forced its way through me. 'What?'

Cromwell leaned his head back against the trunk of the tree. 'You were right. Synesthesia's genetic.'

'Cromwell . . . I . . .' I shook my head, unable to grasp the truth.

'He knew my mum in college.' He laughed without mirth. 'More than knew. From what I can tell, they were together.'

My fragile heart struggled to comprehend what he was saying. Yet it beat fast, the strength of it making me breathless at what had just fallen from Cromwell's mouth. 'Cromwell . . . ' I murmured. 'I don't know what to say. What . . . what happened with them?'

'I don't know.' He sighed. 'I haven't been able to bring myself to ask him. He wants to tell me. I see it in his eyes every day. He told me he wanted to explain . . . but I can't hear it yet.' He lowered his head, red bursting on his cheeks. When he looked up again, he said, 'But he's been helping me. We've been working together every day.'

I frowned, until it dawned on me. 'You're playing the gala?'

379

A flicker of a smile pulled at his mouth. 'Yeah. And I think . . .' He looked into my eyes. 'I think it's good, baby. The symphony I'm composing . . .'

Baby. The endearment circled my head, only to float down and take up its rightful home in my new heart. As it settled I felt calm. Warm and safe beside the boy I loved.

'Easton wrote me a letter.' I closed my eyes, still feeling the sadness it brought me, but . . . 'He's at rest now.' I tried to smile. 'He's no longer taunted by the demons that took away his joy.' My eyes stayed on his grave. And I wondered if he saw us here now, needing to be with him. Missing him so much it hurt.

I turned to Cromwell. 'What color do you see around his grave?'

Cromwell exhaled. 'White,' he said. 'I see white.'

'And what does that mean to you?' My voice was barely a whisper.

'Peace,' he said, a relieved calm to his voice. 'I see it as peace.'

The final tether that had kept me chained to the grief I couldn't release floated away to the dark sky above us. I leaned against Cromwell, sighing in contentment when he put his arm around me and held me close.

We stayed that way until the night grew cold and I grew tired. 'Come on, baby. Time to get you back.' Cromwell picked me up and led me to the car. He put me in his truck then went back for my chair. Sleep pulled me under, and I didn't wake until I was back in my bed. I opened my eyes to Cromwell kissing my cheek. He met my gaze, a plea in his expression. 'Come to the gala.'

My heart fell. 'I don't know, Cromwell. I don't know if I can.'

'I have to go to Charleston. To work with the orchestra. But please come. I need you to see it. I need to know you're there, in the audience ... the girl who brought music back into my life.'

I went to answer, but before I could, Cromwell leaned down and kissed me. He stole my breath and my heart in that one sweet kiss. He walked to the door, then stopped in the doorway. 'I love you, Bonnie. You've changed my life,' he said without looking back, then he walked away.

I was sure he took my heart with him as his footsteps faded away. And I knew that the only way to get it back was to go to Charleston in a few weeks to see him perform.

My boy, who once again had music in his heart.

27

Cromwell

Several weeks later . . .

I sat back in my seat, closed my eyes, and took a deep breath. My chest was tight, but my heart beat like a heavy drum. Adrenaline rushed through me. A switch had flicked on within me the minute I came to Charleston several weeks ago. When I stepped into the rehearsal room and was faced with a fifty-piece orchestra. The orchestra who would be playing my music at the gala.

Music that *I'd* composed.

I shook my head and took a drink of my Jack. I hadn't drunk in weeks. Stopped smoking that day outside the hospital when I'd thrown my packet of cigarettes into the rubbish bin.

But I needed a few shots of Jack right now.

I got up, taking my Jack with me, and walked out of the dressing room and through the corridor into the theater. The sound of the door closing echoed around the vast space. I stared up at the painted ceiling and down to the rows and rows of red velvet seats. I made my way up onto the stage and moved to the front. I stared out over the theater, and my blood spiked with heat.

I focused on a spot in the center of the theater. The chair I'd reserved for Bonnie. Doubt sat like a lead ball in my stomach. I had barely spoken to her in all these weeks. Christmas and New Year had passed. She'd called me on Christmas Day, sounding like the old Bonnie. Her voice was strong, and she told me her heart was beating hard.

But I could hear the thick lacing of sadness in her voice. She'd barely asked about the music. My music. 'I miss you, Cromwell,' she'd whispered. 'Life just isn't the same without you here.'

'I miss you too, baby,' I'd said in response. I'd paused. 'Please come to the gala. Please . . .'

She hadn't said anything to that. Even now, the night before the show, I didn't know if she was coming. But she had to. She had to hear this piece.

I'd written it for her. Because of her. Everything in my life was now all about her.

I didn't want it any other way.

I jumped off the stage and sat on the chair on the front row. I stared up at the theater, at the background that had been constructed for my performance. I sighed and took a long drink of the Jack.

I closed my eyes, inhaling the scent of the theater. I remembered this smell. Lived for it. *You belong on that stage, son.* My father's voice circled my head. *You'll have them captivated the same way you do me.*

The lump that always came to the surface clogged my throat. Then I felt someone drop down beside me. I opened my eyes and saw Lewis. He'd been with me all these weeks. He'd never left my side. Working with me day and night on my symphony. He hadn't talked to me again about what I'd discovered. Just worked with me, composer to composer, synesthete to synesthete.

He understood me more than I ever could have known. He'd felt every note I'd played. And he felt every emotion my music tried to convey. And better still, he'd supported me when I decided to be different. My piece tomorrow night would divide opinion. I knew it. But it had to be done. It was the story I needed to tell, in the only way I knew how.

'You nervous?' Lewis spoke quietly, yet his voice echoed off the walls of the theater like thunder.

I sighed. I didn't answer him at first, but then said, 'Not about the performance . . .'

'You want Bonnie to be here.'

I clenched my jaw. I wasn't good with letting people in. With showing my emotions. But Lewis had seen me compose. He'd helped me all the way. He knew what my piece was about. There was no point in hiding it from him now.

'Yeah.' I shook my head. 'Not sure she will be. Her mum is trying, but she's still in a bad place.' My stomach dropped in sadness. 'Deep down she loves music. But since Easton, it's been lost, and she doesn't know how to get it back.'

'She sees this,' Lewis said, pointing at the stage that tomorrow would be filled with a full orchestra, lights and . . . me. 'She sees you on that stage, conducting a piece inspired by her, and she'll see. Music will find its way to her again.' I turned to face him when he went quiet. 'I've never seen or heard anything like what you've created, Cromwell.' Lewis's voice was husky, and the sound of it made my stomach tense.

I'd been good these past several weeks. Managed to not think of the truth. Of who he was to me. The composing consumed me. My days and minutes were taken up by notes and strings and crescendos. But right here, right now, I couldn't fight it even if I tried.

'You're better than me.' Lewis laughed. 'It's not easy for a composer to admit that. But it's true . . . and it makes me so goddamned proud.' His voice broke off, and I had to grit my teeth together to stop the lump in my throat from growing. My pulse beat faster.

'I was selfish,' he said, his voice raspy. I gripped my bottle of Jack so tightly I was sure it would smash under my hand. Lewis ran his hand through his hair. 'I was young and had the whole world at my feet.' He inhaled deeply, like he needed the break. 'Your mama was someone I didn't expect.' I dropped my eyes to stare at the floor. 'She walked into my life like a tornado and knocked me on my ass.' My hand shook, the amber liquid sloshing around in the bottle. 'And I fell in love with her. Not just a little bit either. She became my whole world.'

Lewis stopped speaking. His eyes were shut, his face was pinched as if he was in pain. He kept his eyes closed as he said, 'But I had my music . . . and I also had drink and drugs. Your mama didn't know about that until later.' He patted his chest. 'It was the emotions. They helped quell the emotions.'

I looked down at the Jack in my hand. I thought of how it was all I drank when I'd lost my dad. When it all became too much.

'My music was starting to get noticed, and the pressure built. And your mama stayed by my side, helping me by just being there and loving me.' I was frozen as he admitted that. I pictured my mum in my head. I tried to imagine her when she was young and carefree. She'd been so quiet and reserved my whole life. I struggled to understand her, but now I was starting to see it made sense. Lewis broke her heart. For the first time in years I felt like I knew her. Then I thought of Bonnie. Because Bonnie was that person for me. The one I let in. The one who helped me through the emotions when they became too much. The one who believed in me. The one who I'd tried to push away. But she stayed beside me. Right now, I felt sorry for Lewis, because he'd lost his Bonnie. My stomach fell as I thought of the distance between Bonnie and me now. The pain of it was unbearable.

'But the more the music consumed me, the more the alcohol and the drugs became the one real focus in my life.

'It went that way for months, until she found me with the drugs.' His face contorted, and his voice lost strength. 'She begged me to stop, but I didn't. I believed at the time I couldn't, because of the music. But I was selfish. And it has been the biggest regret of my life.' He finally met my eyes. 'Until I found out about you.'

'You left her pregnant?' I asked, the black, simmering anger I was feeling showing in my voice.

'I didn't know she was pregnant at first,' he said. 'I was an addict, Cromwell. And your mama did what was best for you both at the time. And that was not having me in your life.' Lewis ran his hand down his face. He looked exhausted. 'I found out she was carrying you when she was six months along.'

'And?'

He met me square-on, let me see the shame in his eyes.

'Nothing. I did nothing, Cromwell.' He blew out a shaky breath. 'It was the biggest mistake of my life.' He leaned forward, and his gaze became lost on the stage. 'My life was the music. It was all I had. Made myself believe it was all I had. Later, I heard your mama had met someone, a British Army officer, when she was pregnant. He'd been stationed over here in the States.'

I tensed. This was the bit that involved my dad.

'I found out she had moved to England to be with him. That they'd married . . . and that you'd been born. A boy.' He looked at me. 'A son.' His voice cracked, and I saw the tears brimming in his eyes. 'It killed me at the time, but like I did with everything else, I drowned the feeling in liquor and drugs.' He sat back in his seat. 'I toured the world, playing packed-out theaters and creating some of the best music of my life.' He sighed. 'I blocked it all out. Hardly ever went home.'

He clasped his hands together. 'Until one day I did, to see a pile of letters. Letters from England.' My stomach flipped. 'They were from your dad, Cromwell.' I fought back the tears that were threatening to fall. I pictured my dad, and all I could see was royal blue. I saw his smile and felt how it was to be around him. How he'd always made everything so much better. How he'd always prided himself on doing the right thing. He was the best of men.

'They were letters from him, telling me all about you.' A tear fell down his cheek. 'And there were pictures. Pictures of you . . .' The lump in my throat grew thicker and my vision blurred. Lewis shook his head. 'I stared at those pictures for so long that my eyes were strained. You, Cromwell. My little boy, with my coloring, my black hair.'

My heart slammed against my chest. 'I fought for years to get sober after that. It was a battle I didn't get a hold of until you were a lot older.' He went quiet. 'I lived for those letters. I lived for those pictures. They became the only real thing in my life . . . and then, one day, a new letter came. One that had a video inside.' Lewis shook his head. 'I've lost count of how many times I watched that video.'

'What was on it?' I asked, voice graveled.

'You.' Lewis wiped a fallen tear from his cheek. 'You playing the piano. Your father's letter told me that you'd never had lessons. But that you could just play.' His eyes became lost to his memories. 'I watched you play, your hands so skillful . . . and the smile on your face and the light in your eyes, and I felt like I'd been hit by a ten-ton truck. Because, there, on that screen, was my son . . . a music-lover just like me.'

I turned my head away. I didn't know if I could hear this. 'Your father told me of the synesthesia. He knew of my tour to Britain, to the Albert Hall, and asked me something I never thought would happen. He asked me to meet you. To help you . . . he thought I should know you. Because of how special you were.' My head fell forward. My dad had been special too. He'd loved me so much. I wished I'd told him how much I'd loved him when he'd been here.

'He knew you had synesthesia too. He knew you'd be able to help me.' My heart squeezed as I thought of the pride my father would have had to swallow to ask Lewis, the father who didn't want me, for help. But he'd done it.

He'd done it for me.

A tear tracked down my cheek.

'That night,' Lewis said, his voice trembling. 'I'd been sober for a few years . . .' He looked at me. It was the first time I'd really looked at him. And I saw myself in his face. I saw the similarities and the shared features. 'When I saw you . . . my son, standing there in front of me, your mama so gracious in letting me meet you after everything I'd done . . . I went home that night and overdosed so badly that I woke up in the hospital with a permanently damaged liver.'

My eyes widened. Lewis's tears were free-falling now. I couldn't take it. I couldn't take all of this. 'Seeing you showed me how much I'd messed up. And my son, who was more talented than I would ever be, didn't know me. Called someone else Dad.' He wiped his face with his hand. 'It destroyed me. And from that moment on, I made myself a promise. That I would do anything I could to help you . . .' Lewis trailed off, and I knew what happened next. 'Cromwell, when I learned of your father . . .'

'Don't,' I said, unable to hear it.

Lewis nodded, and the silence hung heavily between us. 'I've never met a more honorable man in my life. Your father . . .' I choked on the lump. 'He loved you more than anything in this world. And because of that, he allowed me glimpses into your life – something I didn't deserve. Still don't.'

I dropped my head, and the teardrops from my eyes crashed to the floor. 'He should be here right now,' I choked out. 'Seeing this. Me, tomorrow.'

I felt a hand on my back. I tensed. I almost told him to move it, to fuck off, but I didn't. After everything – after Dad, and Bonnie, and Easton – I just let it happen. I needed it. I needed to know I wasn't on my own. I let it all out. On the theater floor where tomorrow I would conduct, I let everything that had been caged up inside me for so long loose.

When my eyes were swollen and my throat was dry, I lifted my head. Lewis kept his hand where it was. 'I have no right to ask anything of you, Cromwell. And I'll understand if you never want more from me than my help over these past weeks.' I met his eyes and saw the desperation there. 'I'm not a good man like your father. And I could never fill his shoes. But if you ever want me, or need me, or would be gracious enough to let me into your life, even just a little bit . . .' He trailed off, and I knew he was struggling to finish. 'Then . . . that would be the greatest gift I'd ever receive.'

As I looked at Lewis, I realized I was tired. I was tired of letting everything get to me. Of carrying all the sadness in my heart and the anger in my gut. I thought of Bonnie and of Easton, and of everything they'd gone through. Of how Easton couldn't cope. I didn't want that for my life. I'd spent three years choking on the anger and sadness . . . the regret of my last words to my dad, and I didn't want to go there again. Bonnie had shown me a new way to be. And I refused to go back.

I took a deep breath. 'I don't know how much I can give you.' It was the truth. Lewis looked like I'd struck him, but he nodded his head. He went to get up. 'But I can . . . try,' I said and felt a new kind of lightness settle in my chest.

Lewis looked back at me and took a quick inhale. Tears built in his eyes. 'Thank you, son.' He started to walk away.

Son.

Son . . .

'Thank you,' I said as he approached the exit. Lewis turned around, frowning. 'For everything you've done, these past months. I . . . I couldn't have done it without you.'

'I did nothing, son. This was all you. And tomorrow night, it'll be all you again.'

I looked down at the Jack Daniels in my hand. 'Will you be okay? Tomorrow?' I'd asked a favor of Lewis, for the sake of the piece. He'd accepted straight away, without thought.

Lewis looked up at the empty stage, which this time tomorrow would be full of musicians like us. 'I'll be up there beside you, Cromwell.' He gave me a tentative smile. 'I imagine I'll be the most okay I've ever been in my life.'

With that he walked out of the door, leaving me alone with my thoughts. I sat there for another hour, playing the piece in my head, replaying how it looked in rehearsals. Just as I was about to leave, I took out my phone and texted Bonnie.

I hope you come tomorrow, baby. It's all for you. I love you.

I pocketed my mobile and walked back to the hotel. And with every breath, I thought of Bonnie's face, her brown eyes sparkling from my music. And I prayed to God that she'd be there.

Hopefully, with a smile once again on her lips.

28

Bonnie

The line was huge as we pulled up to the venue. I stared out of the window and swallowed my nerves. Cromwell was playing in here tonight. I missed him. I missed him more than I ever thought possible. Every day when he wasn't beside me, I felt it more and more. I missed his deep sea-colored eyes. Missed the way he would push my hair back from my face, and I missed the rare smiles I'd sometimes be blessed with.

I missed his hand holding mine.

I missed his kisses.

I missed his music.

But most of all, I simply missed him.

I hadn't realized until he came to Charleston just how much I needed him in my life. He was the air I breathed, the moon at my night.

Cromwell Dean was my sun.

'You ready, Bonnie?'

I nodded at my mama. She helped me from the back seat and into my chair. I'd started walking more and more now. My physical therapy was going well. In a few more weeks I hoped to be walking all the time.

Easton's heart was meshing well with me. But then, I'd always known that would be the case. My brother would never have seen me wrong.

Mama led us toward the doors. But we headed to a different one from everyone else. I realized it was the VIP entrance. I smiled at the man who took our tickets, then my heart started beating loudly in my chest when we were personally led to our seats.

The theater was full to the brim, not a spare seat to be found. I was breathless as I looked at the stage, hearing the telltale sounds of the orchestra warming up behind the heavy red curtain. A certain electricity buzzed in the air, making goosebumps rise on my skin.

When we arrived at our seats, I looked around at everyone dressed in their best. Men wore tuxes, and women wore glamorous dresses. A sense of pride filled my heart. They were all here for Cromwell. Every person was here to hear my Cromwell Dean.

Mama leaned over and took my hand. Her eyes were wide. 'This is . . .' She shook her head, struggling for words.

I held her hand tighter. I couldn't find the words either. The house lights flashed, signaling that the show was about to start. I stared up at the curtain as if I could see through it. I wondered where Cromwell was now. Was he in the wings waiting to be announced? Was he okay? I wanted to run backstage and take his hand.

He hadn't performed in three years.

He must have been so nervous.

I shared that nervousness as the room quieted and the lights dimmed. My breath became trapped in my throat as the curtain lifted and the orchestra was revealed. Applause rang out for the musicians, then died down as we waited . . . waited for the boy I loved with both my old and new hearts more than anything in this world.

I heard my heart beat in my ears, only for it to skip when Cromwell stepped out onto the stage. My hand squeezed my mama's as I drank him in. He was dressed in a perfectly tailored tux. His large frame and tall height made him look like a model as he walked to the podium. The audience's applause ricocheted off the walls as Cromwell stopped center stage. I stopped breathing, seeing his neck tattoos creeping from the collar of his shirt. His piercings glimmered in the light. His black hair was as messy as it always was. And flutters broke out in my chest when I saw his handsome face.

He was nervous. No one else would see it. But I did. I could see him rolling his tongue and rubbing his lips together. I saw his eyes adjust to the light then rove the seats.

I froze as his deep blue eyes fell on me. And then warmth burst inside me as his shoulders relaxed and I saw him exhale. His eyes closed for a moment, and when they reopened, he smiled. A true smile. A wide smile.

A smile of love.

A smile just for me.

Any air that was in my lungs fled as his smile hit my heart. Cromwell bowed then turned to the orchestra. He raised a baton into the air, and in that suspended moment, I realized I was seeing the true Cromwell. The musical proficient that he was born to be. The orchestra waited for his signal, and the lights dropped low.

The symphony started with a single violin. And I gasped. Not at the already heavenly sound, but at the screen above the orchestra. The black screen that, when a note was played, flashed up a color and a shape – a triangle.

Cromwell was showing me. He was showing what it was like for him.

He was showing me the colors he heard.

I watched, mesmerized, as shapes in every color of the rainbow danced across the screen. Strings and woodwinds and brass joined in, following every movement of Cromwell's hand. And I watched, heart full and eyes wide, as Cromwell showed me his soul. I tried to drink it all in, the sounds, the sights, the smells of instruments being played so perfectly. Of Cromwell, at home on that stage, showing the world what he was born to do.

At the end of the second movement, the music died down to a single drum carrying a beat. Cromwell lowered his baton. Then, from stage left, out came Professor Lewis. The audience clapped lightly, unsure what to do at the surprise introduction of the infamous conductor. Cromwell handed Lewis the baton and disappeared into the dark. The drum continued, a steady rhythm . . . just like a heartbeat . . .

A spotlight suddenly flashed onto the upper stage left. Cromwell stood under the spotlight, his decks, laptop, and drum pad in front of him. His headphones were on his ears, making him look every inch the EDM DJ I knew him to be. The drum that was playing was suddenly echoed by Cromwell's synthetic drum.

The strings came in next, a double bass and cello taking the lead. Violins took the melody. Light and pure. Then a song I knew started to play. The pianist to the right was playing the piece I'd seen Cromwell play so long ago, in a music room on a late night . . . falling apart after the last note faded away.

My heart leaped to my throat. Tears swelled in my eyes. The pianist played the song perfectly as Lewis conducted the orchestra with ease. Then the music dropped again, and the faint sound of a song I knew – a song that came from my heart – poured from the speakers above us.

My song.

My voice.

I gasped. My voice singing 'Wings' filled the room. The song was set to a harp and a flute. Serene. Pure.

Beautiful.

My hand went to my mouth as my breathing stuttered. Because this was how he saw me. Then, from the background came the sound of an offbeat heart. My hands shook when I recognized the sound.

It was my heart.

My old heart.

A melody grew louder. One of sadness. The beautiful sound of the clarinet and cello playing side by side made my heart ache. And then it came, the sound of another heart. A much stronger heart.

Easton's heart.

My heart.

My hand fell over my chest, and I felt the beat beneath my palm, in sync with the beat from the speakers. Cromwell threaded electronic beats with the orchestra, the colors a firework display of what he saw in his head when his music played. And I was enraptured. I was drawn into the piece like I was living it. My fight song came next, the song he had played for me so many times in the hospital it had become my anthem. The soundtrack to my hopes and wishes as I lay breathless in bed.

My wish to be forever with him.

The music that I had pushed away for so long seeped into my skin, my flesh, and down to my bones. It didn't stop until it made its way down to my heart and, finally, my soul.

I closed my eyes as the symphony came to its crescendo, the mixture of mediums, modern and old, making me feel alive. I felt like my heart wanted to leap from my chest.

This was why I loved music.

This feeling right now. This harmony. This melody, this perfect symphony . . . and then I heard the guitar, the acoustic guitar finding its way over the crashing of drums and the soaring violins.

My song.

Our song.

'A Wish For Us.'

The tears fell down my face as the rest of the story was told. Because that's what Cromwell was doing. He was telling me it all. From his first composition as a child, to his father, to Easton . . . and to me. He was telling me it all, through music, through song . . . the only way he knew how.

I cried. Chest wracking with my love for Cromwell Dean, the boy I met on the beach in Brighton. The boy I loved with my entire soul. The boy who had created a symphony just for me.

As the last note sailed into the air, cementing Cromwell's place among the musical greats, the audience erupted. People jumped to their feet, applauding the genius that was Cromwell and his symphony.

A program fell to the floor in front of me. When I looked down, I saw the symphony's title: 'A Wish For Us.' And I smiled. I let the tears fall down my cheeks, exorcising the pain, the numbness, and my life without Cromwell.

Cromwell came to the center of the stage. Lewis held out his arm, presenting his son to the audience. The pride in Lewis's eyes was almost my undoing. Cromwell took a deep breath, his eyes searching the crowd. I clapped and clapped, in awe of everything he was. The person he was and the love he inspired in me.

And then his eyes fixed on me. His hand moved to his chest and tapped over his heart, a shy smile on his face. Happiness filled my every cell. Cromwell bowed and left the stage. The applause lasted long after he'd gone. A testimony to the effect his music had on the people who let it into their hearts.

When the theater was clear, my mama pushed us backstage. My heart thundered in my chest as I smoothed my hands over my dress. Musicians moved around backstage, the adrenaline that was surging through them palpable.

And then we turned the corner, and I saw him.

Cromwell was at the end of the hallway, standing against the wall, eyes closed and taking deep breaths. His bow tie was loose and his shirt was open. His sleeves were rolled up to his elbows, showing his tattoos. 'I'll leave you two alone.' My mama's footsteps faded away.

Cromwell opened his eyes. He startled when he saw me. He straightened off the wall, his chest rising and falling in rapid movements, and went to take a step forward, but I held out my hand for him to stop.

He did, and I took a deep breath.

I gripped the chair's arms and pushed myself up. My feet shakily hit the floor . . . and the whole time, I never took my eyes off Cromwell. A proud smile lit up his face when I took a step toward him, my weak legs knowing they had no other choice but to carry me forward. Because they knew, as much as my heart did – I had to be with Cromwell.

He was our home.

My heart beat strong. And I made my way to Cromwell, remembering the symphony he'd created for me. And with every note I remembered, every flash of color that had given me a glimpse into his heart, I pushed on. I pushed and pushed, until I was out of breath . . . but I was before him. I'd made it to him. I'd fought to get here. And I refused to quit now.

I looked up, and Cromwell's shining eyes were fixed on me. 'It was beautiful,' I whispered, my voice cracking.

'Baby.' Cromwell pushed his hand through my hair. I closed my eyes, the touch of him so, so welcomed after so much time apart. And then his lips were on mine, as sweet and as perfect as I remembered them to be.

I felt him. Felt everything about this moment. When he pulled back, I stared into his eyes. 'I love you,' I said, holding on to his wrists. His hands cupped my face.

'I love you too,' he breathed, and closed his eyes. Like he couldn't believe I was here. Like I was his dream come true.

Like I was his living, breathing wish.

When his eyes opened again, he said, 'Come with me.' I nodded. He whisked me up into his arms and held me closely to his chest as he carried me to an elevator. When the doors closed, all I could see and feel and smell was Cromwell. I didn't move my eyes from his. He seemed changed somehow. His shoulders had relaxed, and there was a light in his eyes that I'd never seen before. As if they had been injected with life.

When his eyes fixed on me, I could see nothing but love.

The doors opened and fresh air whooshed around us. Cromwell didn't put me down; he kept me in his strong arms and took me along what I saw was a roof terrace. A blanket of stars stared down at us, not a single cloud in the sky.

'Cromwell . . .' I murmured, feeling overcome at the sight. At everything tonight. At the music, the heartbeats, the symphony . . . and him.

Always him.

Cromwell sat down on a sofa in the center of a small rooftop garden. Water flowed around us, sounding like a tranquil river. Winter flowers of reds and greens in decorative pots surrounded us. It was like a glimpse of heaven. And when Cromwell held me tighter, it felt like coming home.

The rooftop was silent. Only the sound of the street below could be heard in the distance. I blinked up at the stars and wondered if Easton was up there, still tethered somehow to his heart . . . to me.

'It's beautiful up here,' I said and finally turned to Cromwell.

Cromwell was already watching me. He looked at me like I was a gift he couldn't believe he'd received. My chest expanded, letting in more love for him than the minute before. I hadn't been sure that was possible.

'You came,' he whispered, and my pulse fluttered in my throat.

'I came.'

Cromwell leaned in and pressed his lips to mine. The kiss was slow and gentle and held a simple promise – that it wouldn't be our last. When he pulled back I let my forehead fall to his. I breathed in the scent of him and let it inside my body with peace.

I felt my lip quiver, but I pushed through the swell of my emotions to say, 'I want to live.' Cromwell tensed. He pulled back and placed his hands on my cheeks. 'I've been thinking about things. I've had a long time to think about things.' I stared up at the stars. As I looked at the vast sky, I felt so small. A simple stitch on the tapestry that was the world. I swallowed the lump that bobbed in my throat. 'Life is so short, isn't it?'

I turned back to Cromwell. His blue eyes were wide as he patiently waited for what I had to say. 'I've had nothing else to do but think of life, Cromwell. Every facet of it. The good.' I kissed his forehead. 'The bad.' Discovering Easton had died replayed in my head. 'And all that's in between.' I lay back against Cromwell's hard chest. His shirt was open at the top, showing his dark tattoos. My hand reached out to play with one of his buttons. 'And I've decided I want to live.'

Cromwell held me tighter. I looked up into his deep blue eyes, eyes that I once thought turbulent, but now thought serene. 'I don't want life to pass me by.' A sudden picture came to mind. Of me and Cromwell. Of us traveling the world ... of us one day perhaps having a dark-haired blue-eyed child. Just like him. 'I want to embrace everything I can while I still can. New places, new sounds . . . everything. With you.'

'Bonnie,' Cromwell rasped.

I took hold of his hand and lifted it so I could see the tattooed ID on his fingers. The one I now knew was a tribute to his dad. 'Losing people you love can make the world seem very dark. But I've realized that even though they're gone from us physically, they're never truly gone.' I shook my head. I knew I was rambling. I met Cromwell's eyes. 'I love you, Cromwell Dean. And I want to love life with you in it. I don't care where it takes us, as long as it means something. As long as our lives have purpose for those who couldn't be with us along the way.' Cromwell's eyes glistened as I kissed the number on his hand. 'And as long as there's you, and there's music, I know it will be a life *lived*, no matter how long or short.'

'Long,' Cromwell said, his voice husky. 'You'll live a long life. Easton's heart will remain strong.' Cromwell lowered his head and kissed the spot where my new heart lay. It fluttered like a butterfly's wings.

Cromwell kissed me again, and I stared back up at the stars, content to just be. This boy, who was holding me in his arms, was my wish come true. The boy who stood beside me through the hardest trials of my life. And the boy who, when I fell apart, brought me back to me, brought me back to him.

Through music.

Through love.

And through the colors of his soul.

He was, and forever would be, the beat in my heart.

Put simply, he was my entire world. A world in which I intended to stay. I vowed to make it. To never let my heart give up. Because I wanted a life with this boy. I wanted to love and live and laugh.

I was determined. And my beating heart echoed that wish.

Epilogue

Cromwell

Five years later . . .

The sun beamed down on me as I sat on the bench. I closed my eyes and looked up. Warmth spread on my cheeks, and I heard mustard yellows and bronzes. Birds singing and leaves rustling.

Then they came, the notes that always filtered into my brain the brightest. Colors bursting into complex patterns. I opened my eyes and scribbled them down in my notebook.

'Easton!' Violet blue burst into my head as Bonnie's voice carried over the wind. I looked up and saw pink as Bonnie's laugh followed behind. Bonnie came jogging around the tree, her cheeks flushed. She lurched forward, and a yellow-colored giggle burst from behind her.

I smiled as our son, Easton, jumped out from the tree and grabbed her legs. Bonnie turned and scooped him in her arms. She threw him up in the air, and his giggle turned from pale yellow to a shade bright enough to rival the sun.

Bonnie and I had a child. I still couldn't believe it. We married straight after college, and Bonnie came around the world with me wherever I played. After the gala, we were never again apart. Not even for a night. I wasn't ever letting her go.

With her heart, we were never guaranteed time. But we'd got this far. And her heart was strong. I knew in my soul that Bonnie would live a long life. And when a miracle happened and baby Easton was born, I knew she wouldn't ever be leaving us behind.

Farraday was going to defy the odds.

Because this was it. This was the life she had wished for. It was her dream. To be a wife, and a mother. And she was perfect at both. My heart melted when I heard Bonnie start to sing. Violet blue danced into my mind. I couldn't take my eyes from her as she sang to our boy, him looking at her like she was his entire world.

And she was. To us both.

Violet blues and whites and pinks played a lullaby in my head. When she was finished, Easton turned to me, smiling wide, dimples out, and said, 'Papa! Mama sings as blue as the sky.'

My heart swelled as Bonnie laughed and kissed his cheek. Because Easton was like me, in both looks and soul. He was like his Grandad Lewis too, who he loved beyond words. Bonnie put Easton down and he ran to me. I scooped him up in my arms and kissed his chubby cheek. Easton giggled, the sound the most vivid of yellows.

Easton sat on my lap on the bench. Bonnie walked past her brother's grave and ran her hand over the headstone. We came here often, Bonnie unable to be away from her brother for long. Even in death, they were tethered to one another. Their shared heart still beating strong.

And like she'd once told him – she was determined to live a life for them both. And she did. With every breath, she did. She was happy. And because of her, so was I.

Bonnie came beside us and curled into my side. I wrapped my arm around her, and she closed her eyes. 'Hum to me what you've composed.'

So I did. I always did whatever she asked. I'd learned that life was too short to deny her anything. I hummed the colors that had come into my head as I'd sat on this bench, my wife and my son listening in. And I couldn't imagine a life more perfect than this. I composed every day, made music that lived in my heart, living the life I was always meant to live. I had my son, who showed me how to love more than I could ever have known.

And I had my Bonnie. My girl who still inspired the music that came from my heart. The girl who was always by my side. The girl who was the bravest person I knew.

The most beautiful.

The most perfect.

And the girl, that with one single smile, still completely illuminated my world.

I knew, wherever they were, both my dad and Easton would be looking down at us all, smiling. Proud of the people we'd become. Happy at the peace we had found. And content to know that we wouldn't ever waste a single breath.

At that comforting thought, a warm breeze flowed over us, bringing with it a blanket of peace. A bird sang its song from up above, gifting my eyes with bursts of silver. Then a white dove landed on Easton's headstone. It looked directly at us . . .

. . . and I smiled.

Playlist

Without You (feat. Sandro Cavazza) – Avicii, Sandro Cavazza

Symphony (feat. Zara Larsson) – Clean Bandit, Zara Larsson

More Than You Know – Axwell /\ Ingrosso

Back 2 U – Steve Aoki, Boehm, WALK THE MOON

Slow Acid – Calvin Harris

Stargazing (Orchestra Version) – Kygo, Justin Jesso, Bergen Philharmonic Orchestra

Pray To God – Calvin Harris

Without You (feat. Usher) – David Guetta

With Every Heartbeat (feat. Kleerup) – Robyn

Place We Were Made – Maisie Peters

Tired – Alan Walker, Gavin James

Little Do You Know – Alex & Sierra

Cut Me – Chris Medina

Afterglow – Juliander

The Story Never Ends – Lauv

Before – Ulrik Munther

Sunrise – ARTY, April Bender

Colors – Halsey

Day That I Die (feat. Amos Lee) – Zac Brown Band

I Hate That Part – Caroline Glaser

The Heart (Live Room Version) – NEEDTOBREATHE

Ether & Wood – Alela Diane

Take Me Back – Sarah Jarosz
Mozart: Clarinet Concerto In A major – John Barry
Sun Is Shining – Axwell /\ Ingrosso
Sky Full Of Song – Florence + The Machine
Melody – Lost Frequencies, James Blunt
Lullaby – Sigala, Paloma Faith
Psalm 91 (On Eagle' Wings) – Shane & Shane
Falling (Original) – Yiruma (Inspired Cromwell's father's piano piece)
Beloved – Yiruma (Inspired Bonnie's Fight Song)
Mercy – Lewis Capaldi

Acknowledgments

Thank you to my husband, Stephen, for keeping me sane. This past year with you, and our little man, Roman, has been the best of my life. I wouldn't change it for the world!

Roman, I never thought it was possible to love somebody so much. You're the best thing I have ever done in my life. Love you to bits, my little dude!

Mam and Dad, thank you for the continued support.

Samantha, Marc, Taylor, Isaac, Archie, and Elias, love you all.

Thessa, thank you for being the best assistant in the world. You make the best edits, keep me organized and are one kick-ass friend to boot!

Liz, thank you for being my super-agent and friend.

To my fabulous editor, Kia. I couldn't have done it without you. To Sarah, thank you for the fabulous proofread.

Hang Le, thank you once again for the most stunning cover. It *is* this novel! I love everything we create together. Here's to many more!

Neda and Ardent Prose, I am so happy that I jumped on board with you guys. You've made my life infinitely more organized. You kick PR ass!

To my street team, I couldn't ask for better book friends. Thank you for all for everything you do for me. Thank you for reading my work, no matter the genre. I owe you everything.

Jenny and Gitte, you know how I feel about you two ladies. Love you to bits! I truly value everything you've done for me over the years, and continue to do!

Thank you to all the AMAZING bloggers that have supported my career from the start, and the ones who help share my work and shout about it from the rooftops.

And lastly, thank you to the readers. Without you none of this would be possible. Your support still blows me away every single day. We have each other's backs, we're our very own tribe. I cannot wait for the journey to continue!

Follow Tillie At:

https://www.facebook.com/tilliecoleauthor

https://www.facebook.com/groups/tilliecolestreetteam

https://twitter.com/tillie_cole

Instagram: @authortilliecole

Or drop me an email at: authortilliecole@gmail.com

Or check out my website: www.tilliecole.com

Loved what you read?

Read on for a peak at the first chapter of Tillie Cole's heart-wrenching *A Thousand Boy Kisses . . .*

Prologue

Rune

There were exactly four moments that defined my life.
   This was the first.

* * *

Blossom Grove, Georgia
United States of America
Twelve Years Ago
Aged Five

'Jeg vil dra! Nå! Jeg vil reise hjem igjen!' *I shouted as loud as I could, telling my mamma that I wanted to leave, now! I wanted to go back home!*

   'We're not going back home, Rune. And we are not *leaving.* This is our home now,' she replied in English. She crouched down and looked me straight in the eye. 'Rune,' she said softly, 'I know you didn't want to leave Oslo, but your pappa got a new job here in Georgia.' Her hand ran up and down my arm, but it didn't make me feel any better. I didn't want to be in this place, in America.

   I wanted to go back home.

   'Slutt å snakke engelsk!' *I snapped. I hated speaking English. Since we set off for America from Norway, Mamma and Pappa would only speak to me in English. They said I had to practice.*

   I didn't want to!

My mamma stood up and lifted a box off the ground. 'We're in America, Rune. They speak English here. You've been speaking English for as long as you've been speaking Norwegian. It's time to use it.'

I stood my ground, glaring at my mamma as she walked around me into the house. I looked around the small street where we now lived. There were eight houses. They were all big, but they all looked different. Ours was painted red, with white windows and a huge porch. My room was big and it was on the bottom floor. I did think that was kind of cool. Sort of anyway. I'd never slept downstairs before; in Oslo my room was upstairs.

I looked at the houses. All of them were painted bright colors: light blues, yellows, pinks . . . Then I looked at the house next door. Right next door – we shared a patch of grass. Both houses were big, and our yards were too, but there was no fence or wall between them. If I wanted to, I could run into their yard and there'd be nothing to stop me.

The house was bright white, with a porch wrapped right around it. They had rocking chairs and a big chair swing on the front. Their window frames were painted black, and there was a window opposite my bedroom window. Right opposite! I didn't like that. I didn't like that I could see into their bedroom and they could see into mine.

There was a stone on the ground. I kicked it with my foot, watching it roll down the street. I turned to follow my mamma, but then I heard a noise. It was coming from the house next to ours. I looked at their front door, but nobody came out. I was climbing the steps to my porch when I saw some movement from the side of the house – from next door's bedroom window, the one opposite my own.

My hand froze on the rail and I watched as a girl, dressed in a bright blue dress, climbed through the window. She jumped down onto the grass and dusted off her hands on her thighs. I frowned, my eyebrows pulling down, as I waited for her to lift her head. She had brown hair, which was piled up on her head like a bird's nest. She wore a big white bow on the side of it.

When she looked up, she looked right at me. Then she smiled. She smiled at me so big. She waved, fast, then ran forward and stopped in front of me.

She pushed out her hand. 'Hi, my name is Poppy Litchfield, I'm five years old and I live right next door.'

I stared at the girl. She had a funny accent. It made the English words sound different to the way I had learned them back in Norway. The girl – Poppy – had a smudge of mud on her face and bright yellow rain boots on her feet. They had a big red balloon on the side.

She looked weird.

I looked up from her feet and fixed my eyes on her hand. She was still holding it out. I didn't know what to do. I didn't know what she wanted.

Poppy sighed. Shaking her head, she reached for my hand and forced it into hers. She shook them up and down twice and said, 'A handshake. My mamaw says it's only right to shake the hand of new people that you meet.' She pointed at our hands. 'That was a handshake. And that was polite because I don't know you.'

I didn't say anything; for some reason my voice wouldn't work. When I looked down I realized it was because our hands were still joined.

She had mud on her hands too. In fact, she had mud everywhere.

'What's your name?' Poppy asked. Her head was tipped to the side. A small twig was stuck in her hair.

'Hey,' she said, tugging on our hands, 'I asked for your name.'

I cleared my throat. 'My name is Rune, Rune Erik Kristiansen.'

Poppy scrunched her face up, her big pink lips sticking out all funny. 'You sound weird,' she blurted.

417

I snatched my hand away.

'Nei det gjør jeg ikke!' I snapped. Her face screwed up even more.

'What did you just say?' Poppy asked, as I turned to walk into my house. I didn't want to speak to her anymore.

Feeling angry, I spun back around. 'I said, "No, I don't!" I was speaking Norwegian!' I said, in English this time. Poppy's green eyes grew huge.

She stepped closer, and closer again, and asked, 'Norwegian? Like the Vikings? My mamaw read me a book about the Vikings. It said they were from Norway.' Her eyes got even bigger. 'Rune, are you a Viking?' Her voice had gone all squeaky.

It made me feel good. I stuck out my chest. My pappa always said I was a Viking, like all the men in my family. We were big, strong Vikings. 'Ja,' I said. 'We are real Vikings, from Norway.'

A big smile spread across Poppy's face, and a loud girly giggle burst from her mouth. She lifted her hand and pulled on my hair. 'That's why you have long blond hair and crystal-blue eyes. Because you're a Viking. At first I thought you looked like a girl –'

'I'm not a girl!' I butted in, but Poppy didn't seem to care. I ran my hand through my long hair. It came down to my shoulders. All the boys in Oslo had their hair like this.

'– but now I see it's because you're a real-life Viking. Like Thor. He had long blond hair and blue eyes too! You're just like Thor!'

'Ja,' I agreed. 'Thor does. And he's the strongest god of them all.'

Poppy nodded her head, then put her hands on my shoulders. Her face had gone all serious and her voice dropped to a whisper. 'Rune, I don't tell everyone this, but I go on adventures.'

I screwed up my face. I didn't understand. Poppy stepped closer and looked up into my eyes. She squeezed my arms. She tilted her head to the side. She looked all around us, then leaned in to speak.

'I don't normally bring people with me on my journeys, but you're a Viking, and we all know that Vikings grow big and strong, and they are really really good with adventures and exploring, and long walks and capturing baddies and . . . all kinds a things!'

I was still confused, but then Poppy stepped back and held out her hand again.

'Rune,' she said, her voice serious and strong, 'you live right next door, you're a Viking and I just love Vikings. I think we should be best friends.'

'Best friends?' I asked.

Poppy nodded her head and pushed her hand further toward me. Slowly reaching out my own hand, I gripped hold of hers and gave it two shakes, like she'd shown me.

A handshake.

'So now we are best friends?' I asked, as Poppy pulled her hand back.

'Yes!' she said excitedly. 'Poppy and Rune.' She brought her finger to her chin and looked up. Her lips stuck out again, like she was thinking very hard. 'It sounds good, don't you think? "Poppy and Rune, best friends for infinity!"'

I nodded because it did sound good. Poppy put her hand in mine. 'Show me your bedroom! I want to tell you about what adventure we can go on next.' She began to pull me forward, and we ran into the house.

When we pushed through my bedroom door, Poppy rushed straight to my window.

'This is the room exactly opposite mine!'

I nodded my head, and she squealed, running toward me to take my hand in hers again. 'Rune!' she said excitedly, 'we can talk at night, and make walkie-talkies with cans and string. We can whisper our secrets to each other when everyone else is asleep, and we can plan, and play, and . . .'

Poppy kept talking, but I didn't mind. I liked the sound of her voice. I liked her laugh and I liked the big white bow in her hair.

Maybe Georgia won't be so bad after all, *I thought,* not if I have Poppy Litchfield as my very best friend.

* * *

And that was Poppy and me from that day on.
Poppy and Rune.
Best friends for infinity.
Or so I thought.
Funny how things change.